UGLASS

UGLASS

The Intrusive Thoughts Of A Melanin Queen

By Rod Palmer

Black Wren Press
Charleston, SC

BLACK WREN PRESS LLC

LIBRARY OF CONGRESS CATALOGING-IN-PUBLICATION DATA

Names: Palmer, Rod, author.
Title: Uglass: The Intrusive Thoughts Of A Melanin Queen/ Rod Palmer
Description: [South Carolina] : Black Wren Press [2024]
ISBN 979-8-9864282-6-0 (print) | ISBN 979-8-9864282-5-3
LC record available at https://lccn.loc.gov/
LC ebook record available at https://lccn.loc.gov/

Printed in the United States of America

This is a work of fiction. All characters, organizations, and events portrayed in this novel are either products of the author's imagination or are used fictitiously.

Caste is insidious and therefore powerful because it is not hatred, it is not necessarily personal. It is the worn grooves of comforting routines and unthinking expectations, patterns of a social order that have been in place for so long that it looks like the natural order of things… Caste is structure. Caste is ranking. Caste is boundaries that reinforce the fixed assignments based on what people look like.

~Isabele Wilkerson | *Caste: The Origins Of Our Discontents*

CHAPTER 1
OUR FIRST KISS

A one, two, three, uh!
My baby don't mess around
Because she loves me so
And this I know fo sho

I hear our song and immediately turn from my huddle of girlfriends to locate my prom date and bestie, Fletcher. He's with his boys, debonaire in his white tux and diamond studded earrings. I wave the hand that wears the corsage he gave me. "*Fletch*," I call.

Fletcher turns, revealing the grin he'd been hiding all along, but now waves his hands no. "Lee-me 'lone, Tahj!"

We normally clown amongst ourselves, but this is prom. I figured he'd be bashful. But I'm stubborn. I advance with a sassy strut that I picked up from the flag team, then I dance the swim with the enthusiasm of a starstruck white girl from the sixties, the era this song parodies. Hey Ya released a decade prior, but in Atlanta, Outkast is always in. I flail one arm up then go down pinching my nose, as if drowning.

Suddenly Fletcher – with his big, six-foot-four self – is in his bag, doing The Carlton Dance like it's nobody's business.

We go back-to-back with stemmed roses for microphones, lip-syncing *Heeey Ya,* and everyone realizes that they're merely extras in our musical. Fletcher and I have the floor to ourselves by the time the song reaches the breakdown.

> *Shake it, shake, shake it…*
> *Shake it like a Polaroid picture…*

On my own dare, I back into Fletcher like I'm giving myself a soothing back scratch against a tree, not to be mistaken for twerking, unless you're Riley, Miss Ice Spice with straight hair, who reads everything for filth. "Twerk it, girl," Riley cheers.

Riley used to tease me back in the day, calling me Ugl'ass so often it became a nickname, but when she learned that I was modeling for an agency, she switched up and wanted to be friends. I helped her get into modeling. I was blind enough to think that because Riley stopped calling me names she'd stopped the ridicule, but no – she'd hide them in compliments like now, playing hype-man as a slick way to call me fast-natured. "Go Tahj! It's ya birthday. You gone twerk it like it's your birthday!"

If she were truly cheering me on, I wouldn't feel the need to clear my name of the very thing she praises. I'm not throwing it back. I'm throwing it side to side; there's a difference, I wanna say, but the music is too loud for lengthy explanations, so I cup a hand to my mouth and yell, "What*ever!*"

Riley mimes innocence. If throwing the rock and hiding your hand was a person…

Just for spite, I start dancing with a little mo' sauce. I take Fletcher's hands and place them on my waist. Poor Fletcher: we're just friends at this point, so he's suddenly confused, but dancing through it – oblivious that my change in energy is more about Riley than him.

This tiff between Riley and me, though, is but a warm hug compared to how we'd bump heads in years to come. So, why even look all the way back to 2016 senior prom? Because this isn't about Riley; this is about Fletcher and me. It begins here, under the spinning disco globe at prom with me placing Fletcher's hands on my body, and my boy doesn't quite know how to take it.

Our science teacher DJ makes a sneaky track change to Drake's Hotline, with its slow intro. Our eyes meet and an entire conversation transpires in our gaze:

Fletcher beams, *Caught by the slow song, huh?*

I glance around, *Don't make it weird, ok.*

He hugs my waist. *Shiiid…*

I look up at him, eyes blazing, *Kiss me.*

His eyes widen. *Wait, what…*

I look away. *Too slow.*

Our friendship just got even more complicated. The fact that we even went to prom together is complicated in and of itself. For one: Fletcher, at the time, has a girlfriend. He asked me to prom because his girlfriend was twenty-three years old – shamelessly chasing the bag with a barely legal five-star recruit. Fletcher wasn't about to forgo senior prom on account of a girlfriend he couldn't be seen with. Coincidentally, I was asked to prom only by guys I *wouldn't* be seen with, so Fletcher and I solved each other's problem by going together.

And here we are, body to body, and the auto-correct that always makes us look away when our eyes try to expose us, is malfunctioning. Our gaze holds, even while the entire prom chants, *Ever since I left the city, you!*

The friendship boundary has come down. I'm amazed that it hasn't already, in the near four years we've known each other. All the while, I've had my boyfriends and he's had his girlfriends and we're both uber faithful, but Fletcher, by the glean in his eye, is telling me that he's ready to risk it all. Those eyes… the rim traced with those thick lashes of his. I'm ready to tiptoe for his lips when Fletcher's teammate and best friend outside of me, ruins it. Bubby comes out of his chocolate tux like a matador's cape then uses it to fan us. Fletcher and I deny the romantic flames, even while we're standing there engulfed in it.

Bubby, in an improv of a disapproving dad, comments, "Is this what we're doing, Fletch? Tahj?"

If Keenan, the other Musketeer, were there he would've been right alongside Bubby shaking his head in disapproval.

I'm off-limits they say, which is probably why me and Fletcher never dated in high school. The bros made a pact not to let a girl come between them, which I thought unnecessary because I'm neither of their types, although Fletcher seems to forget, whenever we're having fun or just vibing like that, and our side glances get sticky and butterflies stir in my belly.

Nevertheless I'm off limits, which is why when Bubby says he's disappointed, Fletcher's palms draw to his chest in denial. "You know it ain't like that."

Bubby, a doppelganger for the rapper Fabulous, looks me up and down in two head flicks. "Look atchya," he says, as if I'm a despicable sight to behold.

I say, "Don't act like I don't tutor you in three subjects bro."

"Swear you grown," Bubby says.

I playfully cut my eye and strut away — because couldn't nobody tell me I wasn't grown back then. I look back and see Fletcher staring at the switch of my hips until Bubby pops him in the back of the head.

After prom, we have dinner at Ruth Chris with Bubby and his date Soha, who's black and Middle Eastern and happens to be stunning.

After dinner, we pile in Fletcher's car, heads bobbing under the interior light while sipping from red plastic cups of cranberry juice with Everclear that Bubby smuggled from his mother's cabinet.

Bubby has a hotel room and Soha has a curfew, so it isn't long before they leave us. Fletcher and I have nothing else planned, so he starts driving us toward Indian Creek Park to walk and talk the time away until my curfew.

I get this feeling that Fletcher, knowing his best friend is getting sex, feels pressure to score at least something with me. During the entire drive he keeps looking over at me with this slickness in his eyes.

When we arrive at the park, Fletcher takes my hand to help me out of the car, but doesn't let the hand go. We walk and we talk while the low tide whispers over the rocks. Fletcher makes an adjustment to our held hands, interlocking the fingers; the gesture, scandalously romantic. Suddenly we can't even look at each other.

My conscience whispers, *but he has a girlfriend.* I whisper back, *I don't give a fuck.* How can I respect a relationship where Fletcher's girlfriend came onto him with the line: *My, how you've grown.*

I catch Fletcher eyeing me, then I feel forced to comment – although nothing comes to mind but my precise thought. "Why do I get the feeling that you're determined to kiss me tonight?" He loves how straightforward I am, until now.

He frowns. "What? What are you talking about?"

I just smile nervously.

His shoulders droop in defeat. "Okay, you got me." A few steps more and he elaborates, "You could've gone to prom with just about anyone…"

Lies, I think.

"You would've been kissed by some lucky guy tonight, right? It's not fair that you be denied that, just because your date is your friend," he says, his cheeks packed with grins. "You deserve the full prom experience," he says, like a car salesman selling the dream in order to sell the automobile.

"The full prom experience?" I look away. "So you're saying the kiss would be innocent?" My face swings back so fast for the answer, I feel my shoulder-length hair, all mine, splay in an arc. Now it's Fletcher who looks away, rubbing his chin as he pleads the fifth. "I ain't saying all *that…*"

I'm thinking, I'm really about to kiss the guy of my dreams. I engage my core to subdue the butterflies because I don't need nerves ruining the moment by causing me to say or do something goofy. I need to be that girl who graces the modeling stage like the world is hers. I need her poise and I need her confidence. Slyly, I say, "We can't kiss and walk at the same time, bro."

Fletcher stops. I take an extra step then pivot. I shake my hair out of my face. My heart drums.

He cradles my face in his hands. "I like you. I *been* liked you, from moment one."

"Really? I thought maybe I grew on you. People don't see me, right away."

That's when Fletcher says, "Bullshit. You have *got* to be the most beautiful girl in the world."

There's a hint of Everclear on his breath. I give him a sly cut of my eyes, trying to be sexy, trying to be grown, trying to refrain from expressing my disbelief, because every day when I leave my mirror, the world informs me that they don't see me like I see me.

Fletcher sees me. Fletcher: the guy I always imagine in place of the heroes in my romance novels, where we do so much more than kiss. In real life he is my friend and my crush, so I'm full with this feeling of love that is big and broad and vague, but I'm also percolating with a desire that is quite specific and detailed, courtesy of all the smutty books I've consumed. In this moment, Fletcher could've done whatever he wanted with me.

I'm just seventeen going on eighteen, and had only read about this kind of surrender, and suddenly I am the fruition of those racy passages, the protagonist with sweaty palms and body heat surging.

As a reader, disbelief was suspended by my lack of experience, but now disbelief is suspended by the fact of my raised nipples. I'm poised to receive his lips, on prom night, in my self-made satin gown, my hair down, feeling more like a woman than I'd ever felt. Fletcher tilts toward me. Our lips meet oh so gently. The fireworks is even better than fiction.

I thought that Fletcher kissing me under the stars was his anointing me as his girlfriend. The very next day, I learn that it was not. I run into Fletcher – and he's with Gigi, that grown woman, sporting baby-hair edges and sneakers to blend in with teenagers hanging out at the mall. I only know it's her because she's with Fletcher. He never showed me Gigi's pics and I'm seeing why: instant jealousy. She's one of those fitness girls who ties the bottom of their t-shirts to show off her abs.

Obviously, she's seen my pics because she points me out with the aim of her giant soft pretzel. She likely approved the prom date after dismissing me as a possible threat.

I step away from my friends and take a deep breath in preparation to be formally introduced to the girl whose boyfriend I'm in love with.

Gigi says, "Tahj, right? Fletch tells me you're a model." She has this bouncy way about her as if she couldn't keep still even if she tried. "*I* need to start modeling," she says, which is so light-skinned of her to not even question whether she's model material even when her front teeth is gapped like a coin slot.

Fletcher stands there tight-faced, worrying if I have the acting chops to get him through this without incident. The way I begin advising Gigi on modeling, I appear so calm and natural, that Fletcher seems to relax. But then I get that taste of disrespect in my mouth and I know it's about to be some shit. "…Modeling is expensive, at first," I say. "Reason being: they'll have to build your portfolio, but don't worry, the agents will find the work for you." Facetiously, I add, "And don't even worry about the gapped tooth. They've been more accepting of that, lately."

Gigi takes my comment for shade, never mind that it's true. She could fit the straw of a juice box between her front teeth and drink with a smile, but she's mad at me for calling a thing a thing.

Gigi tilts and says, "Who you playing with, though?"

Fletcher, knowing how ratchet she can be, he attempts damage control. "What Tahj means is… Well, what she's trying to say is, like…"

I was so done with Fletcher, watching him do the most to soothe her feelings and not mine, while knowing I had to be feeling like crap for having to smile in Gigi's face after kissing him. It hits me: *I'm the secret.* My next thought: *I'm not about to be anybody's secret.* I glare at Gigi and say, "By the way, thanks for lending me your man for prom."

She politely slides past Fletcher. "Hold up Fletch – 'cause I think this bitch wanna get something off her chest."

Gigi would've mopped the floor with me, if not for my three girlfriends who heard the change in energy and came to my side, although none of us are about that life.

Gigi certainly isn't fooled. "What y'all nerdy broads finna do? Dance battle?" She feints forward as if to fight; we flinch back, as if in flight. Fletcher tugs Gigi back and she turns on him, mushing his face while me and my girls snoop away to safety.

I avoid Fletcher at school and ignore his calls and texts. I was content to be done with him as a crush *and* as a friend.

This was our first falling out, so I wasn't yet aware of how things work with us – that our duty to the friendship would always trump our differences.

There was a big media day at our school. Both local news and national correspondents present, their cameras aimed at the podium where the three five-star athletes from our school take part in the tradition of selecting the universities they'd play for, by way of choosing the hat with its logo.

Fletcher sits before a cluster of microphones, his mom on one side and his dad behind him, but he gets up and walks off camera. No one knows what he's doing until he does it; Fletcher calls me out of the bleachers. Millions of television viewers, Gigi included, get a good look at my complex fashion sense as I descend the bleachers – high-stepping for the bitches who rumored that Fletcher took me to prom as a pity date. This was said by young ladies who go out of their way to call me pretty. I'm suddenly black-up, when I have the guy they want.

I'm rubbing circles on Fletcher's back when he takes the hat with the UGA logo and places it on his head.

Bubby also chooses top-ranked Georgia Bulldogs, which would place them in Athens, Georgia, an hour away from the college I chose, Clark Atlanta. Keenan unfortunately didn't receive any Division One scholarships, so he would go to play for Savannah State. The four of us would be split between three cities, so it feels like the band is breaking up. It feels like this thing between Fletcher and me would never get to reach its potential, and would eventually fade into what could have been.

CHAPTER 2
2018 THE 2ND KISS

I'm in a relationship and so is Fletcher, despite the distance between himself and Gigi. But one thing I notice about us: we're always proving our loyalty to each other, even to the detriment of our respective relationships.

I have a whole boyfriend and yet I'm with Fletcher on an eight-hour drive to Miami Fashion Weekend. This is my first whiff of the big time. As Keenan put it, "It's like she's going p-p-pro, in modeling." Keenan stutters occasionally.

He and Bubby come along because we're a crew, and we're always there for our milestones, although they're too macho to say it. Let them tell it: they're coming along strictly for the Latinas.

We're a fourth of the way down I-75 when…

My boyfriend calls. There's utter silence as my phone rings.

I raise a hard finger and turn in my seat so they can each see that I'm being serious when I say, "Act like y'all got some fucking sense okay?"

Despite their grumbling, I assert a wide-eyed, *"Okay?!"*

Keenan says, "Answer the phone and stop acting g-g-gay." Another thing about Keenan: back then he used to call everything gay.

They play like I'm crazy for warning them, but why, when I answer the call, they start making sex noises as if I'm getting pounded: Bubby claps his palms as Fletcher moans, "Oh, Tahj!"

My head shakes in disbelief; I'm helpless to say anything but, "Oh my God."

Fletcher moans, "Yeah baby, this dick got you calling on God, huh?"

My boyfriend's in my ear telling me to put him on speaker, so I do. He's a good sport about it. "Good one, fellas. Had me going for a sec."

They *know* the gig is up, but still keep the ensemble going anyway. That's the problem with male friends; they play entirely too much. I just look at these fools, shaking my head, repeating, "Oh my God!"

My boyfriend's attitude spins on a dime. "Hold up, Tahj… Why the fuck you keep saying 'Oh my God!?'"

Silence implodes. Three big men suffocate with laughter, withering in their seats and gasping. Fletcher laughs so hard, he starts banging the steering wheel. My smile crumples with embarrassment while I assure Donovan, in a voice so calm, it proves that Fletcher doesn't have me in the buck.

Bubby and Keenan dap so hard, it sounds like a cap gun.

By now I'm laughing at their laughter.

Donovan chuckles through speakerphone while patiently waiting to get his lick back. As the laughter dies down, he chimes in. "I should've known better because my baby's way more vocal than that – at least when *I'm* drilling her!"

My jaw drops like its hinge is broken. I take him off speaker. "Don't be telling our business, baby," I whine.

Bubby folds his arms, browbeating my reflection in the rearview mirror. "Knew you was a lil freak."

I can't bear to look at Fletcher. I say to Donovan, "How you let them get you?" We wrap up our conversation with a sappy exchange of who loves who more.

I end the call with dreamy eyes. "My man is so thorough."

"Ole Donald Glover lookin' ass boy," says Bubby.

Kennan, "Ole mmm… mmm mash-up face boy."

Bubby adds, "Them M words be fuckin' you *up*, cousin."

I slice a look over at Fletcher who's usually the first to glance at me when Bubby teases Keenan about his stuttering; however, Fletcher's mind is elsewhere, gazing in the distance with a lazy hand draped over the steering wheel.

I stare at his profile, just waiting for him to look over at me and question why I'm looking at him. He's so gorgeous whenever he's trying to figure me out. But when Fletcher surfaces from his thoughts, he says, "You wildin' Tahj."

"Wildin' how," I ask.

We're two hours down I-75 and now Fletcher decides to start some mess. "If your man ain't jealous, he ain't for you. You're going out of town with an NFL-bound, chiseled athlete." He flexes, then kisses his bicep for play.

All I said was, "Dude, you are *not* all that."

And Fletcher flips. "You wasn't saying that when we kissed," he says. He'd just outted us for real or maybe he was just… No, the look in his eyes says he's definitely not playing. "Does your boyfriend know that we kissed? Huh?"

"In high school, Fletcher."

"But does he know?"

Keenan says, "Tahj is one of the bros, man. You kiss her in the mouth?"

Bubby adds, "I *been* know they wadn't sticking to the code. Hell, I'm surprised it was only a kiss."

Calmly, I say to Fletcher, "What's the matter, huh? If anyone should be upset it should be me, after that stunt yall pulled."

"I'm just worried about ya, slim," says Fletcher. "Ain't nothing the matter with me."

Bubby tattles, "Yeah it is. Gigi done told him if he went on this trip, it's over."

I touch Fletcher's hand. "And you still came?"

Fletcher's eyes go lazy. "I ain't worried. She bluffing."

That would've been a good stopping point, but Bubby takes a swig of vodka and starts up again. "I pray she *not* bluffing because you don't need no problems like huh." Bubby taps my shoulder. "One time, Fletcher caught her on some sneak shit, stuffing herself with his pullout. Had the nigga crying, thinking he was gone be a daddy."

My mouth falls open in disgust, for the act, and for hearing this from someone other than Fletcher who tells me everything. I ask Fletcher, "And you're still with her?"

"That's exactly what *I* said," Bubby adds. "He know that woman don't mean him no good. He just can't leave."

"She's much older than him," I explain. "She has a psychological advantage."

Fletcher cuts a look that makes me shut up while I'm ahead. Next Fletcher focuses on the rearview mirror. "Bubby! Did *any*body ask you *any* of this shit? That's your problem, bro. You talk too much."

Bubby's brow rises to wrinkle his forehead. "What I'm *not* about to do, is sit up here and let you take your shit out on Tahj. I'm not gone do it."

"Bubby… is you stupid, fella? How am I taking my shit out on Tahj? Before you go assuming shit, maybe you should try asking questions, because you don't know the whole story." Fletcher then proceeds to tell the whole story, detailing the incident in the mall where I all but outted him to Gigi.

Bubby listens intently, but after getting *the whole story*, he pimp slaps the air, "*Fuck* outta here! That changes absolutely nothing."

"Why not," challenges Keenan. "Gotta read between the lines bro. The man's saying that Tajh p-p-put a strain on his relationship, and he could do the same to her, but he won't."

All the while, the car accelerates, Fletcher weaving in and out of lanes. I ask, "Fletch… Can you slow it down a bit?"

A few beats of silence pass, but Fletcher still accelerates, speeding down the interstate like a bat out of hell.

"You heard the lady…" Bubby hauls off and slaps Fletcher in the back of the head. Kapow! "*Slow* this muh fucka down, man. This my life you playin' wit!"

The tires screech and the car swerves. Fletcher yells, "You done fucked up now, Bubby!" We bank right and rumble along the shoulder.

There's horror in Bubby's eyes. "Hey, Fletch. C'mon, bress. Ay, Tahj, talk to ya boy!" Bubby is almost Fletcher's height, but he's a skinny wide receiver, a buck-ninety. Fletcher, a defensive end who gives quarterbacks nightmares, is 260 pounds of shredded muscle.

Bubby jumps out of the car while it's still rolling. Fletcher throws the car in park and hops out. Keenan and I hurry around and crowd Fletcher as he stalks Bubby, who spins around, now trotting backward, trying to talk Fletcher out of it. Bubby also searches along the highway for a weapon to make it a fair fight if it comes to blows. Bubby picks up a rotted plank that breaks off in his grasp.

Fletcher sheds his shirt and whips it to the ground.

I scream at Fletcher and push him in his chest. Fletcher calmly picks me up by the waist, turns around, sets me down out of the way, and then resumes stalking Bubby, ignoring Keenan who also pleads mercy for his cousin.

I grab Fletcher from behind, still screaming at him, and in all the excitement, while I'm holding a shirtless Fletcher back, I'm feeling his bare body and I absolutely melt.

A State Trooper pulls over. A stocky dark-haired man exits his patrol car and approaches with a cowboy grip on his belt. We put our hands up. "Put your damn hands down," he says. "What the hell's going on here?"

Suddenly we hear this sound, like the whistle of a thrown bottle, w-w-w-w-w-w. We duck first, then see that it's only Keenan stuttering, "W-w-we out here looking for berries."

The officer assumes they're fighting over me; out of fear, we don't correct him. He very well could've taken this opportunity to search the car where he would've found the fifth of Vodka, but he recognizes Bubby, the standout sophomore, nicknamed Black Panther, for his leaping catches and open field agility.

The officer issues no citations; he issues a speech, saying he'd been divorced twice and can attest that women are going to do whatever the hell they want, in life. "All we, as men, can do is accept it." The officer isn't satisfied until Fletcher has his shirt back on and we're all smiles.

There's complete silence for miles. Keenan drives. Bubby rides shotgun. I'm in the back leaning on Fletcher. He breaks the silence with an apology, as he should, "That's on me, y'all. I fucked up."

Bubby adds, "We bump heads because we love each other, man. It's supposed to happen this way."

We all know what's coming next. Keenan, with that distant stare and bittered mouth, says, "Y'all niggas is gay."

I close my eyes and pretend to sleep, being a fly on the wall to see how the guys talk without me. It dawns on me that Fletcher wasn't upset until he heard Donovan's comment about our sex life – which is a lie, by the way. I like that Donovan is an attentive lover, but he don't be hittin' it like that.

Bubby asks, "Tahj, you sleep back there?"

I give a soft snore as a yes. Fletcher answers for me. "My girl knocked out."

The car gets quiet again for a while, then Bubby says, "Yo, Fletch… Say, Fletch…?"

Fletcher answers, "Yeah?"

Bubby says, "You luh that gal, ain't it?"

Fletcher doesn't reply. He just pulls me a little tighter and kisses the top of my head.

CHAPTER 3
CHOCOLATE THUNDER

Fletcher, Bubby, and Keenan surround me like they're my security detail as I enter the historic Miami Fashion Weekend to represent my first big-name designer on the runway. Everything is a blur leading up to the big moment. We're getting styled and dressed and suddenly I'm in the same room and breathing the same air with legendary designer, Esmeralda Alamilla. And they expect me not to cry and ruin my makeup.

Miss Alamilla walks the line of girls and then stops right in front of me. She wears a stylish hooded shawl and large gradient shades, which she removes and bites the tip as she tries to figure out what to do with me. My breasts are actually too big to be a runway model, but somehow I've skidded by, all these years; maybe now the gig is up.

Miss Alamilla requests something in Spanish and then reaches back for it. She has assistants helping her; she trembles ever so slightly from the onset of Parkinson's, but her genius still thrives behind the web of wrinkles.

An assistant drops a lily in her waiting palm, which Esmeralda places in my hair and says, with a motherly smile, "Perfecto."

There's so much I could say about my experience at Miami Fashion Weekend. It is truly the warmest day of my modeling life, but I only highlight Miami Fashion Weekend in July, to contrast the nightmare that I experience three months later at New York Fashion Week in September.

In Miami, they put a flower in my hair.

In New York, they shave my hair.

Riley is there too. She'd been snarky with me since my first big show in Miami, and a few other paid shoots I'd had with respectable brands over the summer – versus her recurring Shopify shoots, but at this point in time, Riley's cool again because she's landed a premium gig beside me. We're missing nearly a week of fall semester classes; the question of not going never arises.

The day of the first show, we're all chatting in the dressing room. Suddenly the models stand at attention like soldiers for bunk inspection. In walks famous designer, Georgio Valentini with his mousy hair slicked back, his brow high, but eyes trained low. It's made clear that we do not speak a word to him, nor so much as look him in the eyes. He casually passes through, taking mental notes. He then gathers the stylists and whispers his recommendations.

One stylist b-lines to me. She has me sit in the chair, then swivels me around to face her in the mirror. She squats on level with me. To my mirror reflection, she says, quite lovingly, as if offering a child stick of cotton candy, "We're gonna cut your hair, okay?"

I spot clippers in her hand. I spin away. "Cut my hair?"

She shields me from Valentini's line of sight, and says, "Let's talk quietly." She explains that, as big a figure as Valentini is, he is the pettiest little human she's ever known. "Piss him off and he'll pull every string to make sure you never work a show of this magnitude again."

I take a moment to let it sink in. I sigh and ask, "How much? How much of my hair do you wanna cut?"

The stylist hands me her phone. Seeing a photo of a dark-skinned model she'd styled before, my mouth could barely manage the words, "I'm gonna be bald?"

As soon as I hear the buzz of the electric clippers, it's running down the center of my head. A gasp sticks in my throat, my mouth gaped, but not breathing. Tears spill as my shoulder-length hair rains. I'm robbed of what feels like a body part. This is rape — for someone who has no idea what rape is like.

Riley doesn't offer to hold my hand, nor does she gesture empathy from a distance. She's having a good ole time, chatting with her stylist.

I figure Riley's avoiding me for the optics. The only two black girls huddled in grief might look like the beginnings of a protest, but even later, while we're alone in our shared hotel room, Riley's nonchalant about my anguish.

I'm falling apart in there because there are forearms with more hair than my head. I'm in crisis mode. And what do I do in a crisis? Call momma.

I Facetime her without warning. She'd been expecting my call, with this being my second big-time catwalk — a long way from modeling the gowns for the bridal shop she ran, until she closed the business due to an injury that severed some of the nerves in her right hand.

Momma appears on the screen, aghast. Her hand falls from her mouth as she says, "You let them people cut your hair!" She gets up and then sits down. "Maurice? Come look at this."

Daddy slides into view. "Hey, baby girl," he says. His smile drops at the sight of my scalp. He downplays it with a shrug. "Well, hey… You're beautiful regardless."

I'm crying worse than I had when my hair was raining down at my feet. "I don't wanna be beautiful *regardless*," I cry. Daddy passes the phone to momma like it's hot, so I cry to her. "Nobody else had to cut all their hair off, momma! Only me!" Momma doesn't try to calm me down; she knows her baby. She let me finish so *she* could finish without interruption.

Soon, momma starts setting me straight. "Tahj, you not no Sampson! It ain't in your hair; it's in *you*," Momma says. "That thing you got, baby — ya can't fake it; ya can't make it, and they sure as hell can't take it. When you hit that stage, Tahj, you send a message. You let that lil wet rat, Valentini, know that whatever — *it* — is… you got it!"

I'm smiling by the time we're saying goodbye.

Ever since Riley ended the call with her folks, she'd been sitting on the edge of her bed, sighing and tapping a foot, as if dying to get a word in. Her eyes sparkle with righteousness. "The eyes of the blind will be open, and the ears of the deaf will be unstopped."

Riley's been acting religious ever since her mother got remarried. Her stepfather is a square-pants conservative with a high position in the church, looking like Larry Elder in the face.

Just to piss Riley off, I say, "You *and* King James can kiss my ass, Riley."

Riley gasps, "It's just another way of saying: what'd you *think* was gone happen?"

I draw back. "Obviously, I didn't think they'd shave my head! Or I would've told my agent to kiss my ass."

Riley slaps the back of one hand on the palm of the other. "The low cut… the international look… You're a beautiful dark-skin girl, Tahj, that's your lane."

Instead of jumping fresh on Riley's ass for pairing beautiful and dark skin when she knows better, I merely counter her shade. "You're a pretty light-skinned girl, Riley, but they didn't cut your hair."

"You know I didn't mean it like that." The ensuing silence feels like failure. I fall back on the bed and sigh to show that I've check out of the conversation.

Riley, however, keeps on talking – preaching about the industry, as if she is the teacher and not the student in this. I pass, on all opportunities to correct her to prevent having to tell her about her ass, and having an awkward trip back home.

Minutes in, Riley doesn't even seem to realize that she's talking to herself, so I figured I'd help her out. I turn over, away from her, and say, "I just wish I had my sewing machine." The statement isn't just filler. I sew in real life. I sewed my pink prom dress a year in advance. I sew when I'm stressed; I sew when I'm depressed; I sew as a way to treat myself when I'm broke; I sew when there's a specific need for a piece, or when there's a design in my mind fighting to get out. I sew. It's in my blood. My mother still sews despite her injured hand, and so does two of my aunties and one sweet uncle. My modeling only came about because momma needed the free labor for her bridal shop. Her very own daughter happened to be the perfect little candidate: rail thin with legs like stilts since third grade. I feel a nostalgic smile spread across my face – a smile that Riley thinks she made possible with advice that I wasn't even listening to. She plops down on the bed next to me and rubs my back, saying, "You got this girl."

I acknowledge Riley with a nod, while all along I'm rethinking where I fit in the scheme of fashion. Because if I've got to walk around with an egghead every day just for the few minutes I spend on stage, modeling ain't it. Silently I pledge that beyond this event, my focus is solely on design and that's final.

But baby… the next day when I'm on stage – baldhead and all – I'm feeling myself.

When I hit that catwalk, I'm feeling myself so much that even my errors produce brilliance. On a 180 turn at the end of the runway, I step too wide, but in order to buy a split second to recover, I give a slight shimmy to distract the eyes from the left foot that I drag into balance. The audience eats it up. As I walk back off stage, the artistic director has her high beams set on me. Instead of scolding me, she drops a hand on my shoulder and says, "More of that!"

As I'm in the chute awaiting my next walk, I see Valentini in the back, reaming the director. I'll never know for sure what Valentini says, but he points to the top of the runway where I had hit my move, then points to himself; it's as if saying that *he's* the attraction and he will not have his thunder stolen by some no-name model and her antics.

I go out, stride over stride, in a boned corset top and single-pleat almond pants. I simply give the same ole competitive chin tip and hands flair that us black people do, for a nonverbal whassup. The other models are being vogue, while I'm being dope, and the audience is eating it up like I'm Liberace out there.

Valentini, still red in the face and still giving it to the director, stops midsentence. He surveys the riled audience. Valentini then looks at me on my return strut. My drip makes his face fall slack with awe – makes him forget whatever he was saying to the artistic director.

My head-turn meets his gaze, the audience still thinks I'm performing with this sneer upon my lips, but I'm dead-ass. Why? Because the great Valentini has yielded to me!

Backstage Riley sums it up with her signature shoulder roll, and "Bay-*bee!* My girl showed out!"

I couldn't wait to call Fletcher. I'm in the dressing room with my titties out and the phone wedged between my shoulder and ear, telling Fletcher how I set the catwalk ablaze.

Just hearing, over the phone, the joy this man has for my wins, brings me to tears. I hug the phone to my breast and exhale to hide the fact that I'm crying.

Fletcher's single now, and we've been talking a lot lately because he's been sick over Gigi, who finally broke it off nearly three months after that Miami road trip. Gigi exited their two-year relationship by ghosting Fletcher, and then posting her new boo – some well-off, conditioning coach for the Atlanta Falcons.

Fletcher asks me what I'm doing this weekend because the guys are coming home, on some spur-of-the-moment type of thing. Keenan's father bought a new truck and since Keenan's coming to swap for the hand-me-down, Fletcher and Bubby decided to visit. Since college split us up, the four of us haven't been in the same room together for a while.

Fletcher tells me they plan to go to the theatre to see the new Guardian of the Galaxies movie then turn-up later that night.

I can't let him see me bald, so I lie, "Me and Donovan going out of town."

Fletcher keeps pushing the issue, as if I didn't just explain to him that I can't.

He says, "I'll come a day early."

"I can't," I say.

Fletcher keeps pressuring me to open some part of my schedule, if only just a half hour, to see the guys. "…Or maybe just you and me," he slips in, suggestively. It would be our first time seeing each other since his breakup with Gigi.

Fletcher seems so desperate to see me that I begin to think maybe, since the breakup with Gigi, he's not as okay as he says he is. Maybe he's falling apart. And to keep from seizing and chewing off his tongue, he needs my lips to kiss. For that, he'd need to see me in person. And therein lies the problem. I'm only two days bald and insecure.

People look at me like I'm a cancer patient or a Sudani refugee. And maybe it's because I lack the confidence to make my bald head look like a flex. Whatever the reason, there's no way I can let Fletcher see me like this. I couldn't bear his lies, insisting I'm beautiful, while privately repulsed by me; he'd never be able to unsee it.

I'm on the phone gathering my things in a dressing room full of models that I just recently outshined, and I'm feeling ugly, and telling Fletcher I can't see him this weekend. "I can't... Sorry, Fletch... I just can't."

Fletcher insists, "C'mon, don't do me like that."

"Do you like what, bro? I already had plans. You can't expect me to drop everything, like–"

"I would drop everything for *you*–"

"Likewise! But when there is a need. This is not that. You're talking about going out to the club."

Fletcher sighs; his response comes out quiet and humble. "Tahj, you know me. You know I wouldn't be pressing you if it was simply club night. I'm going through some shit, right now, a'ight? I need you. I'm telling you, I need you."

Fletcher's right. I do know him. I know him well enough to hear the parts he won't say. "*Why* do you need me, Fletcher? Why haven't you needed me like this in two whole years, Fletcher? What's changed?"

Fletcher lets silence speak for him.

"That's what I thought," I say. "I have a boyfriend."

"Didn't I have a girlfriend when...?" The sentence finishes itself, *when we kissed.*

He's sick with heartbreak after losing Gigi for driving to Miami to support me. And I'm sick because my hair won't let me quote-unquote help him. Help *myself*, is what I'd really be doing. Maybe kissing him is a line that I wouldn't cross, for the fact that I have a man. But the fact that I'm bald keeps me from showing up to *toe* that line and let a long hug confess everything that my mouth would deny for as long as I'm committed to someone else. I see myself hugged up with Fletcher, gazing in his eyes, agonizing over what I'm missing out on, on account of my hair, but while I'm daydreaming, I'm not saying anything.

My silence is received as rejection. Fletcher hangs up without a goodbye. And my baldheaded ass sat there feeling somewhat relieved, thinking that maybe not speaking for a while would give my hair time to grow back if I could hold off seeing Fletcher until fall semester break.

After getting dressed, I walk out of Spring Studios at 50 Varick Street with a heap of praise and business cards. Riley, to my surprise, is my biggest cheerleader. She urges me to come meet with "the girls" who're gathering at a restaurant for a feast to end weeks of fasting leading up to Fashion Week, as if it's their very own Ramadan. I'd seen girls measuring their water intake, and eating only a half cucumber for lunch, so I understand why, at the restaurant, the six or seven girls who showed up aren't talking to each other; they're too busy stuffing their faces as if competing in an eating contest. One model, Teagan with the green eyes comes up for air and says, "You guys are *so* lucky."

Riley and me eye each other, thinking maybe she meant that we're merely diversity hires, but Teagan explains, "You guys (black models) don't have to starve yourself. I mean… we're *all* skinny, but we (white models) have to look friggin' sick; that's our assignment."

Seeing her clavicle so painfully pronounced, helps me feel less cheated about my scalp. I try to conjure words of empathy for Teagan, but a gentleman interrupts with a business card scissored between two fingers.

"Dan O'Brien," the man says. "Call me Dano."

I offer my name as reluctantly as I take his card. "Tahj Thompson."

"How long are you here in New York?"

"We leave tomorrow morning."

"Well, I'm here for the third year in a row – becoming sort of a regular thing now," he mumbles. "I'm an anthropologist, specializing in aesthetics."

"Aesthetics?"

"The study of beauty. I run a test I've been doing for a few years. Tested about thirty-something models here just the past couple days."

I'm already dismissing him. "Are you talking about the Golden Ratio?"

Riley chimes in with attitude, "More like *White* Ratio."

I float a palm to her assessment. "Exactly," I say.

Dano, impatiently scratching the back of his neck, drops the hand at his turn to speak. "I'm glad we all feel the same way about it. This new test doesn't measure to a European standard of beauty but a *global* standard of beauty."

Riley huffs and whispers, as if the man can't clearly hear her say, "Trying to lure us into the back of a van, must be."

He smiles. "I don't fault you for thinking that." He has long hair and he wears those serial killer, wire frame glasses. "Thing is, I'm not trying to get anyone into a van – just a rented conference room at the hotel down the street. It's where my equipment is set up." With a coy smile, he adds, "Not to toot my own horn, but I know my shit. And I'm telling you, Tahj, your score will be way up there."

Riley says, "*Her* score. What about mine?"

Dano's head tilts as he appraises Riley. Apparently, he forms an opinion he'd rather keep to himself. His eyes cut to me. "What doya say? Takes just a half-hour."

We pick up and go, leaving half-eaten plates. Riley grills Dano the whole way. "This doesn't make any sense. If it's free, how do you make a living? Where does the money come from?"

"First of all, it isn't just me. Worldwide, there are about seventy-something scientists just like myself. I'm but a pawn on a big ole chess board." Dano sighs and continues, "Where does the money come from, you ask? Where science *always* gets its money: wealthy donors, corporations, big universities… The U.S. government, via grants…" With a curl of his finger he invites us to a secret. "You didn't get this from me, but the world is about to get a whole lot worse for common folks. And the powers that be, are in a rat race to find ways to get people to accept the world that's coming. On the other hand, you've got corporations interested in how this study could impact advertisement, brand recognition, and all that… Finally, you have the science community and wealthy philanthropists who see the humanitarian benefit, to possibly reshape systems that were built on privilege. This study has racked up a bill of over fourteen million dollars. But me, drawing a salary without having to stand in front of a classroom? Priceless."

We're crossing the painted street as I look down at the business card, which says that Dano – this lemon-lot salesman-looking character – has a PhD from Harvard.

As we step up the opposite sidewalk, Riley questions, "How can a study like this be valid? Beauty is so subjective."

"*So* subjective, in fact," Dano says, with a number one raised. "…that those in power can remake beauty in their own image. Think if Egypt were still the greatest empire in the world, everybody would be dyeing their hair black instead of blonde, and buying brown color contacts instead of blue. We've mined through all the subjectivity and found some universal and mathematical consistencies."

Dano is so long-winded with his answers, I decide to keep my questions to myself.

We enter the hotel conference room and he has me scan a QR code for a lengthy survey on my phone browser. He tells Riley, "You can also take the test if you like."

Riley's reply lets me know just how bothered she is that she wasn't nominated. "Ain't nobody worried about your stupid little test."

While I'm doing the survey, Riley's next to me with her legs crossed, ankle rolling, eyes thinned in disgust. "Hey, Danny – or whatever your name is? What, about my face, tells you I won't score high on the–"

"–We can start with the lack of distance between your eyes or the shallow eye sockets, which gives you a flat-faced kinda look; your nasolabial folds are a bit plush–"

"–What about you, sir?" Riley says with two irritated hand claps. "Who are *you* to tell *me* about–"

"–Who am I? The person whose opinion you asked for."

Riley scoffs, "Nasolabial folds. This, coming from somebody who looks like Jeffrey Dahmer or somebody."

To calm Riley, I pat her leg. "Okay, you win," I say.

She points a rigid finger to her chest bone and says, "The only reason I'm here is because I don't want my friend ending up in a meat locker somewhere, messing with you."

Dano seems pleased by the rise he'd gotten out of Riley, but he lets it die there.

I try changing the subject. "Bubby's coming to town this weekend."

"And," Riley frowns.

"Bubby's gonna be rich."

Riley does her booshy girl thing, batting her lashes and throwing her nose in the air. "You'll never catch me with a dude who walks around with his mouth hung open – talmbout some, 'Whassup, shawty.' Uh-uh… Bubby is way too hood for me."

"Really," I say. "Ain't you from Lakewood Heights?"

"Lakewood what? Puh-lease," she says with filth.

Riley's denial is so thorough, I figure it wouldn't be worth the effort to make her admit. "Ok," I relent, although I know for a fact that Riley used to live in the Heights.

"Anyway," says Riley. "Is it just Bubby coming this weekend, or is it Fletcher too?"

I run my hand back over this little bristle of hair on my head and say, "I'm so mad I let them cut my hair. Yes, Fletcher's coming this weekend, and I just lied to him on the phone, saying I'm gonna be out of town."

"On account of your hair?"

"If I went out with the guys, I'd probably end up arguing with Donovan anyway."

Riley comments, "I don't mean no harm, Tahj, but you must be out your rabid-ass mind."

"What?"

Riley swats a hand at my apparent foolishness. "Ain't no way you're this gullible. Fletcher is a future multi-millionaire, and you're gonna cancel seeing him, for a liberal arts major slash short-order cook who does poetry? Where'd you get your picker-meter from,

Tyler Perry movies?" Riley's hands flail out. "Fletcher's ole cradle-robbing, bubble-butt gal done left him needing a shoulder to cry on. It's your time to shine! Shoot, if it were me…" Riley crosses her legs away from me and mumbles something lewd, then checks my reaction.

Nonverbally, I'm daring her to keep playing with me.

"Tahj. I know you not trippin'. You know I would never try to get with Fletcher. This just jokes."

I point, then laugh like my attitude was all a prank, but chiiile… In my mind, I was already measuring the distance to snatch her hair.

A laughing Riley shakes a finger. "Had me going for a second, there."

We return to small talk, but undeniably, the air has changed. We get back to kee-keeing, but an elephant's with us in that hotel lobby, kee-keeing too.

Riley revives the subject again on a more serious note. "I'm just trying to tell you, as a friend. Don't let somebody come along and snatch Fletcher up before you come to your senses."

I complete the survey and Dano guides me into a booth, which is an aluminum frame in the shape of a cube, draped with thin white curtains to soften the lighting from the lamps on the outside. Dano gives a few instructions. "Look straight ahead. Chin up. Hold completely still for me." Many infrared lasers pinpoint my face like I'm the target of fifty assassins.

Dano's curtain silhouette shows him using a stylus pen on a MacBook. He gives more commands, to smile, to open my mouth, to close my mouth, to close my eyes… then he tells me to open my eyes and that it'll be a bit uncomfortable. The lights flash directly into my pupils. Dano then orders me to turn to the side, and it's the same drill, collecting data from *200 nodal points.*

Dano asks me to step out. As I split the white curtain, I find him shaking his head with a cheeky smile that won't go away. "I knew it," he says.

"Knew what," I inquire. "I scored high?"

"I'm fortunate to have found you. And I'm honored to tell you, Miss Thompson, that out of a database of nearly a hundred thousand women, you are the known most beautiful woman in the world."

Just by Dano's delivery, I saw it coming a mile away; still, it hit me a fist in my gut. I'm out of breath with disbelief. "I'm what!"

Riley stands. She comes over with this expression like she's just walked in on her parents doing the nasty. I'm shaking hands with Dano when Riley hugs me from the side and then spins me around. "This… has got to be… poetic justice for you," Riley says, dreamily. "You find out you're the most beautiful woman in the world… and the one person here to witness is a girl who teased you back in the day."

34

CHAPTER 4
2020

Bubby's getting married just a couple of months before he'll become a rich professional athlete. Fletcher, Keenan, and myself are all surprised by Bubby, the playboy of the crew, beating all of us to the altar. What doesn't surprise us is that she's white.

Emily Schnieder is also a collegiate athlete, a UGA volleyball player with a body that Bubby just had to have. Reportedly, Fletcher frowned and said, but that face tho – to which, Bubby replied, *Ya don't fuck the face bro.*

Bubby's comment came four months before going down one knee before Miss Fuck Face at centerfield during a televised game. It was supposed to be just a sex thing, but Emily made Bubby wait and he started liking her in the process. Emily then confided that she's a virgin waiting for marriage, but it wasn't so much that she was a virgin. This devout Mormon, from a nuclear home, and former state cup-stacking champion was the furthest thing from Bubby's mother he could find.

Bubby's still technically broke, so he commissioned me to make the wedding gown for free. I barely finish in time because the wedding is rushed. Either Emily's hurrying to tie the knot before this negro comes to his senses, or maybe it's really the pandemic. She says she wants the wedding underway before public gatherings are banned outright. Bubby, to our surprise, doesn't get cold feet; he's in as much of a rush, as Emily, to wed.

Now, on the wedding day, I'm applying my makeup in the mirror, feeling legit guilt for the conversations that Fletcher, Keenan, and myself have had outside of Bubby's presence. We've been dancing around the idea that maybe the pandemic has him worried that there won't be an NFL to be drafted into, and that maybe Bubby – deep down inside – thinks money is what makes this marriage palatable for Emily, who'd never dated a black guy in her life until she was approached by one who's a future millionaire. As soon as that thought completes in my mind, I force it out.

I lean with the kabuki brush to highlight my cheeks, thinking, this is my friend's big day, and I won't let a shady thought hang around long enough to later slip as a shady comment.

My hair is still short. During the process of growing my hair back, I noticed how short hair serves my face up like a ring cradle puts its gemstone on display. When I look in the mirror I don't see the most beautiful woman in the world. I see Tahj – and I love me some me. There was never a voice of loathing living inside my head; it lives on the outside, in the form of a bitter boyfriend, whose reflection slides into the mirror frame behind me. Donovan is still in street clothes. I say, "Guess you're not coming."

"Let's pretend it's unrelated to the fact that I haven't been cumming at all lately."

I pause my eyeliner pencil, a finger peeling the lower lid, incidentally giving a reaction more telling than an eye-roll. Donovan is in the exact place I met him two years prior: in a low-paying job with a half-finished book of poetry titled *Maladies of Man*. He despises me for surpassing him.

He leans in the doorway and says, "Am I the only person who thinks Bubby's fiancé is ugly? She was over here trying on that gown, looking like The Bride of Chucky."

"Stop it. She's beautiful."

"You're beautiful." The flattery gets no rise out of me. His compliments, of late, have been merely the intro to a dis track. Donovan folds his arms. "But what *is* beauty, though," he narrates, as if he's the voice of a documentary on the subject. "Is it that all the points on your face have impeccable symmetry?" He squints like a sniper. "You're going to the wedding of a guy that wouldn't much smash a chick with 4C hair – didn't fall in love with any of the redbones and half-breeds he done ran through. Oh, but the moment that simpleminded, long-lipped southern negro got him an All-American girl from Cedar Rapids Iowa, he felt like he found him a piece of heaven."

"D!" I eye him in the mirror, lipstick in hand, awaiting the completion of these words: "Enough, alright."

Knowing he's getting on my nerves only makes him eviler. "I have no doubt that Bubby actually sees a beautiful woman. Wanna know why?" Donovan mistakes my weary sigh for a yes. "We don't see with our eyes. The brain only accepts half of what the eye collects. It fills in the gaps by way of cognitive association. With all the images we've been fed, the idealism of whiteness – it gives Emily one hell of a buffer. That's a buffer that you do not have the benefit of – because those who control the images don't look like you. You see, Tahj, these highly successful men you *think* you deserve; they don't scale the white world without wholeheartedly buying into it. They know they won't be invited to the country club with a spook on his arm."

I turn around and lean against the dresser. "Tell that to all the rich men in my DMs just praying for you to fumble."

He looks me up and down as if to comment on my dress. "What cognitive associations do pink and black evoke? To me, it looks amphibious."

I slam the blush on the counter. "Just be outta here when I get back! Maybe sleeping at your place in that little twin-sized bed will humble you."

I shoulder-bump him on the way out. My eyes are dry. Perhaps this is the end. The idea itself brings relief. No more dimming my light for fear of my shine consuming his. No more limiting myself to the places Donovan can afford. At modeling events I find myself managing his feelings instead of networking. At Donovan's poetry events, I have to hear him refer to every woman as goddess, then refer to me as Tahj, because I don't wear sandals and linens. I represent the materialism that he slams with his performances.

What were we thinking? We're just too different. I thought Donovan was deep, but when the bickering began, I realized that he's simply the most eloquent version of an asshole I'd ever met.

I threw myself into my work as a way to figuratively exit the relationship. I've been busy sewing, and busy tutoring Bubby via Facetime to keep him off of academic probation. I'd quit the modeling agency and used the contacts I made during New York Fashion Week to book more shows. Those shows led to more contacts and more shows, and kinda snowballed into a full-time job for this full-time student. With all the contacts I'd gained over the years, I became an agent for others. I picked up a few clients just by approaching them in public and saying, You're pretty. Do you model?

I have so many obligations that, having to tend to a relationship became just another thing on my plate. I used to judge women who entertained casual relationships, and now I find myself open to having one.

When I *do* start looking for love again, one thing's for sure, I'll be leery of men like Donovan because the tongue that's sharp enough to carve a woman a throne, is also sharp enough to slit the queen's throat while she sits upon it. There was a point where he had the most beautiful woman in the world convinced that she'd be hard-pressed to do better than a narcissist whose love language is to project his self-loathing onto his lover.

Hearing myself think it in these terms while driving toward the wedding, helps me decide that I will, in fact, end the relationship.

It would be the first time in a long time that both Fletcher and me would be single. Ironically he's now morphed into the kind of man that I would never date.

Fletcher's become a man of conquest. He's well aware that he's a walking fantasy with his diamond-cut face, a squinter with an inviting smile, the body like A.I. art, all tatted up and animated with the swag of an alpha. He doesn't lie to women; he lets them lie to themselves, so some even know about each other.

They've been letting Fletcher get away with so much that he's become fascinated with the idea of poly relationships – never facing the real issue that Gigi has ruined him, so now he uses a band-aid of many women, over the broken heart he suffered at the hands of one.

He even treats *me* differently now, the way he calls me baby-girl, the thievery in a gaze that undresses me; how he looks at me and licks his lips as if his tongue is living vicariously through his eyes.

His compliments have changed. It used to be, *That skirt is fire*, or him yelling out, *Okay legs!* But now it's *Dayumn*, when I'm working them heels, or when I got my chocolate twins squeezed in a pushup bra, he's licking his lips with a sly, *Fuck around...* I ain't never had an ass to brag about, but let me bend over for any reason, and here go Fletcher: stroking his beard, talkin' about, *Shiiiid…* I never liked men flirting with me in this way, but with Fletcher, I love it – even if he is this way with other women. I'll soon be free to find out what keeps these women fiending him like addicts.

The wedding venue is at The Roof, in Atlanta's Old Fourth Ward, which is the old Sears Roebuck building twice renovated from City Hall East (for as long as I can remember), to the recently renovated Ponce City Market, still preserving the original architecture from a time when milk delivery trucks were as common as Amazon delivery trucks today.

It's an odd venue because of COVID safety protocols; atypical times call for atypical weddings. Open-air ceremonies are deemed safer, so the procession wouldn't see the inside of a church, which seems disappointing, but when I arrive at the rooftop and see the view of Atlanta's cityscape and how the venue is done up quite elegantly with lights strung above and white linens spiraling down the poles of the gazebo and open bar, it's apparent that safety concerns forced them into a better option than their unforced imaginations could fathom.

My purse is stuffed with masks in wedding colors that I sewed for the bridesmaids and groomsmen, which they seem to have no interest in wearing. I have one mask left, with no one to give it to because Fletcher's nowhere in sight.

I'm handing a mask to Bubby's best man, Keenan, who tells me he hasn't seen Fletcher in a minute either, but in a change of subjects, Keenan leans in to tell me, "Hey, look, don't say nothing to nobody about this, Tahj, but… Bubby asked me to be his agent."

It warms my heart to know that Keenan won't be left out, since he's clearly not getting drafted into the NFL. I ask, "You said yes, right?"

"Hell… to-the yeah… shoot. Why bless… a stranger with all that money? Keep it in the family, ya know?"

Over the years Keenan has done therapy and rarely stutters, but now speaks like a man who's out of breath. And since my toxic trait is to mimic the person I'm speaking to, I sorta sound the same. "You know, Kee, I'm… already an agent. If you need… help with contract negotiations… endorsements…" I grip his collar to say, "Don't you hesitate… hear me?"

Keenan replies, "You took the words… right out my mouth. I'm about to cuff my degree in sports management, and what have you… but you got that hands-on, sis. Can't beat that." Keenan looks around conspicuously then asks, "Why don't you talk to Fletcher about being *his* agent?"

"Isn't Fletcher holding out for a top agent, though?"

"I told my boy he reaching, but he don't hear me though. You just stay in his ear. Closed mouths… don't get fed."

Just then, in Keenan's background, I spot this girl we know named Tameka, nicknamed Meek, coming out onto the rooftop, looking around like she was dropped in wonderland. She's one of Fletcher's throwaways who is so stuck on him, that she befriended me for proximity to Fletcher. I say, "Now, who invited her?"

A wide-eyed Keenan, asks, "Who invited who?"

"Meek."

Keenan wrestles a grin into submission. "Well, if anybody can find Fletcher… bet that ole blood-hound can."

I whisper, "She's coming."

"Gotta go." Keenan pivots and marches on, leaving me holding the bag, and that bag is Meek – beautiful girl, nice girl, but sickening as the devil. Being in fashion all my life, I can tell how her anxiety shows up in her appearance, how her makeup isn't thoroughly blended, and how she favors body dresses to avoid the stress of matching pieces together. I always say, give me a week with Tameka and I'll have her polished. The baddie look does not favor her, with its excesses of shine, from hair gel to lip gloss and the bling of designer shades. I'd give her a look that's simplistic and elegant, with matte colors to soften her aura.

"Hey Tahj," she waves.

"Hey Meek. You're early."

"Earlier than this," Meek says. "I been here for a minute; it's that I'm just now coming upstairs."

I ask, "Have you seen Fletcher?"

"Fletcher? Yeah," she says casually, but there's this darting of eyes that gives away her distress.

"Is there something the matter?"

Meek's hand swats limp. "Naw girl it's just…" She resets her thoughts with a sigh. "Guess who *else* is here early?"

"Who?"

"Riley. When is this chick ever early for anything? But here she is, well before time, over at that Dancing Goats Café flirting with Fletcher, with her iced caramel macchiato with chocolate sprinkles on the whipped cream."

I squint. "That's awfully specific, Meek."

"You ought to see Riley: the way she hangs on his every word, the way she toss her hair aside before lowering her mouth onto that straw, like she's showing off how she'd do him."

I now, legit suspect Tameka of stalking. "Again, that's quite specific there, Meek," I say.

"Riley is my friend–"

"–Is she? Or are we making things up again? You only kick it with Riley on occasion because of me, and I haven't been kicking it with her lately. You don't need to make up some sort of narrative. If you wanna be mad at Riley, be mad at her; she gets off on it, actually…"

My mouth: "…And if Riley and Fletcher wanna be together there's nothing you or I can do about it."

My mind: Bullshit!

I calmly help Tameka find a seat, but I take off to go yank Fletcher by the ear. I'm on the elevator pacing because it isn't descending fast enough. I remember Riley once joking-not-joking about what she would do to Fletcher, and now just days ahead of the NFL Combine and two months before he acquires millions, she's flirting over coffee? The way Fletcher's been moving lately, I wouldn't put it past him to sleep with her if the opportunity presented itself.

When the elevator hits bottom, I'm a bullet shot out of its chamber, shouldering through folks like a mother for a lost child, but as soon as I reach the café, my whole energy changes. I'm a casual shopper strolling in, by chance, in a pink mini wrap-cut dress and heels, eyes up, scanning the menu behind the counter.

I see what Meek saw; Riley, across the table from Fletcher, summoning all of her feminine wiles. I wave. They wave back and nothing more, as if neither would invite me over – which is odd.

To heck with it, I say, then I walk over, tickling the air. "Hey, you two. Got something for ya, Fletch." I hand him the mask. To Riley, I say, "Congratulations on qualifying for the Miss Georgia pageant. I'm so happy for you."

Riley, not motioning for a hug, turns her face up to me to say, "Thank you Tahj. You've already congratulated me for that, but I'll take seconds."

Fletcher looks tight-faced like he did that day at the mall with Gigi. I say to him, "Hey, Fletch… Let me know when you get a minute… something I've been meaning to talk to you about."

"I got a minute right now, actually." Fletcher half gets up, but questions it, his eyes stopped on Riley. "We *were* just about to dip, right?"

"You two go right on ahead," Riley says, while pulling her purse strap up her arm.

Fletcher says to me, "We can talk on the way back, bet?"

I turn to go, thinking Fletcher's right behind me, but he'd stopped to discard their trash. I'm waiting at the exit when Riley and her loud perfume passes by; her chin turns to a shoulder in a sassy look-back. "No coffee, Tahj?"

The question is rhetorical, suggesting my visit to the coffee shop was motivated by a different kind of thirst.

Fletcher offers his forearm, like a butler in his tux. He says, "I think I know what you wanna talk about."

"Probably," I say. "But first, what was *that* about?"

"What?"

My response is a face drained of humor.

"Oh, it wadn't nothin' just talking. Funny thing, though…" He pauses with a gait of bewilderment.

"Spit it out," I say.

"Riley… She fucking prayed for me, man. Right there at the table. She said I've lost my way… the partying, the broads…"

Softly, I ask, "Was it real? Or was she just trying to get close to you?"

Fletcher's taken aback. "It felt genuine. And she's right. I gotta…" He sighs, "I gotta do better."

I say, "It just seems kind of suspect to me. I pray for you in silence – not only for your personal wellbeing, but every time you go out on that field I ask God to cover you."

He replies, "I know you do, Tahj."

Riley prayed for him in person. Touché. Internally, I kick myself for not thinking of doing it first.

Fletcher asks, "So where Donovan at?"

I lean away, frowning. "Donovan who?"

"Oh, you finally came to your senses?" For a year now, he'd been telling me to drop Donovan.

"I should've took your advice earlier."

"So, what'd you wanna talk about?"

I hadn't planned on asking Fletcher to be his agent, but since I interrupted his coffee date, saying I needed to talk, it's the only reason I could think of. I start with a slow, singing, "Well, ya know… Bubby made Keenan *his* agent, right?"

"Aw shit." Fletcher's dips, as if his arms suddenly weigh a ton. He begins talking a mile a minute, saying everything but no. He explains how his situation is different from Bubby's, who'd be the first wide receiver taken in the draft, and receiving a max rookie contract, leaving no room for negotiation; therefore, it doesn't matter who

Bubby has for an agent. Fletcher, on the other hand, is a defensive end coming out in a draft year that's stacked with defensive end prospects.

He's a fourth-rounder at best, which sounds weird to me because, for millions of viewers and myself, the eye test reveals that when ten armored men clash in what looks like Medieval battle, often it's Fletcher launching through the melee with a big hit that changes the momentum of the game.

Unlike modeling scouts, NFL scouts do not trust their eyes; their sight is guided by stats, so knowing that only 10% of Fletcher's sacks came in under four seconds tells them to pay attention to Fletcher's wingspan measurement, which falls short of men who historically dominate the position.

Fletcher believes the NFL Combine – an event of athletic drills to test strength, speed, and agility – will produce a new set of stats to force NFL scouts see his worth.

If only beauty had stats. My stat line for the 200 nodal points on a face would remove this awful subjectivity from the eyes of those who don't readily see me as pretty.

"Did you hear what I just said?"

I cut my eyes. "Of course, I heard you." I didn't. "You said everything but no." That's what he won't say. He'd rather me back out and relieve him of the pressure because he doesn't have the nerve to say no to me, but what this negro somehow *does* have the nerve to say to me is, "Why you worried about that little percentage an agent gets when you could have it all?"

I look over at him, and I can't feel my face to know the expression I'm giving – amused, puzzled… willing? All of those things? Fletcher doesn't crack a smile. I say, "You're serious?"

"Dead ass."

I stop and pull him out of the flow of foot traffic. I say, "It pains you that much to say no, that you would rather play with my emotions, than say you don't want me for an agent?"

This man looks me dead in my eyes and says, "I *don't* want you for my agent. I want you for my life."

A sigh lets me know that I had stopped breathing. I look away and my eyes land on wedding guests stuffing onto the elevator in the distance, which prompts me to snatch Fletcher by the hand. "Boy bring your ass on. Groomsman can't be late for the wedding."

"You think I'm playing?"

"We'll talk… later," I say.

We're speedwalking, Fletcher looks over with a sly grin. "So, when is later?"

"Tonight."

"At your place?"

"Ah," I say. "Now I see what you're up to."

He challenges, "What am up to?"

We enter the elevator, feeling lucky that it's empty.

"Speak on it, Tahj," Fletcher asks, playing clueless.

I hit the button and wait for the doors to close before I give my naughty reply. An older lady dressed for a wedding, possibly an auntie of Bubby, hurries toward the elevator. I pray, in silence, that she fails. This elevator is the only privacy Fletcher and I will have for a while. Fletcher tries to reach across me to stop the door. I pull his hand down, and then I'm looking auntie dead in the face as the door slides shut.

"*Tahj*," Fletcher laughs. "That's messed up."

I sneak and text Donovan *it's over*, then I say to Fletcher, "As I was saying: I know what you're up to. You're trying to get me in bed." I back into him. Fletcher lets out a surprised but sexy, "Oh shit." I back him into the elevator wall. His arms envelop me. My head angles back, lips poised. His kiss is warm honey on my lips, his tongue is an orange slice entering my mouth. I churn in his arms to face him for a full, frontal kiss. My body is as activated as that prom night when we kissed under the stars. Fletcher teases back, his eyes darting all over me as if to verify that he's not dreaming. I can't believe it myself. All those years of restraint brings our mouths together in a hot and luscious kiss. He lays my head back and sucks my neck. I'm looking up at the ceiling of an ascending metal box wishing we had more time. He squeezes my buns harder than they'd ever been squeezed, and he says to me, "Let's go somewhere."

That sexy whisper makes a warm light turn on in vijayjay. I want him so bad, I can't even remember the word no, so I say, "But the wedding's about to start…" I take his hanky, swab my lipstick from his lips, and return it to his lapel. I steal one last kiss and say, "Tonight, okay?"

"Tonight? That gives you plenty of time to overthink it, Tahj," Fletcher complains. "I *know* you."

The elevator dings. Fletcher unhands me and we quickly face front, containing ourselves like bottled mischief. While the door parts open, I smooth my dress; Fletcher tugs his suit – and this is what Meek sees.

She stands in the doorway, eyes beaming with the glimpse of Fletcher and me straightening our clothes, and my lipstick oddly missing. I can tell that it rocks Tameka to her core – no matter how she tries to smile it off and say, "I was just about to come looking for y'all."

Fletcher breaks away and hurries toward the groomsmen behind a curtain in the dining area. Meek follows me to the seating area. I spot momma, but the chairs on both sides of her are taken.

Meek has had the same smile painted on her face since the elevator; it sours just a little, as she says, "Must've got you some coffee too, huh?"

She'd said this while looking directly at my bare lips, which hands me the perfect excuse for my lipstick being gone. "I did, actually," I say.

"Mm-hm. I was about to say…"

"It was really good."

Tameka cosigns. "*Okay?* That's my favorite coffee bar. I know their menu by heart." She corners me with a sharp look and says, "So what did you order?"

Suddenly I'm on trial, and I get the distinct feeling that Meek's fixing to swing on me if my answer sounds bogus. What's worse is that I have no clue what's on that café's menu, and I am not a coffee person at all to say what a woman like me *would* fancy. In the ticking time, where I should be thinking of a lie, my mind clouds with a daymare of wedding guests having to pull us apart.

"I forget what it's called, um…" I tap my chin and look up into a fine blue sky for God to get me out of this, and then He reminds me, word for word, when Meek was so specific about Riley's order, so I repeat that. "It was the iced caramel macchiato with chocolate sprinkles on the whipped cream."

She follows me down the rows of folding chairs and sits right beside me. As I apply lipstick in my hand mirror, the tension makes me sick to my stomach.

CHAPTER 5
LEMME PUT THE TIP IN

ubby leans forward to kiss the bride, while his mother prays for an earthquake to prevent her son from effectively giving all his millions to someone who looks like those underqualified women who'd get promoted ahead of her at work. I know how Miss Annette's feeling because she had vented to me, the day she came over to check my progress on the wedding gown. She had said, "Sure as a groundhog's shadow is the signal for a long winter, a white woman jogging is our signal for gentrification." Bubby only knew Emily a few months while black women have to be overqualified, strung along ten years and coming to the altar with a fully formed family. Annette wouldn't say directly to Bubby; she just nitpicks about the wedding. She complained about having to forego the tradition of jumping the broom. Emily overheard and cluelessly offered to incorporate it into the wedding plans, to which Annette had replied, *We not gone play in our ancestors' face!* Annette, recovering from that memory, then looked at me and said, *They not clueless. They now trying to gentrify our men!*

I don't share Annette's sentiments towards white women, but I recognize the anguish she must feel for watching her son finalize his marriage with a kiss to this snow white Caucasian girl's lips, while God does nothing to intervene.

The change from wedding to reception is only a shuffle of chairs. The only members of the bride's family to make the cross-country trip during the pandemic, are the parents, the bride's maids, and six or so bright-eyed Iowans who are clearly sitting in the presence of more black people than they'd ever seen in one place.

Caterers, buttoned up to the neck, bring champagne trays for the dinner toast, and there is a stew of whispers among the guests.

I'm at the table with Meek who's getting on my nerves with all the sly remarks. "My girl Tahj don't play… went right downstairs and sent Riley packing… She say, not today. Not with *my* friend Fletcher. Went and got her*self* some coffee in the process…"

I know how Meek's mind works and I know what she's insinuating, but one of my pet peeves is people dropping hints instead of being direct. I now regret declining Bubby's offer to be in the wedding; I wouldn't have been stuck at a table with Meek. My mouth has the taste of disrespect in it. A few more sly comments from Meek and I'll look over with a smile and politely ask her to shut the fuck up.

The blare of a microphone shuts her up for me. Keenan begs everyone's attention for the toast. Although he talks like a man out of breath, it favors this speech, giving it an unscripted feel. He takes this small gathering on a nostalgic trip back to the dusty roads of Jackson, a small town a half-hour out of Atlanta where he and Bubby grew up – where their last name is mud and they're not expected to become anything in life. Keenan narrates the hard times they'd endured, namely, the unjust incarceration of his brother, along with other calamities this cold world has thrown at them. Keenan then turns to Emily to summarize, "I say all of that, to say… I am a witness, that…" Keenan takes a hard swallow and I know he's struggling not to get ahead of his words, but it gives space for emotion to set in, his eyes glassy with conviction. "God has saw fit to bestow upon you, a man… that is battle tested… a man… that is unwavering. Whatever you find yourself going through… Amari 'Bubby' Turner…?" Keenan's head lowers and shakes. "He'll be right there in the trenches with you… and he will see you through."

Their first dance as Mr. and Mrs. Amari Turner, is to the Beyoncé remake of Etta James's *At Last*.

Emily looks up, her eyes focused solely on Bubby, and she's crying so much that she laughs at her inability to compose herself.

Guests hurry towards the front to take phone pics of the first dance; Meek follows suit, leaving me at the table by myself.

Riley steals Meek's seat, her eyes forward set upon the bride, as she whispers. "*This* bitch… If that idn't the elation of a lottery winner, I don't know what is."

I sigh and say, "I'm just trying to give them the benefit of the doubt. And my support."

Riley asks, "Those two big guys that were standing in the wedding… They're Bubby's teammates, aren't they? What do you know about them?"

"P.J. and Rome? I just know they still got a year left before they're draft-eligible."

"Oh," Riley says, as if she's lost interest. She adds, "I wasn't asking for *me*, by the way. I was asking for my friends here." She looks back, spotting friends at the table behind us, "I'm not sure if you met them before, but… Peyton? Milan? I present to you, Tahj, the most beautiful woman in the world, they say." Riley's stiff head-turn seems lowkey facetious.

The phrase 'they say,' doesn't get by me, either. Still, I smile. "C'mon Riley. Do you *have* to say that every time you introduce me? Look at you… Look at these ladies… You're all beautiful." Beautiful in an uppity, Hamptons sort of way.

Riley changes, suddenly, as if a smug alter-ego emerges to say, "I hope you don't think you took Fletcher's attention away from me earlier."

My mouth falls open. I'm slow to believe my ears. I reply, softly – this being a wedding and all, "Lemme tell you something, Riley. I'm not in competition with no bitch, alright?"

"Tahj," Riley says, with a hand splayed on her chest as if she's the one who was attacked. "You're not hearing me. What I'm trying to tell you, is that I do not have eyes for Fletcher. My man plays professional basketball. Didn't you know? Obviously, you're not even keeping up with my Instagram." Riley waits for a response but then adds, "If you've cut me off as a friend, Tahj, at least let me know."

"Don't play with me, Riley," I say, and turn away, showing her the back of my head.

"See… That's ya problem, right there. Always so quick to think somebody's coming for you."

Once all the ceremonial portions are done, the D.J. kicks it off with something lit, to signify that it's now everyone's party. I'm so eager to surround myself with the bros and leave Riley sitting there looking stupid, that I find myself – not walking toward the guys, but dancing my way over.

I'm stepping like a boss-bitch, and it seems the guys are hyping me up, but at second glance, I realize that they're telling me to turn up the stove. Nothing will satisfy them unless I hit my signature move – at this wedding, in front of all of our mommas. Internally, I'm like nah… but as soon as Gunna comes on the track with that, *Everything litty I love when it's hot.*

I squat, in a wide stance, elbows out, fists rolling back and then swerve… my weight transferring from the bend of one knee to the other. The guys go bananas. I raise up with a hand shading my eyes like ship captain's ahoy, and this is what gets the party going. Iowans scan the party as if realizing that it's true, what they've heard about how black people party.

The football players snatch Bubby away from his bride and bark like dogs and bump chests as if Bubby just scored a touchdown. I wasn't about to get in the middle of that, so I go to Emily, who always seems as eager to win my approval, as I am to show her that she doesn't have to. I give her a big hug and bring her over to the guys for selfies with our new addition to the crew.

The dance floor fills. Drinks go 'round. We're by the roof's edge posing around Bubby and Emily for selfies, raised champagne glasses sparkling against the metropolitan skyline, the moment minted in digital selfies, but in hindsight, it's cemented in our memories as a lesson on how quickly life can turn from triumph to tragedy.

In every picture, I'm hugged up with Fletcher. Naturally, Bubby takes notice, since he has always policed us. When the selfies are done, we disperse and yet Fletcher's arm is still around me. Bubby smirks under a brow of suspicion. He says, "Word?"

The observation makes us giddy and shy, which is all the confirmation Bubby needs.

There's a commotion on the dance floor. Suddenly everyone's riled up like water in hot grease. One of Bubby's thick girl cousins, Ari, is backing it up on the dancefloor, but still, that's not the catch.

A bridesmaid from Emily's side of the family pulls up and tries to give Ari a run for her money, but just doesn't have the cakes to do it. Still, that's not the main reason the party goes berserk.

The kicker, is a young Iowan buck named Clarke, pulling up to Ari, and getting under that big ole rump like a game of limbo, his eyes bugged out with excitement, one arm whipping around in rodeo fashion.

The crowd tightens around the dancefloor. Bubby's mother joins the twerk competition to show that she's still got it even at forty. Bubby pushes through the crowd, yelling, "Oh no you don't!" He snatches his mother by the arm, drives her off the dance floor, and forces her into a seat. "Fuck you think you doing!"

I'm appalled by how Bubby treats his mother. I motion to go over there and talk some sense into him. Fletcher holds me back, his head motioning left, the direction he wants me to follow.

We go to the dining enclosure for the wedding party. There's a curtain behind the table of honor. Fletcher finds where the curtain splits and pulls me through into a makeshift dressing area for the wedding party. There's a body-length mirror, a few chairs, a wicker couch, and a small table where there's a half glass of red wine with lipstick on the rim.

Wasting no time, Fletcher takes me in his arms. Despite the party noise outside, there's an unmistakable quietness in this moment. The seriousness in his eyes, and the tenderness with which he kisses my mouth, tells me he wants me now.

I slip him my tongue, as a reply that I'm down. His kisses travel from lips to chin, to neck, to chest. We wrestle my dress down my shoulders. He pulls my bra down with his teeth to uncover my breasts and suddenly my entire areola is sucked into his mouth. I caress the back of his head, my body aflame with desire. I've only been this aroused three times in my life, all with Fletcher, twice today.

The *me* that reasons and questions, is buried under the me that feeds and lusts. I grind against him such innate appetite, that it's clear that I'm aching to get him inside of me.

The thing that brings me back to reason is the moment we negotiate, with only the eyes, how we should go about it, in this tight space. Standing? No. Bent over a chair? No. Fletcher sits on the wicker couch. I straddle him, and then I say, "Our mothers are out there… What if we get caught." Still, this is not rejection; I'm gauging his need. If he must; I will.

Fletcher squeezes my cheeks so hard, we hear my lips part because I'm so saucy.

He kisses me then pulls away to ask, in the most carnal yet sensual manner, "You want this dick?"

"Mm-hm," I reply. We're panting and whispering sensuously. "I'm so fucking wet."

He heaves upward to struggle with his belt. The moment has arrived, but with it, the smack of reality and all of its implications. I ask, "So what do we do after this? Go back to being friends?"

He gives me a long, passionate kiss, as if hoping by the time the kiss ends I'd forget the question, but it turns out, he's only using the kiss as evidence. "If we could do *that*… are we friends?"

With no smooth segue in sight, I simply out myself and say, "I can't date you."

Fletcher's confused in the drunkenness of lust; he unhands me.

I whisper, "Please don't take your hands off of me."

He frowns, but grips my waist.

I say, "I'm in love with the *old* Fletcher. This version of you, I only wanna…" A hot sigh replaces the word fuck. "But later," I kiss. "Tonight."

"You don't want a relationship? That's *my* line. How you gone treat me like *I'm* the broad?"

I let my eyes fall closed and my head shakes. "You've changed; that's all I'm gone say."

Fletcher takes my breast in his mouth again, but he can tell that the fire is extinguished. He pleads, "Just let me put the tip in, baby."

I pause with a bit lip, like a gameshow contestant deciding whether to bet it all. "C'mon," I say. I start hiking my dress up my legs. Fletcher's just looking, as if he is still the passive observer during all the times he'd imagined this. I urge him, "C'mon, baby." My desire escalates to panic.

Fletcher spreads the flaps of his tux, then digs at his belt. I'm reaching under me to slide my panties to the side, when we hear someone coming. We freeze.

Three shadows approach the curtain. A woman sobs, "I hate you." It's Emily. Her father whines with some excuse. There has been a family incident. They're heading behind the curtain for privacy, but stop and argue where they stand. Fletcher and I remain stock-still, praying they retreat. The mother's hand splits the curtain. I tense; my bare ass exposed, my mouth ready to explain, but the hand comes out of the curtain to point at the accused. "If it wasn't for you…"

Fletcher and I scramble with our clothes as if were on fire, our eyes on the silhouette of the family.

At the time, I had no idea why they're upset, but I'd find out later that it started between Keenan and Emily's father. The man tried to play devil's advocate about the wrongful conviction of Keenan's brother. He kept following Keenan around long after Keenan had deemed the conversation over. Keenan kept walking, thumbing back, saying, "Somebody get this dude." Emily's dad kept following, kept trying to assert another perspective, despite all the holes in the state's investigation, and even the murder victim's family championing the innocence of Keenan's brother, and that the case has been taken up by The Justice Project and is currently in the process of being overturned now that ten years of an innocent man's life has been wasted. The shit apparently hit the fan when Emily's father had said, *But if he was out in the streets past midnight with no good reason, he's guilty of something!*

Keenan called out, "Yo Bubby! Better get ya father-in-law before I knock his old ass out!"

They say the man stood there with arms spread like Jesus, saying, "Gimme your best shot."

That's when the daughter and wife drug him away, and they ended up on the other side of the curtain from me and Fletcher, ready to enter this room for privacy, thinking it's empty since nobody has any business being here.

Quietly, I stand and smooth my dress in the front, then ask Fletcher, "What do we say?"

This fool takes the half glass of red wine from the table and pours it on my dress.

The family enters, bride first, but she's backing in. Only the parents sees us, Fletcher swabbing my wine-stained dress with his hankie. As for my hand cocked to slap Fletcher with, for dousing me with wine, I smoothly redirect that hand to the back of my neck in mach worry.

Emily, in a voice that is low, but smoldering, says, "You just hate the fact that my husband is black—"

"—*Emileee*," the mother says while pointing at the fact that they're not alone.

Emily's head turns, eerily, homing the target of her mother's pointing hand. Emily reddens at the sight of Fletcher and me, standing there astounded by what we'd heard, yet bashful for being nearly caught in the act.

They're caught in the act too. Together we're just five pairs of eyes twitching in our faces, waiting for the reactions of others to see how to go about smoothing this thing over.

Fletcher points from the hip. "We're just gonna…" We scoot by, with mumbled apologies and an unspoken agreement that nothing leaves this room.

"Club soda," Emily's mother says, like it's some speakeasy codeword. "For the stain," she clarifies.

"Thank you… thank you," I bow, while backing through the curtain.

Outside, the atmosphere has tanked, and the D.J.'s whimsical melody sounds like the violins playing to the Titanic's sinking.

Bubby's relatives are beside themselves over the behavior of the bride's father; Emily's kin stands with them, in solidary, against the behavior of Emily's dad.

Thankfully, Meek is nowhere in sight. Fletcher and I grab drinks from the open bar then find a pair of chairs away from everything. I start by saying, "We almost had sex, bro. That's crazy to me."

Fletcher leans away, his eyes slits. "No relationship, though?"

My head shakes, "You got too much going on, fam. And when I say too much, I mean women."

Fletcher's head lay back; his grievance aimed up at the sky. "I'm trying to make you the one, but you'd *rather* be a jump-off? Who does that?"

If we didn't have to keep up appearances for the wedding I would've gotten in Fletcher's face. "*That's* how you phrase it?" I swirl a finger, stirring things in a different direction. "How about we look at this way: you got community dick," I say. "Just because this wedding got you in your feelings, I'm supposed to suddenly fall at your feet? You still got bitches. And you're not about to have me looking like one of *them*."

"You trippin' Tahj."

"Having standards is always considered trippin' by guys like you." Too late to take back the *guys like you*, so I deconstruct it. "I didn't mean it like that. It's just that I want the real you, to come back to me."

He looks away. "Nah, don't try to sugar-coat it."

"Don't do that," I sigh. "As if you don't say things you don't mean – like that time you said, you no longer believe in monogamy. I guess you meant that."

His eyes get sleepy with indifference. "I didn't want a relationship because I was waiting on you. It was always you, from moment one when we met in the ninth grade, but you was with wassaname."

"You know his name," I nudge.

"A year later that boy had you down bad," Fletcher says as he watches me giggle. "Tenth grade, man! And bro had you crying like he done handed you divorce papers and threw you out on the street."

We laugh like only we laugh with each other, so loose and free. I fall over toward Fletcher, knowing he'd catch me. "You so stupid."

Fletcher pipes down, and says, "That was the first time you ever cried in front of me. I wanted to kiss you so bad."

I raise a brow. "You should have."

"But you was hurting."

"So! I would've kissed you back, then acted all innocent, like I didn't know what came over me."

"I was afraid you would've thought I was no better than Dre because… Remember? At the time I was with–"

"–Macy," I say, smugly. "I couldn't stand her ass, but she hated me worse."

Fletcher laughs, "We were never single at the same time, until today and we almost fucked twice."

I cut my eyes, smiling, "Only a man would say it like that."

Fletcher adds, "You think I play the field because Gigi hurt me? No. It was you who hurt me."

I lean forward and look over so he can see the severity of my frown. "How are you trying to put that on me?"

"The time I needed you the most, you fuckin' left me hanging."

"What? When have I *ever* left you hanging?"

"I don't even wanna talk about it." He waves me away, as if it's all too much. Gently I capture his face in my hands, and steer him back to me. We're off to ourselves but visible to everyone, even Meek if she hasn't already left. "I don't care if they see. Fletcher, you can't tell me I hurt you and not say why. Whatever it is, Fletcher, I'd never hurt you intentionally."

All along Fletcher's been looking down, avoiding my gaze; his eyes lift to say, "You intentionally *lied* to me."

I release his face, no longer worthy to hold it because I know what he means, "Look, that wasn't about you. I didn't want you seeing me bald. I panicked. Do you forgive me?"

He smirks and says, "C'mon now, it's not that serious."

"It was that serious for *me*… head looking like a kiwi fruit." I let our giggles dissipate before saying, "I can't wait until tonight. There's so much to talk about. So many things I never said over the years."

A sly Fletcher says, "We can talk *afterwards*."

I frown with a late epiphany. "Wait a minute. How did know I lied?"

Fletcher flicks his head toward the culprit. "Ya girl, Riley told me."

Just then Bubby calls Fletcher to come join the guys. He looks over at me for permission. I say, "Go ahead. I'm a go chill with momma for a minute. We'll talk."

I turn to go. Fletcher touches my arm. I look back. He says, "If we're gonna be friends with benefits, I'm gonna win your heart when you see that I'm not dealing with nobody but you. This is the first day of the rest of our lives and you don't even know it," he says with a smile so wide, it's apparent that he's oblivious that Meek has gotten a running start to shove Fletcher so hard, that he swipes out of view like a phone screen.

Every head rotates and every mouth falls open, in this well-dressed assembly, reminiscent of the Oscars slap; I'm Lupita, glazed over in meme-worthy disbelief.

Fletcher recovers from sprawling to find Meek in his face, berating him. Bridesmaids, groomsmen, and guests alike rush forward, their pleas for peace working against itself, resulting in the chaos they try to prevent.

My mother has to restrain Fletcher's mother, who pleads, "Let me go Letha. Let me show this dizzy bitch I ain't always been saved!"

Fletcher, being tall enough to see completely over Meek, checks for me.

I'm furious, yet satiated with vindication. I lift my palms, serving him the entire scene on a platter. I say, "This is *precisely* what I was talking about!"

Fletcher counters, "You can't put this on me! You know this broad crazy."

Meek looks back at me, then at Fletcher, as if wondering how is it that he's explaining himself to me and not her. She shoves Fletcher to command his attention. "You lied to me!"

The way Fletcher bucks up and yells, makes the crowd flinch. "How the *fuck* I lied to you?! I told you I didn't want no relationship!"

Meek points in my general direction and screams, "I heard you two back there in the back."

Fletcher and I spot each other like deer in headlights; Meek was spying? If the bride's family hadn't thwarted Meek, she might've tackled Fletcher and me and we would've been floundering half-naked, trapped in the curtains like a fishing net.

Fletcher says, "Are you stalking me, now?"

"No," Meek says, two beats before her head shakes. "I wasn't paying you no attention. *Riley* told me."

I thought it was strange, how, in all the commotion, Riley was still seated and poised. If this be the Oscars, she's the Jada in this. Riley must've been furious that I interrupted their little coffee date, so she sent someone crazy enough to do what she wouldn't.

Only after Riley's name is called, *now* she gets up to intervene? And with the gall to put scripture to her lips. "Calm down, Meek. For the fruit of the righteous, is peace."

Meek disregards the advice and starts ranting in second person. "I told myself… Tameka, just let it go. I went all the way downstairs, had my key in the ignition… But no! I am *not* gonna let you keep doing me like this!" Meek points in Fletcher's face, a finger bending the tip of his nose.

Fletcher snatches her hand down. "Ay! Calm your fuckin' ass down!" I see Fletcher glance at his mother and then change his tone. "Meek… Man, listen…" He wipes a hand down his face. "What you don't understand is this: when I say I don't want a relationship, the *with you* is silent."

Meek seems orphaned, by learning that a relationship is not the thing that Fletcher didn't desire. Meek gets a spark to say something else, but the words catch in her throat; the fact that Fletcher never wanted her to begin with, shushes anything she could try to say in return. There's also a hush among the assembly, for it is truly saddening to watch a well-meaning woman come undone, but this is someone's wedding and she was selfish enough to make it about her.

Bubby says, "Somebody get her the fuck outta here."

Me, being the closest friend Meek has in attendance, I come alongside her to guide her away, but first I have some choice words for Fletcher. "The old Fletcher would know when someone needs saving from themselves."

At the sound of my voice, Meek looks up and discovers that I'm the one guiding her away and rubbing her back. She yells, "Get yo *fuckin* hands off me!" She snatches from me so hard that the force yanks me off balance and sends me Crip-walking in those high heels.

Meek centers me in her bloodshot gaze. "Two-faced bitch! I got a mind to go up-side *your* head! So, what's good!"

I recoup my balance to locate Meek coming forward, her hands jittering by her side like she could swing any moment.

I hear my mother call out like a winner at Bingo, "Uh-oh! You got the right one now." She's removing her earrings and kicking off her shoes one by one. Now it's Fletcher's mother holding my momma back.

No one holds Meek back. Fletcher tries to break through to save me, but Bubby and Keenan assume he's trying to put hands on Meek, so they restrain Fletcher. Meek advances towards me and I'm feeling I'm in an arena with a bull.

I back away slowly and try reasoning with her. "Meek… Coming after me isn't gonna change anything."

"All this time, you been playing in my face."

I back into a chair and nearly lose my balance again. Meek seizes the opportunity to rush me. But baby, the way I snatch up that seat and swing, I should've made folding chairs famous years before the Riverboat Brawl. I hit her twice; the second bop ringing her bell so good, it sends her marching the other direction. She dashes toward Fletcher, and takes a wild swing that misses him, but clocks Bubby's cousin, Ari.

Bubby lunges at Meek, but Fletcher grabs Bubby and drives him back. "That's a woman, bro!"

Bubby yells, "But this *my* got damn wedding, Fletch! Fix this! Before I have to do it my way!"

"Say less," Fletcher replies. He corrals Meek with lazy-eyed aggression, to show her how futile it is to struggle against him.

As Fletcher's leaving, with Meek in tow, he looks back; our eyes catch, mine warm with tears. I gulp the frog in my throat and say, "Not tonight… Not ever. Hear me?" And that's the last thing I say to Fletcher, just minutes before the fatal accident.

It's over, it seems. Everyone looks around as if hung over from the adrenaline. Ari holds a cold bottled water to her eye. The D.J. tries to give the party a shot in the arm with an up-tempo song; the caterers get back to work, and I'm sitting there at the table with the mothers of Fletcher, Bubby, Keenan, and my own mother while they take turns lecturing me. Fletcher's mother tells me that sometimes you have to give a man time; her son isn't ready for a relationship. My mother warns, "Pick one. You can't be lovers *and* friends. That's a dangerous game."

Keenan's mother cosigns, "Very d-d-dangerous game." Not a second later, we get proof of just how dangerous a game it is.

We hear, below, engines racing and tires squealing. "Fletcher," yells his mother. We run to the side of the roof that faces the parking lot and see below, cars the size of toys. Meek tries to block the driveway. Fletcher's car climbs the climbs the curb in an attempt to squeeze through. We know that lives are at stake the moment Meek guns it in reverse and clips Fletcher's car on its way out. His back bumper sags.

Fletcher's mother screams louder than all of us combined. Fletcher guns it into traffic and Meek tears off behind; it's a highspeed chase.

We run along the side of the roof's chest-high border, like NASCAR spectators, screaming as Fletcher and Meek weave in and out of traffic. Meek scrapes another car while trying to cut Fletcher off. I'm bawling as I watch.

They create such mayhem on the highway that cars ahead of them take notice and begin pulling over for their own safety. This only gives Fletcher a clear runway to gun it. Perhaps Fletcher was tracking Meek in his rearview because the traffic light ahead turns red seconds before he hit brakes. The entire wedding reception leans over the rooftop; people screaming; tires screaming; horns blaring and there's a loud bang as eighteen-wheeler rams Fletcher's car and sends him fishtailing, the rear right side of his car coming apart in a trail of debris.

Meek's Nissan Altima slides under that same tractor-trailer, her car roof peeling back like a banana, the vehicle folding into itself as it's wiped along the street in a shower of sparks coming from under the jack-knifing truck.

Further ahead, Fletcher seems to gain control of his car, but the back end is too damaged and maybe the brakes no longer work because his car gallops off the road and rams smack into a concrete barrier. The front of his car is crushed like a beer can all the way back to the cockpit.

I'm wailing *No* to the sky as someone holds me to keep me from crumbling. That someone is Riley, who soon needs someone to hold her up as the reality dominoes to her.

I hear Bubby yelling, "Stop that crying y'all! He alright!" I hurry to the edge of the roof, hoping to see some sign of life, in the distance; Fletcher exiting the vehicle maybe? But there's nothing.

Bubby repeats, "He alright, yall. Don't do that!" This is just Bubby's way of dealing with it, using hope as a shield against despair. His new wife and his mother hold him up as he caves in. Fletcher's mother runs towards the elevator. We all take off after her, then go down in groups.

On the ground, Fletcher's mother takes the lead. She's flanked by Keenan and Bubby. I'm right behind them, walking in stride with Emily, my sympathetic hand reached forward, resting on the shoulder of Fletcher's mother. She clutches her cell phone in both hands, having either of two very different phone calls she'd have to make to Fletcher's father.

There's about forty of us walking along the sidewalk in protest, not against systems or governments; it's a protest of hope against what seems to be the inevitable.

I hear, from behind, Riley's voice, "Lamentations twenty-two says, Be not consumed—"

Before I could scream at her, someone else does. "Bitch ain't this all your fault?" Someone then shushes that person with the words, "That's not what we need, right now."

Fletcher's mother, however, finishes the scripture, "Be not consumed …for his compassion never fails." Mrs. Lewis then looks back to say, as a lesson for all. "If grace can be won or lost, then it is not grace." Mrs. Lewis, being of the southern belle type, this is a pleasant way of saying, just let the bitch slide y'all, but Riley doesn't seem to get it; she takes it as an invitation to come lead.

Riley pushes up front beside me, but that's not good enough. She then squeezes herself under Bubby's arm so she's next to Mrs. Lewis with an arm around her. All eyes are on Meek's balled-up car. Good Samaritans have pulled over and exited their cars, their faces bent in horror. The truck driver paces with a cigarette between his lips. He stops to look at us, slowly shaking his head, as a grave warning to not come forward, for the images will surely haunt us for the rest of our lives.

Just across the street from me there is a woman dead, and I know her personally. Moments ago, I hit her with a friggin chair. I cry out in anguish. Emily hugs me.

The feeling among us is that Meek's death is a foreboding of Fletcher's. Keenan's legs give and he squats down, his head shaking. "Not my dawg. Not my dawg, man."

Bubby picks him up. "We gotta keep walking. We gotta keep walking."

Riley, in her infinite wisdom, imparts, "We fix our eyes not on what is seen… Second Corinthians four and eighteen."

Leslie quickens her pace and then trots, probably to get away from Riley's sickening ass, but maybe that's just me, observing as someone who's sick of Riley myself.

Sirens increase, seemingly from all sides.

I stop to remove my high heels, hopping on each foot while the crowd rushes past me. The wedding guests splay into the crowd already at the scene. My skinny self is getting bumped around when I hear Fletcher's mother scream.

The bodies are too tight for me to get through, but I'm tall enough to where I could see Fletcher getting up from sitting on the curb to embrace his mother. My tears of sadness turn into tears of joy. I scream Fletcher's name. He doesn't seem happy to be alive. He's heard of Meek's death, and it's something that will weigh heavily on his conscience, and mine, for a long time.

I struggle to get through the crowd and join them. Bubby, Keenan, and Riley rejoice in a group hug around mother and son.

I see Riley reach up and place a gentle hand on Fletcher's face, announcing, "I prayed while you were racing down the street. And God answered my prayer."

I'm stuck behind a wall of people, on the outside looking in as Riley gives herself credit for saving Fletcher's life when her meddling put it in danger in the first place.

Fletcher towers over them, peering. He asks, "Where's Tahj?" He cups a hand by his mouth and yells, "Yo, Tahj!"

I wave up high. People make a path for me to go join them. Fletcher meets me and hugs me, repeating, "I'm sorry…"

"Don't," I say. "I just thank God you're still here."

My eyes close tight but I feel another presence. I look. And who's right there with us but Riley, rubbing Fletcher's back, as if she's sanctioning our moment.

I'd had enough of the bitch. The twitch, to slap the fuck outta her, had already occurred, but what stops the swing of my hand and the *bitch* on my tongue, is the sight of Emily pointing me out to a police officer. I'm looking dead at the same heifer who's wearing the gown I made for free, when her lil frog lips read: *It was her.*

The officer starts toward me and all I could do is watch. He calls me by name and peels me away from Fletcher. Everyone who was there at the wedding to see that I'd hit Meek with the chair in self-defense, tries to tell this to the officer, but Emily's word seems to carry more weight than all of theirs combined. More officers close in and things almost turn ugly.

Fletcher tries to intervene on my behalf, but Riley holds him back – and doing too much in the process, how she clutches him from the side, an arm around his waist and a palm on his chest.

They fold me into the back of a squad car, supposedly until they can corroborate my story with enough witnesses.

I'm in the back of the squad car sobbing, with a wine stain on my dress, and a snot bubble I can't even wipe because my hands are cuffed behind me. I'm shut in that car for so long that Fletcher's ambulance has time to back in and strap him on a gurney, as a precaution. I'm still handcuffed in that squad car as I watch Mrs. Lewis climb aboard the ambulance with her son, and a fussy Riley barter her way onto the ambulance as well. By the time they let me out of the squad car and remove my cuffs, the ambulance had already disappeared in the distance with Riley in it.

I determine that I no longer fuck with Riley on any level. And if there's any moment that I can pin this decision on, it would be the way she held Fletcher back from helping me. I know how anger has a way of warping memory. But while I was being handcuffed, I swear I saw Riley's hand, on Fletcher's chest, begin to soften and caress. The same chick who 'doesn't have eyes for Fletcher,' seemed to give me this territorial gaze, as if to say, *he mine now*.

BOOK II

CHAPTER 6
FINALLY

A week after the wedding incident, Georgians receive the shock that their pandemic-denying governor has succumbed to mainstream pandemic fears and issued a statewide lockdown. Stores pack with citizens buying food and supplies. Ammunition shelves are bare by noon because of the Southern conservative phobia that the apocalypse is triggered by people not working.

Fletcher had come out of surgery just days before the lockdown announcement. Although he walked away from the car accident, he walked away with a concussion and what doctors call an axial compression injury to his neck, an injury which caused him to miss the NFL Combine that he was betting on to improve his draft status.

If a neck injury and concussion doesn't scare NFL executives from taking a chance on a mere fourth-round prospect, the injury to Fletcher's character does. Although there were no charges beyond traffic citations, the news broadcast billed the car accident as a "domestic incident" involving NFL hopeful, Fletcher Lewis, which resulted in the death of a young woman.

There's virtually no way Fletcher's going to the NFL; therefore, none of the women in Fletcher's call log called. That ambulance ride was the last time anyone had seen or heard from Riley.

It's me, just days after breaking up with Donovan, holding Fletcher's hand before going into his scheduled surgery. It's me, joined in prayer with his family and Pastor Childs. It's me kissing his forehead as he rouses from anesthesia. So, Fletcher says it's me that he wants to spend the lockdown down with.

The only problem is his parents; they would not approve. They sacrificed their empty nest to nurse Fletcher back to health, and have become quite protective of him since the accident. Fletcher can't just drive off; his car was totaled. He'd need my help to ditch his parents, and there's only a twenty-four-hour window before being outside becomes a misdemeanor.

Fletcher's father, being a train control engineer for MARTA makes him an essential worker, so he's gone all day. The moment Mrs. Lewis goes out to get supplies, and Fletcher finds himself in an empty house, he texts, *come get me.*

When I get the text, I'm loading my car with fabric, way across town, so it takes me a while before I'm standing on the brown brick steps with Fletcher opening the door with a casual, "Whassup Slim." No hug. No smile. He hasn't smiled since that tragic day. He's holding a half-eaten protein bar and chewing, which I find slightly irritating because it cancels the celebratory kiss I'd been reliving in my imagination on the drive there.

My lips mash in ridicule. "Always eating. Look at you." Look at him is precisely what I do, as I follow him inside, spying his calves, the shape of large mangoes in skin casing, tapering down to his Nike slides. His shoulders bulge out of a sleeveless cotton T, his arms chunky and veined. I smile with my lips tucked in, just thinking about all I'd do to this man during the lockdown. At the same time, though, I'd have to be okay with not doing it at all because Fletcher is vulnerable. I dare say he's depressed.

Fletcher is one of the most mentally strong people that I know, but still… He blames himself for Meek's death; his dream to play professional football, for which he'd worked so hard all his life, is destroyed. For his athletic scholarship, he had blind-picked Data

Analyst as a major, thinking he'd never have to use it. And now he finds himself staring down forty-plus years of working a job he'll hate. Fletcher's but a young man of twenty-two years, and he's going through what would be a lot for anyone to bear.

I follow him into his room, seeing how the trophy case now mocks him. There's packing boxes stacked in a corner as a result of the move from Athens, Georgia. Fletcher slings a backpack around his shoulders, then points to the suitcase on the bed. "I ain't supposed to lift nothin' over ten pounds. Doctor's orders."

I warn, "Now Fletcher… before I take this suitcase out to the car–"

"–It's not heavy, only the essentials."

I drag it off the bed by the handle and it nearly yanks me to the floor. "You call this not heavy?"

He shrugs.

I sigh. "Anyway, as I was saying…" I rock back and forth on tiptoes and say, "Are you sure about this? Your mother's gonna be pissed – at you *and* me."

"Won't be the first," he smarts. "As far as you: I'll tell momma I twisted your arm."

"Okay, but…"

"But what," Fletcher whines. "Why you stalling, bro? Ain't no telling when momma's coming back."

"Let me put it to you this way: do you still wanna go through with this, knowing that I'm not about to have sex with you?" Biggest lie ever told.

He straightens up tall just to make me feel short. "See… I wasn't even thinking about sex," he says. "–that is, until you come here in ya lil leggings… flat belly in front… lil bubble in the back…" Even when he's kidding, he doesn't smile?

I, on the other hand, am blushing so bad that I look away to hide my face. Fletcher adds, "Even if we don't, I'm gonna enjoy trying."

I try to be serious but struggle to stay in character. "But Fletcher, you're not well. Emotionally," I say, as I sneak a feel with a hand on his chest. Fletcher makes his chest jump under my palm and I damn near spring pee.

He says, "When you say no sex… that means I can't taste you either?"

Just hearing this makes me seize up with a tight shrug.

Ever since the accident, he seems to have returned to the old Fletcher; the Fletcher that I wish to marry and have babies with; the Fletcher with whom I'd been in love since ninth grade. He's the man I've loved throughout college with an hour's distance and other relationships standing in the way. Astoundingly, there's nothing in the way now; no boyfriend for me, no groupies distracting him, no family present with us, as they've been since the accident – not even tuxedo layers to pad the space between us like the times we'd previously kissed. There's so much man standing in front of me, I wonder how to begin; go low, hug his waist, and lay my face against his chest, no. I go high, easing into his body, my head rearing back to gaze up into his eyes; my hands join behind his neck.

He flinches. "Easy baby." The injury.

"Awww, I'm sorry boo-boo." I start kissing him like a woodpecker on valiums, stopping for baby talk. "Poor Fletcher… is the baby hurt?" I woodpecker him again. I'm overdoing it, but I don't care. It's been too long a wait for me to not be free in this moment. I tease away, feeling my eyes uncross to search his face. I study him, waiting for the words that would perfectly capture this moment, but I end up hearing it from him.

"Finally," he sighs.

My sentiments exactly. I notice something that's been missing since the accident. "There's that smile," I say, dreamily.

Suddenly the suitcase isn't impossible to carry. I snatch it up and hurry out the door, bowed under its weight, moving in small hurried steps.

Soon, I'm driving away towards a sun so bright, I lower the visor to shade my eyes. Fletcher's hand is on my thigh. We don't say much. I look over, smiling. He doesn't ask me why; he just smiles too.

I ask, "Are you okay?"

"I'll be alright," he nods.

"I'm gonna take good care of you. Not just the injury."

He nods again.

"You're carrying a lot. I know you think you can carry it all by yourself – and for good reason: you're strong, you're no quitter, you're intelligent…"

Fletcher covers his face with his hands, and it looks like one of those moments he'd alluded to, during our phone conversations, where he feels overwhelmed.

"Fletcher." I give a series of glances, tracking the highway and him. "Baby, talk to me."

His hands drop from his face and he sucks his teeth. "Man, I done went and left my doggone prescriptions."

"What?"

"It's four of them sumbitches. Gotta take 'em every day."

I'm now at a red light staring him down. "You big dummy!"

"Oh, I ain't intelligent no more?"

"You make me sick. What if your mom's at the house?"

His head shakes between shrugging shoulders. "It's not like leaving the scripts behind is an option."

I bust a U-turn and hit the gas, risking a ticket.

Thankfully when we arrive, the driveway is empty. Fletcher unbuckles his seatbelt and says, "I'll be right b–"

"–Hurry!"

I'm parked on the curb, jittering with nerves, checking the rearview mirror every two seconds. We're good, I'm thinking. He should be out any second now, I say, with my eyes in the rearview mirror to see his mother's burgundy Lincoln coupe turn onto the street. My head falls on the rim of the steering wheel, my body heavy with disappointment. Fletcher's mother turns into the driveway as the garage door raises, but she doesn't drive in. She gets out of the car and walks towards me, dressed to the nines on a Tuesday, in a body dress, quarter boots, and choker.

I don't know what else to do but cry. Mrs. Lewis taps on the glass and I lower it. She stoops to the window, her face plump and beautiful, her makeup impeccable. She reaches in and rubs my back. "Bless your heart, sweetie. It's natural to be sad for him, but he's gonna come out of this just fine. Yesterday, we started therapy."

"Therapy?" I turn, surprised, and sniffling.

"That's a good thing, hon. He'll be all the better for it."

Fletcher comes out of the house, sees his mother, and then tries to return, but runs smack into the door he just closed behind him; prescription bottles fall and rattle.

Mrs. Lewis stands upright and says, "Fletcher, what're you doing?" She looks at me and then takes a half-step back from my car. "Tahj? What's going on here?"

I just look ahead and cry some more. Fletcher trots over, explaining while scratching his head. "Hey ma, yeah, uh… I'm staying with Tahj for the lockdown."

Mrs. Lewis stiffens. Only her eyes move as she looks at me, then at Fletcher, perhaps trying to decide which of us to curse out first. "That's fine," she decides.

Fletcher's eyes stretch as wide as mine.

Quite plainly, his mother adds, "Just give me a minute to go get my things." She poses, her eyes fixed on me. "Because there's no way I'm letting Fletcher out of my sight, in his condition."

Fletcher whines, "Man, that little play-play surgery. Ya can hardly even see the incision… I'm in *no* pain."

"That's not what you told the therapist." The paradigm shifts. Fletcher's mouth shuts like a trap, and my head lowers in pity.

"The ailment, is not of the body; the infirmity is of the mind," Leslie says, in true Southern Bell style, straight-faced as she plunges the dagger of flowery words. Suddenly I wonder if the prescriptions were all from the surgery, or is Prozac among the pill bottles bulging in Fletcher's pockets.

Fletcher could gather no more of a reply than, "Why you putting my business out there, ma?"

Leslie shows him a hand to talk to. "I'm not even going to address you. If you do not like the way I'm handling things you are most certainly welcome to take your grievances to Lew." His father, nicknamed the first syllable of his last name. "For now, you be quiet while I have a conversation with Tahj, ok?" Leslie leans in again and says, "Don't misunderstand me. I am not sore at you, beloved. You have yet to learn that you cannot love a man into ascension." In thought, I reason that Donovan is proof of that. Leslie peers at me and says, "I hear out of my son's mouth that he feels most alive when on the football field hurting a man, or in bed having sex with a woman, and I'm supposed to allow this?" She takes my hand, peers into my eyes, and says, "Tahj look, I'm sorry you had to hear that." I'm tuned into her like my life depends on it, watching her red lips and pearly white teeth shape every syllable. "I love the love you have for my son, and it hurts me to reveal that, whatever y'all had planned for this lockdown, wasn't what you thought it was."

My mouth opens, or it was never closed. "But I wasn't–"

She grips my hand tighter, but still lovingly. "Fletcher is his own man. If he decides… he can still get in this car and go with you, but I'm trusting *you* to make the right decision and drive off without him."

With that, Leslie walks toward the house, sidestepping a complaining Fletcher. I realize that everything I wish to have with Fletcher would be so much more fulfilling with his mother's blessing. I welcome Leslie's guidance, but what she does not get to do, is dictate to us. In the time it takes her to scale the steps I decide which this is.

Tears drip from my chin as I put the car in gear and drive off. Fletcher takes off after my car yelling. "Tahj! No!" If only NFL executives could see the speed with which this big defensive end chases my car down in a pair of slides, his place in the NFL would be secure. He snatches the door handle and the passenger door swings open. I see the pebbled asphalt rushing by like rapids. A neighbor's mailbox bats the passenger door closed, and stops Fletcher in his tracks.

INTERLOG
LOCKDOWN

I'm nearly losing my mind alone in my apartment. Isolation was supposed save us from COVID, but who was going to save us from isolation? There're TV commercials for toll free crisis lines; it seems COVID walked so that depression could run.

I would've stayed with my folks, but with my younger brothers still at home, I worried that I wouldn't have a bathroom to myself, nor workspace for sewing. Near the end of two weeks in isolation, though, I would've given anything to be watching soap operas with momma, or feeling like a little girl again, welcoming daddy home from work, or having my brothers Quin and Zay banging at the bathroom door for me to hurry up; our collective boredom causing us to clash.

For the lack of human contact, good or bad, I'm deteriorating. I hadn't seen a whole human in weeks. I go out for a humidifier and see masks up to the eyes; bodies without faces. At home, there are faces without bodies on my Zooms and Skypes with my family, Fletcher, the guys, and a few girlfriends that I'd check on to see how they're holding up.

On this day, my phone calls are done by noon and I find myself being *swallowed up* by the silence.

No one has heard from Riley since Bubby's wedding, and I would've been content to never hear from her again after all the mess she pulled, but after I'd run out of people to call, I'm forced to call Riley.

She answers my Facetime while getting out of bed and unsuccessfully angling her phone away; there's a body next to her. "Hey," she says, as if unsure how this conversation might go, considering her antics at Bubby's wedding.

"How are you?"

"Just waking up," she answers. "Facetiming me this early, girl I must look a mess."

"You call noon early?"

"It's the time zones. I'm three hours behind," Riley explains, as she exits the bedroom and heads down a long hallway. "I'm in Phoenix. My man flew me out as soon as we got word of the lockdown."

"Your man?"

"Gideon Anderson–"

"–Gideon? He white?"

"He's a black all-star NBA player. I tried to tell you at the wedding that I wadn't sweatin' no Fletcher."

I try not to scream. "Whatever."

"But how's Fletcher holding up though?"

"You would know if you called."

Riley glances around conspicuously, then whispers. "I'm not calling some guy from my man's home."

"Fletcher isn't just some guy; he's a friend."

"My man don't play that friend crap, and I'd rather lose a friendship than lose all this," Riley says, as she enters a luxury kitchen of stainless steel and marble, cherry cabinetry edged with crown molding. "So you and Fletcher are finally together?"

I wonder who might've told her. I look away, hiding a smile. "I don't wanna jinx it. Ever since the accident, he's been different. He tells me he's okay, but…"

Riley's eyes stretch. "I can't believe you're sitting here, blushing at the thought of being with Fletcher when he missed out on the NFL? You're a model, Tahj. You should aim higher."

"It was never about that, Riley. What if it's simply that, he's *for* me."

"No he ain't," says Riley. "God would not have given you beauty if he wanted you broke."

I smile to soften the shade I'm about to throw. "I don't mean no harm, Riley, but how are you talking about what God wants? As if He wants you to be shacking up."

Riley laughs. "Bitch where's the shack? This house is so big, and our bedrooms are so far apart, this doesn't even count as shacking up, in the biblical sense."

I'm laughing and wondering if my laughter sounds as facetious as hers.

Riley adds, "You should be living like this too, and I'm mad at you for thinking you have to accept less just because you're dark-skinned." Hearing this, I'm shocked silent. Riley continues, "Since you're so 'real,' why can't we be 'real' about that? *My* complexion isn't a sore spot, so that should go to show you right there. Look at you… don't even know what to say."

I crane away from my phone, frowning. "Girl *puh-lease*. I'm just stuck on how you try to put this on complexion. That's wild to me – but I guess you were dying to get it off your chest, so please do go off, Riley."

Riley tilts with the concern of an empathetic teacher. "I just want what's best for you."

"And you put it on complexion?" I mimic Riley's head tilt, but to show confusion. "Why can't it be, that you and me are just built different? For one: I couldn't do what you did."

"What'd I do?"

"Turn your back on Fletcher the moment a rich nigga put you on a plane."

"That's fair," Riley nods. "But this isn't about my friendship with Fletcher. What I'm fighting for, is my friendship with you." Riley then says, to my wrinkled brow, "Yes, Tahj. I'm going to be on a whole nother echelon now. I'm gonna be vacationing places that Fletcher can't afford you. So, I don't wanna lose our friendship because you can't keep up. You're a fashion model, Tahj, and you're choosing to waste your most valuable years – as a woman – on struggle love?"

"Struggle love?" That did it for me. "Let me get off this phone girl before I cuss you out." I hang up, cutting her off midsentence.

My apartment is silent again. Thoughts become louder. I lay out on the couch thinking of all the things I should've said to Riley during our call. The bitch. How is she even my friend, I wonder. Or maybe we were never really friends, which is why when I quit the agency and moved off campus, we hardly kept tabs on each other, which is how Riley showed up at the wedding with two friends I'd never met.

I start binge-watching Netflix and then I'm napping off and on throughout the day and night. Even my dreams try to quench my thirst for humanity with populated beaches, campus settings, and then there is this one dream at church where I'm sitting in the congregation next to Fletcher. Up high in the choir, I spot Meek in a white robe, not singing *Do Not Pass Me By* with the rest of the choir, but just staring – not at Fletcher, but at me, with a stare that seems to wish death upon me.

I wake up in the thick of night, with an epiphany of guilt for my role in Tameka's death. There was no way I could survive my guilt alone in darkness, so I flick the lamp on my nightstand and Facetime Fletcher with the covers up to my chin, tears in my eyes.

To my surprise, Fletcher's up. He's pouring with sweat. He's in his garage lifting weights, trying to take his mind off of it. And there I was, bringing the tragedy back to him. Fletcher's quiet as I explain how, previous to the dream, I'd only invented my own guilt, punishing myself for going behind that curtain with him, or hitting Meek with the chair. Now having suffered Meek's stare, even in the dream realm, the real reason rose up uncomfortably in my chest and wouldn't go away until I talk about it.

"The look in Meeks eyes, seemed to blame me for not being real with her. I hid my feelings for you from everyone; you included. I should've told the one person who would've felt betrayed if she found out by any means than from my mouth. And for Meek to find out in the way that she did…" My eyes clench in agony; warm tears squeeze through my lashes.

Fletcher grips his face. "This is too much," he says.

His response hurts because it denies me the support I've been giving him when he has weak moments. "Too much?" My voice cracks terribly.

He looks away. "I'm out here in the middle of the night, trying to take my mind *off* of it, Slim."

"What about me? You can't think that you're the only one dealing with guilt–"

"–Guilt!" He bites down and looks away, as if I have no right to feel what I feel. "Look, you wasn't fucking her, alright. I was with her a few days before the wedding."

A few days before telling me he wants me for a wife. I had no idea he was still going back to Tameka.

He wipes sweat with his shirt and then stares in silence for a few beats. "I ain't mean to go off on you, babe. That's the thing: It's hard for me to keep emotions in my chest now. I'm not the same. I'm sorry. Actually I'm sorry for a lot when it comes to you," he says.

I echo confusion. "…Sorry for a lot when it comes to me…?"

"This gone sound weird and shit, but…" I then hear him reciting words that are clearly not his. "…I apologize for objectifying you and for… violating our friendship–"

"–*Friendship?* Wait, what is this?" He looks down as if he's lost something on the floor. Softly, I say, "Answer me, Fletcher."

"The journey that I'm on… There's only one healthy path… And that path… is alone."

"That's not you talking, Fletcher. What is that therapist telling you?"

A tear slips down his cheek. "I love you, Tahj. I swear to *God* I love you."

"This isn't happening," I'm saying, as my head shakes no.

Fletcher says outright, "We can't be together, like that."

Anger swells in my chest like an inflatable raft. "This is *not* coming from the same guy who ran my car down like his life depended on it. No, Fletcher. You let those people get inside of your head. They don't know us. They don't know *me*. Whatever you're going through, Fletcher, we'll go through it together."

Slowly Fletcher's head shakes no and I wanna punch him through the phone. "Tahj," he says. "As much as I want that… for one, it's not fair to you, and number two, it's only going to make me worse." The thing that makes me hit the ceiling is when he says, "We can still be friends."

"You were gonna ditch your family to spend the lockdown with me. How this turnaround?"

"You just don't understand."

"*Make* me understand," I scream.

We talk for about a half hour more but the result is Fletcher standing firm, and me basically pleading for him to give us a chance. I open my mouth to offer a compromise – to suggest we take some time off, that maybe he'll feel differently after the lockdown, which has us all going crazy, but by the time my first word is out, Fletcher's head is already shaking in refusal, which triggers me to absolutely lose it. "You're a *bitch* you know that! A big muscle-bound bitch!"

"Tahj…" His eyes blaze with pain from the stab, and then shock that the wielder of that blade is the one he loves. "Slim…"

"Ain't no Slim!" A somber cry bubbles at the back of my throat. "Not long ago, you was begging me to put the tip in." My cry starts to hiccup, but I fight through it. "You have a few – a few sessions with a therapist. And now – and now, you're sitting here, acting like you know every fuckin' thing."

"Tahj. It's not *like* that, Tahj."

"Mm-mm…" My lips tighten and my head tremors no in refusal of Fletcher trying to make excuses for what he's really doing. "You play with my heart, Fletcher? After all these years? After all we've been through? How dare you!" I go silent, wiping tears in my blanket. In a calm fury, I render a sentencing that's overkill. "I don't care if I never see you again and I mean it. Don't call me. Don't speak to me. Ever again!" I end the call, and refuse his attempts to call me back. He sends a slew of texts. He says he didn't think I'd be upset because I denied him a relationship first; it's the only text that I respond to. I tell him that ever since the accident, the old Fletcher returned and so did my desire to be in a relationship, and now anything less is unacceptable.

Although I'd been sewing throughout the lockdown, my craft is no longer about pleasure; it grasps for survival. I'm a different person on the bench in front of the instrument; I'm Beethoven half deaf and banging the keys out of desperation to hear. I sew at a frantic pace, for long hours in the morning and throughout the night, under the beam of a bending lamp; cutting fabric, pinning the seams, powering through the finger pricks while sunken deep under the hypnosis of the humming machine; the thread spool spinning, the needle pumping, my eyes sandy and cracked for lack of sleep.

It's not even about Fletcher anymore. I begin to see our relationship ending as my karma for being dishonest with Meek. I'm churning out garments that should wear tags that say manufactured by guilt.

I back away from the sewing machine afraid to be consumed by the thing meant to rescue me. I kneel at the couch and leaf through the pile and see wrapped skirts, kimono tops, a dungaree dress, each with some type of flaw, inconsistent stitch density, or puckers at the seams because they're stitched with my last threads of sanity.

The next day, Bubby calls on Facetime. Since the lockdown, it seems it's the only way people want to communicate now. I let the call go to voicemail. I hurry to the bathroom to put on makeup and Facetime him back.

"Whattup Tahj? Fuck's going on with you and Fletcher?"

Obviously, Fletcher's confided in Bubby but I'm unsure as to what extent.

"There's nothing going on with me and Fletcher."

"Who you tellin'? It's *been* something with you two."

I hear Emily in the background. I warn, "I don't wanna see her."

"How many times I done told you, Em thought she was helping," Bubby says, as if it should change my mind.

"Just angle your phone accordingly," I say.

"Anyway… My boy Fletcher hurt. Y'all really not speaking?"

I sigh, as if ready to let the call fade away to boredom.

"He done lost a lot. Losing you could be the straw that breaks the camel's back."

"Nobody's worried about *my* back."

Bubby's head shakes. "What's happening to us? You and Fletcher falling out… Me and Keenan falling out…"

"You and *Kee?* Ain't no way! For what?"

Bubby looks down to hide a smile then raises his head, the smile still strikingly there. "Well, with Keenan being a brand new agent and everything, I told him I'm trying to bring in someone with a little experience to help him."

I say, "If they share the role, they gotta share the bag."

"Exactly. Keenan was so pissed, man… If we was face to face, I swear he would've swung."

"You ain't know that about your own cousin? He's always been like that about money."

"But it's be me putting my body on the line every week. I decide."

I try not to sound too thirsty. "Sooo, you're looking for an agent with a little experience? Got anybody in mind?"

By now, Bubby's smile is at a hundred. "Look at you, acting all clueless and shit."

My mouth falls open. "Don't play with me! On God?"

"On God," Bubby nods. "Just think. A couple months from now, you're gonna be a millionaire. We'll *all* be millionaires–"

"–Millionaires…" What a blessing to have a friend so blessed, and with a heart to bring his friends along. I let it wash over me, then I'm hyperventilating and fanning myself until, "But wait. Me? Not Fletcher?"

"You're the one who helped me stay off of academic probation throughout high school and college. And you never asked for a dime, and never once did you throw it back in my face. Now, as far as Fletcher… We got Fletcher covered. We gone do what we gotta do to get him in the league. Alright?"

"Alright," I say.

Bubby says, "I'm glad you're on board, because we're gonna need your help. You and Fletcher gonna have to work through it. No bro left behind."

I wipe a tear and say, "Thank you, Bubby." It's all I can think to say. "Thank you. You did not have to do this."

"I *did* have to do this. I owe you more than you'll ever know." He smiles, but at the same time, he's eyeing me like a sniper, then squeezes the trigger on something I never would've expected to hear from Bubby. "Between me and you… I'm a married man now because of you. In every woman I ever dealt with, I saw my momma. Although I love her as my mother, I ain't respect her very much outside of that – with her scheming ass. But being friends with you all these years and seeing just how solid you are… how authentic, how consistent… You made me believe I could *love* a woman versus spending a lifetime *tolerating* one." Mind you, he's saying this just outside the presence of his new wife.

"Aw Bubby," I say. "That's the nicest thing anyone has ever said to me."

Bubby swats a hand. "Don't read too much into it though. I gotta get off this phone. A'ight then."

I stare at the blank screen. This is too much. Hearing Bubby's admiration of me, and then looking back through memory and finding moments where I should've seen it. And then there's Fletcher, who I swore never to speak to again, but once again, I'm back in this cycle where our falling out is negated by the responsibility of friendship.

A month after the lockdown, I find myself standing in our old high school football field in the hot sun chatting with Keenan and Bubby as we wait on Fletcher. Their plan to get Fletcher noticed by NFL scouts, I suspect, is also a plan to get Fletcher and me back on speaking terms.

Since the car accident made Fletcher miss the NFL Combine, we're here to facilitate our own combine and post it on social media, hoping it would go viral.

I agree to help as part of the terms of Bubby making me co-agent with Keenan, but I would've done it anyway because Fletcher would've done it for me. Besides, holding a stopwatch in the hot sun doesn't even compare to Fletcher's eight-hour drive to Miami, which cost him a relationship, to support me in my first big-time catwalk.

Still, any thoughts of being with Fletcher romantically, is out of mind – perhaps because he was out of sight – because when he appears in the distance, walking across the grass in his half-T and tights, and I'm seeing that gorgeous brown face and ripped abs, I'm also seeing what I cannot have, and it makes me upset all over again.

Of course, my makeup and hair is perfect. I'm in leggings, with my twins gathered plump in a sports top. I'm telling Bubby and Keenan how I'd gained a few pounds over the lockdown and they swear they can't see it. I happen to pinch my belly right when Fletcher reaches us; he doesn't comment. He's all business. He shoulder bumps the bros, then acknowledges me with a nod and a husky, "A'ight."

We're out in the sun doing drills and filming, sometimes having to do multiple takes. Their old high school coach had given Bubby the keys to the facility where they go in and bring out the tackle sleds. The Georgia sun doesn't give a damn about waiting on summer, and the guys are sweating profusely by the time they have the heavy sleds out on the field and in position for the next drill. I make a T with my hands. "Y'all ain't thirsty? I got a cooler in the car, but I can't carry it way over here."

"My dawg," Bubby celebrates.

Keenan ads, "Don't Tahj be coming through?"

"I'm tired of having to think for you stooges." I'd be lying if I say I wasn't trying to elicit a response from Fletcher.

I spot Fletcher's lazy look-away and wonder if he's holding back a wisecrack, or if he's refusing my humor because he's upset.

Bubby and Keenan nominate Fletcher to escort me to my car and retrieve the cooler, figuring we'd break the ice.

Nonchalantly, Fletcher asks, "Where you parked?"

Naturally, I point at the car, so obviously visible through the chain-linked fence, my lips playfully twisted to mock his question, but I quickly cancel the act, and redo my response like friends on the mend should, with a soft, "It's right over here."

He walks a few paces behind me and I wonder if he's checking me out. Whatever it is he sees in my narrow frame, he seems to love it, or maybe the way he feels for me distorts his vision. We go through the fence and he stands behind me as I open the trunk.

Fletcher hugs me from behind. The nerve of him. I throw his arms off of me. "Too soon," I say, coldly, as I turn to him, but I find Fletcher in tears, his face so wet he had to have been crying the entire time he followed me to the car. He's too distraught to speak.

He turns away, dejected and now it's me holding him from behind. "Fletcher? Fletcher. Talk to me, please." I hurry around to face him. I take the arms I threw off me and place them around me.

His mouth trembles. He whispers. "I can't."

"Breath, okay? Breath."

He sighs twice and looks down at me, his eyes blood-red from crying. He confesses, "I'm having suicidal thoughts."

Our embrace tightens. This answers everything. "I didn't know," I cry. "I didn't know."

He whispers, "*They* don't know," meaning Bubby and Keenan.

I pat his back and shush him softly like a mother to a hurt child. "I'm here for you, Fletcher. I'm here. I'm gone always be here. You hear me?"

He whispers, "I can't do this without you, Tahj. I'm gone die without you."

CHAPTER 7
LATE 2022

"Pardon my tone, Tahj, but… he's without you now… and he still ain't dead," says, Jay, a handsome older gentleman I'd been having a lovely time going out on dates with.

I respond, "When has he ever been without me? We talk all the time." Fletcher and I were still just friends again, now two years since the day he nearly put the tip in. Now that he's playing in the NFL, being just friends is easy with the distance between us. When he returns in the offseason, it's his vow of celibacy that makes being just friends, easy work. I respected his journey, but I had started back dating as a message to Fletcher that my availability to him, is not a given.

"So you invited me to dinner to talk about him? Not us?"

"I'm getting to that." I'm giving the backstory so Jay knows I'm not fading him for some new guy that came along and swept me off my feet.

Jay says, "What round did he get picked? Fifth? Did he even get a million a year?"

"A little over that," I say, then sip from a glass of Castello Del Poggio.

"And Bubby made you his agent – not Fletcher?"

"Their situation was different, plus I was not that kind of agent, then."

"But you knew football," he challenges. "No way you picked up all that knowledge in just the last couple years."

"I used to watch football because of my bros, then I started watching it for myself. Now I watch it for work."

"I ain't gone lie, Tahj. Just hearing you talk football gives me the feelings." He pets the air to calm my inclination to remind him I'm not interested in a relationship. "Calm down, Tahj. I know when I've been friend-zoned. It's you who don't know when *you've* been friend-zoned."

"Fletcher can't friend zone me. We were friends *first*. Plus he buys me things."

"Things like what?" Jay waves off his own question. "Apparently not much, with his family in his pockets; him making a million a year, only."

"*Only*, you say?" I line Jay up in my crosshairs. "I know you have your own firm and whatnot, Jay, but how much can a lawyer really make?"

"The title isn't what pays me. The massive settlements I win for my clients is what pays me–"

"–How much, though?"

Jay replies, "My finances is a rather intimate topic for someone I'm not intimate with… yet."

His *yet* prunes my face, just thinking of the miracle it would have to take for me to wind up in bed with him.

Jay grins. "You think I'm worried about having sex with you? You keep letting me hang around, and there will come a time when you'll be the one pressing *me* for it."

As boundless as his confidence is, somehow I don't find it off-putting; I find it interesting, "Who *are* you, behind this persona? You present this guy who's got it all together, as if you don't have any worries or deal with pain."

He studies me for longer than I'd like. "A piece of advice: Don't show interest in a man's pain. Once you let him see how comforting it is to lay his burdens on you…" He sighs. "Congratulations. You just won yourself the most broken version of that man. Instead, show interest in his resolve; that'll get you the most solid version of him. The bonus for you, is that you get to stay in your femininity; that's your happy place."

I conceal my pride in my rebuttal as un unload it, "I'm gonna have to disagree with you, there, Jay. You act as if women should just sit back and let men fend for themselves. If that's the case, Adam could've done bad all by himself, but no… God made Eve. So, *I'm* saying, if *my* man has to run himself into the ground, to afford me a life of luxury, I don't want it. I want happiness for *us*." I could say more, but my soapbox is already two stacks high.

"Can't argue with the Bible," says Jay. "If you coddle a man, he better be living by that bible too, or it could be disastrous." He takes his snifter, his grasp ejecting the index finger at me. "You was determined to be right about *something* this evening, huh…" He examines me like I'm a piece of work. "A woman who cares just as much about her man's happiness…? You're killing me softly."

"That's no different from literally every woman I know." My frown clears with a revelation. "I think maybe with you, Jay, the money gets in the way."

Coincidentally, the server sets the check down with a bow. I snatch it up. "In fact, let *me* get the check this time."

He looks at me crazy. "Girl, don't you know I got an Omi filet on my plate? Thutty-year-old brandy in my glass?"

I swat the air. "Don't sweat it. Because once you hear why I asked you to dinner, you're gonna demand that I pick up the tab." I see tension in his brow. What I have to say is hard for me too, makes me suddenly slow of speech. "You know… Fletcher recently got the same injury he had in that car accident; his third concussion in two and a half years. And, well, his team cut him, so now he's changing the focus away from football… for his health. He's on his way back to Atlanta… and we're gonna be business partners."

Jay leans inquisitively. "So you expect me to do the math, for the part you're not saying? You and me, going out on dates, has to stop because your old flame is back."

I finally look at the bill. "Yikes," I say.

"Preciate you buying me dinner," Jay says, smugly.

I slip my card in the leather bill holder.

"I guess this is goodbye, then."

"Or you can make me your fashion consultant, like I've been asking you since day one. I could use the money."

"I told you, Tahj, my personal assistant is my fashion consultant. She, kinda, keeps expanding the scope of her job on me. I don't wanna step on toes."

I reply, "I'll bet you she's over fifty."

"Forty-six. Same as me. Why?"

"Because the only thing about you that makes you look over forty, sir, is your wardrobe." And his thinning hairline, I dare not say.

Jay contemplates momentarily then reaches for his phone, saying, "Why don't I call her and we all can work this out.'"

"Actually, I gotta slide."

"Running off to go see Fletcher," Jay says, jokingly.

I sorta shy away and say, "Don't make me lie to you, Jay."

OUR FIRST TIME

I lay on the couch with wine in my glass and lace on my body, knowing good and hell well that within only a few minutes of Fletcher's arrival, the lingerie will be coming off; my open-toed stiletto pumps would be staying on. The lights are low; the glow of candles dance high on the walls as the flames lick about, and the surround sound fills the room with soft melodies that I compiled on iTunes.

My house is clean, my bills are paid, my schedule is clear, my pussy is shaved, and I'm in the mood like never before.

There's a knock at the door. "It's open," I sing. I subdue my smile as Fletcher walks in, astonished by the atmosphere.

I've wanted this so bad for so long, my mind struggles to even process it. I'm caught in this existential moment where I'm looking at the man now, and seeing shades of the boy I met the summer before we started high school. He was already the size of a full-grown man, with his baby face and peach fuzz on his chin. I was school shopping with daddy, coming out of the store when were approached by Fletcher who was going around asking for jumper cables while his mother waited in the car. Daddy had cables and offered to help. Fletcher was all yes sir this; no sir that, so respectful to my daddy and to his own mother. And *foin!* Who would've thought that we'd end up here; but then again, who would've thought that it would take us this long.

He joins me on the couch, my legs in his lap. His eyes take their time traveling the length of me.

I wanna be sexy for him. I want to be everything he desires, while him just being here with me, and with a stretch of time for us to fill however we want, is everything I desire. But we have time to play with. "So…" I say. "Have you talked to Kee since the blowup?"

Bubby intended Legacy Sports Agency as a way to bring his closest friends along, so money would never come between us; nevertheless, money's coming between us. Fletcher's being added as a third partner, so Keenan's bitter for again, having to reduce his shares.

Fletcher says, "Kee not upset about reducing his shares. He's mad that it's me. He'd gladly give up shares if it was for his brother."

I can tell that Fletcher, out of respect, tries to appear more interested in the conversation than the impending sex.

"Interesting," I say, while thinking, *shut up and fuck me.*

I'm about to, he replies via telepathy.

I'd forgotten how that ability turns on whenever we're holding back. He says, "Khalid tryna to use his settlement to buy into the company. Now that I'd make it a four-way split, Kee would lose his majority owner status in order to bring his brother on. *That's* why he's pissed."

I bite my lip and say. "I feel like we're getting way off topic, here."
He smirks. "Oh?"
"Let me get you a glass of wine."

He licks his lips. "Glass of *you*."

I sit up, face to face. I trace a finger along his lips. "Well, I hope you're thirsty."

For starters, I quench him with a kiss, then tease back to marvel at the beauty of him. He pulls me onto his lap. The way our kiss sucks and twists, it seems as if lovemaking has begun, but we have plenty of time. We sigh, overwhelmed. His eyes are still closed and his head sways, maybe to me, maybe to the music, guitar strings under the gentle fingers of H.E.R. His eyes open, ablaze with candlelight as well as an idea. "May I have this dance?"

We meet at the center of my living room floor, our faces smiling and heads shaking at ourselves for doing this. I wrap my arms around his waist and look up into his eyes to convey to this man that I am all his. My hands slip under his shirt, up the wall of abs to grope his chest. He squeezes my buns and it takes everything in me to not break my gaze and go down on him. I feel him growing against me, and it feels like it is everything I hoped it would be, and probably more.

I help Fletcher remove his shirt and then we continue the dance, swaying in the embrace. I detail his chest with kisses. He doesn't try to take over; he let me spoil him.

He inserts two fingers in my mouth. I manage to lower my panties and spread my stance. His wet fingers fondle my swollen lips. I clutch him and kiss his mouth and suck his tongue, shuddering, under waves of pleasure. My hips rock back and forth into his hand, and then back one final time, to escape his fingers before I get too lost in my own pleasure that I forget about pleasing him.

I go down on my knees and soften my mouth. I catch him in my mouth and make half of him disappear. For the part I can't reach facing forward, I run my mouth along the side, head waving in a slow, nonverbal no. I let it fall and spring like a diving board. Fletcher seems ready to lose his mind. I comment, "It really *has* been two years for you."

Fletcher replies, "For you too… right?"

I recapture him in my mouth to avoid the question. I pleasure him until I'm convinced that he's forgotten.

I stretch by bra down, then gather him in my breasts; the reality hits me. "This is crazy," I say in amazement. "Me and you… We're really doing this." I squeeze, then pull away slowly, letting it fall. His masculine sigh is everything to me.

I stand. We start kissing again and I take no initiative to guide us to the next thing, deferring power to him. He picks me up like I'm nothing, and walks backward with me to the couch where he sits, his strong hands raising me higher, up to his mouth like drinking cereal milk from the bowl. Suddenly, I'm standing on my leather couch, my ass seated in his hands while he's slurping me into orbit. I'm sizzling with pleasure; squeezing my breasts and moaning to them.

Fletcher buries his nose in it, then enters me with his tongue and I'm riding his face like a bull. Afraid to climax too soon, I stand straight up on my couch, looking down, watching a line of ooze string away from his lips.

"Dayumn," he says, his eyes as carnal as a wolf's.

I help him out of his pants and then kneel before him but he catches me by my armpits and brings me up into a kiss. He says, "I wanna feel you."

I lead him down the hallway, just thinking about how right this feels; how everything happened the way it should have. Our misfortunes were really our saving graces. If we dated in college, the distance might've ruined us. If we dated in high school, immaturity would've gotten the better of us. We're twenty-four years old now. We'll have proximity on our side, as we'll be sharing an office, and we're now mature enough for a love that could carry us further than we can see into the future.

On the short walk down the hallway, I have a flash vision of us, years from now, reliving this experience with wedding rings on our fingers, the kids in the care of grandparents to afford us this night, our added layers of mother and father falling away with our clothing, revealing man and woman, husband, and wife. I know I'm being overzealous thinking this far ahead, but I treat myself to the thought of it anyway; imagining Fletcher with a little grey in his beard, us with a bit more belly, bonding in coitus where all the newness and thrill has graduated, over time, into a lovemaking that is sweet and gentle and knowing, our expertise honed and our intensity girded by memories spanning many loving years.

On this night, however, it's only here and now. It is us, just now entering that dream, as we enter the bedroom together for our first time.

The room is a vigil. Plotted along the dresser, window sill, and nightstand are more candles; we are golden in the aura of their light. He lifts me. I clamp his waist with my thighs and reach back, my hand under me feeling for him. He's hot and throbbing in my grasp. I begin edging my threshold with the tip and giving myself the shivers. My head's back, mouth open, bearing teeth to the candle-scented air, like a she-lion, high on the pheromones of the alpha. He pops in and we sigh as one. I whisper, "I've dreamed about this for so long."

He smirks. "You sure you can take this wood?"

I give a sassy look as if I'm not worried, but honestly there are concerns. I have to help him spread my cheeks apart just to let him in, and in just a few preliminary strokes to coat himself with my cream, I'm clawing his back at the feel of the stretch.

"Mm-hm," he smiles, knowingly. He clutches me and whispers, "You feel so good to me, baby." I concur, but can't speak because he's scary deep. He takes me on this smooth up-and-down ride like a carousel, but speeds up, as if the ceramic horse, suddenly imbued with life, breaks free and bolts; I'm a bouncing jockey hitting the final stretch of a derby, riding this powerful beast, leaning in the saddle to whisper encouragement, but out of my mouth erupts the name of our creator in a B-flat, "Oh God!"

I thought my dreams of Fletcher had lingered so long that it turned delirious in my mind, but here he is, in the flesh, glaring at me with a bit lip while doing the most with that steady stroke, exacting my wildest imagination.

I'm a storm system; colliding fronts of ecstasy and emotion swirling all tumultuously inside, while I'm being vertically fucked into oblivion; a full-bodied pleasure reverberates down to the toes that I curl and crack. I'm so full with him it feels emotional in a vague sort of way, yet there're very real and tangible passions welling up inside of me, like the flutters of gratitude for being wanted so intensely. My heart is massive with vindication, for the two years I'd chained my romantic feelings to be the friend Fletcher needed in order to get well; there was always the risk of me being made a fool.

It's that feeling of vindication, along with that relentless stroke that hurls me into orgasm. I throw my head back, mouth wide, moaning wildly.

"Look at me," Fletcher demands.

My head snaps straight on command. The sweat beads on his beautiful face and body, reflects candlelight and it looks like he's sweating fire. Now that he has my pleasure-drunken attention, Fletcher looks me in my eyes and for the first time, he tells me, in the midst of my spurting orgasm. "I love you."

"I love *you*." The pleasure, both emotional and physical, is so much that I black out – ten seconds deleted from my existence. I will never remember how I got onto the bed, looking at the ceiling; I only remember Fletcher coming into view, over me, marveling at his work and giving me smiling kisses to my lips and face.

He whispers, "Turn over, baby."

I can't say no to him, but I won't turn over; not now. The next song on the playlist, has a lines where we need to be face to face when the lyrics arrive. I hold Fletcher at bay for about ten seconds until he hears why I can't turn my back to him: the intro of this retro organ, sounding small in the distance but surging to the forefront, arriving in full volume with the abrupt kick drum and snare. I let go of Fletcher's face because I see that he understands the assignment. He lowers to kiss my lips as the rustic voice of Tay-Tay Sutherland eases its way into the first refrain.

We're enraptured in the sounds of the organ and the painfully raspy voice that sings for the agony of the years we could not be together; a voice that sings of dedication and renewal.

Fletcher's already in tears. A few raindrops pelt my cheek. My voice trembles, my eyes blur with tears. "I love you, Fletcher." We mourn the loss of Meek, but rejoice the death that didn't happen, even after the fact. Fletcher embraces me with the same energy as that spring day, sunlight glaring off the back windshield of my car as we embraced, when Fletcher told me that he would die without me. We hush for lyrics that lay us bare.

> *I can't live without you.*
> *I can't live with you, girl.*
> *I can't live – can't live, naw naw*
> *I said I can't live… without you*

As the song fades down, we're face to face, tasting each other's tears, and moaning in orgasm together.

I then hold Fletcher to my breast and coddle him through his last orgasmic quakes. I don't hold it against him for not pulling out; the passion was too overwhelming to stop and reason. My only thought in regard to me possibly becoming pregnant is, *so be it*. Fletcher looks deeply into my eyes and says, "I'm never gonna let you go. You hear me?"

Later that night Fletcher yells, "Tahj… Tahj…"

I spring fully awake, in fight or flight mode, thinking there's an intruder.

"Tahj…" Fletcher's calling my name as plain as day, but he's still asleep, eyes shut, thrashing. Suddenly, he sits up, board stiff, yelling, "No!" It's a nightmare.

I throw my arms around Fletcher and his body damp with sweat. I whisper, "What were you dreaming about?"

Fletcher rubs his eyes and says, "Why do you ask?"

I look at him like he must be joking. "You were tossing and calling my name," I say. "You don't remember the dream?"

Fletcher looks at me as if I'm losing it, then turns away and wraps himself in the covers, saying, "I think you were the one dreaming, babe."

I lay there confused and staring at the back of his head.

CHAPTER 8
OFFICE MATEs

In the morning, we stagger our arrival so it's not obvious, to Keenan, that Fletcher and I rolled out of the same bed. Can't start off being messy, getting out of the same car with twin Starbucks cups, acting all flirty. Fletcher and I decided it's best to keep our relationship on the low, for now, since we're business partners.

I'm already settled at my desk when I see Fletcher down the hallway coming out of the elevator in a grey suit.

Keenan, to my surprise, doesn't seem bitter at all. He greets Fletcher with a handshake that folds into a shoulder bump. "'Sup killa? Ready to take over the world?" Keenan acts as if just last week, he didn't call Fletcher a charity case over the phone.

I hurry over, my legs still sore from last night's lovemaking, yet I give Fletcher the same buddy handshake and shoulder bump he got from Keenan.

All Keenan knows is that me and Fletcher's attempt at a relationship sputtered during the lockdown, and we'd been dating other people ever since.

We spend the morning in three swivel chairs around Keenan's desk, training Fletcher on how to use the talent management software and our database of scouting reports. We explain the interface for our paid cloud service with access to hundreds of thousands of hours of game film to evaluate athletes.

I hear Fletcher humming the song from last night. I give him a look.

He stops, smiling. "What?"

Keenan looks over. "Did I miss something?"

"It's nothing," I say. We get back to work, noticeably trying not to look at each other and expose our secret.

Keenan and I have a secret too. We hadn't done a damn bit of work in two years. As we train Fletcher, I see him slowly picking up clues, like the lack of office clutter and the dead potted plant, which is why Fletcher finally asks, "Okay, so… where's the client list?"

While Keenan and I stammer to answer the first question, Fletcher fires a second, "And why hasn't the phone rang all morning?"

I admit, "Well… we kinda don't have a phone."

Fletcher's face rotates to me. "Don't have a phone?" He looks again at dead plant. A smile grows as slow as a life-cycle demonstration, from an infant kink in his cheek to a grin, to a gate of teeth. "Y'all got to be kidding me. All that shit you was talking Kee… Here it is, more than two years gone by and you ain't eem put a landline phone in this bitch?"

In fact Keenan and I would go months without seeing the inside of this office. I explain, "Bubby got a max contract. Of that, Keenan got over a million and me just under–"

"–So that's it? Y'all planning on riding Bubby's coattails? Not me," Fletcher declares. "Together we should try to out-earn Bubby. Y'all talking about millions. I want *hundreds* of millions." Fletcher tosses his hands up. "No wonder why, whenever I ask how business is going, I never got a straight answer from either of you. Ain't no clients *to* talk about."

"Nah, don't trip. We got clients, big dawg," says Keenan, regrouping his ego like soldiers to defend the front line.

"Who?!" Fletcher's eyes widen like the owl he imitates.

Keenan swivels the mouse and in a few clicks, we're at our client list of six athletes, five of which failed to go pro. Keenan points to the one hopeful who's on a practice squad and still fighting for a roster spot. "Remember o'boy from Virginia Tech, Blake?"

"Blake!" Fletcher rockets up from his seat and walks away – board stiff like Soulja Boy at that viral Breakfast Club interview. *"Blake?"*

Keenan's mouth twists with shame as he looks to me for an ally. In my effort to win back some of the man's pride, I explain, "As pitiful as this list may seem, every one of our clients bring in some kind of revenue."

"How?" Fletcher folds his arms like an Indian chief.

"Obviously, you think an NFL contract is necessary to make money as an agent."

"Talk to 'em Tahj," Keenan booms.

"Every one of our clients was hometown heroes during high school football; they became fixtures in the consciousness of college towns where they played."

"Preach!"

"That's value," I say. "I handle their endorsements; the same thing I've been doing for myself for years."

Fletcher leans towards the computer screen and points to one name on the list. "What kind of endorsement deal are you getting for this Chase Little character, for example?"

"Funny you should ask," I say. Chase has the biggest contract of all. American Red Cross for the Charlotte, NC chapter… blood donorship spokesperson." I pick the next name on the list, "We have Tawon Summers, with a United Negro College Fund endorsement–"

Keenan cuts me off with the stupidest response. "Don't forget about Tyler Monroe…"

My head drops and I sigh in exasperation.

Fletcher, now with a suspect grin, asks, "What endorsements he got?"

I answer with a sigh of defeat, "An endorsement deal with Big Daddy's Barbecue and Used Auto Sales."

Fletcher's laughter throws his head back. He hyperventilates just to gather the breath to yell out, "Not barbecue!"

I float a palm at Fletcher's insolence. "Of course, you would pick the most insignificant thing and focus on that."

Fletcher laughs so hard, he sets a hand on my shoulder for strength. I snatch away and march to my desk. "Tahj," Fletcher calls while wiping tears. "You can't take a joke?"

I point at myself and say, "I *do* my job."

This tickles Fletcher even more. He tries to hold his laughter, causing it to hiss with the force of a popped tire, but he's waving it off. "My bad, Tahj. I'm gonna get it together, I just…"

I just… cut my eyes and pretend to do work.

Fletcher shows confusion, which swings to the other male in the office. "Is this what you have to deal with?"

Keenan replies, "Welcome to my world, bro." His mouth buttons as he catches my glare.

Next, Fletcher flops in a seat, his hands rubbing together as he says, "I can get us going, y'all. Over the last two years, I been on three different teams. I'm legit friends with veteran NFL players coming into their contract year. Three teams means three cities and in each one, I took part in football camps where I've made contacts with some legit up-and-coming players – never once thinking that one day I'd become an agent. In fact, Jamal Richards of the Tennessee Volunteers just texted me this morning."

Keenan raises a finger. "You can't contact college athletes until their final game of eligibility, Fletch. You know that."

"Not true, bro. I can contact them as a friend. I just can't contact them as an agent."

"But you *are* an agent, now."

"Am I?"

"Speaking of," I nod down the hall, where, coming off the elevator, is a Middle Eastern man with a European combover that's as shiny as a vinyl record. He has a briefcase in one hand. The other hand unbuttons the top of his vintage blue tailored suit as he approaches.

Fletcher mumbles, "That's the lawyer? I thought we were going to him; he comes to us?"

I comment, "We get the royal treatment because we're friends of his very rich client, Bubby."

I approach the door, explaining, "Everything we discussed verbally is about to be put into ink, and you'll be, officially, the third operating partner." I pull the lawyer in with a handshake. "Attorney Bashar. Nice seeing you again."

"Tahj," he nods. "Always a pleasure."

Keenan, who had been so upset last week, seems awfully relaxed now, and it worries me.

Bashar passes out the papers, explaining each document. I take my time with each sheet, ensuring that his summaries match what's in print.

Forty-five minutes is spent, by the time a neat stack of documents has our wet signatures and the lawyer is snapping his briefcase closed. Keenan, however, throws in a caveat, "Question…"

Keenan, under the beam of three pairs of eyes, continues, "There's three executives, right… Two men, one woman."

The way he says *one woman* makes me lean with intrigue. "What're you getting at," I say.

"What if two of us were to start dating?"

I ask, "Are you serious, right now?"

Bashar's brow-raise makes his hairline shift back. "C-suite romance?" He spreads a hand. "Any of you involved now?"

Our guilty conscience makes the question an accusation. "No," we answer, maybe a bit too forcefully.

Keenan tattles. "They have a bit of a history. Think of the situation it would put me in if old flames reignite. I have half the stake in this company. Their stakes combined make up the other half. If they share a pillow, they're a team, and their combined power can stalemate anything I try to do with this company."

Fletcher fires, "You haven't *done* much of anything with the company in two years, bruh."

"Regardless," says Keenan. "I want protection."

Bashar gathers his hands on the table. "I'm not sure that you even need my advice on this. It's pretty standard practice that one member of the couple steps down."

Keenan lays a hand softly on the table. "And what happens to that person's stake in the company?"

"If the remaining partners either lack the capital, or the desire to purchase the relinquished shares, it opens the door for a new partner."

Fletcher glances around and says, "Why do I feel like you two had this conversation before?"

Keenan ignores Fletcher and says to the lawyer, "I want that in writing."

"Nah, what you *want*," Fletcher counters. "…is one of *us* out, so you can bring your brother in. Let's be real."

I get up and walk away fuming. I could very well be pregnant with Fletcher's baby and to hear that it would cost me millions if I'm made to step down before Bubby's contract renewal in two more years, is just too much for me.

This marks the day that money starts coming between us.

CHAPTER 9
The Math Ain't Mathing

I didn't just walk away from the table. I left the office altogether and got lunch for the three of us, well sort of.

I return with a bag from a deli down the street. Keenan asks, "You a'ight?"

"Of course," I say as I set the bag on Fletcher's desk. "I'm so alright, Kee, I got you lunch."

Keenan says, "'Preciate ya. What's in the bag?"

"Tuna sandwiches for everybody."

"Tuna?" Keenan looks at me funny. "You know I don't like no tuna."

I raise a hand to my mouth. "You love tuna. I thought it was the pimento you didn't like."

There's this gloom in Keenan's brow that says he thinks I did it on purpose. "Come on Fletch. Lemme show you my favorite little lunch spot around the way."

Fletcher, feeling my foot stepping on his, under the table, declines, saying he'll work through lunch while studying the software. "This is all new to me, and I wanna hit the ground running, ya know?"

I hold my laugh until Keenan leaves then I hop up. Fletcher asks, "The tuna thing was on purpose, huh."

I pull Fletcher by the hand. "There's something I want you to see in the copying room," I say, but my grin is so devious. Fletcher comes along because whatever it is, he thinks he'll like it.

I pull him inside the copying room. "You didn't get a chance to get me from behind last night." I say, while seesawing my panties down my legs.

I start glazing him with my mouth, momentarily getting lost in it, then I rise up, knees popping, lips smiling so fondly at Fletcher who says, "Risking it all, huh?" He thumbs a drip of saliva from my chin and kisses me slowly, the intensity climbing, until he spins me around and bites the side of my neck while snaking himself inside of me. We breathe together in long, slow sips of air.

Risking it all takes on new meaning today. If we're caught, one of us would be forced out before Bubby's contract year and miss out on millions. That multi-million dollar risk, along with the taboo of frolicking in the office, is what has me so turned on. I moan in delight while bent over stacked cases of toner cartridge. There's still sandwiches to be eaten before Keenan returns, or we raise suspicion. I look back at Fletcher and urge him, "You gotta hurry baby." He's so serious in his pleasure, his eyes on my bum, mesmerized no doubt by the creamy entry, the repetitive eating and regurgitating of his dear penis. Pleasure runs down my body like waterdrops.

Fletcher covers my mouth like a hostage and talks dirty to my ear. "You love this dick?" Never with such force have I ever said *Mmm-hmm*. Next, he's convulsing with his head buried on my shoulder, his moans fading like a man falling off of a cliff. I turn around as Fletcher's eyes unroll. I pet his cheek and say, "Don't make that face, baby."

We laugh and embrace. Fletcher just gazes at me with his head shaking. "God, I love you," he says.

"I love you too." I grab my underwear and lead him out. "Come on, baby. Eat your sandwich."

Back at my desk, Fletcher unwraps his sandwich and says, "Fuck what Keenan's talkin' about. If we get caught and one of us is forced to step down, I know a way that neither of us would have to lose anything."

I frown, "I wouldn't bet on that Fletch."

"I could buy the vacated shares, and everything would still be ours if we're husband and wife."

I'm taken aback.

Then Fletcher's taken aback. "You ain't wit it?"

"Oh hell fucking yes, I'm with it… It just caught me off guard, that's all."

With a packed cheek and breadcrumbs on his mouth, Fletcher says, "That's not the proposal, by the way. I'm gonna do it the right way."

I squeeze Fletcher's hands and tell him, "You already know the answer." The thought hits me: I am pretty much a wife, right now.

Fletcher adds, "Ya gotta think about this too – after last night. We could get exposed by a pregnancy."

Not only am I pretty much a wife, but I'm possibly a mother too. With that delightful reminder, we lean across the desk for a kiss, our profiles fitting together like puzzle pieces. My head shakes and tears fall. "Sorry, let me get it together before Keenan comes back." I dab my tears and begin eating like it's work. For a while, we're just chewing and smiling at each other in silence, then it dawns on me. "I like that plan." It's so simple of a solution to all the complicated documents we signed earlier, that I recite the plan just to check for errors. "If we're married, when you buy out my stake in the company, the money still goes back to both of us just like it does now. It really is fool proof."

"I'm tryna tell ya, babe," Fletcher agrees.

I grab a calculator and verbalize the math. "So, this company, right now, is evaluated at 2.5 million dollars and mine is a twenty-five percent stake—"

"Wait," says Fletcher. "2.5 million? Where'd you get 2.5 million from?"

"It was on the documents we signed today."

"Where'd the *documents* get it from then? 2.5 mill? How?"

"Bubby is our client, that's how. He's considered an asset on our books. An asset that will bring at least fifteen million to our bottom line in two years. But 2.5 million is not what you'd pay, though. You're not buying the whole company just my part." I turn the calculator around. "It's only six-hundred-thousand dollars." The heaviness in Fletcher's brow forces me ask, "You got *that*, don't you?"

Fletcher's head shakes. "I got it, but I'm not in a position to come off of it. I got three homes in three different cities, and I'm still paying the mortgage on all of 'em. I didn't anticipate being out of the league, so I'm just now trying to get renters."

"But it's just for the transaction," I say. "It may get held up in escrow for a bit, but as soon as the money hits my bank account, I'll give it right back to you."

Shame pulls down like a shade over Fletcher. "Honestly, baby. I ain't got it, period."

As softly as I can, I say, "You were in the league for about two and a half years, baby. What happened?"

"Taxes happened… That hundred thousand dollar Range Rover parked outside happened. *I* happened…" Fletcher leans back in his seat, his hands sliding back to the edge of the desk. "I hate to ask you this, Tahj, but… maybe we can pool our money." Fletcher gets up and paces away, embarrassed by his request. "Just so we can be free… and I can love you out loud." He walks behind the desk and massages my shoulders.

I reply, "You know I would do it, Fletcher, but… How much do you think that house cost me? I bought it outright. I bought my car… outright. I bought daddy the first brand new truck he's ever had in his life. I paid off bills, student loans." I sigh. "I'm debt free, but cash poor."

Fletcher grips his forehead in frustration. "Dammit!"

"But what was I supposed to do?"

"Baby, I wasn't cursing you." Fletcher swivels my chair around and kneels before me. "I'm not upset with you at all. It's just that something is always in the way of *us*." Fletcher gets up and goes pacing again. "First I was under Gigi's spell for two years. Then you was with Donovan. When that was finally over, the accident happened and my own mental shit got in the way. Just when I think we're finally clear, now it's Kee – our own fuckin' friend in the way?!"

As Fletcher paces back toward me, I meet him face to face, body to body, hand in hand. "We're gonna find a way, my love."

"Fosho," says a determined Fletcher. "We got until the end of December to reel in some top-tier recruits and by April we'll be cashing in on those contracts."

"So, in seven months, we can be a real couple?"

"We're a real couple right now. We'll just gotta do it different for the time being."

When Keenan returns from lunch, I'm at my desk acting normal, as if my future husband isn't across the room looking sexy in his suit; as if we didn't just get in a quicky in the copying room. Keenan, on the way to his desk, frowns and says, "Damn, yo. Soon as I walk in – hit in the face with the smell of tuna."

I sense Fletcher's mischief, as if Keenan's tuna comment dubs as a punchline to our office sex. I cut my eyes at Fletcher, warning him to fuck around and find out.

Keenan glitches, as if to inquire about the tension in the room, but instead walks on, to his desk with a stirring recognition lingering in his brow. He's found himself on the outside of yet another inside joke between Fletcher and me. The ink isn't even dry on the professional conduct clause, and already Keenan's suspicious.

We resume work for the day, actually taking Legacy Sports Agency seriously by compiling a list of potential athletes who'll play their last game in December during Bowl month. My phone rings.

It's Monae, my only fashion client. Between the pandemic and joining Legacy Sports, I let go of my handful of modeling clients, to focus on sports agency, but one day while I was picking up a to-go order and Monae stormed out, saying fuck this job, that she was going back to stripping. I found her outside puffing a cigarette while waiting on an Uber and I asked if she ever thought about modeling.

I never told Keenan that I'm an agenting outside of Legacy Sports, so when I take Monae's call, I turn in my chair and lower my voice while trying to convince Monae that she has no proof that a lingerie brand terminated her contract due to discrimination. The call ends in a stalemate.

Keenan thumbs at me and tells Fletcher, "You see her whispering, right? Must've been her boyfriend."

"Must be," Fletcher cosigns with a smile.

"Whatever, you two."

Keenan calls across the room. "Yo, Fletch. That wasn't a joke, dawg. She got herself a poppa stoppa. J.P. Reynolds or something or other."

Fletcher's periscopes. "No shit?"

"Don't pay Kee no attention," I say. "Jay is just a friend."

Keenan counters, "How is Jay just a friend, when I know for a fact that you done seen him out of his clothes, talkin' about he got a Barack Obama chest."

Jealousy warps Fletcher's smile, as he repeats, "A Barack Obama chest?"

"He's still in shape, but a little saggy," I explain, and then turn. "Key, you're out of control."

Fletcher says, "*Kee's* the one out of control?"

Fletcher and I was just talking about marriage and now he thinks it was all a lie. I wanna cry, but I have to keep my composure or end up exposing Fletcher and me.

Calmly, even jokingly, I say, "Fletcher. Don't play. You heard me talk about Jay before. That's the guy I met at a wedding. I had to actually go *to* the wedding because the gown I made had a train that needed to be pinned in place right before she walked down the aisle. I bumped into Jay and ended up stitching a rip in his shirt. That's how I ended up seeing him with his shirt off." I say to Fletcher, "Is it coming back to you now? Remember I told you he thanked me by taking me out to dinner?"

Keenan says, "Dude must be *still* thanking you because he's *still* taking you out to dinner."

"On business! I'm now his fashion consultant, duh."

Fletcher steps in, "Chill a'ight, before nothing turns into something."

Keenan points. "If she gotta whisper over the phone, big dawg, it's already something. What was y'all talking about?"

Fletcher who suggested we drop the subject, suddenly seems eager for my explanation, which I give, believing only the truth can set me free. "I was not talking to Jay. I was talking to a model named Monae. I'm her agent, and I didn't want you to know that I have a client outside of this company."

Keenan goes quiet; I see him calculating in his mind. "So you're an agent for this company… but also an agent outside the company? You do know, we have a no-contest clause in our contract? If I'm not mistaken, your clients have to come in under *us*."

I get up out of my chair, my eyes on Fletcher but a finger pointing at Keenan. "See? That's why I was whispering. Kee always on some bullshit."

Fletcher says, "No-contest clause, Key? It's not like she got athletes as clients."

Keenan leans back in his chair, his fingers interlocked. "Niggas… always thinking the rules don't apply to them."

I look at Fletcher, checking to see if he witnessed why Keenan deserves the cursing-out I'm prepared to give him. Fletcher pets the air, signaling me to let it go, that it's not worth it. I listen. And for some odd reason, this gets me all giddy inside; I smile and swat a hand at Fletcher like, look-it my future husband… leading and stuff.

CHAPTER 10
LOVE FALLING OFF THE BONE

I could never have imagined being someone's secret. I never imagined there being millions at stake. I'm Fletcher's secret, but he's also my secret, so I guess that makes it even.

I do find it rather sweet thought, stealing kisses in the elevator and our private affections carried out in the open, like the office delivery of a rose bouquet. Fletcher teases me about the flowers, as if they're not from him. Fletcher was never romantic; he says I bring it out of him.

He takes a half day, saying he had to do something for his mother, but tell me why, when I get home from work, I find this man at my stove, naked under an apron. He said he was cooking for me as thanks for all the times I'd cooked for him. The meal was some ole plain-ass spaghetti and salad, but still…

He bathes me. I'm covered to the neck in bubbles, literally bathing in his love and having sweet conversation to the sound of trickling water as he sponges me. I kiss him with such desire, thinking surely we'd be making love, but he says no. Fletcher sits on the floor next to the tub, then looks earnestly into my eyes. "I don't want us to be drunk off sex, and one day wake up sober, wondering what the hell we're doing. I wanna be closer to you mentally and emotionally. By the time we *get* married, I want us to *be* married." He says he wants to be fully open with each other. He's not open about his nightmares, but I don't point it out for fear of ruining the moment.

He put this whole afternoon together and I can't get over it. I just look at him, like he's an enigma. He's too beautiful of a man, and too capable a lover to be this giving. I take his hand and kiss his knuckles. "You are too good to be true."

"No, *you* are… You saved my life."

In my mind, a question arises. Is this a trauma bond? I answer, but we've always had feelings for each other. Meek's death was pivotal, and maybe it makes him hold me tighter and gaze at me longer. And maybe I'm overthinking it. I decide right then and there: I'm just gone shut up and love this man.

Our love is falling off of the bone. Our love has me loving life all the more. Fletcher says that I bring the romance out of him, but he's certainly bringing something out of me. With him, I feel like how wearing the color pink makes me feel: dainty and demure.

There's a definite glow about me. Nothing says it better than me getting an authentic reaction out of my neighbor who has the face of a stone Moai statue and never greets me with more than a grunt. We leave our houses and trot down the steps at the same time. My natural inclination to match a person's energy has gone out the window. I wave and say hello with such life that my neighbor's head turns to the sound of grinding rock and a smile cracks across his stone face.

There's a girl at Dunkin' who is always so transactional, but it always seems as if there's more she'd say to me if not for the watchful eye of an oppressive shift manager. Before I even fix my mouth to order my breakfast wrap and O.J. I'm reading her name badge for the first time. "Jherica," I say. "You're really pretty, you know that?"

She acts like she's in the presence of a celebrity, her eyes widening to circles, her every sentence ending with, uh. "No, *you're* pretty-uh. I follow you on Instagram-uh." I see her glancing in fear of her manager.

"You follow me, but are you following the tutorial?"

Her hands jitter. "You think I can model?"

"Easily," I say. "Just follow the instructions then contact me directly." I slide my card forward under a white-tipped fingernail.

"Thank you-uh," she says.

I leave Dunkin' with this feeling… a feeling that I'm usually quick to put away; this feeling that affirms my calling to empower women. Sports agency was never my choice; it's only more lucrative.

My future husband vows to relieve me of Legacy Sports, so I can pursue my passion. His promise lets me face my calling, like turning my face up to the sun on this fine morning.

In a packed elevator, I'm the only one smiling, like the prize in a cereal box. I bring in canvas paintings and plugin air fresheners to liven the office.

Keenan had taken the day off, so I'm walking around with my shoes off, and sitting in Fletcher's lap. I catch him when he's concentrating hard on work and start getting on his nerves, playing in his hair to distract him, then pretending to be mad when he denies my kiss.

Working together is the only thing that makes this secret relationship tolerable. We spend a lot of time together; however, the time is spent pretending that we're not together. It's the lying that bothers me.

We lie to Keenan. We lie to anyone who could potentially get information back to Keenan. We lie to our families despite their growing suspicions; we lie to mutual friends even outside of Bubby, who's in Philadelphia raising a family and playing for the Eagles, but the one thing that pains me the most is that we can't hold hands in public. Nearly every kiss is behind closed doors, and when in public, it's a dare preceded by a quick scan of the area to ensure that it's safe. That April wedding feels so far away, and my frustration grows every day.

At least I don't have it as bad as Riley. A porn chick posted her ultrasound saying Gideon is the father. I'm hammering a painting on the wall when I ask Fletcher. "Did you check on Riley?"

Fletcher looks up from his work, his snap reaction seems as if he considered lying. "She won't pick up."

"I'm surprised you called her after how she did you. You were in a fatal accident and she forgot you existed as soon as that same knucklehead put her on a flight."

Fletcher's fingertips wiggle at his throat. "I don't return energy. I'm gone be me regardless."

"That approach can leave you looking stupid – showing all this concern for a chick who told me not to date you because you were broke, and that it would be struggle love."

Fletcher smirks and says, "But look whose love is struggling though?"

Later that night, lying awake, I have an epiphany. Fletcher's behind me sleeping so peacefully, and it irritates me that doesn't wake up and ask me what I'm thinking.

Don't wake him, I think. He's tired. He had stayed so late at the office, that dinner was in Tupperware by the time he returned home. Fletcher even brought work home on his laptop. I had unboxed a few outfits sent from a supplier and then modeled them in the extra bedroom that I use as a green screen studio, and Fletcher was still working, his face aglow from his laptop while I photoshopped my backgrounds and sent the images to the clothing company's marketing team for approval.

I was in bed by the time I heard Fletcher's shower running. I was half asleep by the time he got in bed with me.

Considering how much of *our* time he'd given to work, I conclude that he owes me. I shake him. "Fletcher?" My idea can't wait until morning. It's a plan that can soothe our frustration from having to hide our relationship. I shake him again. "Fletcher. Are you awake?"

He so easily rolls me over and throws his heavy arm across me, locking me into a spoon.

The new body position dictates a change in strategy. I begin arching back into him, but pretending as if he's the culprit. "Not tonight ok, Fletcher," I say, as I grind him stiff. "Stop it okay, I'm not in the mood," I say. His heavy breathing stops. I stop. I peek back over my shoulder to find a pair of night eyes looking at me like

I'm crazy. I begin chuckling in a mix of humor and nervous guilt. I look back again and see him still looking at me like I'm a clown, and I burst out in laughter, slapping the bed in mirth.

"Gone with all that noise, Tahj, damn."

I try to hold my laughter and end up snorting – then laugh out loud at my snort.

Fletcher is truly pissed. "Can't you see I'm asleep," he says and tries to turn away.

I crawl on top of him. "Fuck your sleep," I joke. "You don't want me? Huh, Fletcher," I say while grinding on top of him.

He warns, "Keep it up. I'm gone fuck the shit outchya."

I roll my hips, asking, "Are you awake now?"

Fletcher joins his hands behind his head. "Are you sure this is what you want?"

"What I *want*, is a vacation. For us."

"Hold on." He grabs my waist to stop my movement, then we lay on our sides facing each other. "What you mean, vacation? You see how busy I am, right? I'm working as hard as I can, *for us*."

"But you can't take the time to go on a vacation *for us*?"

"How much time?"

"The reason why I wanna go on vacation because I'm tired of feeling like a side-chick."

"I already know babe, but how many days are we talking?"

"Three days. Minimum. I guess."

"So we're supposed to be out of the office for days, at the same damn time? How's that gonna look to Kee?"

"At this point, I don't care how it looks. I'll tell him I'm going on vacation by myself, and you tell him that you have to fly out to handle business with your houses."

He asks, "Where do you suppose we go on vacation?"

"Somewhere."

Fletcher sucks his teeth. "You don't even know. We'll talk about it in the morning."

I turn on my other side, away from him. "You'll be lucky if I talk to you at all in the morning," I say, but with a smile he can't see.

We lay in silence for a while, until Fletcher curses the night. "Shit! Now I'm up."

I fake snore.

"You ain't sleep," he says as he rolls over. I roll again, stopping with my face down on the pillow, still pretending to sleep. I sense him lying there, studying me. Then I feel him moving around, the covers shifting. My eyes are closed. I can't see, but he's not getting up to go to the bathroom or kitchen; he's up to something.

I feel the covers lift away, gently – not enough to wake me if I were really asleep, so I keep pretending. I put on a fake twitch and readjust, but still lying face down in a T-shirt and no panties.

He hovers over me. I feel his heat. Then I feel him working himself inside of me. I pretend to rouse. "Wait, what," I say dreamily.

Suddenly, all at once I feel him sink into me so deep, I cough. He says, "I told you what was gone happen right?"

He's a man of his word.

He sends me to work the next day walking gingerly, stretching, and yawning all afternoon like a housecat.

As I'm in the copying room yawning and stretching, Fletcher peeks in, chuckling. "*Told* you," he says.

I can't even smart back. "Can you pick up dinner tonight? I'm not about to cook; I'm going to bed early."

"I'll bring you dinner," he agrees. "But I'm spending the night at the folks, though." He reaches around me, then hands me a few sheets of paper from the printer tray. "Look this over," he says.

It's tentative bookings for flights and hotel. I would've squeezed him and sucked his mouth if Keenan were not right around the corner. I whisper, "Look at you, coming through for me, baby. Four days? Punta Cana?"

"It's easy on the budget. Rates are reduced during hurricane season." He points to the picture. "But look how beautiful that is."

I look up at him with stars in my eyes and say, "Book it."

CHAPTER 11
THREE-HOLE PUNCHER

"So, not only is Fletcher the latecomer to the company, but the only value he's added so far is a landline phone, yet *he's* the one cracking the whip? The man who lives with his parents?"

"Don't do him like that, Jay." I cut my eye as I reach the measuring tape around him. "Fletcher's got three homes."

We're at Balani Custom Suits, choosing an outfit for Jay's upcoming speaking engagement. "But you *do* get what I'm saying though, right? He needs to be told to stay in his lane a bit. And if you don't wanna have that talk with him, maybe Kevin will."

"It's *Keenan*, for the fiftieth time. Now, you're just doing it on purpose. And I see, you still haven't went to the barber I recommended."

He starts telling me how he has a ten-year relationship with his current barber. "It's a loyalty thing for me," he explains. All the while, he's looking past me, at Monae, who I'd brought along to help. More specifically, he's eyeing Monae's fake butt, which is too overstuffed to jiggle, so it wiggles when she walks.

I tighten the tape around Jay's beltline. "Looks like you *did* gain a little in the waist. No biggie though." I turn and hand the shopping list to Monae and tell her, "Here's the items and the sizes. On this one, if you can't find Olive, go with smoke grey."

Monae walks away with the list, curling a ribbon of hair on a finger. "Olive," Jay says, as if tasting a bitter one. "See, that's that pretty-boy stuff, I'm talking about."

"That color resonates with veterans. It's subconscious." Jay's distracted by Monae in the distance. I whisper, "You ain't slick."

He's so caught, he can't deny it. "Why is she even here?"

"As a witness. Because my man is jealous. Plus I'm training Monae, so she can branch out in her fashion career, which isn't making her much money – which is why I hired her as our secretary."

"I'm just gonna say that jealousy, in a man, is dangerous. If he's making you conduct business with a witness, that's a red flag."

My eyes roll. "He doesn't like the fact that his girlfriend is in the business of taking the clothes off of hotshot lawyers – especially one that used to take me out on dates."

Jay clears his throat. "I'm starting to think that your new boyfriend and Fletcher are the same person."

"*I'm* starting to think *you're* attracted to trans women."

The fright in Jay's eyes tells me he had no idea that Monae was trans, but also that Monae's standing right behind me!

I turn. Monae curls her finger. "Can I talk to you for a minute, Boss Lady?" I follow her to the other side of the store between racks. She yells in whispers, "Don't ever out me again, here me? Not in the streets. And not on the job."

I feel attacked. "Where's this coming from? You're open about it. I've seen you tell guys–"

"–Broke guys!" She points in the direction of Jay. "That's my money you're messing with."

"My bad, *dang*," I vent. "Didn't think it was a big deal."

"Wait…" Monae looks as if she remembers leaving the oven on at home. "Did you out me to your partners?"

"I plan to! You're Keenan's type. What if he tries to get with you?"

"What's his type. The stripper type," Monae says, daring me to confirm.

Her tats and implants makes it hell to find her modeling gigs, which is why I hired her as our secretary. "I'm telling them. I don't care what you say."

"And you'll be the third job I sue for discrimination!" Monae abouts face and then marches away.

I return to Jay, who now looks worried as he stares at an alert on his phone. "Somebody just went in my house. Can we take a rain check? We still got a few days before the event."

I reply, "No, *you* got a few days. I'm gonna be in the Punta Cana, remember?"

Jay starts buttoning his cufflinks. "Come with me, then."

I freeze up, wondering how I'd explain to an already jealous Fletcher, me ending up at Jay's house. "Give me your bank card," I say, with my hand out, tickling for it.

He frowns, as if I'd asked for his left kidney, but he hands the card over anyway. I give Monae Jay's card along with the keys to my car. "Get everything on the list and then meet us at Jay's house. I'll text you the directions."

I hurry out of the store with Jay. Even in his haste, he's a gentleman, rushing to open the door for me. By the time he scrambles back to the driver's side and flops in the seat, he's on a call with his assistant. "Sarah? Your code was entered in the alarm system. You're at my house? ... You *know* not to go in my house unless I'm with you or I send you... Just stay put until I get there."

I'd never seen him upset until now. I ask, "Now that you know it's only your personal assistant, how is it still a problem?"

"It just makes me uneasy."

"You gave an alarm code to someone you don't trust?"

Jay pounds the horn and then speeds around a car trying to parallel park.

I'm confused by his distress, yet I try to lighten the mood. "You act like there's a body under your floorboards or something."

Jay bites down on the first thing he wanted to say, then he sighs and gives a gentler response. "I love your sense of humor, Tahj, but not now, ok?"

We're quiet for the rest of the drive, even when I see him turn left onto Northside Parkway, and into Sandy Springs where there are mansions starting in the tens of millions. Internally I'm going *what the heck* but outwardly, I'm as quiet as a mouse. His home would put some resorts to shame. A wrought iron fence slides open in front of a long tile driveway. Jay's Audi sedan has no business parking where a Rolls Royce should.

I expect to wait in the car, but Jay gets out, hurries over and opens my door. I follow him, wondering if this is all a ploy to show off his wealth. The sedan looks like an electric Barbie Car, dwarfed by a mansion as tall as the slim columnar trees plotted along the estate. Jay goes in first and leaves the door open for me.

I'm dumbfounded by the interior, especially by this abstract centerpiece of crystal rods in the shape of a flying carpet or giant stingray. The staircase is ascending platforms suspended apparently by nothing, or perhaps by some incantation spell. The right wall is decorated with a façade that has smokey streams running across it, like the surface of a gas planet like Jupiter or Saturn. I hear Jay and Sarah talking quietly.

I hear her say. "Don't ask me what I was thinking. I don't know." Her glance finds me the instant I come into view. I'd seen her once before. Her hair was in braids then, but now it's combed out and parted down the middle, like a storm cloud tamed around her small brown face and thick lips, ablaze in crimson. She wears a short-sleeve mermaid dress and open-toed pumps. I spot the pedicure and manicure. Sarah looks as if she stopped by on her way to a soiree, but no; she glowed up for Jay. Sarah blushes at her own folly and I hear her say, "I'm so embarrassed. You don't even notice." Sarah backs away.

Jay picks her hand out of her folded arms and comes closer a step. His demeanor, and his voice, softens. "Of course I notice, Sarah. You look good to me."

My lips makes a silent oooh, and I start backing away. Monae's text comes in, so I trot outside to meet her. By the time I return to the mansion to leave the clothing and the platinum card on the nearest table, Jay and Sarah are sitting and talking quietly. I want so badly to be nosey, but respectfully, I hurry out of there with my head turned away, refusing to look.

It's Monae's first day and Keenan's already simping. He gives me the I-9s and W-2s to get her processed, then he does a short orientation on company policies, all the while, eyeing Monae's cleavage.

Next she's paired with me at my desk for her training. I have but one day before vacation to train Monae on how to operate the switchboard landline and the scheduling software, but Keenan keeps happening by my desk with his obvious reaches. "What's that fragrance, if you don't mind my asking?"

Monae – always quick to put men on the defensive, replies, "Now, why would I tell you my fragrance? Are you gonna buy some for yourself?"

Keenan tenses. "Ay, I ain't with that gay shit."

The quickness with which my head turns to Monae…

The slur doesn't seem to bother her. She smiles. "I was about to say… So, are you asking me for my fragrance so you can buy it for some other chick?"

When Keenan's enamored with a woman, he turns bashful and country-sounding. "Aw girl. I was just askin'. No real meanin' to it."

Monique's eyes thin, as she says, "I wouldn't want you getting that fragrance for Missus Keenan and be thinking about me when you're with her."

I glance over at Fletcher. He's just tuning in and wondering how we got here. I shrug stupid. Our gaze hardens when we hear Keenan stutter; the man hadn't stuttered in years, now sounding like a helicopter.

"W-w-w-well you see… I don't d-d-don't–"

Monae, in amazement, points her long, curved fingernail. "Oooh, you stutter *too?* I used to stutter so bad that my eyes would roll up."

Keenan's mouth falls open. "Really?"

I see red cartoon hearts pulsating in their eyes. Keenan has no idea what he's getting himself into, but if I tell him about Monae it would get us sued, so I try another strategy. "I hate to break this up.

But Monae, you have the right to know that *this* is the man who tried to garnish your modeling royalties."

Monae looks him up and down. "Garnish my whet? Aw *hell* naw. You got me messed up."

Keenan pouts, "Tahj… how you gone say that?"

Monae dismisses Keenan, swiveling her chair back around to our training session her head erect, her blue contacts focused solely on work, "Did you hear something, Tahj? This office shole is quiet."

Keenan wanders on, shoulders slumped. "You a hater, Tahj." As quick as Keenan resumes work, he stops. He seems to tip an imaginary hat when he says, "By the way, there *is* no Mrs. Keenan. I reckon I'll find her soon enough if the good Lawd see fit."

Monae twists her lips. "*Mmm*," she says, as if her interest is piqued. Keenan is by no accounts ugly, but he's lost his edges to the weight gain since college football and now has a rounder face and the neck rolls of an adult baby. Perhaps it's the money that piques Monae's interest.

As the morning ages, however, it seems as if Monae has her eyes on a loftier prize. She sashays over to Fletcher's desk, twirling her hair, like she usually does when she's flirting. "Do you mind if I borrow your three-hole puncher." My blood pressure spikes for her emphasis on *three-hole* – which is one more hole than I'm willing to give, and one more than Monae has to give.

I study my future husband like a sniper. Nonchalantly, he hands her the hole puncher with a *here ya go*, but as she goes away switching in her leather pants, Fletcher and Keenan look at each other and grin. I'm so mad I wanna hit him in the side of the head with my paperweight.

I honestly didn't think that either man would find Monae attractive. She can't even take side-angle pictures in her photoshoots because of her long torso and fake butt. Keenan and Fletcher had always been famous for trolling mismatching thighs; maybe they only made fun of it when I was around.

When lunchtime rolls around, Keenan's thirsty ass says, "Where're we all going for lunch?"

I say, "I don't know where you and Fletcher are going, but Monae and me are gonna take off on our own."

"Are we," Monae asks, with a wrinkled brow.

"Yes," I say as I pick up my purse.

On the walk down the hall towards the elevator, I'm dead silent as Monae muses about Fletcher. "Oh my God, that Fletcher is *too* fine. I don't see how you work with him. He got a woman?"

"Yes." My only words.

Monae, with a sassy look-away, says, "Girl he so fine, I don't even care."

"Trust me, you're not his type."

"That's what they *all* say, until they get this top."

I bite down so hard, I'm liable to crunch my teeth like ice. As soon as we board the elevator, I go in on Monae. "You got in my face the other day, now I'm getting in yours. Lemme tell you something Mo! You can kee-kee all you want, in Keenan's face, but don't bring that shit around Fletcher, you hear me?" The other lady in the elevator slides to the corner, afraid to catch a stray.

Monae sings, "Ooooh, yall fuckiiiin."

"No we're not," I say.

Monae's eyes thin. "So why is he not fair game?"

"You just fuck around and find out." I then straighten my jacket with a refreshing deep breath and say, "Now, where do you wanna go for lunch? It's on me."

CHAPTER 12
PUNTA CANA

Punta Cana has me looking different, perhaps for its proximity to the equator. The sky's blue is saturated. The noon sun is not yellow; it's hot white, and when I close my eyes and look at the sun, the pink from the back of my eyelid is neon. I study my arms and the back of my hands. I study myself in my clamshell mirror while checking my makeup for pictures. My melanin has never been popping like this.

It's like God's been tampering with the exposure slider. I study the faces of the Afro-Dominican drivers lined outside of the airport waiting to shuttle tourists to their villas and I see it in them too. My makeup is suddenly all wrong.

I'm solo in all my social media posts. Ever since the flight, I ensured that Fletcher isn't reflected in the passenger window for a paid promotion selfie of me contemplating the clouds, my wet lips soaked in sunlight, courtesy of a lip gloss from an upstart beauty company that has secured a partnership with Fantasia Barrino. I'm solo in the pictures at the Punta Cana International Airport, leaning against a pillar, wearing KatEye reflector shades, my Aerbud chord tucked into a lime green sports top by Joja, and the sneaker raised against the pillar clearly displays the logo of the black owned sneaker company, SIA Collective. Fletcher aims the camera and snaps photos at four different angles to feature each of the four brands.

During the shuttle ride to the villa I could tell Fletcher's bothered. I had begged him to leave his laptop, but here I am, using our time for work.

The moment I finish editing the airport shots, I jam my phone in my bag and leap on Fletcher in the backseat of our taxi, dotting him with kisses.

He pulls away from my kiss, but holds my face there, and says, "Let's get tore up tonight and have drunk sex."

My rolling eyes stop at the corners. "Maybe I can't."

The epiphany catches Fletcher with his mouth open. "Oh yeah, I forgot."

"I packed a pregnancy test, though. I figured it best we find out while on vacation." He strokes the side of my face and gazes in my eyes.

As soon as we enter our oceanfront villa and set the bags down, I dig for the at-home pregnancy test and take it to the bathroom. Fletcher sits on the edge of the bed, cracking his knuckles while he waits.

After a while, I come out heartbroken, the test down by my side, my head shaking no. Fletcher kisses my forehead, then we cuddle on the bed, not a word spoken. The distant calls of seagulls and the frothy unrolling of the ocean into the shore, lulls us to sleep.

After a nap, we go out and walk in white sand along the sapphire ocean, Fletcher, barebacked; me in a bathing suit with a sarong wrap blowing in the same wind that rustles the tops of coconut trees. It's our first time out in public with the freedom to hold hands and stop for long kisses.

His big gorgeous self looks at me and says, "I wanna take you out dancing."

"Tonight? We got a dune buggy excursion early tomorrow." Fletcher seems distracted, so I say, "Do you hear me?"

He says, "Did you see how buddy was looking at you?"

"No."

"I was like damn dude."

"Are you sure he was looking at me?"

Fletcher then says, "You probably never notice when Jay looks at you like that."

"He doesn't look at me like *you* look at Monae."

Fletcher frowns. "Girl please. If I'm looking at Monae, I'm laughing inside. She looks funny to me."

"She doesn't look funny to Keenan, nor Jay, but you're the exception?"

"Jay was looking?"

"Not anymore. He and his assistant are kinda dating now. She had it bad for him all along, apparently."

"He may have settled for his assistant but you're the one he wants."

I stop with my toes deep in sand, my arms out. "Is this what you wanna do? You wanna argue on our first romantic getaway?"

His brow lifts, "Who arguing? I'm just talking."

I say, "Your jealousy offends me. It tells me you don't think I'm solid. I don't have a past. You do. But you don't see *me* acting all jealous."

Fletcher slumps in dismay. "Wow… the hypocrisy."

My eyes spread so wide it hurt. "Hyp-*oc*-risy?"

"You question me about Monae, but I can't question you about Jay?"

Internally I'm like, *Got me there…* but before admitting I'm wrong, I'd rather march away, stomping the sand as if I'm sicka *his* shit.

Fletcher laughs. "Look atchya: actin' all mad because you know I'm right." He catches me from behind, scoops me up in his arms like a damsel and spins me around. Playfully, I scream, "Get off of me! You're crazy!"

I laugh so hard, my legs kick out straight and I see my sandy toes and a turning backdrop of a tropical paradise. When Fletcher sets me down, I'm literally dizzy with joy as I kiss my future husband. Even now, whenever I think back to this moment in time, I sit with it. I don't stain this moment by thinking of all the shit that happens afterward. I just let the memory fade down like the ending of a song, where I'm just grateful for the vibe.

Later that night, our plan is still to get smashed and have sex, so we're at a club, the atmosphere filled with Salsa music and bar chatter. I'm tipsy and measuring my sips to keep the buzz at its current level, where I'm loose and the music moves through me – got me dancing in my barstool. Also when I'm tipsy, I get really touchy; I can't laugh without leaning on Fletcher nor get his attention without petting his leg.

I know Fletcher's feeling it too because he gets in his feelings when he's drunk. He gazes at me and tells me, "You know I love you, right? But…"

I cut my eyes, because every time 'I love you' precedes a but, we argue. "Can we not do this tonight?" I look straight down in my glass and draw a long sip of green margarita through a red straw. When I look up, Fletcher's still waiting for his turn to speak. I sigh, "You're about to fuck up our whole night bro, but go ahead if you must."

He squints and says, "You're always brutally honest when you're drunk. So, this is the perfect opportunity for me." Fletcher folds his arms. "For these last couple years while I was in the league… we never really talked about other people." Fletcher licks his lips and asks, "Did you have sex with anybody?"

I pout, "Why are you doing this?"

Fletcher takes this as a yes. "With who? Was it just one time or was it a thing? How long after I left did you start seeing him?"

"Whoa, there," I say. "I didn't even answer your question."

He sips and smiles, patience borne of stubbornness.

"Just don't act crazy when I give you what you asked for." My fingers rap the bar top. "The guy–"

"–*Thee* guy? Just one?"

"The guy's office was in the same building as our agency. He flirted for six months before I finally agreed to a date. The more I got to know him, the more he irritated my soul."

"How so?"

"I was never pressed for a relationship, and that's frustrating to a guy who thinks *he's* the prize."

Fletcher frowns. "How could he possibly stand next to you and think he's the prize?"

"Money." P.S. I don't quite know why I'm lying here – maybe because the truth is embarrassing, but that guy was actually a brokie and a minute man.

Fletcher smiles, but his eyes do not smile with the rest of his face; this tells me he's angry. He asks, "Y'all still keep in touch?"

I sigh, "Okay this is the last question I'm gonna answer. No, we don't keep in touch. It didn't end well. He told me the pussy was mid, and that I looked like a pretty bitch in Blackface."

Fletcher smiles and points, "I know you're drunk when you say words like pussy."

I counter, "I'm not drunk; I'm feeling good."

"You like guys with money, don't you?"

"I had a million dollars in income that year, and you want me to keep on dating the Donovans of the world?"

Flecther rotates away in his stool but looks over at me. "I'm gonna have you living in a mansion. Promise. You won't have to work at all."

"It's not about that Fletcher," I say, and then watch my words bounce off of him with no effect. "I wanna work. You know I wanna empower women through fashion."

"You say that now. But once the money starts coming in, you're gonna wanna be a woman of leisure."

"Woman of leisure," I parrot. "Wait, I only know of one person who really says that."

"I've always wanted to take care of you, Tahj."

"Always? At one time it was Gigi, remember?"

"Fuck Gigi." His brow turns mad as an eagle's.

I raise my hand. "My turn," I say. "Since we're discussing exes, let me ask you this: what was it about Gigi that had you so gone like that?"

"How many times I done told you?"

"Told me what? You always mumble on to the next subject." I take Fletcher's hands to let him know I'm being serious and vulnerable when I say, "I'm not asking because I'm jealous. I'm asking because I wanna know what you like," I smile. "Was it the fitness lifestyle? At the gym, flexing in the mirror together; or some days opening the fridge and finding a surprise protein shake with a note attached?" Apparently, I'm the only one who finds the joke funny. I chuckle while Fletcher just stares at me like I play too much.

I get off of my stool and stand between his knees where we're the same height, my eyes searching the soul of this beautifully complicated man, under neon lights, with a backdrop of the dance floor, people smiling and jerking to a Merengue tune; none of it distracts me. I'm giving soap opera levels of soliloquy to a man with a soap opera name. "Fletcher, you know I love you. And I want nothing more in this world than to be your wife. What you get with a Mrs. Tahj Lewis, is a woman who is obsessed with making sure that Mr. Lewis isn't wanting for an-ē-thing." I kiss his lips, then continue. "Just like, for you, how it fills you up inside to take care of me. It fills me up inside to take care of you, in the ways that a woman takes care of a man. Please don't deny me that."

Fletcher lowers his head and gives in. "Alright," he says. "But I promise you, it's not the answer you're looking for."

"To know the depths of you, is what I'm looking for."

Fletcher stares hard, questioning it, even up to the moment he clears his throat. "It was not so much about Gigi. This goes all the way back to rec football. She was the coach's daughter, daddy's girl, so she was always around, handing out Gatorade, and cheering from the sidelines. All the boys on the team had a crush on her."

"All?"

"All. She looked like a young Rhianna–"

"–So, yall's crush on her was really a crush on Rhianna?"

He shrugs. "I think it was more that she was unattainable," Fletcher smiles. "She was older than us, she had a woman's body, and me and the guys were all going through puberty, horny as fuck. At football practice, the only girl in sight was her. I can't tell you how many dudes I laid out in practice just to impress Gigi."

My hand covers my mouth, "Oh my God, are you hearing yourself?" I remember Fletcher's mother revealing what he said to the therapist, that he feels most alive when on the football field hurting a man or having sex with a woman. The juxtaposition of sex and football must've begun at practice with pubescent boys hurting each other to impress a young lady who was, in their eyes, a sex symbol. I wonder how many of Fletcher's teammates turned out like him.

I get a hit of déjà vu: something about pubescent boys, then I remember where it came from: Donovan reciting one of his poems, spewing all sorts of trigger-porn, calling the American Dream a colonizers lie, saying how our identities were ripped from our minds, so we identify with those who colonized, and that's why beauty is blue-eyed. He'd also went on to say something about carnal desire being a high yellow nymph roaming the wet dreams of pubescent boys. The coincidence of Fletcher independently describing a team of pubescent boys' collective infatuation with a high-yellow girl who they sexualize for her resemblance to Rihanna, is wild to me. Then I wonder: who appoints sex symbols and why are they not appointing ones who look like me? Whose allure could I draw from? What I draw is a blank. There're a lot more famous *men* my complexion, than women, come to think of it…

"Are you okay, babe?"

"What?" I was so far in my head, I forgot I was at a bar in Punta Cana. I would've explained to Fletcher what I was thinking, but there's no version of my thoughts that doesn't come off as weird. I *am* being weird, I gather, because normally I don't even *think* words like juxtaposition, so lemme shut up. "I was just thinking about something…"

"Obviously… What, though?"

"Well… You just explained your attraction to her, but that doesn't explain why you kept holding on, after you learned that Gigi was a bad girlfriend."

"The chemistry."

I lean forward with intrigue. "Chemistry, as in?"

"The sex, ok. She a *fool* in that reverse cowgirl," he says, and immediately regrets it. "Girl, I'm just messing with you," he says, while grinning like a fox.

"No, you're not." I tilt and ask, "Gina's your best?" I'm smiling but crying inside. I got the truth and it hurts.

"You're my best," he says. I fold my arms, not buying it one bit. Fletcher handles my waist. "Real talk. You don't have to be an acrobat, Tahj. You take me places I ain't never been."

I withdraw from him and face front in my stool, and say, "Let's just change the subject because you're starting to piss me off."

"Babe… I can't believe you' acting like this." He stares in confusion, but he's staring at the side of my face because I refuse to look at him. He shrugs and says, "Fuck it, then. We'll change the subject."

It's my idea, but I'm too pissed to talk about anything else.

"Let me trip you out, though," Fletcher offers. "Kee and Monae fuckin'."

With lazy eyes, I say, "Trust me, they're not."

"How can you be so sure?"

"Because Monae thinks Kee is a square."

Fletcher smirks and says, "So, why would Keenan take the time out of his day to tell me that, while executives can't be in a relationship, an executive and an employee *can* have a relationship. Who do you think he was talking about? We only got one employee."

"Monae isn't his type, trust me."

Fletcher stiffens. "Wasn't she a stripper? Kee love skrippaz, now that he can afford 'em. They stay in his pockets, though."

I add, "Monae's no different. He's gonna have to dig deep in them pockets before he can hit that." I hear myself, and then ask myself, "Wait, what am I saying?"

"Huh?" Fletcher squints at me, as if confused but he pushes past it to get off what he wants to say. "Normally I would try to talk Kee out of it, but nah. He wanna put money over our friendship, so fuck him. I'll let him fall on his own sword."

I nearly spill my drink, doubling over laughing. "Fall on *her* sword!"

Fletcher laughs but still doesn't get it. He adds, "Remember that chick Champaigne down at Magic City? Kee coughed up all that bread and still ain't get no ass."

Yet another unwitting assist from Fletcher. I slap the bar top in mirth, as I manage to say, "Ass is about *all* he can get from Monae."

Fletcher leans in, studying the layers of my laughter. "What're you saying?" His smile shrinks, as he solves the riddle. "Tahj! O'girl is a fuckin' man?!"

I'm shaking my head and saying, "No. No."

"She a dude?"

"She's a woman," I insist.

He raises one eyebrow. "But was she *born* a woman?"

"No one is born a woman," I say.

"Now you playing games. Was she born *female?*"

I say, "I'm not about to sit here and speculate, Fletcher. We came here to dance." I hop off of my barstool and take Fletcher's hand.

He uses my grip to pull me back and hold me captive. "You knew this about Monae? How could you keep it from Keenan?"

"I have to. *We* have to. We out her, and she'll sue us like she's done two previous jobs. Besides, why should we look out for Keenan while he tries to cut us out of millions? Kee wants to be so hung up on the rules, *we're* gonna stick to the rules too and protect Monae's identity."

"*Damn,*" Fletcher says. "Coming to my desk, talking about some damn three-hole-puncher."

My head whips to Fletcher. "That's the first thing out of your mouth, after finding out?" My head turns back slowly, as I stare off in the distance. "You were really holding onto that, huh?"

"Girl don't play with me." Fletcher downs his shot, then shakes his head. "The irony, though… as much as Keenan like to call everything gay."

I pull Fletcher's hand and we angle through the bodies until we're near the center of the dance floor. The rhythm of the guitar and maracas is so feisty, that our two-step can't keep pace so we try the Merengue. We press palms, as if pushing a wall with short, choppy steps, the hips and torso twisting in opposite directions. I smile so wide I feel the air on my teeth, as I tell Fletcher, "Look at your big, built self tryna show out."

We just about get it down pat when the song changes. Suddenly, it's the Salsa. Again we mimic. Our Salsa is mild and bland, but we're having the time of our lives, laughing at our missteps under swirling disco lights. The salsa's quick back-and-forth steps make Fletcher look like he's being jerked around. He laughs at me too. I can't see myself but I'm almost certain that, with my layered tassel party dress and long legs, I'm dancing with the grace of an emu.

A gentleman about my height with an open shirt and hairy chest, tries to cut in. He holds his hand out for me and tells Fletcher, "I show you, my 'priend."

Fletcher doesn't budge. My eyes flare, "Be nice."

The gentleman points at a lady partner on standby for Fletcher. Keeping it one hundred, the bitch is *bad*. She has a ponytail down her back, legs that never skipped their day at the gym, and her waist – what waist? Now it's me who won't budge.

Fletcher mocks. "Be nice."

So we dance adjacent with our Dominican partners, hips rocking like speed-walkers. Fletcher's hands drop from her shoulders to her waist. I look over but look away before Fletcher catches me. My partner notices the rivalry, so he tries to help me win.

I didn't think I knew how to spin properly, especially not in high heels, but my partner raises my hand over my head, and with a firm hand on my waist, guides me through the turn and we finish in-step – speedwalking forward and back, two steps a piece. Fletcher looks over at me. I could tell he's pissed. His partner spins into him, that ponytail whipping Fletcher in the face. I rear back laughing, but then I notice how she apologizes, her face angled up at him, the focus in her eyes, a hand on Fletcher's chest. Now *I'm* pissed.

My dance partner spins me again, but he keeps me turning. The tassels on my dress spin so fast they look like planetary rings. I'm utterly amazed; Fletcher's utterly pissed. He thinks I'm being swept off my feet. My partner pulls me in and dips me. I lay back on the strength of his arm, one leg flies up so free I'm sure I flashed panties.

Fletcher breaks character and comes over with a knifed hand against the man's shoulder. "A'ight, bruh. We done."

The man tries to explain. Fletcher walks into him, bumping the man with his chest. This man who is so graceful on his feet, falls back on his rump like a toddler failing at his first steps.

"*Fletcher*," I scold, as I attempt to help the man up. People crowd us, looking to help, but Fletcher thinks they're descending upon him. "And *what*," he yells. "I'll beat the shit outta all yall!"

"No," I say to them with wide eyes and a show of ten fingers. "He doesn't mean that!" I turn to Fletcher and begin pushing him in his chest, urging him to go, but he acts as if he really wants to take on the three guys in front of him, oblivious of the three more men behind him. I scream, "Fletcher look!"

He looks back at the sight of three more men and says, "Aw damn."

We hurry out of the club. Thankfully no one follows us.

Our buzz is gone by our return to the villa. The hotel's minimart is still open so we buy rum and soda to carry upstairs.

We enter the suite, arguing. "You're supposed to protect me. Not put me in danger."

"I *was* protecting you. I was protecting *your honor*," he annunciates.

"That's the stamp you wanna put on this? You're outta control. How about that!"

After a few shots, we're no longer arguing. Somehow we're laughing – well, Fletcher's laughing. "Baby, you was scared-er than a mug." He tries to hug me. I wiggle away, but he reels me in again. "Naw for real, babe. I'm sorry I put you through that."

"You think *I* was scared. What about you, when you saw those guys coming up from behind – talking 'bout some: 'Aw damn.'" I overdo the impersonation with a dim-witted look.

Fletcher laughs so hard he falls back on the bed with me in his arms. I let out a little scream as we tumble. Fletcher adds, "You call *me* jealous – as if my dance partner didn't have you shook."

I'm smiling by now. "I gotta hand it to her. She was bad."

"I mean, bad as fuck."

I cease all laughter and cut my eyes. "And you was all up on her, dancing like a big ole transformer robot. I wanted to wind that ponytail around my hand and yank the meat out her head."

Fletcher laughs, but he's all too ready to use my comment as evidence against me. "See? You felt the same way *I* felt. I just acted on it."

"No, Fletcher we are not the same."

"How do you think I felt when I saw you dancing like you're living your best life, or like dis nigga done stole your heart or somethin–"

"–Really," I browbeat. "Is that what you saw?"

"I'll show you what I saw." Fletcher gets up for a demonstration; that's how I know he's really drunk. He mimics my spin, with a cartoonish smile across his face.

I'm denying it while at the same time dying laughing at the accuracy. "I was not doing all of that!"

"Aw baby, you was doing *way* too much. And when he dipped you? This was you…" He demonstrates by flopping back on the bed with a leg raised. "Then you had the leg out like this – lil foot all pointy and shit."

I grip my stomach. "Not the foot!" We laugh to our hearts' content. Then I roll on top of him, saying, "Admit it. You're a jealous lover."

"That ain't it. I'm jealous *with you*," he says. "I ain't never been in love like this before. When I was out there in them streets, my heart was safe. Near one of them had the power to hurt me. Now I've got everything invested in you, and it scares me: the fact that you're my everything."

My head lay on his broad chest, my ear to his heart. "You're *my* everything…" Hearing myself, I stop short. I'd said it so comfortably. In all my years, I've always been afraid of being anyone's everything, or vice versa. I get up for another drink. Fletcher reaches for me and misses. While pouring a shot, I look him in the eyes to deliver my revelation. "Doesn't that sound toxic?"

"Toxic…" His nose wrinkles as if the word is a fart.

I feel my eyes go alight. "Well, yeah. Come to think of it… My love for you is so… forceful. I'm afraid that we have a trauma bond, you know, with… Meek, and everything…"

Fletcher, who'd recently got up, plops back down on the bed with this abandoned look on his face.

Fearing maybe I'd hit a sore spot, I hurry next to him. "I'm sorry, Fletch. It just came out."

Fletcher looks down and talks to his open hands. "You just said what the therapist said. I didn't wanna tell you this, but she said a relationship with you cannot work; that I might run away from *you* in order to run away from *it*. Or that we could become so enmeshed that it could lead to irrational behavior, insecurity… jealousy… That's the real reason I stepped away from you."

He gets up and paces away. I let him. It seems the physical distance would serve him better than my embrace. He pours another shot and throws it back.

"You know what," I begin, while still unsure how to say what I wanna say. "That answers one nagging question."

"What question," he asks, somewhat timidly.

I respond somewhat timidly, "The way things played out… had me wondering why you were only interested in a relationship once football was taken away."

"I was afraid to love you. That's the only reason. But those two years taught me that I couldn't love nobody else."

"Your fear of loving me… is that why you want a kid so bad… to anchor you in the relationship? Am I not reason enough?" I look away to hide my face. "Your mother told me you said that you feel most alive either hurting people on the field or having sex with a woman, so it makes me wonder… when you make love to me, Fletcher, what are you really pouring into me?"

Fletcher swallows and turns away. I think he's upset, but no. He starts looking through his things. He returns with something cuffed behind his back. "Tahj. I was gonna wait until dinner tomorrow, but I have to show you this now." He gets down on one knee and presents a ring. "It's not much. I'm gone get you a better ring when—"

"—It's perfect." A tear falls faster than I can catch it with a blink.

"All I know, Slim, is that you are the air that I breathe. I pray that you'll never question my love again," he whispers. "Be my wife."

I buckle over Fletcher and hold his head against my belly. "Yes," I say. "Yes, baby."

He stands and places the ring on my finger. We're wobbly from the alcohol.

We lie down facing each other. In the background to Fletcher's pillowed face, curtains blow at the balcony door. I'm hearing the relentless waves. We're so close, our eyes cross to keep each other in focus, and I can't help but think that Fletcher's cockeyed glare beams with the anticipation of the *second* best sex of his life.

My next thought: it's time Gigi meets her match. Writing this helps me realize that this is probably one of the thirstiest moments of my entire life, mounting a man with the intent to become his best.

I blame the alcohol. What else would make me crawl onto him like a leopard, even giving a love bite to his neck.

Being future Mrs. Lewis feels like an alter ego. She's a woman who's not about to be second to no bitch – in no way shape or form.

I shimmy down on him, my eyes closed, my mouth ajar with a long sigh, for the indulgence of being filled with him. I'm roll my hips, slowly. I'm barely getting started but I notice Fletcher moaning as if he's never felt anything this good in his life. He remembers over-sharing about Gigi, and now he's putting on, to try to reassure me that I'm his best. I smile fondly at him and his sweet, considerate lie, but my goal is to make an honest man of him.

I turn around, mounting him in reverse cowgirl. I hadn't done this position with Fletcher before, so it's obvious what I'm doing, but the liquor has robbed me of all my fucks to give but this one. I'm riding at the pace of a slow jam, but slowly picking up the pace, climbing through the levels until I'm romping to the pace of an aggressive trap beat. I look back and see his eyes stretched to the whites like this ride is getting out of control. I tuck my lip and turn up even more. I'm going crazy, pouncing on him, pounding my own insides to the point of pain, pounding until my hips kink and my thighs burn from the reps. I'm watching my own sweat drip from my chin and dot the sheets as I try to hammer my future husband into the mattress. I fully believe it's authentic when Fletcher yells out, "Aw baby! What're you *doing* to me?" I feel him quaking and pulsing inside of me. I get up in the nick of time. His pole is a sprinkler. Fletcher's yelling, bucking, and thrashing with his eyes shut as if he's having a nightmare of being mauled by a bear. I collapse next to him and now his body is stiff as a board, trembling as if he'd been tazed. I kiss his neck. His eyes slam to the corners, at me. "Don't touch me," he says through clenched teeth.

I whisper to his ear. "Nobody… you hear me? Nobody can fuck with me."

Over the next few days, I'm wearing my ring everywhere and taking pictures of my ring hand that I can't showoff to anyone but myself. We have a couple's massage and go on a snorkeling adventure around the coral, although I can't swim a lick. It's after this snorkeling adventure where we're back at the room trying to get in a nap before our second dune buggy tour. The glass sliding door is open, so the ocean is our lullaby. "Babe," I hear from behind. Fletcher tells me to turn around and face him. I do. He looks hurt. "It's really hard for me to ask this of you, but… lemme hold something until later."

"Okay, I say."

"Only ten," he says.

I suck my teeth. "You know you don't have to ask for that." I'm thinking he means ten dollars because it's cash-only at half the places in the vicinity. I point to my purse. "It's right over there, babe."

Fletcher smirks and says, "Babe… Um… I mean then thousand."

I try not to appear shocked. "I just thought that when you said 'only' I was thinking…"

"Actually, I'm in a bind, ya see. I'm good for it. I promise."

"Okay." Approval comes out like a reflex, but I go with it. "I can transfer it to you later."

"Thank you." He kisses me. "Good lookin' out." We resume our position, with Fletcher holding me from behind. In a few minutes he's sleeping, but me: I'm still laying there with his heavy arm around me and my eyes wide open, unable to sleep.

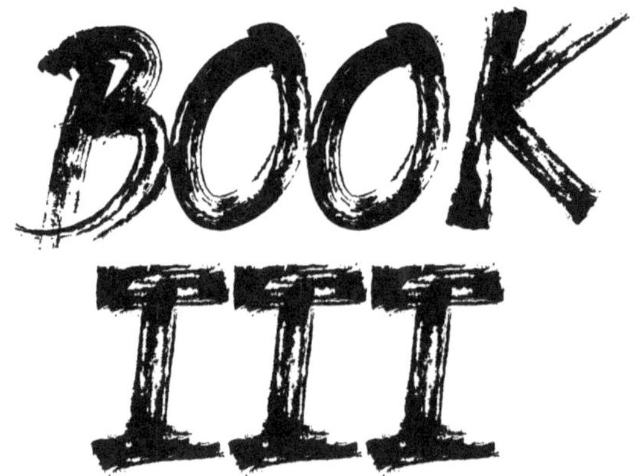

CHAPTER 13
GIMME MY MONEY

It's December 2022, and the agency is really starting to feel like work. Fletcher has lunch delivered so that no one leaves the office because the hour is being used for a meeting he's conducting. I'm only half-listening while eating a butternut squash soup and a baguette from Panera.

At this point, he's *forty thousand dollars* in the hole with me, so I'm hard of hearing on any topic besides that debt.

Fletcher paces the office like a general briefing his troops. "A thousand athletes we've fully vetted. Aside from studying their stats and measurables, we've studied their history and their social media, so once we have the green light to contact them as agents, our conversations will feel organic. It's the only edge we'll have against the big agencies who'll also be courting these very same athletes the moment they play their final game of eligibility. Depending on how many top recruits we acquire, by signing day in April, we can create a whole new life for us." On that note, Fletcher makes eye contact with me to nail the double meaning.

A good recruiting class would mean that Fletcher and I could afford to buyout my stake in the company so we can marry.

However, the idea of marrying Fletcher no longer gives me butterflies. I love Fletcher. I love him dearly, but I'm not even sure if paying back my loans can fully revive us to where we were. He's too comfortable asking me for money and that says something about him, as a man, and as the type of husband he'll be – and because of that, quite frankly, the dick doesn't even hit the same anymore.

Keenan approaches with his phone out and a bone to pick. "I sat here and listened to you all this time, wondering when were you gonna mention this?" He hands Fletcher the phone. "Ain't that your Draft Kings username? Body Snatcher Ninety-Four, your college jersey number?"

My attention is piqued, because I hear Fletcher going on and on about Draft Kings all the time. It's some form of sports betting app that's been stealing his attention from me, of late.

Fletcher wiggles a low hand. "Ay, Kee. We'll talk about that later. We're on business time."

Keenan sprouts a half smile. "But this *is* business. We're agents. We can't bet on sports."

"That's where you're wrong," says Fletcher. "It says it plain as day in the NFL code of conduct that we *can't* bet on the outcome of games, but we *can* bet on player performance – but again – I'm trying to discuss Legacy Sports' business."

"Me too," a wide-eyed Keenan says. "Aren't you using our talent evaluation software to help you win?" Keenan smiles. "Our software. Our hundred thousand dollars."

I spit out my sip of water in such a powerful spray that it suspends in mist. "A hundred thousand dollars!" And I'm hearing this from someone else?!

Fletcher's hung head lifts to me. "Tahj, this isn't what it looks like. All this money is accounted for – which brings me to my next point." In absence of a drum roll, there's only Monae's gum popping. "I'm throwing a Peach Bowl bash. Athletes get in free. Many of the athletes on our draft board are right here in Atlanta…"

I release my held breath, calming myself because I'm so hot about that hundred thousand dollars, that I can't hear anything he says until he mentions money again. "That money I got from the winnings, I gotta use it to rent a club, pay staff, and I'm paying for a couple of celebrity walk-throughs to boost the attendance."

I suck my teeth so loud it sounds like the flick of a lighter.

Keenan echoes, "Peach Bowl bash…?"

"Here me out," says Fletcher. "We'll get athletes in the door just hours after their eligibility is up, so we get first dibs on courting them."

"Smart," Keenan says. "Question though: how much revenue do you expect this party to bring in?"

Fletcher dips forward, "Revenue for who! *You?* You out yo got damn mind, Kee, if you think I'm finna give you a cut after I put up all of *my* money?"

A current shoots through me on the phrase 'my money.' I fire a pen across the office. All three heads turn to me as the pen hits the far wall and rolls on the floor. I couldn't curse Fletcher out and expose us, but I had to do something. I play clueless by looking away and rubbing the back of my neck.

Fletcher adds, "I created a whole nother business, a party promotion business. All proceeds go to sole proprietor: *me.*"

I sling another pen and then stare ahead in space, thinking Fletcher must be thee boldest nigga in the city. Pounding his chest about *his* money, in front of the person who lent him half of her savings?

Monae says, "Boss lady… You alright over there?"

Nonchalantly, I reply, "I'm good, why?"

"Because you throwing stuff, like…" her head lops forward and wiggles at my apparent cluelessness.

Keenan restarts, "But Fletch–"

"–But Fletch, nothing, Kee. Stop it, man. You greedy!"

Keenan retreats to his desk, a hand raised in surrender. "A'ight, bro. Have it your way."

Fletcher takes it as a threat, but he doesn't reply.

We work the remainder of the day in strained silence.

At the end of the day, Fletcher tails me to my house. I storm in and sit fast like a game of musical chairs. "When were you gonna tell me? Huh?"

Fletcher closes the door behind him and stands there like a visitor. "Look… babe… I don't have a hundred thousand dollars. They take taxes off top. I got more like fifty thousand. And if I pay you back your forty, I'm left in a position where I'd have to come back to you again."

"And you think that's better than lying to me?"

"Right or wrong, it's what I thought."

"Fuck what you thought, bro! Run me my bread!"

Fletcher peers from behind a pointed finger. "See, that's that mouth—"

"—I get it from my momma. And what…"

Fletcher smiles and shakes his head. "Calm ya little ass down, alright? I was hoping we could sit down and discuss this with respect."

"My mouth doesn't even approach the level of disrespect, on your part, for hiding money you owe me."

"I know what it looks like—"

"—*Looks like*," I clap. "…you're about to *not* pay me back, *and* try to feed me some bullshit!"

"Can I finish? Huh, babe? Can I finish?"

He takes a seat on the couch beside me, massaging my leg, while I resist the urge to bite that hand and ragdoll it like a Pitbull. He says, "The money I make from this party is going towards our wedding." I fold my arms and cut my eyes, to which a bashful Fletcher explains, "I got Bubby coming through. His team is on a bye week, so he's available; that's one celebrity name. If everything works out, I'm gonna have Brittany Renner do a walk-through; that's two celebrities. And I'm bringing in D.J. K-Dubb so you know it's gonna be lit."

"How much is all this gonna cost?"

"Everything. Most of the money's gotta be used for a deposit, which I get right back."

I huff. "So you're not gonna pay me even a little bit?"

"All you can see is the money."

"Seeing money, and seeing money that's owed to me, is two different things!"

"See the *vision*, baby. This can be the start of our own thing. Keenan's my dawg and everything, but maybe not for long if we stay in business together."

I sign stop like a crossing guard. "Now I *know* you're crazy. Leave the company before Bubby's contract renewal and walk away from more than two million apiece?"

"Did I say walk away from that? You not even hearing me." Fletcher lifts up from his seat to remove his jacket.

I say, "What do you think you're doing with that? No suh. You are not about to lie to me then lay with me."

Fletcher studies me for a moment. "Now I'm seeing the real you," he says.

"*This* is the real me now that I'm upset? So, it wasn't the real me who kept lending you money?"

His eyes thin. "Is this fun for you? Cutting a man down?"

I squeeze my brow with a hand, my head shaking at the realization of perhaps a toxic cycle that I'm in. "Lord, how did I end up in this situation again? I'm in love with a man that I gotta take care of. I can't even come spend the night at his house. He ain't *got* no damn house. Promising me the world, but come to find out, 'the world' he's promising is looking more and more like just dick."

Fletcher's eyes turn evil. "Just dick? You sure? Because you don't suck it like it's just dick. You be riding the shit like it's a chariot to heaven."

I'm in shock. I'd never heard or even imagined Fletcher speaking to me that way.

"Look at you," he says. "You can dish it, but can't take it."

I remember that foul mouth that Donovan had and I'm not about to endure that again. I point to the door. "I think you should go."

To my surprise, Fletcher gets up without hesitation, apology, or remorse. "I ain't your little boy, ya here," he says as he walks toward the door. He steps through the doorway and stands on the other side, adding, "I'm gone take this money and do what the fuck I gotta do. When it works out, you gone love me for it, and I'm gone forgive you for the shit you said today. Because one thing you *don't* do to me is—"

—*Bam*, goes the door that I slam in his face.

CHAPTER 14
BELIEF

"This is the one: the jacket I want you to design an outfit around."

"It's an odd one," I say, while staring the jacket down, my mind forming equations. I realize that Jay is just standing there. I urge, "Are you gonna put it on or what?"

Jay takes the jacket by the hanger and holds it to his body. "This little thing can't get around my shoulders."

"Grab one your size, duh."

"They only *had* one in my size, so I bought it. It's sitting in my closet at home."

My palms turn up. "Why didn't we just meet there?"

"Because," Jay frowns. "You acted so weird last time you came to my house – plus this time there's no Monae, either? Your boyfriend is still jealous, ain't he?"

"Just let me worry about him, okay?"

Jay returns the jacket to the rack, then targets me with a look of concern. "Wanna talk about it?"

"Talk about what?"

"Obviously, something's up. You're not being your usual chatty self."

"Me, chatty? I'm not chatty," I say as I walk through the door he opens for me.

"We haven't talked in months and you don't ask about Sarah and me?"

A Pomeranian trots by. The woman holding the leash has all the fixings – top, bottom, legs, face. Jay doesn't turn or even wince. I kid, "You didn't see that?"

Jay's eyes go lazy. "Sarah's got me blind to other women."

I crane back, impressed. "Thought she was a bit old for your taste."

"I've been looking for what I want. But what I needed found *me*."

I freeze. "So you two are together now?"

"We've kissed, we've cuddled in bed, but still haven't… Her husband passed some years ago. Apparently, he left some big shoes to fill, so she really wants to take her time to make sure I'm that guy."

I tail Jay enroute to his home and we keep the conversation going by phone. His voice, over Bluetooth, fills the interior of my car. He brings me up to speed on his relationship with Sarah, and I realize that I never really heard him talk this much about himself. He then says, "I hate to admit, Tahj, that you were absolutely right. I've been chasing younger women, and they were less interested in me and more interested in what I could do for them. But with Sarah, all she wants is my love and my time."

We reach his home and get out of our cars and continue the conversation. I ask, "Is Sarah here?"

"No. She's just getting back from a trip to her hometown, a small town in Texas, called Wimberley."

"Will she have a problem with us, alone in your house?"

"She's not so quick to jump to conclusions or to question my loyalty."

"Whew. Wish I could say the same about my man, or even myself," I say, as I walk through the door held open for me. My conscience shows me myself, entering this rich man's house complaining about my man; not a good look.

Jay closes the door behind us. "So, he doesn't know that you're… doing business with me, right now?"

"He lost the right for me to have to check in with him." I pivot to let Jay catch up, so he can lead me to his closet. He's paused in shock, so I elaborate, "He owes me money. And what's so messed up is that he has the money to pay me back but refuses until he gets a return on an investment he made."

"Disrespectful," Jay comments as he walks past. I follow him further into the home, listening to Jay talk about how a man should never borrow from his woman, how he should've gotten a bank loan or find joint-venture investors, then he adds, "I remember telling you once, that when you invite a man's pain and he sees how comfortable it is to lay his burdens on you, that it sets the tone for the relationship."

"Are you saying it's my fault he won't pay me back?"

"Try not to be defensive here, Tahj. Just a few minutes ago, I told you that you were right about the money getting in the way of my past relationships."

Hearing that, I let down my defense in a sigh. "Okay, you were right, Jay," I admit. "One hundred percent."

"The closet's in my bedroom." He leads down the hallway. "How much did you give him?"

Ashamed to admit to forty thousand, I reply, "Ten thousand." The look on Jay's face washes with disappointment, so I explain, "When he asks, it's like I don't even know how to say no."

"Hell, had I known you were incapable of saying no, I would a *been* asked for the draws." We enter the bedroom laughing even while I'm cognizant that a sex joke is something I probably should've checked him for. "Alright, Jay, you runnin' out," I say, but my comment's heat is stolen by the sight of this immaculate master bedroom.

I enter, turning in observation. "Wow, look at this." There's soft recessed lighting and a false ceiling that's a network of ovals. The bed is fit for a palace. I can't help but run a hand across it.

Jay says, "I hate to tell you this, but no shoes in the bedroom."

I step out of my shoes and feel the plush area rug under my feet. "What in the world," I say. "Is it mink?"

"It's synthetic," Jay says. "I ain't killin' no animals so my stepping out of bed feels like I'm walking on clouds."

The headboard design seems Hindu-inspired. "What're all these stones," I inquire.

"Amethysts. It's said to aid in deep sleep."

"Nice." I pivot and say, "So, let's see you in that jacket."

His closet is the size of my living room. I card through the hangers and lay matches across the ottoman.

Jay says, "I'll send you your fee plus ten thousand."

"No Jay. It's my man's responsibility."

"And he will fail you. I know his type."

"I'm telling you, Jay, I'll send the money right back."

"Do it, and you're fired as my fashion consultant." He's so stern and full of conviction; it's like I'm getting a glimpse of how he sways a jury in court. "Ten thousand is like five dollars to me. Repay me by not lending him anything again."

I leave the closet and sit on the edge of the bed as he comes out modeling the options I laid out for him. He gets two thumbs down. Jay says, "I wanna get this over with pretty soon because although Sarah said she was going back to her place to get settled, ya never know."

While Jay's speaking to me, I have a moment – a moment where I see him differently – a moment I'm familiar with because it happened with Donovan, who I was not initially attracted to, but after a while of seeing him on campus and talking over the phone, my bosom filled with glitter. Here, alone with Jay in his bedroom, he begins to sparkle before my eyes, not romantically, because of the age gap, but just hearing about the relationship he has with Sarah shows me his emotional stability versus the unstable emotional attachment I'm in with Fletcher, a man who went from the psychological abuse of an older Gigi to a field of women who required very little of him, so Fletcher has never loved properly to know how to love me. Jay has had a ten-year marriage – a beautiful marriage, is how he describes it – where his wife became an ambitious woman who refused to move herself and the children out of Little Rock when Jay decided to relocate his practice. I'm not attracted to Jay, but I see, in him, the qualities I wish Fletcher had.

"Did you hear what I just said?"

I reply, "I heard you." Actually, I didn't.

He squints at me, in a quick but fleeting examination that makes me suddenly aware of myself, how I must look sitting lazily on his bed, admiring him. Did he notice? I hope not, because my heart is fully with Fletcher, my future husband; I'm just realizing how much work Fletcher and I have before us, if our relationship is to endure.

The bed is so soft, I can't resist lying down, thinking if Fletcher could see me now, lying barefoot in another man's bed, he'd flip his lid. This *bed*, though. I bet when Jay's not home, angels descend from heaven to steal naps here. I turn on my side, my back to the doorway as I call out to Jay who is deep in the closet. "My goodness," I say. "What is this bed made of?"

A woman's voice responds, "Cashmere and lamb's wool."

I spazz and roll clean off the bed, hitting the floor like a log. "Hi Sarah," I say, with jubilee. Sarah watches my head pop up from the side of the bed, with a glare that wants for a Whack-A-Mole hammer to bash me back down. But then a smile breaks. "Hi Tahj. I go out of town and suddenly here you are lying in Jay's bed." Her smile scares me.

Jay comes out of the closet, investigating the thud. "You alright?" His head turns to where my eyes are aimed. "Sarah? I thought you were–"

"–First things first," Sarah says, with her approach. "I missed you." She throws her arms around his neck and kisses him. "I came to surprise you, but *got* surprised, huh?" Jay starts to explain, but Sarah puts a finger to his lips. "I'm sure you weren't thinking about how this might look to me. But I'm sure you're aware now. I'm a bit hungry, so I'll be in the kitchen." She plants another kiss on his lips and leaves us there speechless.

I pace and vent, "I'm so embarrassed."

Jay whispers. "What'd she say to you?"

"Nothing really. She just stated the obvious."

Jay smiles and shakes his head. "See what I mean? Another woman would've hit the roof, then try to use my mistake as leverage to dictate." Jay looks around, perplexed with hands on hips. "My mind's made up. I'm gonna marry this woman."

I'm in awe for witnessing the moment a man ends his search for *the one*. It's a rare sight, like an endangered snow leopard emerging from the camouflage of snowy underbrush.

Jay says, "I'm gonna need a ring. You're my fashion consultant. Help me pick out a ring. A hundred K is a good budget, you think?"

I show palms, not wanting any parts of it. "How do you think she'd feel about me picking out her ring?"

"You're right." Jay points with the flick of his head. "You go on ahead. I'll be out in a sec."

On the walk to Sarah, I'm dreading having to bear Sarah smiling through her desire to kill me, or conversing about the weather, and not whether I'm fucking her man, or me potentially blurting out that I'm not, in response to being offered a beverage.

I get to the living room and learn that there's nothing to worry about. Sarah's so cool I wonder if she's upset at all. We sip wine and play fashion judge while Jay models the outfits I'd laid out. We hit it off so well that I begin to feel fake for not telling her that Jay's giving me ten thousand dollars.

At one point, Sarah excuses herself to the restroom and I say, to Jay, "I see why you wanna marry her. But for you, the defining moment was her *not* going off on you?" I try not to appear too invested in his response.

"Well, yes." He stares in bliss, as if the reason is so innate that he'd never captioned it in words. "She believes in me."

Me: a half hour later…

"I believe in you, Fletcher," I say, while looking intently into his eyes. "I'm not gonna trip about the money no more. I trust that you're doing what's best for us." With a fingertip tapping his chest, I say, "You've got the heart, and you've got the smarts to do anything you put your mind to, and I'm honored that your mind and your heart is focused on me. I believe you gone take that money and multiply it, king."

Fletcher looks stunned, as if he'd never had a woman outside of his mother speak to him this way. I sit Fletcher down on the couch. He buries his face in my belly, his gratitude muffled by my sweater dress. My mind is blown by the impact that a woman's belief can have on a man.

I capture his face and gaze in his eyes. "What is it, baby?"

His eyes widen. "The pressure," he says. He sets a hand on his sternum, afraid something'll jump out. "I don't wanna fail you." His shoulders slump. "And right now I got all kinds of hang-ups with this party. The club's forcing me to use their pricey security staff. I got the flyers made, but now Brittany's backing out. I gotta find somebody else, then pay to have new flyers made – to name a few."

"C'mon, Fletch," I say. "You know good and well my belief in you isn't riding on the outcome of some party, bro."

"Thank you," Fletcher says. He's so relieved, he relaxes against the back of the couch. "Thank you for believing in me. That's all I ever wanted, but ya don't think about the anxiety that comes with it," he says, as he reaches a hand into his suit and rubs his chest.

I slide my dress down one shoulder. "I got something for anxiety."

"No thank you." He's looking down in his lap not even noticing that I'm undressing.

"You sure? You might wanna take this."

He looks up and sees that 'this' is a tit in my hand.

This lovemaking hits different. We're re-consummating our love under new sanctions. From above, Fletcher looks at me as if I'm a new creature. He's more patient and attentive, not the dominant lover that I'm used to.

I'm so stimulated, I begin to worry that maybe something's going on with me, and that worry folds across my brow. My mouth stays open; my moaning is small and singing. Fletcher bends to my sound like a violinist, frowning in the concentration of making music while also basking in the pleasure of the melody emitting from his instrument: me. By the end of it, I'm writhing in pleasure, clawing his muscled back. It's the sweetest little climax I'll ever have – also the quietest, my held breath releasing in shudders. I clutch Fletcher's face and peer into his eyes, searching his soul. I try to tell him how good he feels to me, but somehow it feels wrong to speak. This lovemaking is sacred, it's blessed, and Fletcher knows it too. He sinks into me, deeply, and with such care.

Fletcher gazes upon me with such intention and calm that I question what I'm feeling below: he's pulsating. The moisture changes. I'm getting a hint of chlorine. Yup, he came in me. What a letdown, after an evening that went so well for us. Gently, I ask what I already know. "You nut?"

His answer is nonverbal. He tremors as he squeezes out his last drop. The disrespect. I'm on birth control now because of the first pregnancy scare, but still…

Fletcher lay on his side, running his fingers over my hair, as if being nutted in, is something I should bond over. I stare at the ceiling considering the stark contrast between two men.

Sarah tells Jay that she believes in him and the first thing Jay wanna do is shop for a hundred thousand dollar ring.

I tell Fletcher that I believe in him and the first thing he wanna do is buss in me?

"What were you thinking," I ask.

Fletcher raises up on an elbow. "I'm thinking that our love is bigger than just us."

I turn to face him. "Wife first, then mother."

Fletcher just looks at me baffled for a few moments, then he turns over and goes silent, as if to charge my attitude to the mental illness called womanhood.

CHAPTER 15
WOMAN TO WOMAN

The next day at the office, I get a call from Sarah. She asks if we can have lunch. I leave the office on my own and Fletcher thinks it's because I'm still upset with him.

I wear my engagement ring to a Vietnamese-style restaurant, coming in bundled on this early December day where the chill feels like winter's warning shot.

Sarah waves from behind an open menu, her micro braids bound and draped over a shoulder.

We begin with small talk as we order our food; the tension mounting – for me, at least. I usually suck at ignoring the elephant in the room, but today I'm doing quite well: growth, I guess. But maybe not, because it's me who starts doing too much when I look at Sarah with a cheeky smile and say, "You look really pretty in box braids."

Sarah's hands come together, as if playtime is over. "I'll get right to it, Tahj. What's your relationship with J.P.?"

My smile sags with embarrassment. "I know what you saw yesterday looked bad, but I assure you: we are just friends."

"My inquiry isn't so much about what I saw. It's about the ten thousand dollars J.P. transferred to your account."

Sarah folds her arms, awaiting an explanation, but I would never disrespect Letha May Thompson, who always told me to never explain myself to nare bitch. So, I match Sarah's folded arms and say, "Whatever Jay told you, go with that. I'm not the one in a relationship with you. He is."

Sarah's nostrils flare but she's otherwise calm, as she says, "Are you getting smart with me? Because I will throw the contents of this glass at your face and smack the hell outta you before you get wet." My clap-back is still loading when Sarah cuts me off, a half-smile issuing the words, "But I'd prefer to handle this like adults. So, let me back it up a bit, so you can understand that I didn't call you here on some woman-to-woman type thing. The thing is, I'm worried about Jay. Even to this day, he's paranoid about me being at his house without him, and I think I found out why."

My eyes are wide but I'm all ears.

Sarah adds, "Someone's trying to kill him."

"Trying to kill him?" I do-over in a whisper, "Trying to kill him?"

"Have you seen him acting weird – seen anyone sketchy hanging around?"

"First of all, I think you're being paranoid, mam. Who would want to kill him? And for what?"

"For what? I don't know, but maybe I'll have a clue when you tell me what service you provide that's worth over ten thousand dollars to him."

I slide my ring hand on the table. "I don't know what you're trying to imply, but I have a fiancé."

"I'm not asking you if it's sexual; I'm asking if it's illegal. You take a trip to the Dominican Republic a month ago, and the next time you see J.P. he's giving you ten thousand dollars?"

I sit upright with my hands in my lap and say, "Forget Jay for a second and look at *me*. What do you think *I* would be involved in? Drugs? Running numbers? C'mon."

"You look as unassuming as any white-collar criminal. Maybe you carry cash payments to the doctors that help him win damn near every case he brings to trial, which could explain why Jay, a lawyer who works primarily in disability cases, has the net worth of Hollywood lawyers who litigate cases in the hundreds of millions per suit. Did you know that Jay has a private jet?"

I didn't now, and quite frankly I'm baffled. "Does Jay know you're going around asking questions like this? You sound like the feds."

Sarah laughs, but snaps out of it with a look of ridicule. "How do you sound," she says. "You're talking to a woman who's worried because the last time I was in love, I had to suffer losing my husband."

"I'm sorry to hear."

"We were stationed in Germany at the time…" Sarah dabs her eyes with tissue. "He was ran over by a car that was driven by one of the soldier's under his charge. The soldier was abusive to his wife, so while he was deployed, my husband arranged for his family to be moved back to the states for their safety. The soldier returned from deployment to find an empty house and that's when he snapped." Sarah takes a moment. She looks down, shaking her head. "I didn't think I would ever find love again. Now that I have – well now that I *believe* I have – I'm afraid I might lose Jay in the same way. His clients are almost exclusively veterans. They're highly trained and sometimes unstable, and that can make for hazardous working conditions. Even though you haven't answered my question yet – and probably won't – I just wanted you to know where I'm coming from." Sarah grabs her purse, saying, "I won't waste any more of your time. Excuse me, while I go end the relationship–"

"No wait," I say. "Look, my service is fashion. It really is. The ten thousand dollars was about… Well, I was running my mouth to Jay about how I lent ten thousand dollars to someone who refuses to pay it back. Jay sent me the money to erase my mistake."

Sarah looks as if she doesn't believe me. "That's what it was?"

"It's the truth. I didn't want the money. I threatened to send it right back, but he said 'If you do, you're fired as my fashion consultant'," I say, impersonating Jay.

Sarah smiles. "That's him, alright." She sighs and explains, "My paranoia came about one day when I heard Jay threaten someone over the phone, but it sounded to me like the person threatened him first. There was the mention of a name." She licks her lips and says, "Have you ever heard Jay mention the name Ace?"

My head shakes. "I can't say that I have. Believe it or not, Jay has always been really surface level with me. I tell him all my business but he doesn't talk much about his, except for when it comes to you."

"Thank you," Sarah says. "This helps. Maybe it's nothing. Maybe I'm just being paranoid."

We lighten the conversation, just chatting in general, until me and my big mouth: "I probably shouldn't tell you this, but… You and Jay have been going together for just a few months now, and guess what… Jay's already shopping for an engagement ring."

To my surprise, Sarah looks at me as if she'd seen a ghost.

BOOK IV

CHAPTER 16
RILEY

Months Prior

Here's the issue – and for the record, I don't know all the details of Riley's life, but I'm giving it how I eventually heard it from Riley's closest confidant named Joslyn.

Earlier that day, Riley was at a panel interview at some women's event. She's a legit fashion model, a longtime girlfriend of a professional athlete, plus she has Miss Georgia finalist on her resume, over which, she has built a platform worthy of being a panel guest at events like this.

Near the end of the event, the audience buzzes and there is a domino of phone screens lighting up across the assembly. The host notices the unrest but continues with the last of her cue card questions.

It isn't until the event is over and Riley is setting up her little self-published books at a table when a fan surprises her with a hug, but uses the embrace to whisper, "You might wanna see this."

This being a phone placed in Riley's hand, showing a viral trending video selfie of Gideon's mistress, a cat-eyed porn star with white hair and bee-stung lips, posting an ultrasound. "I told you, Gideon Anderson," she says with a seductive smile. "I told you I would expose you, choir boy." Riley, blanched and speechless, wanders through the crowd, leaving all of her things behind.

Riley stands at the window gazing, her eyes raw with tears. I'm one of many concerned friends who saw the video and tried to call Riley, blowing up her phone. Gideon's mansion is otherwise quiet.

And then the front door opens. Gideon calls Riley's name. She can hear the length of his stride hurrying up the stairs and down the hallway. When that tall beanstalk, Gideon, ducks through the doorway, Riley doesn't move.

Gideon approaches, his brow slinked with worry. "You wasn't answering, baby. I thought maybe you'd done went and done something to yourself."

Not a muscle moves but for the turn of Riley's head, to stare at Gideon, who stands there looking like a stretched boy, his nappy box fade squared around a baby face, his nervous hands stuffed in his pockets. Riley asks, "Is it true?"

Gideon's head shakes no, but it's a conflicted no. "It's not that simple."

"I'm leaving." Riley walks. Nothing left to talk about. She opens a suitcase on the bed and begins filling it, stomping to and from the closet.

All the while, Gideon pleads. "I love you. I need you right now more than ever."

"You *need* me?" Riley would've slapped him if not for the armload of clothing. "If *you* need me, that's *your* incentive. What's mine? I shouldn't be shacking up with you in the first place. It's not right."

"Let's *make* it right, then." Gideon pleads, "Let's get married. Isn't that what you want?"

"If you'd marry me because *I* want it; I don't want it."

"Of course I wanna marry you, I just wasn't in no hurry."

Riley's lazy-eyes says she's not convinced. She stuffs another item in the yawning suitcase.

Gideon takes her hand and says, "I can make it go away."

What Riley ended up telling me, is the same story she eventually told a million viewers during a relationship podcast (as a P.R. move) with megachurch bishop T.S. Randolph and his wife. Riley, while holding hands affectionately with Gideon, said, that the porn star, Animae Doll, lied for clout. Gideon did not have an affair, Riley added, but the ordeal served as a teaching moment on the lengths people will go, to exploit the rich and famous.

Gideon paid Animae Doll to abort the baby and to go on Live and say she lied. The million Gideon paid out is nothing compared to the millions Gideon stood to lose if Nike dropped his sneaker deal.

Gideon's agent demanded a meeting and insisted that Riley join Gideon at his dinner table opposite of Gary Goldman and his wife of a quarter century.

Gary demanded that before would even attempt to go groveling to Nike, he wanted to meet and make sure there wouldn't be any setbacks. The meeting is to ensure that the porn chick, Anna Sokolov, was compensated well enough to keep quiet, and that Riley was all-in and committed to keeping a united front to restore Gideon's image.

While the men discuss the abortion and hush money, Riley studies the reaction of Goldman's wife, her deviously beautiful face peeking through a split curtain of blonde hair. This talk of scandal and the façade of public image seems all too familiar to her.

Riley, tired of not speaking, finally says, "So… Mrs. Goldman… What do you do?"

The woman bites her fingertip and smiles as if she'd rather not say. "PR." She lets a few seconds tick before adding, with a secretive wink. "Is that the Mutu painting that's caught your eye? Let me show you around."

They spend some time in the living room for show, then wander down the hallway where Riley, releases the question she'd been holding back. "Is it all worth it?"

What *it all* means, warrants no clarification between women who see themselves in each other. "They all cheat," Mrs. Goldman says.

"But you can still have love. You can still have passionate, undying love in your life like I do – but not with your husband."

Riley glitches. "Say what?" She whispers, "So you have… someone else?"

"Men who are obsessed with wealth and power, will never be obsessed with you; it's the men who fix cars and clean pools. They live check to check, and maybe that's why they savor every moment with you like there's a chance there won't be another."

Riley's head shakes slowly. "I will never do that."

"I didn't think *I* would. But there came a time when I was mommy to four children, and Gary's wife to everyone else. Then someone looked at me and saw Christina. I hired that personal trainer and handed him a non-disclosure." They tour the in-home movie theatre, then the enclosed pool, Mrs. Goldman doing all the talking. "You know about the Currys, right? The dad who was a professional basketball player and his two sons who followed his footsteps? Well, we're really close with that family. I offered Sonya, the mother, my advice, but she didn't listen. Now, they're going through a divorce and she may get next to nothing because she didn't know how to handle herself when she finally met a man that gives her butterflies."

"I'm not chasing butterflies, Mrs. Goldman. I'm chasing God's favor. I'm not judging you, but in the wedding vows, the word love is not a feeling or a condition. It's a command – a direct order, regardless of how we feel inside. All I want, aside from being well taken care of, is to be a good mother and wife, and to honor my vows, because *my* joy ultimately comes from honoring God." Oddly, I do believe that Riley believes herself when she says this.

Christina sighs in appraisal of Riley. "So innocent… So green…" She sighs and adds, "Gideon is gonna chew you up and spit you out."

Later that night while getting ready for bed, Gideon asks, "What was you and Miss Christina talking about?"

Riley ponders the truth, but walks around it like it's the corner of the bed. "Their home. It's impressive, didn't you see? Gary's just an agent, though, so how is he… Well, *does* he make more than you?"

Riley slides under the sheets and turns off the lamp, her back turned to hide how invested she is in the answer to her question.

Gideon replies, "I'm one athlete. Gary breaks bread with more than forty athletes. Makes sense?"

It makes more sense to Riley than Gideon could ever imagine. Riley knows of one sports agent, in particular, that she'd been feverishly attracted to since high school, and especially during college when he was considered one of the top defensive ends in the nation. During those days, the only thing that kept Riley from pursuing Fletcher was her friendship with me.

When Fletcher entered the NFL and a relationship with me hadn't materialized, Riley saw her green light to "reconnect" whenever Fletcher's team traveled to Riley's city, Phoenix, to play the Cardinals. Back then, Riley had her doubts about Gideon ever marrying her, so she thought it wise to stay close to the heart of another professional athlete.

Never once had Fletcher mentioned he was catching up with Riley when he traveled to Phoenix. It was supposedly all innocent, except for the way Riley would glow-up for their casual luncheons.

When Fletcher got dropped out of professional football and said he was going to be an agent, Riley believed that any relationship with Fletcher would be a serious downgrade from the life she was becoming accustomed to with Gideon, so she let the friendship go, just like she did when Fletcher had the accident and his football career was considered over before it started.

Now in light of how well sports agency pays Gideon's agent, Mr. Goldman, Riley figures it's time to reconnect with Fletcher again. Her fiancé had cheated, and in all likelihood, his promise of marriage is only a means to repair his image.

Nevertheless, Riley and Gideon are inseparable in the months following the scandal. They do a slew of photoshoots and post themselves out together in hopes that everyone would see a power couple so in love that the porn chick scandal becomes a distant memory.

Behind the scenes, however, things aren't the best. Not only does Riley have her feelings of betrayal to contend, but the porn chick is still a problem.

Riley's competitiveness towards me would never allow her to share that she'd received such low treatment from a man, but I found out, through other means that, Miss Animae Doll not only didn't go away, but she would become such a pervasive force, that she'd make her way into their bed.

On the night in question, Gideon and Riley were partying in Los Angeles. By being Gideon's fiancé, Riley has celebrity friends, and honestly, I sometimes envy her for the parties she's invited to, often taking pictures arm-in-arm with A-listers; this night is no different.

I remember her Instagram posts at the film festival and the afterparty, including an intimate video selfie in the backseat of their limo, their eyes thin and red. Riley obviously had been drinking, but something was different.

She rarely drinks, but I know how she acts when she's tipsy and this wasn't it. She was acting dreamy, or psychedelic in that selfie video. Riley would never knowingly take drugs, so I say she was slipped a Molly; what transpires later at the hotel proves it.

She and Gideon enter their L.A. suite in a lip lock, wrestling their clothes off and wiping the dresser clean as they feel their way through the room and onto the bed.

Riley squirms and heaves from mere kisses on her neck and chest. The way she would later explain it to Joslyn, is that her erogenous zone was her entire body, and every spot Gideon's lips landed, kept on kissing and eventually she felt like there were many warm lips continuously kissing her all over. A love bite to Riley's tush is so surreal, she could mentally replicate the dental record.

There's a knock at the door. "Ignore it," Riley commands. Gideon disobeys and goes to it. Riley thrashes and whines. "What're you doing? Make love to me!" She leans back on her elbows, watching Gideon at the doorway talking – no, whispering – to a woman.

Animae Doll steps in and sheds a long coat to reveal her arctic white body decorated in lace. She wears a collar around her neck. She hands Gideon the leash and goes down on all fours. Gideon tugs her along, whistling and kissing as if Animae is a pet dog.

Riley doesn't take it sitting down. She's up cursing and trying to kick Anna, but Gideon blocks her. Animae sits obediently on her haunches, panting with her pink tongue hanging out of her mouth.

Gideon pins Riley's arms to the bed. "Chill, baby. Chill."

Riley yells, "Wait! You invited her! That damn dog?"

"She's not a dog," Gideon vehemently denies. "She's a goddess, okay, an ancient goddess of winter who morphs into her spirit animal, a magical Siberian Husky that can—" Gideon stops at the sight of Riley's face, contortioned with a mixture of disbelief and disgust. Gideon simplifies, "White people shit, okay. Just go with it."

Riley, however, doesn't just go with it. She doesn't relax until Gideon ducks his head between her thighs. Riley's drug-induced pleasure is astronomical. Despite the moral war waging in Riley, all she could do is lay there, imprisoned by pleasure. Her eyes clap shut, refusing to acknowledge Animae who watches, alert as a bird dog.

Gideon calls his mistress. Animae walks on two feet. Her body epitomizes her name, with its cartoonish proportions, her red corset squeezing her waist like pastry dough, her breasts so full the skin is stretched thin, revealing the scrawl of tiny blue veins.

Anna massages Riley's belly. Her blistered lips make the shape of an O, which she lowers down onto Riley's brown nipple. Riley moans all the more.

Gideon raises up, his glazed lips saying, "See. It's not so bad. You wanna get married, this is the terms. We can be one big happy family."

He resumes his meticulous mouthing, like a kitten to a bowl of milk. Riley's protest comes out in a moaning cadence. "It's over Gideon. I swear, it's over." Yet when Gideon lifts his head, Riley chastises him, "Don't stop!"

Riley's so lost in it, she doesn't notice Gideon and Anna changing places, until Gideon comments, "Bet she can do it way better than I can."

Riley's eyes spring wide and she looks down between her spread legs and finds Anna's electric blue eyes, set in her white fleshy face. Riley protests, "Gideon, I don't like this."

Anna says, with her thick Russian accent, "I give you pleasure like you never experience."

Riley cries, "Gideon! Get her!"

Anna slicks her white hair behind her ear and licks her blistered lips in preparation to descend them upon Riley's clitoris.

Riley thrust both feet into Anna's chest, screaming, *"Bitch!"* Anna lands in a sitting position on the floor, but her head whips back and punches a crater in the wall; a line of crimson-red blood slips from a nostril.

Anna whimpers like a puppy while Gideon coddles her.

Since Anna's the one with the bloody nose, Gideon decides to leave with her, but he stops to give Riley a speech. "You want me to treat *you* like a fucking dog? Huh? Because, if Anna's out, then it's on you."

Riley counters, "I'll never wear a dog collar for no man. For even *God*, I'd need a detailed explanation."

Gideon says, "You're wearing a collar now, Riley. Your collar isn't around your neck, baby; it's on your finger." Gideon squats next to Riley and says, "You wanna live good, right? So, what are you willing to do for it? You want me to put up millions to fuck around and lose in a divorce? What do I get out of the deal?"

Riley replies, "You get loyalty and respect – something I'm not getting from you."

Gideon comes to his senses and his head hangs. "This was a bad idea. And I'm sorry, Riley. Really, I am. Look, you don't ever have to see Anna again, okay? But *I* do. Take it or leave it."

The next morning, Riley sits on the bed, her knees drawn to her chest while she stares at the crater in the wall. She's alone in the hotel room; Gideon still hasn't returned.

Her eyes squint because the morning sun is bright at the windows; she also squints because she's actually considering Gideon's ultimatum.

She ain't no fool. She's got a few years invested already. She'll go along with Gideon having a mistress if it results in marriage. Riley has done her homework; the state of Arizona is one of nine states under Community Property divorce laws. Neither her morals, nor her parents, would let her have a baby out of wedlock for an eighteen-year drip, so marriage is the only way. Her church won't shun her for divorcing a philandering husband, and in the state of Arizona, she can sever the marriage early on and still be set for life. Then she can focus on finding real love, for once.

A call comes in. Riley checks her phone, expecting Gideon, but it's Fletcher. Riley fumbles to answer. Her smile could be heard through the phone when she answers, "Fletcher! Hey, you."

"Whassup, Riley. How you been?"

"I'm good," Riley says. "Better now, hearing your voice."

Fletcher says, "I hate to call you for the first time in a long time asking for a favor, but I'm in a bind. You see I got this big party, right–"

"–Big party? Business must be good."

"It's pretty good," Fletcher says. "But here's the thing: I need a celebrity bottle girl. Britney Renner canceled on me."

"Don't make me jump through this phone, Fletcher. You see me as sloppy seconds to a Britney Renner?"

Fletcher replies, "Aw naw, sweetheart. Britney was convenient because she's local. I wanted you from the start, but the logistics was a problem. You're way across the country."

Riley repeats the part that resonates most, "Wanted me from the start, huh? Boy, you speaking *volumes* right now."

Fletcher's thrown off momentarily by the obvious flirting from a woman who's engaged to be married. Fletcher keeps it business, though. "I know you're big time now, so the pay is chump-change to you, so what I'm really asking is for you to come through for an old friend."

"Mmm… I don't know."

Fletcher adds, "C'mon, now Riley. You're overdue for a visit back home. I'm paying for your flight, by the way." Yes, this is not an error: Fletcher is paying money he owes me, to Riley, the girl he'd been secretly meeting when his teams traveled to Phoenix. Fletcher and I were not together during that timeframe, so no foul, but the fact that neither ever mentioned their little luncheons to me, I consider that moving funny.

"C'mon now," Fletcher coaxes, as he awaits the verdict.

The verdict, Riley delivers with her signature, flirty shoulder roll and, "Bay-bee… If it's *you* flying me out, how can I refuse?"

When the call ends, Fletcher's on one side, frowning at his phone, wondering if Riley done lost her mind.

On the other end of the severed call, Riley's clear across the country, in her L.A. suite, holding the phone to her breast. "This is no coincidence," she whispers, her eyes darting. "Already, God? I just prayed to You last night."

Riley's God apparently doesn't know that Fletcher was already engaged to be married to me.

CHAPTER 17
WHEN IT HITS THE FAN

It's the day that Fletcher's been getting on everybody's nerves about. The club is packed. Many who attended the annual Peach Bowl game at the nearby Mercedes Benz Stadium came here for the party advertised over the radio and on flyers as the Peach Bowl Bash.

There are as many athletes there as projected. So, what follows athletes like chicks to a mother hen? Groupies.

They range, in age, from about eighteen to twenty-eight and they are everywhere, fighting for the attention of future millionaires, crowding them like ants and twerking for attention, so when I'm simply doing my job courting the athletes, the groupies mistake me for competition. Mind you, I'm dressed professionally, like a stewardess minus the scarf, and yet while up in VIP chatting with projected first-round quarterback Warren Favors, a chick in a sheer catsuit with censor dots over the nipples walks up and says, "I know this bitch ain't in my seat."

I reply, "This *bitch*… is hosting this event. And if you can't go sit yourself down somewhere, I'll have security help you with that."

She studies Warren, whose posture shows alignment with me. "Warren," the chick scolds. "So, this what you on? Huh? Bitches that look like Draymond Green in the face?"

Warren throws his arm out to bar me from getting up. He tells the thot, "Fuck's wrong with you! Get outta here!"

She goes away saying, "You lame, bro!"

Some of the athletes also mistake me for a groupie. I spot a guy with a head of long dreadlocks and a neck big as a thigh. The arm tattoo of an RIP, tells me it's none other than Georgia running back, Jacoby Lynch, for whom I'd watched hours of film and memorized his stats. I figure I'd approach in such a way that he couldn't mistake me for a groupie, reciting his athletic virtues. "Fastest straight-line acceleration in the draft… Decent yards after contact… Bet the Cardinals can use that get-off speed for their spread offense. I can convince them to take you early in the second round."

He just bops to the music. He doesn't look at me, his eyes busy tracking every exotic-looking chick on two legs.

I add, "That's millions more in your pocket if you were to get with our agency."

His eyes had sliced to me on the words *get with*. "I know *you* trippin'," he says and walks away as if I'm obviously not on his level.

I consider following him to have an in-depth discussion on why his dreads smell like ass, but that would've been unprofessional.

I slide up to an FSU defensive back with my pitch. He's watching two thirsty chicks on the dance floor shimmying in a game of batting titties. The young man dismisses my entire spiel and only looks over to ask, "You like girls?"

I see Riley prancing around with her champagne buckets. Some of the same athletes who disrespected me, are different with her. They fall at her feet, offering to carry the bucket for her. I see one guy pull her down into the seat next to him. Monae, who's also working as a bottle girl, has guys all over her as well, and it shows in the wad of tips I saw her counting in the back, and in the amount of phone numbers she's collected.

The big guys, however, are a lot nicer to me. The offensive and defensive linemen, nearly three hundred pounds apiece, seem delighted when I approach. Especially this brown-haired left tackle,

Josh Andrews who has tape-up so clean, I'd bet my last dollar that his barber is in da hood. I explain, "… It's as if NFL scouts don't even realize that 90% of your run blocks climb to the second level. *We* see it because we build our own scouting reports; that's what's so special about our agency–"

"–I hate to cut you off there," Josh says. "But you said you're an agent?" To my nod he responds, "You're *my* agent, then," he says. "And that's only because you're so hot."

This makes my day, but at the same time, it makes me upset, because the first compliment I get comes from a white guy. It makes me wanna go around slapping every brotha in the building.

I have a great time talking with Josh and, quite honestly, he makes three hundred pounds look good, since he's six foot six inches tall. He has this whole comedic schtick about his "hard body" that has me laughing the entire time. He flexes his bicep and, to my surprise, there's a blurry line in the shape of a muscle. He braces and tells me to punch his stomach to see how hard it is. I give him a pretty good shot and it feels like punching a tire. Josh comedically buckles and makes his eyes cross. I turn away laughing and that's when my eyes land on Fletcher's jealous stare.

My eyes stretch, *Jealousy? Really?* I figure he's trying to turn the tables because I'm upset with him for paying Riley money he owes me. Because there's no way in hell Fletcher thinks I'm actually flirting with Josh.

I tell Josh he's something else, then turn to go confront Fletcher, but run into Bubby whose smile shows off a diamond grill. I hug my brother. I squeeze him because I miss him so. Fletcher is still in the distance – not approaching to welcome his best friend, but still staring – as if he takes issue with me hugging Bubby. Bubby steps aside and introduces me to the teammate he'd brought along. Before I could think of what to say, thee Jalen Hurts is kissing my hand, and I'm absolutely star-struck. "Such a pleasure to meet you Jalen."

With the shape of his lips still warm on my hand, he says, "The pleasure is all mine." He has this look that I would recognize even if I were blind. I hate the term melanin worship because it sounds fetishy, when all the unabashed worship of light and biracial women is accepted as normal.

Bubby leaves abruptly. This was a setup. Bubby, like everyone else, thinks I'm single, which is why he conveniently left Jalen and me alone to entertain each other.

Being the consummate hostess that I am, I say, "Let me escort you to Bubby's VIP section." I flag down Monae to bring some bottles. Jalen uses my distraction to his advantage; he hooks my arm like a gentleman. I don't look, but I feel Fletcher's glare burning a hole in my back as Jalen and I walk away.

The club parts like the Red Sea as we walk through; they're in awe of Jalen. And because of him, they're quite intrigued by me as well, like, who's the chick on his arm though?

While going up the steps to the VIP section, Jalen says, "My agent is a black woman."

"Word? That's dope!"

We take our seats. "She's the first black female agent to represent an NFL draft pick."

"Say what! Y'all made history, bro?" It takes me a second to realize. "But you just got in the league, so… what does that make me? The second?"

"I believe so," Jalen says.

I deflate right there in my seat. "That's crazy though, for this to be 2021. The fact that there's still firsts for black women, is mind-blowing."

"Mind-blowing, huh," Jalen repeats. "Those same words had come to me; it was about something else, though." His eyes say that the something else is me.

"I see what you did there." I'm blushing so hard I have to cover my mouth and look away. "Thank you for the compliment," I add.

"You got a man, I bet."

I nod yes with a large grin on my face, just observing this handsome… multimillionaire… gentleman… who uses his celebrity status to support black women… And I'm about to turn him down for a nigga who won't even pay me back and has been acting jealous all night – but he mines, and I'm gone stick beside him.

Monae approaches the steps with the champagne, but she's rudely intercepted. Riley sneaks up and tugs Monae's weave on one side. When Monae turns to the side where her hair was tugged, Riley dips to the other side, snatches the champagne bucket and darts up the steps. Monae is left with a fist drawn and her target out of reach.

Riley enters the VIP section just as Monae yells from the bottom. "Never again in your fuckin' life, bitch!"

Riley, wearing a stink-face, comments, "They should do a better job of vetting the staff around here." She then lights up with a smile. "Oh my gosh! Mr. Jalen Hurts. Why, I had no idea you had graced us with your presence."

Dangling on the end of Riley's outstretched arm is a hand for Jalen to kiss, which tells me that Riley saw when Jalen kissed my hand earlier.

Jalen takes Riley's hand and only shakes it. I turn away to hide a face ready to bust with laughter.

"I'm Riley. You might've seen me on the flyer for this party." She slings her hair back, adding, "Miss Georgia beauty pageant finalist… I don't do this kind of thing, the clubs and all, but I'm helping out my friend, Tahj here."

Jalen takes the bucket. "'Preciate it, Miss Riley."

Riley takes the liberty of having a seat. "Pardon me, but my feet are killing me."

Jalen promptly sets the champagne down and helps Riley up, saying, "If you'll excuse us, Miss Riley? I'm nice… But I ain't *that* nice."

Riley says, "Why, I never!" She pinches her dress downward and walks away with a hard switch.

Jalen asks, "Is she always like this?"

"Always," I say. "I don't know how a star basketball player like Gideon Anderson puts up with her, Riley's his fiancé."

Jalen jerks away. "Ain't no way! He know his lady out here in a tiny dress, acting single?"

"There was a scandal. She and her fiancé recovered from it – I thought. Seeing how she's acting tonight, I just don't know anymore."

Fletcher emerges at the top of the steps and sees me relaxed, leaning towards Jalen Hurts with my legs crossed. The look in Fletcher's eye says he heard me say, *I just don't know anymore,* but thinks I was talking about us.

While Bubby introduces Jalen and Fletcher, I try to slip away, but Jalen calls me back. "Tahj, you're leaving? I thought we was vibing."

With one foot on the first stair, and feeling the jealous beam of Fletcher's eyes, I panic. "Vibing? Go'head with that, bro. I don't know what made you think that," I say and then escape down the steps. I hurry through the club, phone in hand, texting Fletcher. I go to the kitchen just to decompress, but find Keenan in the middle of a skirmish between Riley and Monae.

Riley launches a tin cup of bar straws, punctuating, "Bitch!" The cup doesn't reach Monae because it clocks Keenan in the back of the head; thin straws shower like confetti.

Kee turns and yells, "Ay! Yall gone stop this!"

Monae, behind the guard of a seasoned slap boxer, yells, "Oh, you wanna throw shit?" Monae one-ups her by throwing a wild punch, but Keenan spins around just in time for Monae's knuckles to rake down the front of his face, peeling his bottom lip inside out. Keenan staggers with his eyes glazed and his knees locked.

I set my phone down and jump in like a double Dutch turn, using my back to block Riley, then steering a punch-drunk Keenan by the collars to obstruct Monae. Monae calms down and starts apologizing to Keenan. She soon looks out from that apology to yell, "Bitch look what you done made me did!"

Riley mocks, "Made you *did?* Girl you sound just as ignorant as you look."

"*Call* me ignorant one more time!"

"I ain't got to call you ignorant, just look at you. Tatted up like a damn stripper. We are not the same. I model."

Monae walks forward, clapping. "You ain't saying nothin' bitch *I* model!"

"Model what? Halloween costumes?"

I escort Riley out. I walk her toward the back office of this rented club for her to cool down, but halfway there, I realize that I'd left my phone on the kitchen counter, so I double back.

As I'm closing in on the kitchen, I see, through the round window of the stainless steel kitchen door, Keenan and Monae embraced and kissing. My legs nearly give out. I start gasping with a hand pressed to my sternum. It looks like a first kiss, though, how they stop and smile with such wonder in their eyes.

I about-face and march away, leaving my phone, knowing Fletcher will accuse me of ignoring his texts after allegedly flirting with Jalen.

I return to the back office with Riley, then I plop down in a rollie chair and rest my head in my hands. Riley blows off steam while refreshing her makeup in a handheld mirror. "I don't know how y'all put up with that Monae." Riley puckers her red lips in the mirror adding, "Y'all got an ex-stripper answering the phones? She's just so ghetto and aggressive."

Riley's venting to me and I can't vent back because my relationship with Fletcher is a secret. Nor can I vent about Keenan and Monae because Monae's penis is also a secret. Then it dawns on me, "You're calling Monae aggressive? Didn't you tackle her for a champagne bucket?"

"Look at her and look at me," Riley says. "You don't have someone like her deliver bottles to a star like Jalen."

"Looks like you did more than deliver champagne. You were cheesing all in his face," I say. "Aren't you engaged?"

"Well…" Riley stops short as if reminded that she has a whole wedding date on the calendar. "Gideon doesn't want a wife; he wants a pet dog." At the time, I had no way of knowing that her statement was to be taken literally. Riley starts tearing up.

I sit Riley down in my chair and grab another for myself. "Wanna talk about it?"

Riley wipes her tears and says, "I put on like I have this perfect little life, but it's far from it. Gideon is an insufferable man. The wedding is just damage control, so he won't lose his sneaker deal."

"Don't waste anymore of your time or his, Riley," I say. "Leave him."

Riley looks at me as if she'd never heard such foolishness in her life. "Leave him and do what? Model? You know as well as I do, that modeling is all glamour and no money. What do you suggest I do, go back home and live with my folks? I have a lifestyle, Tahj…" Riley sighs. "A woman like me needs a plan B."

"For a woman like you, plan B is another man, I'm sure."

Riley cranes back, frowning, "What… am I supposed to be ashamed?"

"Is that why you're here? Looking for the next rich athlete? I see you loving the attention."

"You're not helping, Tahj." Riley gets up and paces away.

"I am trying to *help* you see that you're better than that."

"I am a woman of leisure, Tahj. I'm not like you. And quite frankly, I don't have a Bubby in my corner to put me in a position of wealth."

"Wealth? What wealth?"

"I know how much agents make. Gideon's agent's richer than him. Just tonight, between you, Fletcher, and Keenan, you've recruited, what, forty athletes?"

"We can't get athletes drunk and sign them in a club, Riley. This is first contact. We still gotta meet their folks."

Without a deep breath or contemplative pause, Riley fires, "So, what's up with you and Fletcher?"

The question bristles my neck-hairs. "What *about* me and Fletcher?"

Riley unloads, "I know you two had a thing, but it never really materialized, and now I'm just kinda wondering if any of those old feelings resurfaced since you see each other every day, now that you're business partners."

"Which is precisely why we can't go there."

"So you can't date him even if you wanted to?" Riley stops and smirks. "You mean to tell me, you never tried it out? Aren't you curious…?"

I cross my legs. "Curious about what?"

Riley, with a slow look-away, says, "I heard, the dick is stupendous."

There's no denying now that Riley wants him. I could risk it all and tell Riley that Fletcher and I are engaged to be married, but on second thought, Riley can't be trusted. She's your friend until you have something she wants; she could sabotage me by exposing

Fletcher and me to Keenan. "Stupendous? That's the word you use?"

"Lie to me and say you never thought about it."

"Fletcher has someone," I say.

Riley leans back, eyeing me. "Maybe that's what he tells you. Fletcher told *me* he was single, but celibate."

"I don't know why he would say that," I reply. "But believe me when I say, Riley, that Fletcher doesn't want *you.*"

Riley's face is a batch of riddles. "Tahj. Your experience of Fletcher is totally different from my experience of him. He doesn't even tell you everything."

"Or maybe he lied to you about being celibate."

"If so, let's look at the lies, then. If he's telling you he's in a relationship, it closes the door for you. If he's telling me he's single – celibate or not – it's a lie that opens the door for me."

My hand tomahawks forward. "Let me stop you right there–"

Riley rockets out of her seat. "No, let me stop *you* right there okay, Tahj! I'm tired of tap dancing around your little infatuation with Fletcher!"

"Infatuation," I parrot, as I rise from my chair.

"When Fletcher was in the NFL, every time his teams played in Phoenix, he came to see me! I'll bet you didn't know that!"

It hit me like a hammer. Riley, just as stunned by the fact that she'd said it, trots for the door, fleeing the shame of her own betrayal. I suddenly can't catch my breath, and I'm woozy, reaching back, and feeling for my chair like a pregnant woman lowering into a seat.

Riley looks back from the doorway. "I love you, Tahj, but at the same time, you're childish when it comes to Fletcher. For one, you can't date him because you're business partners. Number two: you've got Jalen friggin Hurts cheesing in your face all night. You're gonna be alright, silly."

It's not so much Riley telling me, in so many words, that she's coming after my man; it's finding out what Fletcher had been hiding. All this time he'd been keeping the door open for Riley, then paid for her cross-country flight with my fucking money!

Once I recover, I stamp out of the office and through the club, swimming through bodies like a shark out for blood. I burst through the kitchen's double doors and swipe my phone. I browse his messages. He accused me of playing with him. In a later text, he says, Two can play at that game.

I come out of the kitchen like a locomotive, phone in hand, hunting Fletcher, to jack him up if I find him cheesing with some chick in an attempt to make me jealous.

I run into Josh, who has some friends with him saying they're all interested in making me their agent. I can't just walk away from that. I calm my spirit and enter their phone numbers in my contact list.

I resume the hunt. I spot Bubby and then ask if he's seen Fletcher.

"I just left him out back." Bubby leads me through the club. I follow him, knowing good and well I couldn't unload on Fletcher in Bubby's presence.

We go out the back door near the dumpster, but Fletcher's gone. Bubby points to an upside-down bucket. "He was sitting right there." I turn to leave, but Bubby stops me. "But look. Lemme holla at you for a sec Tahj."

I sit down on the bucket, figuring I should calm down anyway. I'm so upset the cold doesn't even affect me.

"Lotta shit going on," Bubby says.

"Like what," I ask.

"But first, tell me what happened witchya boy, though."

"Fuck Fletcher," I say.

"Wait, what? I mean Jalen. Why you brush him off?"

"Oh that," I sigh. "I'm here to work. I can't spend all night chatting with him."

"Spend the night chatting with him, you may end up not having to work *ever*."

I suck my teeth. "This is what you wanted to talk about?"

Bubby takes a sip from his cup. "I'm fuckin' up, man. I'm talking about my marriage. Em moved back to Iowa."

"What! Why?"

"I screamed at her." He periscopes to me. "Just one time. Now she wanna act like I'm a fuckin' monster… Said she needs space."

"She doesn't want space," I declare. "She's testing your resolve. If you fought hard enough, she would've stayed."

He paces away, head shaking. "She took my baby, man. That's all I'm living for, right now."

"You said it was only one time, right? One time isn't gonna make her forget that you're a good man," I say, ready to be done with it and resume my hunt for Fletcher.

"Am I? I'm a good friend. That shit don't translate to being a good husband. You know I got mommy issues."

"Don't get down on yourself. For one, you're a good provider–"

"–She seems to want me to provide from a distance, alimony… child support. All she needed was a reason. Now, she's milking that one incident for all its worth. There's no talking to her. Before marriage, Em never judged me; now she looks at me like a prejudiced white person would look at me: as a threat. This is who's raising my kids."

I let his comment breathe for a moment and say, "You're closer to the situation than I am, so if you see it that way, I can't dismiss it. But do you think just maybe, now almost three years into the relationship, she's had time to see some things that gives her reason to doubt you?"

"Ever since the baby came she been–"

"–I was just about to say postpartum."

With a head jerk, Bubby says, "You can't tell me about no postpartum, bro. My momma had four kids and did it all by herself."

"And that's the problem. You're bothered because Emily can't endure what your mother did?"

"Em is weak. Let's call it what it is."

"Do you hear yourself, Bubby? If you don't step it up for Emily, how are you any different from the men who didn't step up for your mother?"

Bubby's drink hits the asphalt and he grabs his head with both hands. "Damn Tahj. You ain't had to tell me about my ass like *that*."

I scrub circles on his back. "I could be wrong, but–"

"–No, you're right. Because when you said that shit, it hit me in my chest. And I ain't never seen myself in that way, but it's true."

I try to leave Bubby with something to think about. "You say your lil man is all you're living for, right? Then you would do anything get him back right?"

"Anything."

"How about counseling, just for yourself? Then you come to Em with the receipts – not just talk. Women, across the board, respect action."

"Bet," he says.

"You can cry if you want to. You're safe with me," I say.

Bubby cuts his eyes at me as if I'm ridiculous.

Just then, the girl in the sheer bodysuit with censor dots over the nipples walks by, on her way to her car. "Bitch," she says in passing.

I yell, "Ya *momma's* a bitch." And that's the end of it.

Bubby grins. "What's that about?"

"I had a run-in with her earlier. The bitch said I look like Draymond Green in the face."

Bubby nearly falls forward, snorting with laughter, and apologizing. "Nah, you caught me off guard," he explains.

I observe with hands on hips. "Oh it's *that* funny, is it?"

Bubby recovers and says, "Don't let the haters get to you, Tahj. You're beautiful. Anybody can see that. And if they can't see it, that's their problem."

I feel my face registering this eerie familiarity. "Funny how everyone says it like you just said it, as if you're all reading from the same script."

Bubby bites down on denial like a mouthguard. "Don't play me like that. You that chick, Tahj. You even got the test to prove it."

"Everyone doesn't see what I see in the mirror – at least not right away. I know why my relationships start out as friendships. My looks tend to grow on people. But walking through a club like this, though, the shock, the instant rejection… That's why I don't do clubs."

Bubby, being a friend cheering up another friend, says, "Your looks didn't have to grow on Jalen. He saw it on site, just as I did when *I* first saw you back in the day."

"Stop lyin, Bubby." My lips twist in ridicule.

Bubby shuffles to face me. "What reason I got to lie to you?"

I do nothing but stare at him.

"Okay, I'm lying," Bubby sighs.

"Obviously," I say. "We know you're color-struck."

"I got a preference. Get it right."

"They *all* call it a preference, Bubby."

"A'ight," Bubby relents. "Actually, this is something I thought about for a long time. It's like this: the way I see it…" He squints and says, "When a chick is like, dark, it looks, to me, like their exposure is inverted. Like the negative of a photo."

"Eye-opening," I say, my eyes wide as proof.

"That's just how I see it. How is that my fault?"

"No one's blaming you. I never heard that before, so thank you; it explains a lot."

"I used to think people would go out of their way to call you pretty just to make you feel good. I see your beauty now, though. I may never see it like Jalen sees it, but you pretty to me, *real* pretty – add to that, you're soft and feminine and smelling good all the time… you're cool as fuck; a woman I can trip with, talk football with… A woman who could speak life to my mutha fucking soul – like you did a minute ago – and like you've done for so many years." Bubby's head shakes. "Baby that takes you from pretty to gorgeous."

I nudge him. "Thanks, big bro. But you gotta chill with that, a'ight? I ain't come out here to get all teary-eyed," I say with a side hug. "Fun chatting, but I gotta get back to work."

We go inside and separate into the crowd. I navigate aimlessly through the club, not even looking for Fletcher anymore, but looking at everyone; looking at how they look at me, wishing I never asked Bubby's color-struck behind that question.

I always figured that when men look at me they see beauty, but some reject it, like a woman might pass over a pretty bag, for an ugly one because it has a designer label. Earlier when I had walked through the club on Jalen Hurts' arm, I was convinced that people saw me differently because his status became my designer label, so to speak. This "designer" theory was the only way I could explain how sometimes a guy would walk past me, on their way to court a light-skinned chick with far-apart eyes and big gums.

After talking to Bubby, I'm feeling self-conscious for the first time in who knows how long. Bro said I looked like the negative of a photo, and I can't get over it. I'm shouldering my way through a packed club looking people dead in the face, wondering if this one – or that one – also sees me as some apparition of inverted light. But that's not visual; it's psychological, isn't it? Has to be, I'm thinking. Either way, they got me fucked up. I am literally the most beautiful woman in the world, but a light-skinned bottle girl who seems to have a touch of Down Syndrome in the face, is their chosen one?

It doesn't help matters that when I spot Fletcher, in a circle with the guys, he has his arm around Riley. The way Fletcher looks at me reminds me of his text saying two can play at that game.

CHAPTER 18
NOT BALLS

I approach Fletcher as calmly as I can. I fold my arms so my right hand won't get away from me and slap the hell outta Riley. "Can I talk to you for a minute?" I don't even raise my voice above the music, but Fletcher reads my lips just fine.

I about-face then walk. Fletcher tells the guys and Riley that he'll be right back."

I open the office door. As Fletcher enters, I slam the door so fast, I clip his hand. He's wide-eyed, rubbing his knuckles when I get in his chest and say, "You've been playing in my fucking face all these years!"

"What? All what years?"

I'm hands on hips weaving with my words. "Were you ever gonna tell me?"

"Tell you what!"

"Every time your team traveled to Phoenix you saw Riley." I palm his chest. "The same yellow *bitch* you just had your arm around. The bitch you flew out on *my* dime!"

"If Brit never canceled, Riley wouldn't be here now. Don't act like you don't know that. And when did you become the type of woman who's pressed about another bitch?"

"Another?" I reset my stance like I'm about to go up-side his head.

"You' trippin'," Fletcher says, behind a pointed finger.

I slap his hand and point my own in its place. "Were you seeing her? Yes or no!"

Fletcher backs away calmly but with a warning in his eyes. "Ay look, you got one more time to put your hands on me."

I clap in frustration. "Answer me!"

"You act like having lunch with a friend is a crime?"

"*You* thought it was a crime, obviously, if it's a secret!"

"Bet I wasn't cheesing in her face like you was with Jalen."

My head tilts calmly, but I imagine my eyes are fixed like a crazy woman's. "Oh, that's your angle? How about, I'm sorry Tahj. I fucked up, Tahj."

Fletcher straightens up tall just to look down at me through the slits of his eyes. "I didn't tell you about Riley because I knew you couldn't take it."

I draw back, frowning. "How do you figure?"

Fletcher pockets his hands and says, "You're bitter towards her."

"Bitter!"

"You don't think she would be where she is today if she wasn't light-complected. You don't give her no credit," Fletcher says, while looking everywhere but at me. "She's a good woman. A good, Christian woman who only wants what's best for me, and here's the thing: she wants what's best for me, but it's not because she wants me." Before I could show Fletcher just how clueless he is, he adds, "But I'll tell you one muh-fuckin thing: I better not catch you up in Jalen's face again tonight… Tahj, I will fold that lil nigga up like a wallet, and they gone take me away in handcuffs. Baby, I'm tellin' you," he says with fast-blinking eyes and a frowned mouth.

I've seen him like this before… summer break, sophomore year… choke-slammed a drunken heckler from a rival college.

I have to be careful because I know I got a mouth, and I don't want him to get out of control to where I can't even talk to him —

because I need answers. Calmly, I say, "Let me play your game," I say. "Because you think I have a problem with Riley because she is – as you say – light-complected," I mock. "Maybe you're triggered by Jalen for the same reason you're triggered by Jay. *You*, sir, have an issue with rich niggas. You' big as a damn wrestler, but they make you feel small."

"Girl, you out yo damn mind!"

"What is it then?"

Fletcher brims with anger, his chest all swole, his eyes crossed with rage like the character Deebo in this old movie, Friday, that my dad has watched a thousand times to date. Fletcher yanks up a chair and hurls it, screaming, "Rah!"

I scream. The chair is thrown with such force that it crunches against the wall. Fletcher takes hold of my upper arms, his lips talking over a fence of clenched teeth. "I ain't worried 'bout no nigga! But I'll tell you one thing: I don't play about what's *mines!*"

The horror and tears filling my eyes makes Fletcher aware of himself. He unhands me but the damage is done. "Baby. I'm sorry babe," he pleads.

Tears jet down my cheeks and I'm squealing like a popped raft. He's all over me, trying to help me into a seat. "No, no, no, no, baby. Come here, baby." He's like a big kid rushing to clean up his mess before he gets a whooping.

He hugs me and I wriggle away, yelling, "You don't *touch* me!" He truly gave me a scare and my tears are real, but at the same time, I should be ashamed of how bad I put on. There was never a moment where I felt he would do more than what he did, but there I was, giving distraught victim; giving white girl tears and everything. "You want me to be your little punching bag? Is that what you want?!" I get up and head towards the door. "Let me get the hell away from you."

"No, let *me* get away." He takes a long step towards the door, his feet coming together in a soldiers ten-hut. "See?" His smile screams desperation. "*I'll* go. You stay. Can I get you something baby? Want some champagne?"

I wipe an eye with the heel of my hand, my head shaking yes. Fletcher slips out and closes the door.

The anger he displayed was appalling, but I must admit: the guilt he felt, and the way he scrambled to make it up to me was kinda adorable, come to think. I review the argument in my head, thinking about the part we never got back to, where Fletcher said, in so many words, that Riley makes me insecure or that I'm jealous of her. I hope that's not what I'm giving off, whenever I call out her bullshit. Jealous of Riley? No one can ever take what's mine; they can only show me that it wasn't mine to begin with, and make way for what God truly wants for me.

Fletcher returns with a champagne bottle and glass. His pouring hand trembles like he's diffusing a bomb. "I'm gone say only this: I was so mad, I didn't know what I was doing, babe. And I'm sorry, but you wadn't no victim when you slapped my hand and pushed me in my chest… the way you goaded me? Calling me small? This might be a red flag moment for you, but it's one for me too."

I glare and say, "Whatever."

He walks away, but as soon as he touches the door handle, he stops and says, "By the way, I ran into Isaiah Wynn." Isaiah Wynn is a veteran Tight End for the Atlanta Falcons. "He said he was looking for a new agent. Looks like it's gonna be me." Fletcher waits for my reaction, then says, "You don't know what that means?"

I sigh and say, "Enlighten me please."

"He's already in the league. We don't have to wait for the draft. I could get him signed as early as tomorrow, and the commissions alone could buy you out and we can get married."

I nod.

Fletcher turns to leave but I call him back. "Fletcher?" He turns, seemingly with the hope of an apology from my lips. Lips that I twist in rebellion. "I saw Keenan and Mo kissing."

"Fuck," he says and then backs out of the room with his head shaking.

I was prepared to sit in this back office and sulk, but the acquisition of Isaiah Wynn and the possibility of being married soon, changes my mood. I could be Mrs. Lewis, and I'd have the freedom to focus on my calling, which is not sports agency; it's fashion.

I go from blaming Fletcher to now blaming our situation. Because when you think about it, all of our problems stem from our relationship having to be secret. Bubby would not have tried to hook me up with Jalen, nor would Riley be standing in my face telling me she'd heard that Fletcher's dick game is stupendous. And my future husband would never have gripped my arms like he did because the frustration that drove him to it, wouldn't exist.

I gaze into the future, a smile spreading across my face when a call comes in. I answer, "What's up, Jay? Kinda late to be calling, ain't it?"

Jay sniffles and sighs. Crying? "Sarah's dying," he says.

"What? What do you mean, dying? What happened?"

"It's an aggressive cancer. It has hopscotched through her family for generations. She heard about some genetic testing and went to see if she was susceptible. Lo and behold, she already had it. Next thing you know, she's too weak to get out of bed and her son and daughter are now taking her back to her hometown to die."

All along I'm saying how sorry I am, but also hearing just how futile my words must sound to him. I'm so sorry for Sarah; I recall the last time we talked, and I find a clue there. "I think she already knew," I say. Jay goes quiet, and although it's over the phone, I feel like I can see his face, the way his confusion registers in a stern gaze. I say, "The last time I talked to Sarah, I told her you said you wanted to marry her, and she looked like she'd seen a ghost."

Jay sobs, "That explains it." He pulls himself together and says, "When I had asked her to marry me, she said no. Maybe she didn't want me to bear the burden of caring for her in her last days…"

I sit in the office, talking to Jay for another hour. Fletcher had checked on me once, and I covered the phone to respond to him. If he knew I was talking to Jay, I wonder if he would've gripped my arms again.

It's closing time. Time to clear everybody out, have staff clean up, and get off the clock, or Fletcher pays a higher rental fee. The place looks like a concert after the headliner's final set. The lights are brought up, security ushers people towards the exits, and bartenders are busy wiping down the bar. Fletcher's going around directing it all. The club is half empty, stragglers still hunting for someone to take home, while finishing their last-call drinks. Music still plays, but at half volume, which is why I'm able to hear a sharp *bitch* coming from the VIP section upstairs. Monae and Riley are at it again.

I hurry towards them. Keenan blows past me, full sprint, scaling the VIP staircase three steps at a time. By the time I'm upstairs, Keenan is behind Monae holding her back. The skirmish has calmed down without a punch having landed, but apparently, what had set it off in the first place, is Riley had spit in Monae's face.

They're now separated and throwing insults instead of hands.

"Try it again," Monae dares. "I promise you, I will ball your mouf up in my hand."

Riley sneaks around Bubby and dashes a full glass of champagne that misses Monae and splashes Keenan. He covers his face and howls, "My eyes!"

Keenan, however, couldn't cover his eyes without letting go of Monae, who promptly charges Riley. Riley tries to hide behind Bubby, but Bubby steps back with his hands up, taunting, "Wanna throw drinks, huh?" When Monae has Riley's mouth balled up in her fist, as promised, Bubby teases, "That's what the fuck you get."

Monae uses the grip on Riley's mouth to drive her back and butt her head against the wall while talking to the beat. "You threw that drink in *my - man's - face… huh - bitch?!*"

Out of nowhere, Fletcher lunges through and pulls Monae off of Riley. He then passes Monae on to Bubby, saying, "Take her downstairs, bro."

Fletcher sits on the couch and tends to Riley, who's crying and has lipstick smeared around her mouth like clown paint. She doesn't even try to get up; clearly wanting no parts of Monae, so Fletcher feels it's safe to leave Riley and come help Jalen and me with Keenan, whose eyes are still stinging.

I'm helping Keenan hold his head back while Jalen tries to flush his eyes out by pouring from a bottled water. Keenan shouts, "It's not workin' yall!"

Riley locates a stack of bar napkins and comes towards us, apologizing to Keenan.

Behind us, Bubby has finally convinced Monae to go with him downstairs.

I thought it was funny how, while Riley's doing all this crying and apologizing to Keenan, she keeps cutting her eyes toward Bubby and Monae who are now at the top of the steps.

Before I know it, Riley takes off.

I yell, "Monae, look out!"

Moane turns with wide eyes, at the exact moment that Riley's foot digs into her bubble butt. Monae goes sliding on her back. I scream, "What the fuck, Riley!"

Bubby snatches her by the armpits. "What did you do!"

Riley cries, "It was an accident!"

Fletcher yells, "Don't nobody call the police or I get charged extra!" I look at him like he's stupid. I wouldn't mind seeing Riley taken away in cuffs after what she did.

We're having this exchange as if Monae is not sliding downstairs on her back, her head going rat-tat-tat down every stairstep.

When Monae finally stops at the bottom, she's motionless. We go downstairs in such a rush, we nearly suffer the same fate as a group. Bubby stumbles out front. He puts a hand over her nose. "She breathing."

I overhear Riley who's on the phone. *We need an ambulance. A young lady has slipped and fell down the stairs. And she's not moving…*

Bubby tries to sit Monae up. I yell, "Don't!" I kneel next to Monae, explaining, as if I am the paramedic I once saw on TV, "Don't lift her. There's possibly bleeding on the brain."

Monae's skirt is scrunched up, her panties showing. I thought about pulling Monae's skirt down to cover her, but I let it be, as a form of dry-snitching; this way Keenan could find out without us getting sued.

Lo and behold, Keenan tries to cover his girlfriend by straightening her skirt, but he stops. "Wait, what?" He rubs his tender eyes and stretches them as if he doesn't believe what he sees. A fresh look confirms. "Awwwww hell naw!"

Bubby peeks too. His head shakes to his singing caption, "Not *balls.*"

I pull Monae's skirt and chastise, "Show some respect."

Keenan, again, hollers in agony, "Awww *heeell* naw!"

Bubby scratches his head as he puts two and two together. "Wait… upstairs… didn't shawty say you was her man?"

Keenan lunges. "I'll kill the bitch!" Bubby tries to hold Keenan back, but can't do it without the help of Jalen and Fletcher. Keenan's eyes, red from the sting of wine, makes him look demon-possessed; furthermore, the strength he shows against three full-grown athletes, makes me wonder if only a priest and holy water would calm him down.

Monae comes-to. She lifts her head, her eyes finding the commotion.

I say, "You were out for a while there."

Monae spots Keenan being held back and her cheek torques with embarrassment. "He saw, ain't it," Monae asks, as if Keenan isn't being held back like a bulldog, barking out every homophobic slur in the book.

"Ya think?"

"Next order of business," Monae says, with a raised finger. "Where that bitch, Riley?"

Just then everyone looks around; Riley's nowhere in sight. Monae hops up. I try to stop her but she shakes me off. "You wanna sneak a bitch? huh? Let's go head up!" She goes around the entire club, disappearing to the back to check every closet and bathroom stall.

With Monae out of sight, Keenan now sits at a table without having to be detained, but he's crying like a baby. When his big head rears back, the back of his neck bulges like baby fat, as he hollers in despair.

Bubby and Fletcher try to console him but at the same time, they can't figure out why Keenan is so distraught. I clarify, "I saw them kissing earlier."

Fletcher, as if he's hearing this for the first time, says, "Damn… It's not that bad, bro. It was just a kiss, right?"

Keenan pauses, looks at Fletcher then cries harder.

Bubby rubs his chin. "She said Kee was her man, dawg. Had to been more than a kiss." Bubby nudges Keenan. "He give you head? Huh, Kee? Lil bro give you top?"

I yell, "Stop this, Bubby! You play entirely too much!" So does Fletcher, who walks away stiff, holding his laughter. I tell Keenan, "Don't pay Bubby no attention Kee. He drunk."

Bubby fights a smile when he says, "*Had* to been just head. Balls right there, bro, how you miss it?"

Keenan bangs the table. "It was dark!"

We all faint, in spirit. Physically, we're a wax museum, frozen in the horror of hearing Keenan's confirmation.

Jalen unfreezes first. "I'm out," he says and walks away stiff as if propelled by a windup key at his back.

Keenan explains that before tonight he hadn't gotten anything more than hugs and half-nude pics. He mentions the kiss in the kitchen; he says Monae declined his offer to spend the night, citing, *that time of the month.* Keenan adds, "Later on, she pulled me into the pantry with the lights off. And then she–"

"*–He,*" Bubby corrects. "*He!*"

Keenan turns on him. "I'll knock your got damn head off, Bubby! Keep playing with me!"

Bubby backs away with palms up. "C'mon cousin…" Bubby taps his chest with a fist. "We family – and that's bigger than you being gay, a'ight?"

The only thing that could've stopped Keenan from jumping fresh on Bubby's ass, happens. Monae returns, after ending her search for Riley.

All eyes are on Keenan and Bubby, so we hear Monae before we see her. "Kee? I just wanna say I'm sorry."

Suddenly, Bubby, who Keenan just threatened, has to join Fletcher in holding Keenan back. I jump in front of Monae, pushing her back and telling her to chill.

Keenan yells, under the strain of bullrushing two men, "I want all my money back too!"

Monae bats her lashes in sass. "It was not a loan, my Teddy Bear. It was a gift."

"Stop it Monae," I say. "Just go!"

Keenan starts hurling gay slurs again.

It seems whatever hope Monae had of salvaging the relationship dissipates while hearing the insults, which she avenges by taunting him. Monae turns around, puts a curve in her back, and starts wiggling her stuffed booty. "You want your money back, Kee? Wasn't it worth it?"

Kee, like the athlete who got a scholarship for his power running style, starts driving Bubby and Fletcher back. Monae, fearing he'd break free, takes off trotting and teasing.

Just then Riley runs in, her phone waving. "Clear the way for the gurney!" Riley obviously thinks Monae is still lying unconscious at the bottom of the stairs, and doesn't realize that she and Monae are running toward each other – that is – until Monae snatches Riley by the throat and draws a fist. Riley shuts her eyes and pleads, "Don't hit me! I'm the one who called the ambulance!"

Monae's drawn fist fails to launch. "Ambulance, you say?" It's all Monae needed to hear. She unhands Riley and withers to the floor, saying, "Girl I'm too hurt to fight."

Paramedics roll the gurney in. Red lights strobe outside. Monae lay out on the floor, writhing in mach pain. "My neck! My back! Oh my God, I'm seeing double!"

We approach the EMTs, snitching on Monae, how she'd just run laps around the club in search of Riley; how she'd been twerking and jacked Riley up, just seconds ago.

The EMTs seem apprehensive. They start asking questions. Monae lays her *self* on the gurney and folds her arms over her chest as if she's in a coffin, wailing in agony. The EMTs relent and say that they have to take Monae in. "…As a precaution," they say.

CHAPTER 19
YOU'VE BEEN SERVED

I keep going back and forth about the night before. One minute I'm happy about the possibility of marriage. The next minute, I'm disillusioned by Fletcher's jealousy and anger. They say a man's first heartbreak becomes the window in which he sees every subsequent relationship, so perhaps Fletcher's jealousy is his fear that I'd betray him like Gigi. He denies this, of course.

We pull up to the office together, which is a risk. It's midday; we'd all taken the first half of the day off to recover from last night's party, but the only thing we'd replenished was sleep; I'm still upset. Although I slept in Fletcher's arms, this morning when he returned from running errands, we had a rerun of last night's argument.

Now we sit in Fletcher's car in the parking garage, dressed down for the half day. It's a warm day for the brand new winter, so I'm in camo print pants and a U neck tank top. Fletcher's arms bulge in a beige knit shirt, and he's looking so sexy in his ballcap, his mustache and beard sharp around the lips he licks occasionally while petitioning for my love.

"Like we already said: our issues stem from the fact that our relationship has to be secret."

I could very well say that, him lying about Riley had nothing to do with that, but I'm ready to let him win just so I can kiss his lips and be up under him later this evening.

Fletcher says, "Do you know where I went this morning?" My silent treatment is so thorough, I don't even let out a what. Fletcher reaches into the glove compartment, pulls out a bank envelope and sets it on my lap. "That's everything: my deposit plus everything I made from the party last night. It's everything you gave me, plus some."

My frown loses its battle with a smile. I card through the bills while Fletcher gazes ahead and says, "I believe we fell in love the day we met. How do you let one screw-up convince you that we've been wrong for all these years?"

He glances over and catches me gazing at his mouth. "Girl if you don't stop playing with me…" Our lips meet in the middle, above the console. It's no ordinary kiss. It is free of the debt that has been stuck in the back of my mind for months. It's intense with desire, how the lips press and tug, the roaming hands, the tension of wanting to escalate to more, despite the danger of being seen. "We gotta chill, baby," Fletcher says. "Keenan can pull up at any time." He kisses me again for good measure. "Luh you, girl."

I spread the money in my hands like a fan. "I wanna treat you tonight," I say. "Let's go somewhere fancy, maybe go out dancing…"

"We still gotta be careful, for now. I just gotta find Isaiah Wynn a team and all this hiding shit's gonna be a thing of the past."

We lock lips again, but stop as soon as we see a car coming. It's not Keenan. We sigh relief. We watch the car come up the ramp and turn, the shine of ceiling lights crawling over the vehicle as it passes in front of us, carrying our eyes across our car hood, right to left, where we discover Keenan standing there, watching us like a stalker in a slasher movie. He doesn't have a machete, but a cell phone aimed at us. My heart drops in my belly. We have no idea how long he's been there or how much he's seen.

Fletcher gets out. "Whassup big dawg. You good?"

"I'm good," Keenan says. He dips to look at me through the open car door. "Tahj… *You* good?" I nod. Facetiously, Keenan says, "I guess everybody good, then."

I get out of the car and we head toward the entrance; Fletcher and I in our casual attire, for the half-day, and Keenan in a suit; he's all business. Fletcher and I can feel the question coming, but Keenan doesn't ask until we unlock the office and go in.

He's at his desk composing an email when he lifts his head to say, "Since when did you two start carpooling?"

"Only today," I say. "I had to drop my car off at the dealer for a recall."

Keenan smirks. "I'm tired of pretending like yall not fucking – because who yall *really* fuckin' is me."

"Don't trip, Kee," says Fletcher. "You know you just mad about last night."

"Not just mad nigga, I'm livid. When I got home, and was washing the skin off my dick, it occurred to me, *Tahj*, that you had to know. You're Monae's agent."

"That doesn't mean I ever looked under her clothes."

"I found a picture of Monae modeling on a site for trans lingerie, lace panties with a hole for the ding-a-ling. You didn't know about that gig?"

Fletcher feels me ready to admit, so he jumps in. "Tahj has her modeling women's clothes. That's it. She don't know about nothing else. But look, Keenan. Even if Tahj knew, she couldn't tell you anyway, or Monae could sue us."

Keenan leans back and interlocks his fingers in resistance to anything we have to say. "We'll revisit this later."

"Good. Because we got work to do," Fletcher says, as he drops a folder on the desk. "I printed out a spreadsheet. These are the athletes that Tahj and me got an expressed interest from. I wanna get everybody on one list, put them in the scheduling system so we don't overlap, then we can try to seal as many deals as we can. Gimme your list, Kee."

"My *list*…" Kee's brow raises over lazy eyes. "What list?"

Fletcher studies Keenan with about as much regard as he'd give a daub of doo-doo. "Bruh, you mean to tell me you was out there shucking and jiving with all those athletes and ain't get no contacts?"

I huff and say, "He's not even trying."

"That's not my role." Keenan sets five fingertips on the desktop. "I'm the one who has the dual degree in business and sports management. I oversee everything."

I'm hot, at this point. "Oversee! What have you done?!"

Fletcher faces me and tries to calm me down. "The man's going through something right now."

I yell, "*I'm* going through something if we're doing all the work, so he can get paid twice as much as us, just because he's Bubby's cousin."

Keenan stands up and straightens his suit. "I just got an email back from security. Since you wanna act like that, I'm gonna go down there and request surveillance from the parking garage. What would I see?"

"Nothing," I shout.

He grows a smirk. "You sure yall wasn't kissing?"

I say, "Don't mistake me for you and Monae."

Fletcher palms his face. "C'mon, Tahj, that was low."

I peek out from around Fletcher's wide body and say to Keenan, "What's low, is Keenan trying to cut his own friends out of millions… gay ass."

Keenan points and says, "Fletcher, control ya bitch."

The word bitch pops like a gunshot. Never in anger has one of the bros called me that. Fletcher dares, "*Say* it again! I'll knock your ass clean the-fuck out, Kee. I know you going through some shit right now, but don't try me."

Keenan straightens his suit and says, "I'm about to go downstairs to security. They say without some sort of subpoena, it'll take three business days for them to get the video off the server. So, in these next three days, you two can figure out which one of you is gonna step down."

I flex my claws and pace away, fuming.

As Keenan reaches the door, it opens toward him. A slim white guy in a comb-over and polo shirt says, "Keenan S. Turner?"

"That's me."

"You've been served." He hands Kee a letter and splits.

A baffled Keenan says, "What? This gotta be a mistake." Keenan shuffles back inside, looking the letter over. "How this bitch got a lawyer already? She done racked up a hospital bill of damn near twenty thousand dollars just last night?" He reads a portion aloud. "Requesting immediate payment and subsequent compensation for ongoing care and rehabilitation… until which time pain and suffering can be determined…" Keenan looks up with a grin and says, "I'm about to let this lawyer know they need to be suing you, Fletcher. She got injured at *your* party."

Fletcher's head hangs in defeat.

I say, "But Riley is the one who did it."

Keenan's head shakes. "Doesn't matter. It was in the workplace, done by someone Fletcher employed. Fletch? Did you get insurance to cover this type of thing? *Nope*," Keenan taunts.

Fletcher catches a dizzy spell. He wobbles over to a seat. I say, "Leave him alone, Kee."

Keenan chuckles. "Yeah… thought you was smart huh… started your own business to keep all the profit for yourself, huh…Ya can't make this stuff up!" Keenan laughs all the way down the hall, on his way to security.

Fletcher doubles over, complaining that his head hurts. I fan him with a manila folder. "We're gonna be alright," I say.

"Monae wasn't even thinking about playing hurt until she saw the ambulance. I told y'all not to call no police… meaning no ambulance… no nothing."

The same manilla folder I'd been fanning him with, is what I use to bat him in the side of the head. "Who y'all? Riley called the ambulance."

"After you said Monae was bleeding on the brain, like you' some doctor," Fletcher pouts.

I place my hands on my hips to say, "You should be the last one to take a head injury lightly, with all them concussions you had."

The cut, in Fletchers eyes, should've sliced me in two. I watch him take the hit and forgive my ignorance. I didn't know the issue of his concussions to be a sore spot. "Don't talk to me, Tahj," he says. He just vents to himself. "I get hit with this bill, as soon as things start working in our favor?"

"I'm gonna talk to Bubby," I say.

"I'm not about to ask Bubby for no money."

"This is bigger than your pride, Fletcher. This lawsuit is basically the death of our wedding."

Fletcher folds his arms and reasserts, "I ain't asking Bubby for no money."

I make praying hands, praying to keep from slapping him when I say, "So, where's all this pride when you ask *me* for money?"

Fletcher staches the manilla folder. "I paid you back didn't I?" He begins fanning himself with the folder. "How am I supposed to pay this hospital bill when I gave all the money to you?"

I look away as if he's Madusa. Because there ain't no way in hell I'm giving up the money that he just paid me back.

BOOK V

CHAPTER 20

APRIL 2023: BELIEVING IS SEEING

A vein thumps at Gideon's temple and his eyes fill red as he watches the video on his agent's phone. Athletes get unknowingly recorded all the time. Since Jalen Hurts is captured in the clip, it racks up millions of views over a couple of months before it found its way to a Nike marketing executive.

Gary Goldman says, "We'd just renewed the sneaker deal. That was the pathway to getting your other endorsements back." Gary writes a figure on a memo pad and slides it across the table to Gideon, saying, "This is how much your bitch cost you."

At home, Gideon's temple vein is still there when he enters his kitchen. Riley pulls a ceramic casserole dish out of the oven. "I made Chicken Cacciatore, you're favorite." She inhales the fumes. "Smells good, doesn't it?"

Gideon just stands there watching her, remembering how seeing Riley in the kitchen with that beautiful long hair and red lip-sticked smile would make him feel like everything was right with the world. The fact that the meal wouldn't taste worth a damn, is beside the point. After seeing that video, Gideon feels differently about Riley. Feeling different, makes Riley look different.

Riley approaches her fiancé and asks, "Are you okay?"

The blind belief that she's pure, soft, feminine, and civilized always made him see it. Gideon was always leery, though, because Riley had her beginnings in da hood, and a wild animal is never truly tamed. It's hard to believe that the same woman happily making him dinner like a dutiful homemaker, is the same woman parading herself in a black club, in a tight dress.

Riley removes her oven mitts one hand at a time. "Gideon? Is there something the matter?"

Still, he just looks at Riley, watching her change right before her eyes, from good, Christian girl to bottle-girl, remaking her in the image of her one error. Being less moral makes her less beautiful. Only now does Gideon see what Dano saw at first sight, how Riley's nasolabial lobes are a bit plush, how Riley's filled eye-sockets give her a flat-faced look, and the fact that her eyes are a bit close together makes Riley look like she has, perhaps, a drop of Down Syndrome high up in her family tree.

Riley unties her apron and begins folding it nervously. "My love. Why are you standing there looking at me like you're crazy?"

Gideon says, "Because I thought I had a fiancé – not a fucking bottle girl."

Riley blanches, her mouth opens, just breathing. "I... But Gideon, I…"

"You said you were homesick!"

"Gideon, I'm sorry. I agreed to a walkthrough, but they switched up on me at the last second."

"If you thought you were doing a walk-through, you would have told me. You lied because you were doing something you knew I wouldn't approve of." His fist slams the counter. "*My* fiancé! A bottle girl? Switching your ass in a little skirt like some ghetto trick?"

Riley's falling apart. "I was depressed. I felt cheated. You had just brought that dog to our bedroom and–"

"–That *dog*, is more woman than you'll ever be."

"Baby!" Tears race down Riley's face. She tries to embrace, but he pushes her back.

Gideon raises a hard finger. "I left enough money in your account to fly you back to Atlanta and to transport all of your things."

Riley's hands clench in prayer. "Don't do this, Gideon. *Please!* What I did doesn't even compare to what you put me through! You got another woman pregnant, paid for the abortion, gave her hush money, and then you brought her to our bedroom? I forgave *all* of that. And I'm even trying to live down the fact that you're still seeing her, for god sakes!"

He backs away with his hands up. "It's above me now. You gotta go," he says. "Anna would never lie to me like you did."

Riley whips her apron to the floor. "You can't tolerate the thought of me waitressing in a club, but you're okay with Anna having sex with other men for a living?"

"It's art. It's sexual freedom."

"Oh please! If it's sexual freedom for her, then being a bottle girl in a tight skirt is sexual freedom for me too."

"Not it's not. Because you lied."

"*I* lied? I found out about Anna through her posting an ultrasound of your fetus? And you wanna talk about lies? You begged me to stay, and here you are, now acting like I can't hold a light to a dog from a goat village in Russia? The same chick who blackmailed you with her pregnancy?"

Gideon stares at her and says, "I'd rather a woman from a goat village than a sista-girl from the ghetto. Anna may have come from poverty, but she didn't come from ignorance."

A week later, Riley's back in Atlanta sharing the experience word for word with her friend Joslyn. I, myself, have known of Joslyn since college. We've found ourselves in the same circles, here and there. I got the impression that Joslyn changed like radio stations depending on who she's around. I now know that it's not because she's wishy-washy; it's that she's urged to make people around her comfortable. It's why she's that person you want to tell your business to, with her smooth voice, and her easy brown face, draped with sun-kissed, micro locks.

Joslyn, even while hearing about a "mayonnaise-white" porn star sitting like a dog while Riley and Gideon make love, Joslyn hadn't even flinched in scorn.

Joslyn slowly pulls her curtain of dreads behind an ear and says, "Don't take it to heart, Riley. Any man would be lucky to have you. Thing is: Gideon is not any man. He's an awful person. He has to be better just to be worthy of you. And a porn chick is just easier for a man who wants a woman that he doesn't have to respect."

Riley pauses while sawing her chicken and waffles. "Have you been hearing me? He somehow has the utmost respect for her. Everything she does, he sees it in the best possible light. Anna could turn around and eat her own shit out the toilet and Gideon would call it sophisticated."

Joslyn chuckles, which makes Riley hear herself again and chuckle too. Joslyn says, "You were perfect all this time. Working one shift at a club ain't no reason for a breakup. He took that opportunity because he knows that a good woman like yourself may never give him another reason."

Riley says, "You should've heard him whilst I was packing my things – talking about how he's done with black women. For the rest of his life he's gonna blame us for him marrying outside his race, instead of admitting that that's what he always wanted. He'll say we don't know how to be submissive, while leaving out that his idea of submissiveness is wearing an actual leash."

Joslyn floats a palm. "See? We not crazy. We know when the game is fixed. He went and got the whitest one he could find, too."

"Whiter than Taylor Swift. You ought to see her."

"I did see her, in the ultrasound video, remember?"

Riley adds, "In person, though, she's about as white as Tahj is black."

Joslyn squints, "You so messy. Isn't Tahj your friend?"

"Not no more. I had to tell her about her ass, because she thought Fletcher was off limits on account of her infatuation with him?"

"Infatuation? If their business partner caught them kissing, they're probably doing more behind closed doors."

Riley wags a finger. "Kissing is *all* they did, trust me. Tahj has been sweating Fletcher since high school; she probably got fed up and forced herself on him. I'll bet Fletcher will be relieved when Tahj finally steps down."

"Don't be so sure. Did you ask Fletcher if they were together?"

"I don't have to," says Riley. "He's still celibate."

Joslyn gazes into space. "How are we, as women, letting a man that fine get away with being celibate?"

"Remember the accident where Meek died?"

Joslyn's head shakes. "That's why I be tellin' yall, good dick don't prosper."

"*Jos-lyn*," Riley gasps, but with a smile.

"I don't wanna be driven insane," Joslyn explains. "I'll take fine man with average meat any day. That way, I can still be myself."

Riley replies, "It'll only drive you fool, if you're not what he wants. But let's reel it back a little bit, okay, because I'm not about to sit here discussing my man's junk."

"Your man? Is that wishful thinking, or? Lemme guess: you're trying to speak it into existence."

Riley tilts a little and says, "I don't have to wish nothing. If I want him, I will have him."

Joslyn frowns, "Are you even his type? Look at Tahj."

Riley smooths her hands down her lap, staring. "Have you ever been to a party or event where there's a room full of rich athletes and their significant others? Not nare girlfriend, fiancé, or spouse, ever looked like Tahj."

"We're not talking about them. We're talking about Fletcher likes."

Riley clears her throat. "And I'm telling *you*, that men are adept at being happy with whoever will have them. Ya never know what a man really likes until he can afford it."

"Now Riley…" Joslyn's brow raises, only because her head dips to say, "Do you hear yourself? You sound disgusting, right now. If brothas unanimously prefer light skin, it's not about the skin tone, it's about their self-hatred. And capitalizing on their self-hatred is not the flex you think it is."

Riley tilts and says, "*Now* you wanna be judgmental? On top of that, you wanna judge me? Not men?"

Joslyn frowns with her palms up. "Why would I judge men based on how you think the world works? Out here, beauty is beauty. Out here, Fletcher isn't even celibate, that's only what he tells *you*."

Casually Riley says, "Whatever." But then Riley reads into Joslyn's comment, and something comes over her. With a hard look and claws flexed, as if tensed to lunge at the wrong answer of this question, Riley asks, "What do you know about Fletcher?"

"I'll tell you what I know about *men*. Men see what they want and they go hard for it. Is he going after you?" Joslyn rears back in her seat with her hands up, smiling. "I'm just trying to save you from the disappointment."

Riley bats her large lashes. "As I said. I want him, so I will have him."

"And what about Tahj?"

Riley shrugs. "What *about* Tahj?"

I scratch my nose, thinking someone must be talking about me. I'm in a prosecco gown with frosted beading on Chantilly lace. My wedding gown is the one dress I won't make myself, so I'm downtown in a bridal shop that's seemingly overpriced to recover the monies spent on the magnificent interior design.

The white pillars and ceiling mosaic are a play on ancient Rome, and I'm fretting in the mirror like an African princess who has traveled the Mediterranean to ally through marriage; world domination slipping away from her beloved Egypt and yet I feel just as stressed as Cleopatra. Truth is, Fletcher and I are now leery about getting married, but we won't say it.

At first, everything was going according to plan. Keenan made a concession. Since I had recruited so many athletes, he agreed that I didn't have to step down until after we cash the checks from the draft signings. Draft day was good to us. We got six athletes signed to NFL teams, two as high as the second round. Fletcher and I now have the money to buy out my share of the company and pay for the wedding, but what we couldn't plan for, is Fletcher's emotional health slowly declining ever since he left the NFL. It has led to drinking and impulsive spending.

As soon as the check from Isaiah Wynn's signing hit the bank, Fletcher went out and bought a home when I already have a home, paid in full. He's been running up credit card debt trying to keep up with his friends, two Atlanta Falcon players, DJ and Greedy. Fletcher's been buying jewelry, limited edition Jordans for eleven thousand dollars, gold chains, and watches. Not only has Fletcher been spending at the pace of rich athletes, he's been out in the streets as if he's single like them.

I've stormed into Magic City strip club in a housecoat and bonnet, and dragged Fletcher out by his ear. I've been dragging Fletcher to church every week, often nudging him to keep him awake during service.

I thought there was someone else. Late one night I surprised Fletcher, expecting to find him with another woman. Instead, I found Fletcher lying on the floor in silk boxers and one foot of socks. He was so drunk I had to slap him awake; the other woman was the bottle.

He refused to talk about it. I was stunned because I thought we could talk about anything. Maybe Fletcher fears that if I knew just how damaged he was, I'd sacrifice *us* in order to save *him*. I tried to convince him to try AA, but he refused.

When I say I tried everything, I *myself* sought counseling for insight on how to support him, but the therapist refused to counsel Fletcher vicariously through me.

I went to our pastor and he told me to pray; I sucked my teeth on the way out. As a last resort, I went to Fletcher's mother. Fletcher turned on me. He tried to use that as a reason to break up with me, and I let him. But the next day, this nigga came to the house, kissed my lips, and went straight to my refrigerator like nothing happened.

I let it ride, though knowing full well Fletcher can't be a husband if he's struggling to be just a man. He's dead-set on marriage, though. I think it's the financial pressure, as the deadline approaches for me to step down. I doubt he even has the money now, because after all that spending, he unexpectedly had to pay Monae an out-of-court settlement. As far as the wedding, he hasn't put up any money.

I made all the deposits for the catering company, the cake maker, and the photographer, and now I'm trying on gowns in the mirror, wondering what am I even doing.

I leave the bridal shop with the phone to my ear, canceling a later appointment as I drive toward Fletcher's house, a two-story Tudor-style home in Buckhead.

When I slip my key in the door, I hear them hollering. Who but Greedy, yelling, *Run that shit back nigga. Run that shit back!* When I open the door, they freeze like the Pause Challenge. Greedy, with that big Thanos head of his, is frozen with his chest puffed out. The room is rancid with the smell of weed. There's open to-go containers and drink cups on the table and floor. DJ's mouth is open but silent, as if I'd snatched the laughter right out of his belly. Fletcher's in a stool holding a game controller, his smile shriveling at the sight of me.

I say, facetiously, "Did I come at a bad time?"

"Actually, yeah," Fletcher says, as if he's standing up for his friends.

My eyes widen to take in all the audacity. "I guess I'll just go back out and continue looking for a maker of my gown by my fucking self, then!" Fletcher palms his forehead; I taunt his agony, "Oh you forgot? I just called and cancelled my appointments because you're here playing video games?!"

Fletcher says, "If you can call to cancel appointments, you could've called to remind me."

Before I could say his phone was off, Greedy says, "That's what she won't do. She want you to slip and fall, so she can stand over you."

At first I'm stunned. My brow raises at the sight of Greedy standing up for his friend.

DJ cosigns, "Fletcher can't *make* you happy, T. Nobody can, if you're not happy within yourself ma."

My brow, already raised to the limit, raises even higher, as I study DJ with my lips folded in, wondering how a guy with four children from three baby mommas has the gall to form an opinion.

"Chill, y'all," urges Fletcher.

I gather my hands and say, "Is that what you tell them? Huh, Fletcher?" I examine his friends. "Actually, I thank you, DJ, Greedy… Thank you for telling me what Fletcher doesn't have the heart to tell me. All I get is stood up."

Fletcher says, "They don't know nothing about us. All they know is that every time you show up, you're pissed."

I take out my phone and start recording, saying, "Wouldn't anybody be pissed if they're getting screwed out of two and a half million dollars?"

Fletcher frowns. "Wait. Why are you recording?"

"I was at Legacy Sports Agency first. The only reason *I'm* vacating *my* partner seat is because of our agreement that once you own my shares, I'd still possess it by way of marriage, by living in the household that receives its income. Wasn't that the agreement?"

The way DJ and Greedy's heads periscope to each other, I can tell this is their first time hearing this.

"Don't get it twisted," says Fletcher. "First and foremost, marrying you is about love." Fletcher reaches for my phone. "C'mon with that phone, Tahj. What're you doing?"

"This is me, trying my best to not get fucked over. I've been talking to a lawyer."

"What lawyer? Jay, I bet."

"I have actually been consulting with the law offices of None-ya Damn-Business."

Again, I raise the phone to Fletcher's face. Again, I ask, "Was that, or was that not, our agreement?"

"Yes, damn. I'm not gone lie when it comes to you."

I stop recording and shove the phone in my purse. "I only hope you stop lying to yourself." My face turns hot and my eyes fill with tears. "I love you so much, Fletcher, that I would break my own heart in order to heal yours." Fletcher takes me in his arms and holds me, while Greedy and DJ quietly make their exit. Fletcher lifts my chin and kisses my lips. He asks, "Who am I gonna love, but you? Huh, baby?" He kisses my face and neck and chest, whispering words to my body. "I love you, girl," he says, but it feels desperate, like he hopes to make love as a distraction from our truth, that this isn't working.

Fletcher picks me up by my bottom. We're face to face. I plead, "Talk to me, Fletcher."

He kisses me and says, "I simply forgot about today, babe. Don't make it more than what it is."

"When I say talk to me, don't make it *less* than what it is. It's not about today. What's going on in here," I say as I palm his chest.

He carries me to the bedroom, lays me down and looks at me. Like the hero in the billionaire romances I used to read, he is intensely present with me, but behind those eyes, there is a part of him that I can't reach, a part of him that I want so desperately for him to reveal to me. I whisper, "Let me in."

He dips to my breasts, his veined arms tighten to support his weight. I stare at the ceiling, having my belly kissed when I say, "If you can leave me hanging emotionally, and take what you want, physically, this'll be our last time."

I thought he'd stop; he ignores me. He goes further down and starts kissing me through my panties. I try to reject pleasure to prove a point, which works for all of five seconds, but the way I hold his head and grind his mouth makes breakup sex look like makeup sex.

He pulls my panties aside and admires what he sees. He takes his time licking and nibbling, driving me insane with both pleasure and mixed emotions.

He climbs up to look at me and say, "You not going nowhere." He tries to enter me, but I shake my head no, and roll him on his back. This being our last time, I wanna kiss and savor every inch of his beautiful body. As I peck his chest and abs I'm so turned on that by the time I have him in my mouth, it's like I'm possessed. I'm different. At least my throat is different. I take as much as I can in my mouth and it seems like a new chamber opens up and I take him further; a new skill, unlocked. I'm a throat queen, now. If this were not our last time, I don't know that I would've tried it. But if sex is his love language, maybe opening up my throat, lends to Fletcher opening up his heart. Carefully, I test my limits even further, my throat stuffed with cock; unable to breathe through my mouth, unable to swallow, I use a fist to catch the saliva running down his shaft, and coat him with it. Fletcher absolutely loves it. I gag hard and it pleases him even more. He grips the sheets. His moan is so unhinged that I know he's too lost in pleasure to even hear himself. Although it hurt me, I push down and gag again because it feels so good to him. Fletcher grips his head with both hands.

He doesn't look at me again until he's inside of me, as if within the hallway of a woman is where is power resides. "You not going nowhere," he tells me, then kisses my lips.

I run my hands down his muscled back and squeeze his buns to pull him deeper, my eyes never leaving his gaze. I place my hand over his heart and whisper, "Tell me where it hurts, baby."

Fletcher takes my hand from his heart and pins to the side of his head. "There's no peace in there," he says, while stroking me slowly.

The dick is so good I forget what I wanted to say. If pleasure were a lake, I'd be so deep in it that my ears would be popping; I swim up to its blurry surface to speak. "Tell me," I whisper.

Fletcher lowers, as if to hide his face, but he's still stroking and grinding; using pleasure to cover his pain, – the physical to escape the emotional. "I need you, baby," is all he says.

I suck his ear, whispering, "I'm here for you."

He let me roll him over. He lifts for my breasts, but I deny him, pressing my palms flat against his, like we're on opposite sides of a virtual wall. That wall is Fletcher's alcoholism, and the trauma that he tries to drown it with.

I keep quiet for fear of spoiling the sex. Our fingers clench. I brace against his hands and ride him in silence, my eyes closed, feeling for the angle and pace that would set me off.

"That's right, baby," Fletcher says, and I wonder if he's pleased with my work, or the fact that I stopped talking.

Fletcher pops me on the butt. "Stay right there," meaning on all fours, moving just enough to let him roll out from under me. As he positions himself behind me, I say, "For real, Fletcher… you need help. I'll go with you."

Fletcher grabs my waist and angles my arc so deep that I thought he'd use my back as a sliding board. He looks and admires. "That's right, baby… I love that."

Sex is just another substance that helps him deal with it all. He starts off too aggressive. "*You* my medicine, baby." He picks up the pace. I wait to see if his pace would level off or if I'd have to stop him. He starts pounding, and I'm bouncing off of him like a paddle-ball, and it hurts. "Fletcher," I say. He ignores me. I reach back, placing a hand on his abs to hold him off. "Fletcher... chill," I beg. Fletcher moves my hand away and pounds for a few seconds more before pulling out, moaning curse words, and batting his nut out on my cheeks.

Fletcher collapses, bringing me down with him. We lay on our sides, Fletcher behind me. He clutches me in an intimate spoon — intimate for him. I lay there, feeling slightly disrespected.

Fletcher fades off to sleep. I quietly roll out of bed and get dressed. I kiss his sleeping face and then leave him, and our relationship, right where he lay.

CHAPTER 21
STEPPING DOWN

Keenan tucks a gun in his waist and gets out of the car. Obviously, he'd been stalking Monae because it's just days after she left from under her auntie's roof and into a condo, courtesy of Fletcher's out-of-court settlement.

Keenan rings the doorbell. He feels himself getting antsy as he hears Monae's footsteps approach the door, but he keeps calm. When Monae looks through the doorbell camera, she finds a smiling Keenan.

Monae asks, "Do I need to call the police?"

Keenan replies, "Talking ain't no crime."

"Stalking is. How do you know where I live?"

Keenan smiles and says, "I would've simply asked you, if you didn't change your number."

"What do you want?"

"Didn't I just tell you? I wanna talk."

On the other side of the door, Monae's neck swerves on the words, "I'm listening."

Keenan's head lowers and shakes. "Monae, Monae, Monae… You know I wanna do more than talk."

"I remember you wanting to kill me–"

"–And ever since, I haven't been able to get you out of my mind. Nobody ever made me feel like you. Nobody."

Monae goes quiet on the other side. When she does speak, although Keenan can't see her face, he hears the vulnerability in her voice. "I felt like… like we were falling in love."

"That part," Keenan smiles. "You got me standing out here like a dope fiend, baby, let me in."

Monae says, "This isn't about the money you gave me?"

Keenan replies. "You mean the money I *loaned* you?" Keenan licks his lips and says, "Well, it sorta is about that. I know of a way you can work off the debt, but you can't be messing with nobody else. Only me."

"Sounds like a relationship."

"No. I could never be in a relationship with somebody like you – at least not what *I* call a relationship. But if that's your definition, I can hold up my end."

Monae opens the door with a seductive smile on her lips. She twirls a ribbon of hair, posing with her legs crossed to bolster her augmented hips in a pair of tiny cloth shorts.

Keenan looks her over with a bit lip. "I missed you."

Monae says, "I missed *you*. You not gone kiss me?"

Keenan winces at the thought of it. "After a couple drinks. You got liquor?"

Monae nods yes and takes a deep breath. "I'm gone trust you, okay? Because my gut is telling me, I shouldn't do this."

The instant Monae turns to go get drinks. Keenan steps into a punch at the back of Monae's head. She sprawls and hits the floor with a slide. She lifts up groggy.

Keenan shuts the door behind him and says, "You should've listened to your gut, bitch!"

Monae crawls backward, begging, "Please!"

Keenan draws the gun out of his belt. Monae screams. Keenan helps her up and points the gun at her head. "Scream one more time, and I'll drop your ass."

Monae pleads. "You don't have to do this. You have your whole life in front of you."

Keenan grips Monae's chin. "What life in front of me? You *ruined* my life!" By the grip on Monae's chin, he drives her back into the wall with a thud. A picture frame jars loose and hits the floor. Keenan blasts, through clenched teeth, "You wanna play games with niggas, huh?"

Monae pleads for her life. Keenan slaps her with the back of his hand, recaptures her chin in his grasp, then slams her into the wall again. "You deceived me! I found out who you really were, after... I found out, after…" Keenan seems light-headed as if he might faint. Keenan takes a deep breath and says, "I found out who you really were, after you…" Anger lifts, revealing brokenness under its veil. "… after you had my heart. That's not fair."

Keenan now looks as if he'd use the gun on himself. But then Monae notices something else; Keenan lowkey inhales her perfume. Monae slowly, gently, places her hand on the hand that grips her chin, and pulls it down. They're suddenly in a trance. Keenan just breathes. A tear slips. He looks away. Monae raises her hand to his face and let her fingers graze over his eyes, closing them. Monae inches closer; hesitant, but determined. Keenan's mouth awaits. Monae noses closer. She gently closes her mouth on his bottom lip. Keenan then joins in the kiss, his eyes still closed, the passion gaining intensity. Keenan caresses the back of Monae's neck. She flinches. She still aches from the punch. Keenan's eyes open to find Monae's eyes looking into his. She whispers, "You hurt me."

"I'm sorry," Keenan says. "I'm fighting with this… I don't *want* to hurt you."

They didn't expect me to bring my own lawyer to the table. We're at the office of attorney Omar Bashar. Keenan and Fletcher are already seated as I walk in with Mr. John Patterson esquire, affectionately known as Jay.

Jay pulls out my chair for me. As I'm lowering into my seat, I see Fletcher's jealous ass steaming like a kettle. I know how Fletcher's mind works. He's taking this to the extreme, accusing me, via telepathy, of having an affair with Jay, and that's why I broke it off with him. I say broke it off, but Fletcher and I made love that day and we'd been speaking to each other every day since. I'd been experiencing what I call empty bed syndrome, so I would call him every night at bedtime because having him with me, if even over the phone, helps me sleep. Being, technically, without him brings forth the idea of eventually having to love someone else, which feels impossible to me. Furthermore, just the night before, Fletcher began to open up. He told me, one night over the phone that when he got cut from the NFL, a part of him died – the part of him that holds all the other parts together. That bit of vulnerability was all I needed to feel that there's hope for his rehabilitation and our relationship. It's a hope that was still glowing about me when I rolled out of bed that morning, even as I got dressed to go step down as a partner and transact the sale of my share of the company, without the marriage as a financial fail-safe. I couldn't imagine that, in the end, I would be leaving this transaction, wishing to never see Fletcher's face again.

Jay sits quietly as Bashar passes out the documents and goes over the new evaluation of the company. "Since our most recent evaluation of 2.4 million, there has been acquisitions of several athletes and a lucrative draft. Legacy Sports is now evaluated at 8.8 million dollars; therefore, Tahj's twenty-five percent ownership will go for 2.2 million."

I'm taken aback by the figure. It's what I would get paid, even after taking in all that money from the draft signings and the Isaiah Wynn contract. All this time, we'd been biting our nails over Bubby's big contract day, but I'm walking away with that amount anyway. A smile spans clear across my face; I look over at Fletcher and he's the polar opposite of me; he looks as if he's lost an uncle. I'm reminded that what I get paid has to come out of Fletcher.

Attorney Bashar looks around the table, asking, "Everyone good with the figures?"

Jay sees the smile on my face and he nods with a smile of his own, in genuine happiness for me.

The meeting continues, but Fletcher's still stuck, holding the documents up to his face, squinting as if there's an issue with his eyesight. I knew right then and there that Fletcher didn't have the money.

Jay halts Attorney Bashar, and says, "What I'm not seeing is any mention of a severance package." My gaze swerves to Jay, impressed by his bargain.

Bashar glowers and says, "Because there isn't one."

I swerve the other way, to Bashar, looking at him like he must be crazy.

Jay interlocks his fingers and argues, "Neither is there a rule about someone having to step down as a result of an office romance."

"Doesn't have to be. It's an industry standard that…" Bashar stops with his own foot in his mouth.

Jay points, "How long, Bashar, have you been a lawyer? Because you had to know that I was baiting you to say just that." Jay looks as if he's holding a strong poker hand. "Speaking of industry standards… Isn't it also an industry standard for a parting executive to receive a severance of one year's salary?"

Bashar replies, "My five-year-old son is older than Legacy Sports Agency. This is a new company–"

Jay pounds the table. "A new company you evaluated just shy of ten million dollars!"

Bashar cuts his eyes. "Where do you think you are, pounding my desk like that?"

Jay resets his shoulders. "I *know* where I am: I'm in the drivers' seat. We'll take it to court."

Bashar turns to me. "Tahj, I'm telling you, it's best to settle this now. All he's trying to do, is drag things out to increase his fees."

"What fees," I say.

"It's pro bono," Jay adds.

Bashar's targets Jay with a stare. "All style, no substance. I eat lawyers like you."

Jay grins. "Well, you can start by eating my dick."

I snort with laughter. Keenan knifes a hand across the table. "Ay, y'all go on somewhere with that gay shit." (The audacity…)

I keep quiet. Fletcher's still staring at the document, stroking his beard.

Jay admits, "Of course, Bashar, in court, you would win." Just as Bashar looks around the table boastingly, Jay adds, "But some wins are really losses. And some losses are actually wins. If you've been following the situation in Philadelphia, Amari Turner (Bubby) is likely to get resigned a year early, as training camp ends. I can hold this matter up in court long enough to where Tahj, here, is still technically an owner to cash in on the proceeds of Amari Turner's contract. Or, you pay us one million in severance and we can put this all behind us today."

Bashar counters, "*Half* a million."

Kennan settles it. "Seven fifty. I'll pay that myself just so I don't have to look at her face another day."

Fletcher votes, "I say drag it out; take it to court."

Keenan's head swivels to look at his lifelong friend, as if he's the ops. "Wanna know what you sound like, Fletcher? You sound like a nigga that don't got 2.2 million dollars."

Fletcher punches his hand and says, "Why are we even doing this, bro? We're friends, supposedly!"

Keenan sets an open hand on his chest. "Friends don't do what y'all did to me. First of all, I knew y'all was messing around from day one. I was gone let that ride forever. But y'all ruined my life, then got the nerve to be kissing in the garage the very next day?"

"Keenan," I say, softly, but he cuts me off.

"You knew! I'm not sure if Fletcher knew. But you knew!" He rears back in his seat. "Y'all thought I was being gracious by giving yall a few months to cash in on the draft, but nah. I was just raising the price. I knew Legacy Sports' value would skyrocket after the draft, and that Fletcher wouldn't be able to pay it." Keenan, with a snide grin, turns to Fletcher. "How much you got, big dawg? You got the 2.2?"

Slowly Fletcher tips forward, eyes wide as he says, "I can put somethin' *on* it."

"No layaways here, bruh," says Keenan. "Y'all hold up a sec. I'll be right back." Keenan gets up and leaves. We're all confused except for Bashar who takes the opportunity to check his phone.

Keenan returns with his brother, who'd changed his name to Khalid while in prison. Like Keenan, he has that big baby head, but with an early receding hairline and a prison-grade neck tattoo peeking out of his crisp collar shirt.

Fletcher looks down and starts mumbling to himself. "Everybody's getting what they want. Everybody except me. Tahj is getting her money and her freedom because she never really wanted to do this in the first place. Keenan gets to bring his brother on as a partner. What do I gain? I tripled this company's value damn near single-handedly and *I'm* the one who gets fucked!" Fletcher rocks back and forth in his seat, desperate to break something. "Ain't no way. Ain't no fuckin' way!"

I walk briskly around the table toward Fletcher. Jay's eyes follow me as if he can't believe what he's seeing. "Tahj! Let him be. You're just opening the door for him to ask you for the money." Jay now knows that it was Fletcher who borrowed money before; I never mentioned, to Jay, that Fletcher had paid me back.

Eyes never leaving Jay, Fletcher gets up and says, "Somebody get this nigga before I slap the shit outta him!"

The threat of violence makes everyone stand; Jay, Keenan, his brother, and Bashar are suddenly activated.

Jay starts unbuttoning his suit like he's about to do something. "You think I'm supposed to be scared of you?"

I warn, "Jay, you're making him worse!"

Jay really thinks he's fighting for my honor, but I fear that he'll mess around and get himself choke-slammed through the conference table. I get in the way, my back turned to Jay as I plead with Fletcher to calm down.

Keenan warns, "Better chill out, old school. This is *not* a drill, right now."

"This is an *act*," Jay insists. "He does his caged animal bit, knowing Tahj would do anything to make it stop – even buying her share of the company from herself!"

I yell, "Jay *please!*"

Khalid points at Fletcher and says, "Yall get big man the hell outta here."

Fletcher turns. "*You* get me outta here, you bad!"

Khalid reasons, "Y'all making the lady upset."

Fletcher then looks down at my distress and begins to calm down, for my sake.

I announce, "Give us a minute. In fact give us thirty minutes." I take Fletcher's hand and walk him towards the door. As we pass by Jay, the man stands there with his chest puffed out, wishing Fletcher would.

Just when I think we're in the clear, Jay mumbles, "Better try Jesus."

Now, why'd he say that… Fletcher snaps! Fletcher lunges so fast it's like he was dashed out of a bucket.

Turns out, it's not an attack; only a feint. But it sets off a chain reaction, starting with Jay's knee-jerk reflex to flail his arms while stepping back. His pen goes flying. Jay drops into his chair, instead of falling, which seems like disaster averted, but the force tips the chair back and then it tips over. We sigh collectively as if it's over but no… Jay's legs fold back like a latch and the momentum takes him another half rotation, his suit flapped up his back like a peeled banana. I see nothing but shoe bottoms and ass – the worst possible position from which to issue a threat. "*That* did it," says Jay. "You done messed up now!"

Whenever I remember this day, I laugh myself to tears, but in real time, I'm livid while leading Fletcher out of the office. I speedwalk with a forward lean, arms stiff at my sides, mouth chewing Fletcher out. "What is your problem! You always go too far, Fletcher! How hard is it to act like an adult…!"

Fletcher asks, "Where you going?"

I stop only to look back and bark, "To the bank!"

Fletcher, two paces behind me, says, "I can't tell you how much I appreciate this."

I stop. Not even looking back, I say, "Don't even *thank* me, right now, Fletcher! Don't even speak!" Again, I start speedwalking and chastising. We reach the opposite sidewalk and I'm digging my wallet out of my purse in advance.

Fletcher says, "If it bothers you this much, forget it then."

I stuff my wallet back in my purse and spin. "You ain't said nothin' but a word." I walk in the opposite direction, my head not even turning to appraise Fletcher as I breeze past him.

When I do look back over my shoulder, I see that he's rooted to the spot, his head hung. I turn around and walk back, passing him again while saying, "You got one more time to play with me."

As I approach the bank entrance, I get a glimpse of my glass door reflection, my skin radiant under an April sun, in my taupe, skin-tight maxi dress, my Tao earrings swinging with my aggressive walk. Fletcher makes a late attempt to hurry and open the door for me, but it goes awfully wrong; we're momentarily wedged in the doorway like two stooges before stumbling inside. Irritatedly, I ask, "How short are you?"

Fletcher stammers, "Well ya see I kinda…"

I yell, "How much!"

"A milly. 1.2, to be exact."

Heads rotate with us as we go to the velvet-roped line, spatting in whispers. "You gotta come better than that, Fletcher." My head shakes. "I told you about your spending…" Here's where I say some words I wish I could have back. "Spending like athletes don't make you one."

Fletcher says, "Yeah, kick me when I'm down."

I turn. "How did you get down? You beat yourself with your own hand."

Fletcher counters, "Is it possible to help me, without humiliating me?"

A crazed laughter escapes me. I cover my mouth and remove the hand just enough to say, "I'm buying my company from myself. What's more humiliating than that?" The branch manager approaches. I throw a hand, stopping him in his tracks. "I know. I know. I apologize," I say, my head-turn spreading the apology across all waiting patrons. "We're okay, I Promise." I suspect that the other black customers are embarrassed by my behavior.

I quiet down and face front. It's Fletcher who keeps whispering over my shoulder. "I know why you're acting like this…" As if having to come off of 1.2 million dollars isn't a solid reason. "It's the wedding," he whispers. "You was right… I *was* acting different. I was afraid of marriage." He winces. "Well, not afraid of marriage. I was afraid of…"

I look back, "Marrying me?"

"No. Afraid of *me*. You know I'm a mess, babe, but I try to hold it together for you. It's like wearing a mask… So, imagine the real me behind that mask, looking through the eyeholes at a woman I don't deserve… That day you found me; I wasn't trying to drink myself to death… but I wasn't trying *not* to."

I look back over my shoulder. "I'm just now hearing this? Whispered over my shoulder in line at the bank?" Coming off of a million dollars, perhaps, makes a mouth brutally honest, because I would have never been able to look coldly at Fletcher after he admitted trying to drink himself to death, and say, "I don't want a man who needs me. I wanna be swooned, Fletcher. I want to be cherished. I want to be…"

Next, says a bank teller who dangles a Kleenex for me. "Thank you," I say as I dot the corners of my eyes. "I need to make a transfer please." The process is more complicated than I thought. For a transfer that large, the banker asks us a ton of mandated questions, which only wears my patience.

After the transaction is done and we're heading out, Fletcher keeps thanking me, which is just as irritating as all the banker's questions and disclosures about money laundering and criminal enterprise.

What really sets me off is when we're leaving the bank, Fletcher stops me to say, "After we're finished with the lawyers, let's go down to the courthouse. We'll have a ceremony later, but let's get married now. I owe you that."

"You owe me marriage?!" I'm shouting just a few feet away from the branch manager to whom I'd promised to behave. I fold my arms. "Is that how you think a woman wants to be asked! You don't owe me marriage. You owe me a million dollars." A cry rises in my throat but I shape it into words, sobbing, "And you wanna get married as a way to clear your fucking debt?!" I swipe the back of my hand across my crying eyes.

The branch manager tries to get me to calm down, while Fletcher tries to apologize. I place both hands on my head to try to keep out the noise. My throat starts closing, and all I could do to breathe, is to scream at the top of my lungs.

CHAPTER 22
GUESS WHO'S COMING FOR DINNER

Who would've thought… Riley frequenting a bar that is also frequented by rich athletes: TopGolf on Ellsworth. Riley doesn't know a thing about golf, not even how to dress the part. She's in a split-hem *tennis* tank made famous by Serena Williams. Riley shows skin like she's newly single and ready to mingle. It must've been hard for her to resist wearing heels, just like it's hard for me to be subjective while telling the events of this day; the details of which I do not have all. But I do know that Riley bypasses the hostess stand, not wanting to be seated. She walks with her head on a swivel as if looking for someone in particular.

Fletcher will later deny inviting Riley, so I'll go with the narrative that Riley's there by coincidence while an oblivious Fletcher is in the hitting bay measuring his golf swing.

DJ and Greedy wring their necks, bedazzled by the baddie in a tennis tank, perusing the establishment. Greedy taps DJ, but DJ's already tapping him. *"Nigga…"*

Greedy gives a warning eye. "Stop looking at my future wife, boy."

DJ sighs, with wanting eyes. "Exquisite… She not even thick, but it's a'ight. Chicks like her make thick look ignorant."

Greedy frowns at his friend and says, "You be saying the stupidest shit, dawg."

Fletcher returns from his shot and finds his friends, per usual, salivating over some redbone. This redbone, however, is familiar. "Good ole, Riley," says Fletcher.

Both heads rotate. "You know her?"

"It's Riley. Y'all heard me talk about her."

"*That's* Riley?" Greedy rubs his chin. "The Riley who was engaged to Gideon Anderson? Gotta have a lotta dough to get with her, I bet."

"She'll never say it's about money, but… Ever since college she dated dudes who came from rich families, or older, more established men."

"You must've got with Tahj because Riley was out of your reach, back then."

Fletcher responds. "You must be out yo rabid-assed mind if you think Riley badder than Tahj."

Greedy's face breaks like a puzzle. "Love really *is* blind."

"As a bat," DJ seconds.

Fletcher adds, "Don't get me wrong. She official, but Riley never really fazed me like that. Tahj, though?" Fletcher's head shakes while gazing at me in his mind's eye.

DJ drops a hand on the table. "We brought you here to get your mind *off* of Tahj. Bet *Riley* could get your mind off of her." DJ adds, "According to you, Fletch, Tahj and Riley ain't friends no more, so what's in the way now?"

"The fact that she *my* friend. But y'all suggesting I rebound with her?"

Greedy's big head turns slowly. "A chick like that could never be a rebound. You supposed to *wife* that."

Fletcher glances left and right, smiling. "Don't you remember me telling you about her?"

Greedy puts a fist to his mouth. "Bruh! She tried to give you some. And you said no to *that?*"

"She was trying to cheat on Gideon with me. Plus she was friends with Tahj. You call that wife material, Greedy?" Fletcher turns to his other friend. "How is that quality, DJ?"

"Because it is," DJ asserts. "Gideon cheated first. And Tahj lil angry ass probably had it coming," DJ concludes, because the only version of me he gets, is the one Fletcher vents about; moreover, in person, they sense my rejection of Fletcher trying to make DJ and Greedy the new Keenan and Bubby.

Greedy nudges Fletcher. "Invite her over, man, what's the matter with you!"

Fletcher leaves their section and returns with Riley. The first thing she says is, "You must be Greedy."

He smiles, honored that his name precedes him. "How you know?"

Riley points like a tattling child. "Because I had heard that you got a big Thanos head."

Everyone laughs. Greedy points. "You mean, she got a sense of humor *too?*"

Only in the presence of a man that she wants, is Riley suddenly a comedian – suddenly pigeon-toed too, which always irked me. Riley says, "I can't take credit for that joke… *Fletcher,*" she tattles, with a nudge.

DJ says, "And Fletcher got it from Tahj. Tahj used to call Greedy that."

Riley's hand thrusts like a punch, but it's only a hand-puppet with the mouth shutting. "We not gone talk about Tahj today, okurrr? That chapter's done." Riley leans back into Fletcher with a shimmy, adding, "But baybeee… the book is just getting good."

When I ask Fletcher how could he, he says he never did. He says he just looked up one day and realized that what he and Riley had was, for all intents and purposes, a relationship, but he never says this without reminding me that I was the one who broke it off with him.

Fletcher says he never sought her out. Riley always had a legit reason to be around him. Since she knew so many players in the

NBA via Gideon, she tried to help Fletcher recruit basketball players, to add a new dimension to Legacy Sports.

Things changed when Riley nagged Fletcher to worship with her one Sunday. Fletcher said yes, out of feelings of obligation, since Riley's been such a big help with his recruiting efforts.

After church, Fletcher finds himself having dinner with her parents, and wondering who is this innocent, soft-spoken girl who looks just like Riley. She's different at her church and around her parents. And her parents couldn't be more different from each other. Fletcher suspects that Miss Brenda is disapproving of him; perhaps fearful of dark grandbabies. She moves about the kitchen with an apron over her Sunday dress, serving everyone and mumbling scriptures as a means to shade Fletcher indirectly.

Riley's box-headed stepfather is the polar opposite of his shade-throwing wife. Phillip's too direct. His steak knife paused from cutting roast, he looks up to ask, "So how long have you and my daughter been seeing each other?"

Fletcher smirks and mumbles stupid, afraid to make a liar out of their sweet little Riley who must've told her folks that they were in a relationship.

After dinner, Fletcher's out on the deck smoking a cigar with Phillip, the man urging him to spare Riley all the hurt Gideon put her through. To Fletcher's surprise, the man says his stepdaughter is a virgin holding out for marriage because she doesn't want to repeat the mistakes of her mother.

Phillip stands and offers a handshake to adjourn their meeting, and over that handshake, the man looks Fletcher in the eyes and says, "If you're impatient about sex, be also impatient about marriage. Problem solved. Amen?"

On the way out, Fletcher thanks Miss Brenda for being such a gracious host. Riley follows him out to the porch. "Fletcher, hey…"

Fletcher's eyes sharpen as he looks over his shoulder. "You told them we're together?"

Riley stops in her tracks and replies. "I didn't tell them that, but that's how they took it–"

"–You tried it," Fletcher says. It's all he can fix his mouth to say because Riley's been so good to him, helping Fletcher in business, bringing home-cooked meals by the office, and praying over his struggles with alcohol. Her goodness has robbed Fletcher of his agency to hurt Riley by telling her that his feelings for her are merely platonic.

Fletcher gets in his car. Riley stays on the porch with her hands gathered in front, her cheeks wearing the blush of embarrassment as she watches him drive away.

Fletcher goes straight home. He declines Riley's calls and ignores her texts. He'd tolerated Riley playing him too close, but this time she went too far, using her parents as a way to apply pressure. Fletcher decides to use this incident as his way out.

This is the part Fletcher never liked about being single. After Gigi, he'd always been on the giving end of some woman's pain, which fills him with guilt, and there's only two known remedies to soothe his guilt: another woman, or the bottle. He puckers his lips for the latter, and turns the bottle up. Fletcher shuts himself in the house for the remainder of the evening.

After hours of her calls going unanswered and texts piling in queue, Riley shows up at Fletcher's doorstep; her face glistened with tears. She frantically rings the doorbell.

By now, Fletcher's good and drunk. He's laid back on the couch, knees spread wide in sweatpants and no shirt. He's too drunk to think straight when he hears the doorbell. He stumbles all the way to the door, assuming it's an Amazon package despite the aggressive ringing. "I'm coming man, *damn*," Fletcher slurs.

As soon as Fletcher turns the deadbolt, Riley snatches the door open and Fletcher comes tumbling out, nearly pulling Riley down with him. Riley jerks away. "Get off me," she screams. Fletcher hits the ground and rolls. Riley yells, "That's what you get! You wanna shut me out?! I'm about to show you how it feels to be shut out!" Riley goes in and locks Fletcher out of his own house.

Fletcher bangs on the door and yells from the other side. "Girl open this damn doh! I'm out here with no shirt on – neighbors lookin' and shit…"

Riley spots his keys on the coffee table; he has no way to get in. "Drunk ass," she fires. "You should be glad somebody even wants your behind!"

Fletcher says, "Let me in. Let's talk, Riley."

"Why did you lead me on, Fletcher?"

"Riley," Fletcher blasts. "I'm finna break this got damn door down if you don't quit playing with me!"

Riley pleads, "All I did was try to love you."

"I'm stuck on Tahj, so… I don't know what to tell ya."

Riley, now with an eye to the peephole says, "She dumped you. You need to get over her."

Fletcher stiffens and looks around, bird-twitching in confusion. "What? Ain't no getting over her. Ever."

Riley backs away from the door in horror and screams at the top of her lungs.

Fletcher yells, "Dafuck? Riley! Hey! If you start breaking shit in there, I'm callin' twelve."

"Call them with what," Riley blasts. "Your phone is on the coffee table! You're more worried about your stuff than you're worried about me?"

Fletcher leans on the door for balance, cups a hand against it, and says, "No, no. I'm not saying that, Riley. Riley, I *do* care about you, I just… Hey, can you please just open the door so we can talk?"

"You say you care about me? Okay, well, then if that's the case you should–"

"–*Hey,*" Fletcher yells in frustration. "Let me tell you one mutha fuckin' thing, Riley! This ain't what we doing, okay! Back up from the got damn door," Fletcher warns, as he backs away for a running start. "Get away from the door," Fletcher yells, "…or get run the-fuck over. Don't say I didn't warn you!"

Fletcher takes off like the door is a quarterback in his sights. Coming full speed, Fletcher lowers his shoulder for the hit, but the door swings open like a matador's cape. Fletcher comes diving through and faceplants on the wood floor; he's out cold.

Frantically, Riley runs over, screaming, "Fletcher! Fletcher?" She kneels next to him and tries to wake him. His grogginess is a combination of drunkenness and having his stars knocked into orbit above his head.

Riley cries and apologizes as she tries to help Fletcher stay conscious, but then she turns quiet suddenly; an awful calm comes down over her. She crawls on top of Fletcher who's in and out of consciousness and mumbling things. Riley puts a finger to his lips and shushes him softly, "Shshsh… Don't worry, baby. I got you," she whispers. Riley kisses his lips oh so gently. "I'm gonna take good care of you, okay."

She shimmies his sweatpants down and has a moment of awe for what is revealed. She looks back. The front door is wide open, but if she gets up for the door, she'll miss her chance if Fletcher comes to. Even now, he's not conscious enough to know that something's not right, but he *is* conscious enough to stiffen in Riley's soft grasp. Then again, he's so out of it that he thinks it's me. "Tahj… I missed you, so much," he mumbles.

Riley has Fletcher straddled, with a hand under her sundress, probing herself for entry.

Fletcher realizes that it isn't me. "Stop," he says. He shoves his hand under her dress in attempt to block her, but then he feels that soft, fleshy mollusk on the back of his knuckles and retracts his hand, pleading mercy. "Don't do this, Riley. No."

"Let me…" she says. She's coming apart internally, sniffling and suppressing her cries. "Let me take care of you." She already has him in her folds, sex already a fact. And the part I can never live down is that Fletcher, in the moment, had the awareness to know what was happening, and the strength to throw Riley off of him, but didn't do it for fear of hurting her.

Fletcher grips her arms, ready to toss her off of him, but his mere grasp hurts her. She cries, "You're hurting me." This renders Fletcher powerless, unable to hurt her even while she violates him.

He tries to talk her out of it. "What if I was doing this to you? How would *you* feel? I would go to jail for it."

Riley, with tears dripping from her chin, collapses on top of him, whispering to his ear, "Please… Please love me back."

Fletcher, just as passively as he'd let Riley force her way into his life, he let her force him inside of her body. Riley shudders from the surge of pleasure. She buries her crying face in the crook of his neck.

Fletcher just lays there, summoning all of his power to resist, for as long as he could, the inevitability of drowning in pleasure. Already the acoustics of it crowds his ears; the ruffle of clothing, and the spackle of her goo spreading down the length of him.

Fletcher stares at the ceiling like he's deceased, while Riley desperately, yet methodically, hunches, in an attempt to resuscitate the dead.

CHAPTER 23
MYSTERY WOMAN

For the first time in a month, I call Fletcher. It picks up on the first ring. I start by clearing my throat of the pride I had to swallow just to make this call. I say, "Fletcher? Hey, um… You got a minute?" There's silence. I figure the phone picked up by accident, but no. There's something intentional about that silence; I get the feeling that there's a woman on the other end — some chick with her face lit by the phone screen bearing my contact, Slim Shady, and hearing the guardedness in my voice, asking, "Fletcher? Are you there?" I would have never guessed that the woman on the other end was Riley, lying beside a napping Fletcher.

The line goes dead and I'm sitting on the floor with a baby in my arms, stiff as stone, my heart thumping.

Bubby asks, "Everything a'ight?"

I'm holding his one-year-old, who reaches up and nearly snags my lip. "I don't know… I think his phone was picked up by a woman." I see Bubby nodding as if not disgusted in the least, so I add, "It's been only a month."

"That's like dog years for a man, Tahj. A month to you is like six months for him. Bro had to smash something for his sanity. Ya gotta look past that."

"I'm not trying to be with Fletcher. I'm not. I can't do a man who makes me feel stupid for being with him. But if he can move on this quick, it makes me question, what did we really have?" I stuff my phone in my purse on the floor beside me. I stand the baby up with his feet in my lap; he has a firm grip on my thumbs. He begins laughing and pumping his legs as if trying to jump. I begin singing his name, "Jeremiah… Jeremiah…" He laughs and snorts, which makes me and Bubby laugh. Emily comes in and takes Jeremiah from me, saying it's nap time. No shade. Me and Emily have been good. We put that wedding incident behind us ever since she became pregnant.

I'm watching Emily exit the room with Jeremiah, when I say, "I want these beautiful babies to grow up knowing who their auntie is. I may have come to Philly for fashion week and everything, but *they* are the main reason," I say. Bubby's eyeing me already. He knows there's more to the story, so I out myself. "I thought you and Jalen hung out all the time."

We break out in giggles.

"You ain't slick," Bubby says.

"Of course not. I was being obvious."

Bubby points, "How are you mad at Fletcher, but you out here trying to get with Jalen?"

"It's not like I'm tryna give him some. I'm not even ready to move on. I owe the man an apology, for fading him at the club that night."

Bubby says, "Jalen and me… we been chillin' less lately. In fact, our last time out was a double date. He got him a lil shawty now."

"Not a big deal," I say. Sheeit, I'm wounded.

"Wanna know who his girl reminds me of?" Bubby starts snapping his fingers to jog his memory. "Who's the chick that sing that song, Shea Butter Baby?"

"Ari Lennox." I suck my teeth. "Look at you… You're just trying to let me know that his new girlfriend is dark. I'm not surprised," I say.

Bubby takes out his phone.

I say, "Don't call that man. He got somebody."

"Nah, I'm tryna get Fletcher on the phone." Bubby puts the phone to his ear and immediately takes it away. "Straight to voicemail."

I hold my cry for the remainder of my visit and all the way back to the hotel. I still love Fletcher deeply. I've been in different stages of loving him ever since the ninth grade, so I don't know how to *not* love him. He never cheated, so the possibility of a relationship, I figured, was still open. I thought I had more time than a month before he started entertaining other women. I thought he would be focusing on getting better in order to win me back.

After our big blowup, I needed a period of not talking to Fletcher; it was like I couldn't speak to him without bleeding.

Fletcher didn't want to speak to me either, after I'd turned his failure in the NFL as a weapon in an argument, and then screamed in his face after he revealed the depths of his depression. That whole conversation needs a do-over. The moment I complete that thought, my phone rings.

I lift my head off the pillow and look. It's a call from Riley. I speak to the ringing phone, "Why are you calling, Riley? I don't fuck with you." Ever since December when she expressed interest in Fletcher, our friendship has been a wrap. I send the call to voicemail.

Since the phone is there in my hand I try calling Fletcher. Again the call goes straight to voicemail. This time, I leave a message, "I'm just calling because, well… I'm sorry, for one. I had said some things and… You've been real heavy on my heart, lately, I… I don't wanna say everything in voicemail, but… Can you call me? Maybe we can set up a time to meet, and talk, okay? Talk to you later. Bye."

I hang up and stare at the phone. In the upper corner of the screen, I see Riley's voicemail waiting; I check it just for kicks.

The message isn't actually a message. It's background noise as if she'd dialed me by accident. There's a man in the background. I hear sheets, as if they're in bed. Riley whines, *Talk to me, please.*

I hear the man's sleepy groan – not the words he issues. But that voice! I know, without a doubt that the voice is Fletcher's. My head shakes. "No! No!"

His voice is heavy with sleep. *Leave me alone,* he says.

I hear Riley's hand slide across the sheets toward the phone to end the call.

This was no accident. She wanted me to hear this. I redial, phone trembling in my hands, my breathing shallower with each subsequent call that goes directly to voicemail. I think it wise not to threaten Riley over voicemail so it couldn't be used to convict me for her murder – because I swear I had every intention of killing this bitch.

Riley's in bed with Fletcher, and I'm all the way out in Philly, unable to pull up. I'm cursing Riley and Fletcher out as if they're right there in the room. "You better be glad I'm way out here, because if I was there I would ring your fucking neck. Just you wait, snake bitch! And you, Fletcher? Ooh, you dirty son of a bitch. A month? Huh? A month after I give you a *fucking! Million! Dollars!*" I hear myself yelling and figure I should calm down in this suite before I really lose it and start breaking these people's shit.

I make a distress call to Jay. When he picks up, I'm crying so bad, he can't understand a word I'm saying. He asks, "What happened? Are you hurt?"

All I could say is, "Can you come get me?"

"Don't you know it's a Sunday? Lemme see if I can get my pilot on the phone."

CHAPTER 24
KNIGHT IN SHINING ARMOR

I pack my suitcase in tears. In just over a couple hours Jay has a driver picking me up in front of my hotel and in a matter of fifteen minutes, Jay greets me at a private airstrip.

The man looks totally different. I'd seen him only once since the day he represented me, and now he looks years younger. His hairline isn't thinning, it's full and styled into a head of neat, soft naps. He's beginning a beard, like a light shadow that's carved razor-sharp along his cheekbones. For once, he isn't wearing a suit. A grey, knit shirt settles into the creases of his shoulders and chest. He wears shades and a platinum chain; he's worn neither as long as I've known him.

Jay hugs me and holds me. I say thank you, with my face against his shoulder.

"I'm just glad you're okay." He then tips the driver and leads me through the private hangar.

Midflight, so much time has passed since my meltdown over the phone, I'm calm. I've already confessed why I was so upset, and he's giving me a speech. "I told you about men like Fletcher. He has no self-control. He found himself with a beautiful young lady and gave in to the moment. The moment will always be bigger than anything he values in life," Jay says. "But you don't need me to tell you that, though. He's already shown you."

I sigh and look away, the most attitude I can give a man who's flying halfway across the country and back for me.

Jay adds, "With that being said, though, if you still wanna go confront him, I'm going with you."

I say, "That's just gonna make Fletcher come after you."

"That's what I want him to do," says Jay. "After what happened at the office, I owe him one."

My eyes slant to him. "Don't play."

"You better *ask* somebody." Jay's smirk says that he's joking, only because I'm laughing.

"Jay, let's review what happened last time okay," I say with a finger twirling back in rewind. "Fletcher jumped at you and the next thing you know, all I saw was shoes and ass."

We laugh until we're crying and weak. I hold my belly and slap my knee, then I realize I'm laughing by myself. I look over at Jay and he's eyeing me with a dead face. Laughter cranks up again. I'm digging tissue out of my purse and wiping my eyes. I reach over and wipe Jay's face and suddenly there's a glitch in time. I realize how close we are, with me leaning over him to wipe his face.

He says, "Laughter is just what you needed, huh?" He licks his lips and says, "Do you realize, Tahj, that I always know what you need."

No woman needs to be told what it can do to your heart when a man comes to your rescue, especially when you're at your lowest. I feel his hand grasp my elbow. He moves closer. I try not to panic as his face approaches, but he angles up to kiss my forehead. We sit quietly for a spell. There's suddenly a bit of turbulence. I don't know that I would've stopped him if he'd went for my lips because kissing him would've served as revenge against Fletcher.

Just to break the silence, I say, "So we're just gonna pretend that you don't look like a whole new person today?"

He pinches the chest of his shirt, smirking, "Well, you know…"

I look him over and ask, "So how'd this come about?"

"I finally went to that barber you recommended. I should've went a long time ago."

I giggle and say, "When I arrived at the hangar and saw you, I was like who is this? Did Jay send his son?"

"Man let me tell you," says Jay. "These young ladies are coming after *me* now. The compliments… The head turns – and not just when I step out of the Rolls Royce either."

My eyes roll. "Alright, Mr. Big Head."

"I say that, but I'm really not interested in younger women anymore. After Sarah, I think I should be looking for women more my age who've already been in a good marriage. They're more mature; they're no stranger to compromise. They're not trying to use my money to be the envy of their friends. Older women are done with the bullshit. They want something lasting and meaningful." He raises a finger. "But they still gotta be fine though."

I actually touch my sternum, feeling for what might be a flutter of jealousy there because what Jay says he wants, isn't me. Internally, I ask myself, *Am I trippin' right now?* I shudder to shake off the feeling. I start speaking just to take my mind out of that space, but end up saying something I wanted to say to Jay for a while now. "I know Sarah's passing… how sudden… it cut you deep, Jay. And I feel guilty to this day because maybe I wasn't really there for you like you're always there for me."

Jay takes my hand but doesn't look at me when he says, "You were there. No need to feel guilty."

After the flight, Jay drives me to my home, where my car is. He totes my suitcases inside then takes my hands in his. "If you still want to go to Fletcher's place I'll go with you, or maybe I'll follow you."

I hug him and say, "Thank you, Jay, for everything."

We pull back from the hug and he's holding my waist, a bit handsy, I think, but I allow it. "You still haven't said if you're going through with it or not." He lowers his gaze and says, "How about this: either you go confront Fletcher just to get your feelings hurt even more, or come with me and see this big surprise I have waiting for you."

"Big surprise?" I swat the air. "There ain't no surprise, Jay. You just don't want me to go to Fletcher's house."

"No really. It's been over a month in the making."

"I would love to, Jay, but I'm just tired," I lie.

Jay replies, "Have you thought of how much pleasure Riley would get from watching you crying your eyes out on the front steps? Come with me, Tahj. I promise you, this is bigger than anything anyone's ever given you, except for life itself."

I'm taken aback by the thought of Riley looking out the window at me acting hysterical like a crazy ex. At the same time my curiosity about this big surprise locks in. "Well, since you put it that way…"

I go with Jay. He drives us close to the heart of downtown. All along, I'm doubting that this surprise is even real. I say, "There's no surprise is there? You're doing this so I won't go to Fletcher."

"Nope," says Jay. As I said, this has *been* in the making and it's still not quite done. You wanting to confront Fletcher is only forcing my hand to show you early."

Jay parks in front of this closed-down brewery that appears to be undergoing renovations. He could hardly contain his smile.

"What, Jay? What is it?" There's no luxury car adorned with a bow. Nothing in the area stands out to me.

Jay comes around to the passenger side to let me out. I rise out of the car, "Ok, you can tell me now."

Jay, with this lollypop smile, walks towards the construction site and opens a chain-linked fence that obstructs the sidewalk. The brewery is being gutted out. There's a large construction waste bin off to the side. Jay guides me through the fence. "This is all yours."

"What? What're you talking about?"

He stabs a key in a bar lock through the door handles. He opens the doors, and flicks on the lights. "I was gonna wait until it was all the way done."

It seems not far from being done. There's brand-new flooring, recessed lighting, and a counter where a register could go.

"*Talk*, Jay! What is this?"

"It could be a retail store. It could be a bridal shop. Whatever you wanna make it. The reno and a two-year lease is on me. You raked in three million this year; you'll need the tax write-offs. If you don't want it for yourself, sublease it and pocket the money." Jay studies my nonreaction and says to it, "I guess I should've gotten you a Louis Vuitton bag instead."

"No way," I say, distractedly, because I'm so overwhelmed, creeping forward on Bambi legs as I scan the place. "This is me? Stop playing!" I turn around and step backward. "Stop playing, Jay."

Jay says, "I know you're traveling and attending fashion events to get a feel for where you belong in the industry, but I'm like, why? You know where you belong. You've been an agent, a model, *my* fashion consultant… but the one thing you never stopped doing is design. Bring your best designs out of that closet of yours, we'll present it to a manufacturer and work on a distribution deal. This can be your flagship store, right here."

My eyes are wet. I throw myself into Jay for a hug. Accidentally we lean to the same shoulder and find ourselves face to face. This man has been my knight in shining armor on my darkest day; he's giving me life with this gift; plus he lookin' *foyn*. I say screw it. I plant my lips on his, not so much romantically, but on pure, unabashed gratitude. But the biggest surprise is not my very own flagship store; it's the wave of emotion that passes through me the moment our lips touch. Jay gives me the feeling I wish Fletcher could give: the feeling of being cherished.

Jay retreats just enough to say. "I ain't trickin' Tahj. That's not what this is. I did this because you mean so much to me. And *because* you mean so much to me… it kills me that you never got this from any man you've been in a relationship with. Even if they didn't have the means to do something like this, the least they could've done was to handle your heart with care. And they didn't do that either."

Those words send a hundred arrows to my heart. My eyes are a well of tears. I'm crying and trembling, so kissing him again isn't even feasible. Jay pulls me close, rubs my back, and whispers, "It's ok Tahj. Let it go. You're safe with me."

CHAPTER 25
ROSES ON ASPHALT

Fletcher, who never checks his voicemails, finally does. He got my only message, the one I left *before* learning that Riley was in his bed; therefore, Fletcher calls me, thinking I'm still looking to apologize to him. I let him keep on thinking that.

I agree to meet, just to see if Fletcher's capable of lying to my face. If he's honest, there's still a chance for our love even after sleeping with Riley. We were on a break; things happen – like me kissing Jay.

This conversation would also determine how I manage my friendship with Jay – whether we put any expectations out in front of us, or not.

Fletcher said he'd meet me where I am. Where I am, is at a fashion industry summit at Flourish, By Legends, a top-tier event space, yet somehow the event manages to be lowkey rinky-dink with the miscues and disorganization, but it's all love out here, as black fashion entrepreneurs gather in solidarity.

The event starts with a catwalk rotation introducing the models by name; that's where I spot Monae. She struts down the runway, miraculously healed now that she's gotten Fletcher's settlement check.

I see old classmates from CAU, now growing in the industry; I'm seeing girls who came up through the same modeling agency as me. One of the vendors, for example, is an old college classmate with an unforgettable name – like, who the hell names their child Temperance. She'd always say, proudly, that it's Latin. But if you look it up, you see that it's not Latin for goddess or beauty like most girl names; it means the same thing it means in English: self-restraint.

Temperance has gone way off track from fashion. She does property staging and interior design for businesses.

"I'm starting a store, ya know," I say, as I flip through her portfolio. "This is damn good work." Her work is so good, in fact, that I verbally guarantee her the business of designing my store. We exchange business cards and I promise to call Temperance when the structural work is done.

Temperance asks, "I know it's not finished and whatnot, but can I have a look at the space anyway just to see what I'm working with?"

"Anytime," I say. "My schedule is wide open these days."

I move on and make my rounds. Having been an agent for as long as I've been an adult, ya girl ain't never scared to rub elbows.

Soon I'm smiling in the face of the keynote speaker, designer Jayla Adeyemi. She's dark like me, so we're instant kins.

There comes a point when I'm speaking and it seems she's not even listening, but just eyeing me from various angles as if she might hit on me. She cuts me off midsentence, "Who is your agent?"

I pause before saying, "I'm not a model, actually."

"But *did* you model?"

My eyes wonder. I spot Monae in the background.

Jayla adds, "I know a model when I see one. Look at how you stand."

I counter, "But right now my focus is–"

She pokes my midriff-exposed belly. "Can you drop ten pounds in two weeks?"

"But my ass is just now coming in." The joke bombs, I wipe it out of the air. "Just kidding. I can drop weight, but what kind of work are we talking?"

"How does a cover shoot with Touché magazine sound? You and another model flank me on a throne. Plus I got two more shows for this season's lineup." Jayla peeks around me, signaling to someone that she'll be right there. She slips me her card. "Sleep on it. You got until tomorrow to decide."

Jayla squeezes my hand and takes off. I turn and take off in the direction I last spotted Monae. I get a text from Fletcher that he's five minutes away. I'm supposed to meet him outside since he doesn't have tickets to get in. I look up from my phone and suddenly Monae's standing in front of me, her eyes wide behind lightly tinted summer shades. Monae says, "I just came to see if we were on speaking terms."

With no real heat on it, I say, "I see you're up and at em the moment you got your check."

Monae looks away scratching her head so I know the shade is coming. "I thought you came over here to talk about the fact that we still have a year left on our contract."

My head shakes. "No we don't. If you didn't change your phone number I would've called you to let you go as my client for conduct detrimental to my brand."

Monae just nods.

I try turning her focus to the bright side, "I see you're moving up in the world, though. The catwalk is what you always wanted right? And here you are – even with the body tatts, and the stuffed-crust booty…"

Monae goes away laughing. "Oh God…" I'm laughing too. She returns saying, "I know you ain't called my booty no stuffed crust." She places her hands on her hips. "Yeah, technically, I'm on the catwalk, but this ain't how I want it. I don't want to be their little trans token for their diversity theme. I wanna grace the stage as a woman."

"I don't see the issue. You look just like a woman–"

"–I *am* a woman. Don't play." Monae says with batting lashes.

"Slip of the tongue, girl."

Monae squints. "Question, though. How could you terminate our contract for conduct detrimental to the brand, when technically, my conduct happened while I was working for Fletcher. And I did not scam Fletcher; I was really hurt."

"The fight with Riley went viral."

Monae replies, "And it's *still* on-sight if I ever see the bitch again. She snuck me and kicked me smooth down them stairs. I don't care if I spot her in a church, a funeral, or at a wedding. I'm on her ass like stank on shit."

"It's not worth the trouble, Monae."

Monae's head cocks so far to the side, it looks like she's listening to her shoulder. "Look who talking? You must not know."

"Must not know what?"

Monae straightens upright. "You should feel the same way I feel about Riley, because the moment you and Fletcher broke up, she started showing up at the office all dressed up, bringing him home-cooked meals and everything, child."

I try not to show that I'm bothered by Monae saying things that would make it harder for me to get back with Fletcher and still be able look myself in the mirror. The idea of Fletcher (as Bubby said) smashing some chick, who happens to be Riley, is an easier pill to swallow than the idea of them behaving like they're in an actual relationship.

I challenge, "You talk like you still work there. You don't know what you're talking about."

Monae says, "If I don't know what I'm talking about, ask the guys if Riley isn't trying to get a position down at the agency. This bitch not only trying to take your man; she tryna take your whole life."

"You're making this up because you want me to hate Riley as much as you do." Monae returns a look of scorn, to which I reply, "I'm supposed to talk to Fletcher in just a few minutes. What if he denies all of it? Give me proof so I can catch him in a lie. So, again. How do you know all this?"

"Okay, I'm gone tell you." Monae's eyes thin behind her shades. "But you can't tell *nobody*, hear me?" Monae looks around, twirling her hair. "I'm seeing Keenan… and he tells me everything."

I'm staggered by this. "You and Keenan? How is that possible?"

Monae lowers her sunglasses to reveal a bloodshot eye. "I don't know that it *is* possible, Tahj. Every time he sleeps with me, he wanna turn around and fight me."

"I'm so sorry to hear that, Mo. And you're still with him?"

Monae shrugs. "We're in love."

I vent, "I would never think that Keenan could hit a woman."

"He's conflicted inside. He's not fighting me; he's fighting himself."

"Have you reported it?" Monae looks away. I lean, chasing her eyes. "You gotta report it, Monae. Because I promise you: one day, he's gonna go too far one day – and I hate to think what could happen."

Monae blinks fast to beat back her tears. "Don't lose no sleep over me, Tahj. I'm good." Monae slips her shades back on her face. "Gotta go." She turns and goes backstage in preparation for the next set.

I check my phone and see Fletcher's text. I hurry outside and wait by the valet stand, and spot Fletcher parking in the back row. I approach him because if this turns into an argument we'd have privacy out among rows of cars.

I'm popping gum and I'm ready. My tongue is so sharpened from cursing him out so many times in my mind, that I'm sure the final product would be brilliant. He carries a bouquet of roses. I meet him halfway, cat walking between a row of cars. He looks me over like a meal, his eyes zeroing in on my cross-strap midriff. He says, "Girl you know you bad. Comin' out here witchya lil midriff. You know that's my weakness."

I glance. "Grey sweatpants? Really?" Not to mention the V-neck showing off the canyon down the middle of his chest.

Fletcher hands me the bouquet in this beautiful glazed vase. He says, "Can I go first?"

I inhale the aroma of red roses and set it down at my feet.

Fletcher says, "I know you said you didn't like how things went down, and… you wanna maybe clear the air, and that doesn't mean you wanna necessarily change your mind about us. Look, I don't blame you if the sight of me still makes you wanna scream. I just want you to know that, I only picked up a drink once since that day. I haven't really been rockin' with DJ and Greedy, like that."

I say, "Why are you telling me this?"

"Because I want you to know that I'm over here getting my shit together." He seems so earnest and contrite, I just wish he was not lying through his teeth.

Deep down, I wanna play clueless and give in to him. I don't wanna be here standing before the man I love, looking at the ground to avoid his eyes, and feeling like I have to keep my hands to myself.

Fletcher adds, "And I'm gonna give you your money back sooner than you think. I acquired an NBA player. Their free agent signing period starts in June."

Inconspicuously, I ask, "And you haven't been with anyone else?"

Fletcher smiles as if my accusation is adorable. "Bubby told me, you thought a woman picked up my phone. That was me, baby. I just wasn't in the right headspace to talk to you. That's why I turned my phone off."

Lies. I'm furious inside. "So, you were alone? You haven't slept with anyone since we broke up?"

Fletcher smiles and says, "Where's all this coming from?"

With a straight face, I lie and say, "I talked to Riley."

Fletcher buckles as if gut-punched.

"And you're standing here acting like you're getting your shit together, lying to my face!"

"Wait, Tahj. Hold up. It's not what you think."

"If it was some random chick, maybe I could get past it, but my friend? Why?"

Fletcher says, "What happened with Riley doesn't count."

"How the fuck does it not count?!"

"I was too drunk to consent. She forced herself on me."

I let out a crazed laughter. "Your big strong self couldn't fight off little ole Riley?"

"I was damn near passed out."

I take out my phone and play my voicemail. "You hear that? That's the sound of bedsheets. How did she get all the way in your bedroom *to* force herself on you?"

"It didn't happen in the bedroom. She wouldn't leave. She followed me there afterwards." Fletcher's eyes widen at my phone still playing the message. "Did you hear that? You hear me tell her to leave me alone? I was cursing her out the whole time." He pulls out his phone, scrolling through pages of texts, "Wanna see where she apologized for what she did to me?"

"No. I wanna know why you're acting as if Riley slipped and fell on your dick – when I know for a fact that she's been coming by the office and bringing you home-cooked meals." Fletcher stiffens, as if caught. I say, "Didn't think I knew?"

He responds, "I didn't lead her on, if that's what you're implying."

"Regardless, it happened. You come to me with flowers, but with no intention of disclosing any of this? Didn't you think I would eventually find out? Did you think I could somehow get past this? Would you be able to get past it if I fucked Jay?"

Fletcher takes a long blink, his eyes still closed when he begins, "Wait, what?"

I raise a finger. "Don't get selective hearing. I said *if.*"

Fletcher's head shakes. "But why would you even say that? The situations don't match. Riley was your friend, but Jay was never a friend of mine, so using him as a comparison seems mighty forced. Y'all fucked?"

"No." I would've been stuck had he asked if we kissed.

Fletcher points as if he's seen a ghost. "That's a real soft no, Tahj. Did you?" His brow contorts. "*Did* you?" He keeps repeating the question while inching forward until he's towering over me. He repeats the question again as if he doesn't hear me denying it over and over again.

"How many times do I have to tell you, no!"

Towering over me, Fletcher whispers. "Did you give Jay my pussy?"

I place my hands on his chest to give us some space. "I haven't had sex with anyone. If you don't believe me, I can give you definitive proof. And once you see that your curve is still there, I can go back to being mad at you afterwards, ya feel me?"

Fletcher's eyes are closed, but not blissfully. Internally, he's wrestling with something. This nigga backs away, hands up, talmbout, "I don't want to be touched."

I'm like, "You bring me flowers in grey sweatpants, telling me how you're getting your act together, for what? So we can shake hands?"

"I was violated," he says. "And this doesn't feel any different."

Before I know it, I'm saying, "Man gat-damn, Fletcher! You *stay* in turmoil, bro. Something always got you fucked up!"

"If you think you can control me with sex, then *you* got me fucked up."

I point to the stick of dynamite bulging in his sweatpants. "Can't you see how ya mans down there threw me off a bit? Or maybe I thought–"

"–You *thought…*" He taps his temple with a finger. "…you thought that I didn't have any self-control. You don't think I'm a real person."

Suddenly, the puzzle comes together in my mind. His behavior is more telling than seeing any apology texts from Riley. Fletcher's exhibiting the traits of a victim, using a subsequent encounter as a chance to reclaim his power.

I would've explained to Fletcher that I understand, and I would've asked him to share the experience, and I would listen and not judge him, but Fletcher's acting out and ranting.

I'm standing there watching this guy crash out over nothing; dick still hard in his sweats, as he marches over to the flower vase that I set on the asphalt. Fletcher raises the glazed vase straight above his head and smashes it on the concrete. "Maybe I should go back to hoeing," he exclaims as he jumps in truck and slams the door. He peels off, leaving the broken clay vase and scattered roses in his wake.

When I return to Jay later on that day, I'm half there, thinking about how truly sorry I feel for Fletcher. But at the same time, I saw precisely the kind of drama that I don't need in my life.

With Jay, I see precisely the kind of calm discernment that I *do* need in my life. Of course, I say nothing about meeting Fletcher, but I tell Jay about the Fashion Industry Summit, particularly about Jayla's offer to model for her.

I'm in his closet sliding hangers, sorting out a few ensembles for him. "I just don't know what to do," I say. "How can I turn down an opportunity to be on the cover of Touché? Then she invited me to two shows. And I ain't no slouch when it comes to the runway. I could have everyone buzzing about me. The store won't be done for a while, so maybe there's time to…" I pause and look to the doorway because Jay's so quiet. He's just standing there, staring me down.

"Do what you want," Jay says. "But it sounds like you're leaving *your* dream and entering Jayla's."

I shake my head in awe of him. "You're so right. How do you *do* that?"

"How do I do what?"

"Take something so complicated and make it so simple. You don't add to my stress; you make it go away."

"I thought you fed off of stress, and that's why you're drawn to what's-his-name." Jay approaches slowly, intently. "Maybe you're finally ready to enter your soft era."

Just hearing it makes me close my eyes and bask in my imagination. I open my eyes and Jay's right there in front of me. He tries to take me in his arms, but I lift the hanger between us and say, "Try this on." I step around him, then glance back at the stack of outfits lying across the ottoman. "Try those on too."

Now all I'd have to do is lay back and play fashion judge. I've been eyeing this magnificent bed this whole visit. I desire it like I desire a lover. I stand at the foot of the bed, feeling the synthetic mink rug between my toes for a bit of foreplay. I stretch all the way out on the bed and claw the sheets like a housecat. By the time Jay comes out in his second outfit, I'm blinking off to sleep.

The sleep was so good I wake up drooling and not knowing where or *when* I am. I see dusk out the window and mistake it for dawn. I jerk upward into a sitting position thinking I'm in seventh grade missing the school bus, but then I remember that I'm a whole grown-ass woman.

Jay lay beside me. My movement rouses him. I return to my pillow, turned away. He scoots closer behind me, and asks, "Are you okay?"

"Yeah," I say.

He kisses me in the opening of my backless dress and feels me tense up, so he doesn't do it again. He starts running his hand along my body, my arms, my waist, and my belly. He asks, "Is this okay, me touching you? I'll stop if it's not."

"You're okay." I say with my mouth, but in my mind I'm saying, I hope this man doesn't think I'm about to have sex with him.

Jay says, "I know you're not over him. I think you *want* to be over him though."

He waits for a response that I'm not about to give.

Jay, in his deep soothing voice, says, "I can help you."

The way his hand glides over my body, I think I know what he means. I don't know what to say. I just hope that my silence is taken as rejection.

But then Jay leans in, his breath hot on the back of my neck when he says, "Let *me* do *you*."

I haven't had any in a while, so the idea of getting off without catching another body, sounds intriguing.

"I will do you as many times as you need before you're ready to take that next step." He kisses the back of my neck. I moan intentionally, to be taken as a yes.

I let Jay turn me over. I'm not ready to be intimate, but at the same time, I'm thinking, I'm about to get my pussy sucked by someone who has twenty years of experience over any man who has done it to me before, so there's some curiosity there, some anticipation. And judging by the mastery of his hands caressing my body, I'm guessing that this is about to be sublime.

It starts out like research to me, observing how a man of his years approaches making love to a woman. He savors every moment, the kiss of my lips, the gaze in my eyes, the care in how he takes down my dress, the hand now venturing to my breasts, not squeezing but gathering them gently. He doesn't go straight for the nipples but licks carefully around the outer curves. I never knew that area to be so sensitive.

He's in no rush to get to the main event. His patience, however, has a double edge. For one, I'm feeling every fiber of pleasure to the fullest; on the other hand, the anticipation is driving me insane.

He plots warm kisses in a trail down my belly, and then my inner thighs. I'm trembling by the time he raises my legs and positions his head between them. He wets a peace sign, then massages the lips with his fingers. I'm so revved up with anticipation that my exhale, exhales. My clit sheds its hood. Jay whispers, "There it is." He spits on it and then captures it in his mouth.

Oh, the long, slow, slurps has me calling his name out loud – has me lifting my head trying to see how he makes this level of pleasure even possible. He lifts my bottom clear off the bed in the cradle of his hands, and puts his face in it. He turns me over and starts eating me from the back. I'm moaning in broken pitch, and then my soul leaves my body when, as I'm climaxing, he starts going to town, licking my crack with his whole tongue. My mouth opens forward like a large freshwater bass, and out comes a long, singing opera note.

It was so good, that I find myself afterward lying next to him, finger-drawing circles on his chest while campaigning for the next time. "A few more soirees of this, and I think I *will* be over Fletcher."

CHAPTER 26
PEEP SHOW

There comes a point where I realize that I'm becoming addicted. Ever since that Saturday matinee in an empty theatre with a leg tossed over the back of a chair and Jay slurping me like hot soup, you couldn't pay me to wear pants around this man. It's all skirts for easy access. I also keep spare underwear in my purse and glove compartment.

I even went into the sex store, cloaked in a hoodie, to get some sprayable fragrances and flavors for him to enjoy. Jay's plan is working, it seems; my desire to be with Fletcher, is slowly fading.

I did see Fletcher again, one evening. He was speaking in codes but our telepathy was shot. He tried to seduce me, but I was able to resist him. If not for my soirees with Jay, Fletcher would have surely folded me up on his couch.

He said he needs someone to talk to but all I do is argue, *but you just wanna beat me over the head with my mistakes.*

Try therapy, I smart.

He counters, *If I can't talk to you, who do you think I'm pouring my heart out to?*

I scream, *Be with Riley, then!* I was done.

One morning, Monae called, saying she needed to talk, but wouldn't discuss it over the phone. I prepared myself to hear that maybe Fletcher has Riley pregnant.

It's starting to feel really funny, Monae and me, being friends again. Our friendship was over when she scammed Fletcher, but after learning of the abuse, I keep in touch, out of concern for her safety.

We're at Lennox Square Mall, in the Burberry store going from rack to rack, carding through summer wear while chitchatting. I break the seal on my topic first. "Are you alright?"

"I just be chillin' girl, staying out these streets."

I give lazy eyes. "You know what I mean."

Monae pauses. "Oh, that? That ain't nothin'."

"Until it's something," I counter.

"We're doing good. Kee asked me if I wanna move."

"Move? As in…"

"To another state. Together. He said he can hire somebody to help Fletcher run the company day to day."

I say, "Well the next time something happens, you gotta report it, okay. And if not for your own safety, do it for the money."

Monae looks up from the halter top held to her torso. "What money?"

"Take pictures every time it happens, so you can have a solid civil case to sue for damages. For someone who makes as much money as Keenan, you can get about a million dollar settlement, according to Jay."

Monae smirks and says, "You know what, Tahj? You're starting to get on my nerves talking about Jay *this* Jay *that* – for everything."

My head trembles no. "Girl please, I do not do that."

"How not? I've been standing here listening to you do it the whole time."

I make my mouth smack and say, "Anyway… What do you have to tell me?"

"*Girl…*" Monae's head shakes. "You not gone like this, but… Fletcher and Riley are now official."

I hardly flinch. "It doesn't surprise me. He bonds over trauma, dating his rapist comes as no surprise. God bless them," I say.

Monae punches her hand. "Whet? I'm trying to get you to ride out with me and pull up on the bitch. She done took your man and you talmbout some: God bless 'em? I know you lyin'."

"That's not even my style. I don't pull up."

"You pulled up on me in the elevator that day when you thought I wanted Fletcher."

"It didn't go down like that," I say.

Monae sighs, "Girl, Jay got your nose so wide open, it don't make no sense."

I roll my eyes. "You're just determined to get on my nerves today."

"Okay, so, back to what I was saying. Keenan confronted Fletcher about it. He said that was messed up how Fletcher did you – messing with someone you used to call friend."

"Keenan said that? Keenan who hates my guts?"

"If not for you, Keenan would've never met the love of his life," Monae says, with batting lashes. "But wait: let me tell you *how* it went down…"

To summarize Monae's report, when Keenan confronted Fletcher, Fletcher explained how Riley took advantage of him when he was drunk. Fletcher felt so violated, he cut her off completely, but a week later, after smashing the vases of roses while arguing with me, Fletcher got drunk and called Riley over. Monae says, "Little did Riley know, Fletcher was planning his get-back. Riley took off them clothes, and Fletcher turned her lil yellow ass over and went Ham!" Monique adds, "Riley couldn't take the dick," so she started crying. In Fletcher's mind, he was no longer the victim, but *she* was. Fletcher felt terrible. He felt *so* terrible, in fact," says Monae. "He was willing to do anything to make it up to Riley, even if it meant being with her," Monae says with pursed lips. "And that's what he did."

I'd been wearing a look of disgust throughout the telling. "That's gotta be the saddest story ever about how a relationship was formed."

Monae says, "Well, I ain't got no room to talk because baby me and Keenan got them beat."

A call comes in. Monae rolls her eyes because she could tell by my smile that it's Jay. After a few pleasantries, I'm saying, "Yeah, I can be there in an hour."

I look down at my half-T and stylish ripped jeans and say, "I gotta change outfits." I buy a tennis skirt, and take it straight to the dressing room. Monae stands at the door, chastising me. You gotta change clothes just to go have lunch with your man? You're weird."

My weird-ass heads on over to that courthouse. Jay waits at the top of the steps, leaning on the rail. His phone is to his ear, so I figured he missed my text.

I get out and start walking towards him. He spots me, then starts hurrying down the steps as if something's wrong. He swerves my kiss and gives a side hug, which he uses to spin me around and guide me in the direction from which I came.

I ask, "Where do you want to have lunch?"

"Nowhere," he says. "I thought you knew to dress a little more… grown."

"Why? When I didn't plan on getting out of the car. We're going to a restaurant."

"You see all these people leaving the courthouse on lunch break? Where do you think they're going? To any restaurant, café, or bistro that we might go to. These are judges and lawyers. I'd have to go right back in that courtroom after lunch and face them." He looks around conspicuously, and says, "They give me enough shit about my new look. I'm not about to have them calling me a sugar daddy too."

I smirk and shake my head, but not for humor. Because Jay is one comment away from me telling him about his ass.

He asks, "Where're you parked?"

I tiptoe and point. "Over there, in the back."

His head tosses the other direction. "We'll go to my car." He's already texting his assistant to bring us lunch.

I smile at his car, and say, "Not the Rollie."

He opens the passenger door for me. "I drive the Rolls Royce for intimidation."

He goes around to the driver's side and gets in. "The lawyer I'm facing today… Never seen anything like her. I'm getting my ass handed to me."

"You're having a bad day," I say. "Is that why you wanted me to come by? To support you… emotionally?"

"Well, yeah," he says. "Also, I just want her to see how beautiful my girl is. Make her feel small."

"What," I say in delightful confusion.

His arm reaches across the seat. His hand goes under my tennis skirt. I say, with no effort to stop him, "You stay playin' in my pussy, Jay. But it's always you doing me. That's not cool." It's pathetic actually, to be with a man who requires nothing of me – knowing he's merely a placeholder for the man I really want, but Fletcher makes me so emotionally unhinged that I would scream at the top of my lungs in the lobby of a bank. Sometimes being with Jay makes me feel like maybe chaos is better than being with someone like him, even though he's better *for* me; he doesn't move my emotional needle. With Jay, my desire for him only arises when I'm getting something I want: private jet service, a storefront renovation, dining at five-star restaurants, the designer purse full of cash just the other day, and the best fellatio on the face of this earth.

My knees are up against the dashboard of a Rolls Royce, squirming in my seat because his fingers are so good it makes me wonder if he has a pussy of his own to play with. He dips his fingers, wetting them and then rolls my clit under his slimy touch. My back arcs against the seat, my eyes shut tight as I moan, "Dayumn, Jay. How did you get so *good* at this?" I turn my head and open my eyes, really looking for an answer, but I see that Jay is distracted, his eyes fixed on something. "What're you looking at," I inquire.

"There she is," he says.

"Who?"

"The lawyer who's kicking my ass right now. Brown hair, long khaki skirt, all by herself… not being social… not on the phone. She's leaning against a pillar eating a fucking Yoplait yogurt with a plastic spoon." Jay's two middle fingers reach inside of me. My hips curve, helping him reach a spot I'd only read about before experiencing it with him. I lift the front of my tennis skirt to see. He has my vulva gripped like a briefcase handle, the two middle fingers missing to the last knuckle. The feeling is so immense, that I wanna warn him that I'm about to lose control. Still, he keeps talking. "She knows what we're doing, but she's trying not to stare… Uh, oh. There she goes." Jay giggles. I imagine from this lonely woman's vantage point, observing me with my head tilted back, my mouth as wide open as a morning yawn. Jay laughs, "Did you see that, Tahj?"

My head lay to the side to look at him. I'm panting as if I'd ran laps. "How could I?"

Jay taps my leg. "My assistant's coming. Straighten up."

I do no more than pull my skirt down. So when his assistant arrives to hand us to-go bags through the driver's side window, the young man sees my head laid off to the side and my chest heaving, which forces him to asks, "Is she okay?"

"Asthma attack," explains Jay. "Just took the inhaler; she's coming around."

By the time I gain my wits about me and I'm sipping soda and eating curly fries, I revisit the subject of this rival lawyer. "You asked me to have lunch with you, just to put on a peep show for her?"

"I expected to have lunch at a restaurant, remember?"

Softly, and without anger, I say, "When we're together, I'd like the focus to be on us."

"It was. That's why I didn't stop just because someone was looking. It just so happens to work in my favor. When we go back in that courtroom, maybe she'll be uncomfortable. Maybe she'll be off her game."

"You'd go that far to win?"

"You have no *idea* how far I'd go to win."

"Would you cheat, to win?"

"That wasn't cheating. Just a little manipulation, that's all."

"A little manipulation? Is that what you're doing to *me*?"

The way Jay turns to me I could tell that he feels attacked. "Look, you already said you didn't like my focus being elsewhere and I respect that. It should've ended there, but you wanna take that one thing and run with it?"

"I wasn't about to run with anything." Actually, I was, but since he headed me off, it renders me silent. That silence floats on for a few beats until I say, "You can't manipulate me into loving you."

"Love? You think I want *love* from you? I want *access* to you. Let's get it straight."

I'm so shocked, I'm stupid too because I can't speak. I'd never heard anything so cold leave his mouth.

Jay adds, "It is in *your* best interest to fall in love. Life with me would be a lot more pleasant for you, if ya did."

Before I say anything, I just look at him. Just in case he's talking reckless, I give him a few moments to come to his senses and take it back, but he doesn't. He's standing on business, so I follow suit. "Thank you Jay, for getting me all the way together. Now that I know what this is, I can tell you right now, I don't want it."

He reaches. "Tahj."

I snatch my hand. "Don't touch me! Old ass."

"I'll be that," he says. "But from now on, you can eat your *own* pussy."

"Dirty old man. I can't believe I fuck witchyou." I open the door and step out of the car.

Jay says, "And ya better not slam my door!"

"Fuck you!" Rolls Royce or not, I slammed that door so hard I pooted.

I start speedwalking to my car, just rolling the words around in my head. Access? Access to me...? Fuck he think this is? He thinks I'm supposed to bow to him because he has money? Fuck that. I have money too. I'm good.

It's just disheartening because I thought that Jay and I were above these kinds of blowups. To hear this wise, mature man tell me to eat my own pussy, was disappointing. Maybe more disappointing is what I'm *not* hearing: his footsteps coming after me. I look back and I see him, framed by the drivers' side window, his hand tickling goodbye with the same fingers he had inside of me. I flick him off in return.

He thinks I'm playing. All I needed was for him to give me a window. My middle finger, is me leaping out of that window. Jay doesn't know it, but our little so-called relationship is definitely over. Forever.

As soon as I get in my car, I get a call coming in. The contact says Temperance. "Shit," I say. "The store."

CHAPTER 27
THE DEBT

Six months later, Fletcher calls and asks to meet in person so he can return my 1.2 million dollars. It feels like the closing of a chapter because Jay and I, at this point, we're locked in; he's my man. That blowup we had was our only one. We made up the same day, and our relationship has been beautiful, but he's been hinting at marriage, and I don't know about all that.

It's December, and the grand opening for my boutique had already come and gone. Bubby flew out because he knew that the other two Musketeers weren't coming, for obvious reasons. With Fletcher not so much as reaching out via congratulatory text, helped me decide that I would never entertain any ideas of being with him ever again.

Besides, life's good. I'm loving my work, and I love the fact that Momma's running the store with me. Her biggest regret was closing down her boutique, so mine gives her new life; she adores Jay because of it. My dad had his reservations about Jay's age, but now they're pals. I once overheard Daddy thanking Jay for being so good to his only girl.

I feel like I'm fulfilling my purpose. I'm attending women empowerment summits. The girls who model my clothing all look up to me, and in just six months, I'm already making a name for myself on the local fashion scene. I may not have the lover I always wanted, but with Jay, I'm living the life I always wanted.

Fletcher and Riley are now a serious couple, so there appears to be no regrets on either side.

When I meet Fletcher at the bank, I make it a point to show how unbothered I am. While sitting through the lengthy transaction, our conversation stays surface-level.

On the way out, the chill bites us as soon as our shoes hit the grit of the sidewalk. We share an awkward hug and go our separate ways. I walk away with my eyes wide and lost, *So, that's it?*

I look back over the shoulder of my red tweed jacket and see that Fletcher's turned too. He's wearing an uncomfortable-looking smirk, through which he says, "How about we celebrate?"

I smile.

I follow Fletcher's Range Rover in the Porsche Cayenne Coupe that Jay bought for me. We end up at a bar called the Bookhouse Pub on Ponce De Leon Ave. We choose high tables away from the bar. Fletcher doesn't pull out my chair for me, which is something I wouldn't have given a thought, had I never been with a man like Jay; however, after all this time, I still look at Fletcher thinking, *damn* he fine.

I order a martini. Fletcher orders a sweet tea, extra lemon. My brow wrinkles. Fletcher explains, "I don't drink. At all."

We browse the menu for a while, adding small talk. I say, "Why are you looking all up-and-through that menu just to end up with a cheeseburger?"

He laughs. "You know me—" *babe* nearly slipped out.

We place our orders and surrender our menus to the waiter. I say, "Look at us." I see Fletcher glitch on the word *us*, so I rush to clarify, "We're all grown up now. Seems like just yesterday, we were in high school clowning in the hallways or chillin' at the mall. Now we're entrepreneurs… We're doing really well, financially—"

"—*Really* well, financially for you," Fletcher says. "I mean, look at you… You even look different."

My brow climbs. "Different how?"

Conversation gets thrown off by the arrival of our drinks.

Fletcher starts stirring his tea, as if he has no intentions of revisiting my question.

I press, "You said I look different?"

"Like royalty… Like you should have servants at your beck and call. Obviously, Jay takes really good care of you."

My eyes thin and I turn away like an unamused cat.

"I never stood a chance, huh," Fletcher complains.

"Don't you *even*… Money had nothing to do with it."

"I just got one question," Fletcher asks, with the gait of a fox. "While we were together… did anything ever happen between you and Jay?"

"Really?" With no real heat, I say, "If I knew you were inviting me here to question my loyalty, I would've taken my ass on home. You're still jealous? I thought you evolved."

"I have. I've evolved enough to admit that I'm having a bitter moment, and I apologize." Fletcher sighs and says, "The whole time we were at the bank, I was just watching you, in awe of you… seeing how soft and demure you've become. No matter how fiercely I loved you, I was in the way of *this* woman. It's looking like Jay is the right man for you and I don't know how to take that."

"Wow," I say, softly. "I couldn't imagine the old Fletcher with this level of accountability. Was *I* in the way of *this* Fletcher? I could easily say that Riley is the right woman for you." I sip my pineapple martini before adding, "And it's not like you're the only one who has bitter moments. You don't think I'm ticked off that Riley gets this version of you? Why couldn't you get it together for me?"

The food arrives, and we get off track while interacting with the server about our meals and drinks, and in the back of my mind, I'm just wondering how Fletcher will answer the question. I don't see much of Riley and Fletcher, but I hear, through Monae, how Fletcher dotes on her and showers her with gifts, now that he makes a fifty-fifty split with Keenan. I was his provider and caretaker, in a sense, but Riley gets to be a woman of leisure? I can't help feeling like I prepared Fletcher for her.

Once the waiter leaves, I can see that Fletcher hasn't forgotten the question, a question he seems to have been waiting all his life to answer. His hands slide out across the table, and it takes me a second to realize what he's doing. I place my hands in his and watch his eyes close and head bow. "Dear Lord, we thank you for the meal you have set before us…"

My head is not bowed and my eyes are not closed; they're open wide with wonder. Where was *this* man while we were together?

As soon as I hear *amen*, I blink – frontin' like my eyes were closed the whole time.

Fletcher picks a French fry from his plate and says, "I didn't get myself together for Riley. If it's for Riley or for you, or anyone but myself, it's bound to fail." He's chewing one fry and pointing another when he says, "So here's how it happened: I was such a wreck, I thought I needed football again. I knew it was a longshot, but I was desperate. Since teams worried about my concussions, I sought out a specialist to clear me. I failed the short-term memory assessment. I then went through a series of interviews. Then Dr. Feldman ordered an MRI of my head, my brain…"

I lean in, worried.

Fletcher says, "I'm going to tell you something that I haven't told anyone – not Bubby, not Riley, not even Momma and Daddy. So please don't repeat it."

"Fletch, you're scaring me."

"I'm telling you because it's the only way to explain what was going on with me while we were together, okay? I have Chronic Traumatic Encephalopathy."

I mouth Oh my God. With a name that long and all the secrecy, I figure it must be tragic.

Fletcher smiles. "Did you even hear me? It's only CTE."

"That's what I thought you said." I dab my eyes with my dinner napkin.

"Believe the horror stories, but know that there's levels."

"But isn't CTE only diagnosable postmortem?"

"I don't have a diagnosis. I have a professional opinion based on clues in the MRI and the interviews. It explains everything, my lack of impulse control, the drinking, the jealousy, the anger, the depression."

I cover my mouth. My life was a lie. My surviving Fletcher story is really his surviving CTE story.

"Just knowing that it was my brain, and not me," Fletcher says. "That was the game changer."

Fearfully, I ask, "So, does this condition deteriorate or... What's gonna happen to you?"

"My life is gonna be as normal as anybody else's, just with*out* alcohol, *with* daily meditation and the grace of God."

I stare ahead, but look back, revising the past. "All the things I blamed you for... The things I held against you... None of it was your fault."

"Regardless, I did those things. And the regret weighs on me. I may have just repaid you a million U.S. dollars, Tahj, but I feel like I owe you a million more in love."

Hearing this, I'm not okay, but I hold it together like a cracked vase, chin resting on fist, wondering if Fletcher invited me here looking to unpack the fact that we're still in love. I feeling vulnerable, so I back into my emotional safehouse: humor. I should be gazing in his eyes and confessing my feelings; instead, I deliver a punchline with a coy smile and a wink. "Since you owe me a million in love, I'll text you the drop-off location. And it better be all there."

Fletcher bites his smile and rubs his hands together like Birdman. "I see you got jokes."

"No, you got jokes. Coming out of your mouth like that as if you're not in a whole relationship – with my ex-friend." I wasn't even thinking that, so I wonder how it got out of my mouth. Again, I clean it up with humor, an uneven brow and a tongue-in-cheek, "Are you happy though?"

Fletcher mocks, "Are *you* happy?"

"I'm decided," I say, hoping his takeaway would be that I didn't say yes.

Fletcher huffs, "Decided... with that old man?"

Mildly triggered, I take a deep breath because I don't play about our age gap. For the last half-year it's been me, getting people all the way together when they mistake us for father and daughter, so naturally, I respond with a little heat. "Well, that old man got me feeling like a young man could never."

Fletcher frowns, "I know you're not talkin' about–"

"–Emotionally, bro. Getchya mind out the gutter."

As if Fletcher's ego is his jacket, he tugs it and says, "I was about to *say*…"

My eyes roll.

Fletcher says, "To answer your question. Am I happy? First of all, you asked it like you was expecting me to say no… Yes I'm happy."

"Yet you're telling me you owe me love?"

"I see what this is," Fletcher says. What you wanna hear, is anything along the lines of me being the ex who's miserable without you. How about this: for me, Tahj, you are definitely the one that got away, but that doesn't mean I can't still be happy, amen? In your eyes, Riley is merely the sum of all the things she's done to you. She's actually a lot more than that. She's really good to me, she's supportive…"

I raise a stiff hand. "Let me stop you right there. I'm not about to sit here and listen to you brag about her, bro. If you were any other ex you'd be dead to me for what you did. You borrow a million dollars then went and got with my friend? You should thank me for not showing up at your bedside with a boxcutter."

Fletcher jokingly rubs his throat, echoing, "Come to my bedside with a *box* cutter…"

"I thought about it, actually," I say, casually. "There ain't too many chicks I know, that could still be cordial with you, much less having dinner witchyo monkey ass. I took that heartbreak on the chin and I *ate* that shit."

Fletcher takes a timely bite of his burger, figuring he'll keep his mouth busy while I vent.

"But no… I would take no satisfaction in you being down bad about us. Before we became a couple, we were friends for how many years? So, naturally, I want what's best for you. And with that being said, I'll say this: I think you should tell Riley about your condition."

A lazy-eyed Fletcher's says, "I'm not doing that. I'm not doin' it."

"She can help. She can be a second set of eyes for you. You two *are* in a serious relationship, right? Most likely she's gonna be your wife pretty soon so…"

Fletcher cuts his eyes and says, "Are you being messy, right now?"

After just being called out for being messy, here I go, "If not your wife, Riley will soon be your baby momma because your pull-out game is weak."

I sip martini and watch his head go back with laughter, even raising a knee. Fletcher recovers to say, "Nah, my pull-out game is only weak with *you*."

Now it's me giggling like a chessy cat. It goes on for so long, I can't even keep it sexy no more. I'm like, "Fletcher, why you' so *stu*pid?" And it's not so much his timing or delivery. I'm laughing at how he managed to shade Riley and compliment me in the same breath. I'm laughing because it feels so satisfying to hear Fletcher – in so many words – that I'm still his best lover. If Jay was outside peeking through the storefront glass, seeing how I'm kee-keeing in Fletcher's face, he'd never let me live this down.

I came here expecting closure, but messed around and got my heart buss open. I am *not* over Fletcher; there's no denying it. Now I gotta get through another 15-20 minutes of dinner without exposing myself.

Fletcher says, "Did you hear what I just said?"

"Huh?" I was so deep in my thoughts, I didn't even know he was talking. I say, "I missed that. Sorry, I was distracted." Distracted by the fact that I've never stopped loving you.

Fletcher pardons me with a smile. "I was saying, that I won't tell Riley about my condition because she won't let me breathe as it is. Why? Because she's insecure. And *because* she's so insecure I have to…" Fletcher stops and sighs, "Actually, I'm ashamed to say all the things I have to do, to reassure her that I won't drag her like Gideon did."

I counter with a strong, "*Or* she's afraid to lose you like she got you."

"Stop it," Fletcher swats. "You and I were not together, when–"

"–When she raped you?"

Fletcher's face goes dead. "Anyway. It's not only Riley getting on my nerves, it's her stepdad too. He stay in our business, plus he be trying to recruit me."

"Recruit you?"

"Since I'm recognizable, because of football, he wants me to be a leader in the Black Evangelical Community."

My eyes widen over a slick smile. "A leader in the Black Evangelical Community?"

Fletcher adds. "I don't fuck wit him, though… Ole Leprechaun shoes ass nigga."

There I am, kee-keeing again. Fletcher stops me with a look. I say, "What?"

He turns serious. "Another thing is… They're pressuring us to get married."

"What's the rush?"

"They think Riley's still a virgin holding out for marriage."

I dip forward on both words: "A virgin? Riley?"

Fletcher shows both palms. "All I can say, is that their church pressures her to keep up a certain image."

"What church concerns themselves with who you're fucking?"

"Riley's stepdad brought us to the prophet to bless our relationship – I thought. Come to find out, this nigga was approving our relationship."

I'm lean way in scorn. "Boy, whet! What've you gotten yourself into? What kind of church is this?"

"The kind of church that's members only. They don't open their doors to the public. They only accept new members by referral."

"You know what that is?" I start snapping my fingers as a way to call the word to me. "A cult. That's what it is. You better get out while you can."

"It ain't no cult."

"Are you sure?"

"Go on somewhere with that, Tahj."

"Are you *sure?*"

"Tahj…." We stare each other down, rooted in our opinions. The stare-down is broken by the server setting down the check. Fletcher quickly hands over his card in an attempt to beat me to the punch.

He then smirks at me and my folded arms, realizing I never even reached for my card.

"Well damn," he says, playfully. "You used to, at least, fake-try to pay."

The comment spurs a few memories that we reminisce over for a spell. Then we get up and leave the bar with me on Fletcher's arm. We chat and giggle to the sound of our sidewalk stroll.

Fletcher says, "It's that time of year again. The Peach Bowl Bash is right around the corner. You coming?"

"Is it still at Club Ultra?"

"Yeah."

I ask a question without words, engaging our telepathy again to see if it still works. *Will Riley be there?*

He confirms with a look-away.

My car chirps, signaling our departure. I turn and say, "I'm glad we talked… This is the closure we needed."

Fletcher huffs. "There can't be no closure between us."

"Excuse me?" I'm acting surprised when it's the response I hoped for. I'm thinking, if this man takes me in his arms and tells me he can't live without me, there's no telling what I would do.

Fletcher looks into my eyes like he would look upon a horizon, and says, "Don't you know, that if I'd went to that doctor sooner, we'd still be together?"

I try to avoid emotional infidelity by way of the eyes, so I look down. He licks his lips and I get that private little thrill, so I look down at the ground to see his caramel burnt tips shuffle close to my red pumps. He lifts my face. My pulse drums.

I provide a fail-safe by kissing my fingertips, and then I reach forward, transposing the kiss to Fletcher's lips. Fletcher gently pulls my hand down and closes in. I refuse to look away. We linger on the other side of that line we just crossed. We're only cheating if we're going back, but the emotions that spill into this kiss feels like the beginning of our happily ever after. The kiss fastens for the length of a long inhale. The release has us catching our breath.

I have so much to say, but Fletcher beats me to it, "I'm sorry," he says. "I just had to do that. I'm not trying to–"

"–Not trying to what?!" My pressure spikes, because with that kiss we gave our hearts and now it seems as if Fletcher's trying to take his back. "You don't fucking kiss me and then tell me what it's not!"

Fletcher's shocked. I see his thoughts spinning like a slot machine and landing on, "Did you think we were gonna have an affair?"

My hands flair out. "An affair? Really?! You know me better than that, Fletcher, and I'm insulted that you would even think–"

"–So you must've thought I was leaving her," he says, frowning. "My loyalty won't let me–"

"–*That* was loyalty?"

"That was me wishing I could go back and do right by you." Fletcher pinches his nose bridge and drops the hand with a sigh. "I want you listen to me for a minute, okay… When I got better, I was so excited to become capable of giving you the love you deserve, that I couldn't hold it in. Kee was calling me gay for pouring my heart out to him, telling him how I was gonna move heaven and earth to be with you again. I was so excited that Kee had to grab me by the shoulders and shake me to get my attention. Nothing could've prepared me for what Kee had to say."

"What could Kee possibly tell you about me," I ask, but then realize that Keenan could've told Fletcher anything I told Monae, with her big mouth.

"Kee said that you was sleeping with Jay." Fletcher throws his arms up and let them flop at his sides. "Ain't that the same man you was telling me not to worry about?"

"I would've never went there with Jay if you didn't go there with Riley."

Fletcher counters, "And there would've never been a second time with Riley if I hadn't found out that Jay was suckin' your pussy all around town!" Fletcher gathers himself with a deep breath. "I'm sorry."

My hands spread away, ironing out all the back and forth to say, "Look, it's best that I just go. You made your point."

"I have *not* made my point," he declares. He approaches, towering over me. He takes my face in his hands, looks deep into my eyes, and says, "My *point* is this: if Riley ever gives me a reason –

the slightest reason – I'm coming for you. And we're going to be together like we're supposed to be."

He'd said it with such conviction, I never believed anything more than those words. He plants his lips on mine, for the last time, then gazes into my eyes to say something, but words fail him. He walks away with his kiss still wet on my lips, leaving me hot and sprawled against the side of my car.

CHAPTER 28
YOU MUST REALLY LOVE ME

For having shared a kiss with another man, I'm sick with guilt whenever I'm in Jay's presence. This goes on for weeks. I begin catering to him as penance. I ask for advice even when I don't need it because I know how Jay loves to be consulted. I become so agreeable that he would stop and stare in disbelief.

He starts showering me with more money and more gifts. I struggle to remember the last time I spent a dollar of mine. The spa gift cards start piling up because the boutique keeps me busy. Jay says I should spend less time at the boutique and more time being pampered. I explain that I spend a lot of time at the boutique just so Momma would feel like a partner instead of an employee. Jay had encouraged me to have a talk with Momma.

And it's taking me all day because the store was busy early, plus I don't know how to begin.

Momma takes her lunch in the office, so I figure there's no better opportunity. I ask Uncle Sirus to watch the floor, then I go find Momma eating leftover neckbones and watching her soaps.

I sigh and say, "Momma we need to talk."

She doesn't even turn in her chair. "Gone nah! I'm watching my stories."

"This is serious, momma."

She swivels to me, her head cocked in resistance. "You finna write me up?" Her mouth twitches to keep a smile from breaking. "You got until the end of this commercial break."

"What I wanna tell you is, I'm decreasing my hours."

Momma counters, "*Therefore*, what I wanna tell *you* is, I'm not increasing my hours to make up for yours."

"Did I ask you to increase your hours? If anything, you should decrease yours too."

Momma's brow raises but she turns an ear, waiting to hear the catch.

I can't help blushing when I say, "Jay wants me to enter my soft era. If I'm always stressed, how can I be his peace?"

"That's not what he means, Tahj. What Jay's trying to say is, if you're always stressed, how can you be his piece?"

"Ma, I just said that. I'm asking you to have brunch and spa days with me, and you're playing."

"You think yo daddy bout to let Jay finance my soft era too?"

"We can be like best friends, ya know?"

"What happened to all your friends anyway?"

"You know what happened." They changed as soon as I got the commission check from Bubby's rookie contract; ordered up a two-thousand-dollar restaurant bill then pressured me into paying it.

Momma swivels her chair around to the TV, narrating, "Look, Tahj. Macy done come back from the dead. Her husband, Jack, has amnesia and is now married to Kate, but Jack is about to see Macy again for the first time, so maybe he'll remember that Macy is his true love…"

I quietly back out of the room and leave her talking to herself.

I know Momma. She resists change, even for the better. If she thinks I'm about to beg her to have spa days with me, she's got another thing coming. I'll just come in only twice a week, looking refreshed and radiant, just to make Momma long-eyed, then maybe then she'd give in to this lifestyle. Living stress-free and getting pampered, I would love that for momma as much as I love it for myself. My life is about to be so good; I feel stupid for kissing Fletcher, I'm thinking, as I go out front.

I bump into Uncle Sirus, who places his pinky finger at the corner of his mouth and says, "Your old man out here."

I cut my eyes at Uncle Sirus, on the way to Jay. I throw my arms around Jay's neck and kiss in the middle of the sales floor, which is something I never do. "How'd the doctor's appointment go?"

"I'm healthy as a bull." Jay then whispers, "Did you talk to her?"

I pull Jay along. "I'll tell you on the way. I've got a surprise for you."

He lights up. "For me?"

I cut my eyes and say, "Don't act too surprised, dang… as if I don't do for my man."

I drive us onto I-85. The stereo's turned up. I dance in my seat like I'm a whole music video, flirting away, tickling under his chin as I lip-sync sexy lyrics. Jay looks at me like he's having one of those moments when he realizes just how young I am. Internally, though, I'm trying to convince myself that this surprise gift is not out of guilt for kissing Fletcher a month prior.

Jay asks, "What could this surprise possibly be if we have to drive to it? You know it can be lingerie every single time, and I'll never be disappointed."

I point ahead. "You see that?"

"What?" He looks, oblivious.

"You're looking right at it. Let me stop before we pass it." I slow down and veer onto the shoulder not far from the Civic Center when Jay finally recognizes himself on a billboard with his partners in the same marquee image from his website.

Jay grabs his head with both hands. "You did this?"

My smile hardens with sarcasm. "Uh, yeah."

"For me?" His torso rings around to get a better look at the billboard; he then unwinds and faces forward, gazing at the train of cars swooshing by. "You must really love me," he says.

"I wanted you to see it before you left town." I pause to reprocess what Jay had said, and then pop him on the arm. "Of course, I love you, Jay. Why you say it like that?"

Distractedly, he massages the arm I popped. "What do you mean?"

"Like you don't already know. What do you think this is?"

He faces me and says, "Obviously it came out wrong. I love you – point-blank, period – as you young folks like to say." He kisses the smile he produces on my lips, but the smile is just me pretending that I'm over it so I don't spoil his surprise.

I try to leave it alone, but on the way back, I find myself asking, "Do you remember our first argument? You told me that love was optional – all you wanted was access to me."

"I remember," Jay says – and that's it.

"Well? Is that still true?"

"It was true when I said it."

"How about now? Do you feel bad about saying that?"

His phone rings. "I feel bad that that was once my truth." He raises the phone. "I gotta take this." He answers the phone and I can hear the person on the other end yelling. Jay tries to calm them. "Hold on, hold on. What happened?" Jay listens a while, then says, "I take a half-day and this happens? Don't do shit until I get there. Nobody talks to Ace. No call, no text, no nothing, you hear me?"

I remember Sarah mentioning that name. She thought this Ace person was trying to kill Jay.

Jay tells me to step on it. His emergency kills our conversation, but it doesn't stop me from wondering.

We say I love you all the time. So how could the idea of me being genuinely in love, give him such a splash in the face? Has he been operating under the precepts of a sugar daddy relationship? Is his generosity serving as a monthly allowance for the young chick on his arm? Did he think of the sex 1.5 times a month, as services rendered? Did he think all the affection and romance was us pretending we were not in a relationship of convenience?

Later that day, after closing time, we're in the office doing payroll when I bring this to Momma. She acts as if she doesn't hear me.

"Hey Tahj, do me a favor right quick."

"Yeah, what?"

Momma points to the doorway, her eyes targeting something down the hall, as she says, "If you don't mind, baby, gone over there and sit your 'tarted ass down somewhere." Momma wheezes with laughter.

I'm chuckling too. "I can't believe I fell for that." She used to do that to me when I was a girl.

"No, but seriously," Momma says. "He ain't no different from no other man. The problem with your generation is yall want men to understand yall. They not. They can't." Suddenly Momma double-takes. "Where's all this coming from, anyway?"

I sigh and flop back in my chair. "I saw Fletcher recently."

"That was about the debt, wasn't it?" Momma covers her mouth. "Did y'all…"

"No."

Momma sighs. "I was about to *say*… I ain't raised no tramp."

I say, "We only kissed."

"Tramp!"

"Momma!"

"I swear I don't know what that boy got dangling between his legs because he be having yall girls acting crazy." Momma starts fake crying. "And I don't wanna see my baby's car folded up under some big ole tractor-trailer."

I show weary eyes. "Can you be serious for a minute?"

"Girl, you the one telling jokes, talkin' about you kissed Fletcher, and wondering if Jay loves you. But here's the gag: Jay came by the house and asked me and Maurice for our blessings."

The thought of marriage slaps me dizzy. "Really?"

Momma says, "You worried about the look on Jay's face? You should see *your* face right now."

"It's not that, I just… It's just sudden. Did he say when he was gonna ask?"

"When it didn't happen on Christmas day, it made me wonder if everything's still alright."

I shrug. "He's been the same with me."

"He's waiting on New Year's, then. Marry that man, Tahj. You can't go wrong with a good man because, in the end, he's gonna make you right for choosing him."

"Make me right for choosing him," I parrot.

"Isn't he? Ever since you got with Jay, your life has been nothing but better. He don't ask much of you, yet he wants to spoil you. You're sitting up here, trying to make up some reason to go back to Fletcher, and that's a mistake. I swear, I wanna judge you so bad, but I can't; you learned this from me. I went and married *my* headache: yo daddy." Momma smiles nostalgically.

"And it worked out just fine."

"Your daddy has a touch of bipolar. I tried to heal him with my love."

"And did," I sass.

"But it cost. Not only did it cost me, it's costing you. The idea of love that you developed through me, got you thinking your true love is a man who drives you insane."

We go outside where momma is required to be on the phone with daddy until she makes it safely to her car, so we wave our goodbyes.

I walk away regretting having brought this to momma; she makes it harder for me to lie to myself. *Yes*, I am looking for any reason I can to be with my true love.

I shut myself in my car and text Fletcher, *Hey, can u talk?*

Fletcher replies, *Will u stop texting my man?*

I remember Fletcher telling me how insecure Riley is. If she's gatekeeping his phone, my only recourse is to see him in person.

I've been walking around with the flyer to his 2nd annual Peach Bowl Bash, which takes place on tomorrow, Saturday, December thirtieth, which is a day and a night before Jay is gonna pop the question.

CHAPTER 29
SOMETHING AIN'T RIGHT

It seems so sudden that I find myself here, in a fixer-upper wearing a headwrap to protect my hair. I have a paint roller, and the drywall is half-covered in taupe. I scan the renovation, and it seems to be coming together nicely. It's a lot of work, but a blessed undertaking because what I know, without a doubt, is that this house is ours – ours as in Fletcher and me.

Speaking of… I look down the hallway and see Fletcher, the half of him revealed by the half-open door. I walk towards him. As I advance down the hallway I begin noticing little imperfections, like cobwebs, a loose floorboard, and a small ceiling ring, the remnants of a leak.

Fletcher hears my footsteps and hurries to push what looks like a deep freezer up against the wall. By the time I reach the end of the hallway, Flether's coming out of the room, a hand behind him shutting the door as if to hide what's inside. I get only a glimpse. It looks like a bassinet of some kind. I saw hair. A sleeping child inside, maybe?

Fletcher's a bit thinner. He looks stressed. "No electricity's getting to this room," he says. "Gotta check the breaker box." I follow him to the washroom where he takes out a screwdriver and begins removing the panel.

I say, "Are you sure you know what you're doing?"

"How hard could it be," he replies.

"But that's electricity, Fletcher."

Fletcher sets down his screwdriver. "Baby," he says with a smirk. He massages my belly, which is swollen with child. "Do you really think I would put my family at risk?" I realize that Fletcher's looking more than a bit thin; he looks drained. The baby kicks; our eyes go ablaze and we kiss.

"I trust you," I say. "But don't expect me to sit here and watch." I turn to go and Fletcher gives me a pat on the butt. I return to painting the living room wall in smoke grey (I could've sworn it was taupe).

Oddly, the door at the end of the hallway is ajar again. I set the paint roller in its pan and go towards it, determined to find out what Fletcher was trying to hide earlier.

The hallway looks even worse, with cracked paint and dry rot spreading along the baseboards. I arrive at the end of the hallway and reach for the doorknob.

Behind me, Fletcher warns, "Tahj! You're not supposed to go in there."

I look back at him as I defiantly push the door open and go in. The thing I thought I saw, was not a baby bassinet at all. It's a casket! Fletcher runs down the hallway, yelling No! I approach the open casket anyway, knowing how afraid I am of dead people. Lying in the casket is Riley. I freeze where I stand, tears welling. She looks waxy. There's a line of stitches across her throat where it was slit. I turn and Fletcher's at the door, his face bent with empathy for what I must be going through to have seen it. But there's something else I notice. Each time I set eyes on Fletcher, he looks worse. He looks sickly and his lips are dry. Referring to Riley's cut throat, I ask, "Who did this?"

"She did," Fletcher says and then takes me in his arms. I try not to appear scornful of him. Up close I see, beneath the carpet of his hair, that his scalp is made of tin.

I wake up.

It was just a dream. My heart's thumping, my eyes darting. I lay there for a long while, as still as a log, while emotional storms wage on inside.

This is the day that I plan to risk it all for the love of my life and I have a chilling dream like this? Maybe the deteriorating house with Riley's corpse in it represents the relationship we'd have if we have to hurt others to be together: a relationship decaying, like the house, with guilt and maybe even karma. I lay there soul-searching for a good half-hour straight, only to end up dismissing it all as just a dream.

I get out of bed with neither a yawn nor a stretch. I steep my ginger tea and then pull out my laptop to work on designs.

The one person missing from the dream shows up at my door unannounced. Jay hands me a flute of white roses. He says, "I was on my way to the office to get some records together; couldn't resist stopping by."

I notice that the area where his hairline is filled in, is thinning, which is odd because in the dream, it was Fletcher's hair thinning. I turn around from setting the vase on the counter and Jay catches me by the shoulders. "Tahj," he says, followed by a long pause. Every time he speaks now, it feels like he might go down on one knee.

"What," I smile, my stomach in ties. I can say yes, even though I plan to put my heart on the line for Fletcher later on tonight. And if Fletcher's adamant about staying with Riley as long as she doesn't give him a reason to leave, I can turn right around and follow through with marrying Jay. I can have a life of relative comfort and happiness. And maybe the fire that burns for Fletcher, over time, will reduce to ash. I look him in the eyes. "What is it, Jay?"

"You know what? I feel bad for letting business cut into our weekend," Jay says. "So I figured after I finish up at the office, I could treat you to brunch."

Softly, I reply, "I don't wanna be another thing on your to-do list."

"But my pilot can't get me off the ground until two, this afternoon. I got time."

Private admission: the surprise roses sickens me. Jay's sweet effort to right a wrong that was beyond his control to begin with, sickens me. How stupid will I feel tonight, under neon club lights, shoving through the crowd to pour my heart out, over trap music, to a man who doesn't treat me this well.

Jay, being so obliviously devoted, fills me with a guilt that makes me feel unworthy of his embrace. I back away, saying, "I'll be fine. Let's just make the most of the time we'll have in Mara Largo." It's an odd New Year's destination, but Jay swears they're beginning to rival Time Square.

Jay produces a sly grin to mask his feelings of rejection. "You act as if being with you is work."

"It's just that, ever since you got that phone call, you've been stressed; I don't wanna add to it."

"Stressed? I don't know the meaning of the word."

"Yeah… about that phone call… You mentioned a name: Ace. Who is he, anyway?"

The name hits him like smelling salt, how Jay blinks through his confusion. "Why do you ask?"

"Sarah, bless her soul, she mentioned that name."

"Sarah?"

"She thought this person meant to do you harm, so it worries me when I hear that name."

"Ace is an old nickname. Did she know the real name? What else she say?"

"She thought it was suspicious how you're a lawyer, and you have your own private plane."

"Really?" He looks away and returns; his brow unchanged. "Look no further than the legendary Willie Gary, right here in Atlanta. He has a private plane and we're both lawyers who specialize in the same types of cases." He peers at me as if to see if I'm convinced. "Are you okay?"

"Should I not be?"

"You look hungry," he giggles. "I'll send you an Uber Eats." He leaves me with a kiss, sweet man.

He won't return until tomorrow morning, so I don't even have to fashion an excuse to be out tonight. I pick up the flyer to Fletcher's party and stare at it, reassuring myself that this is something I have to do.

CHAPTER 30
White Chinchilla

The bouncers call the baddies to the front of the line. Apparently, you have to be either light-skinned, or thick-thick to skip ahead, like first-class passengers at an airport. The world's most beautiful woman is passed over and left shivering in line like a basic bitch.

Keenan pops out of the club and looks down the line, counting heads, perhaps worried about the club's capacity. He sees me, and says, "Tahj! What you doing waiting in line?" He pops the bouncer on his shoulder, chastising, "Got this baddie waiting out here in the cold, man?"

I'm speechless the whole time, as Keenan escorts me in, apologizing for the stupidity of his staff.

Mind you, the last time I'd seen Keenan he was paying out a million dollars of his own money just to sever ties with me. Either Keenan's not upset anymore because he ended up falling in love with Monae, on account of me, or he knows that I know, and he's nice out of fear that I'd out him.

I notice he's not looking at me, but out over the crowd. He only glances when he says, "You see Bubby? He was right over there."

I shake my head, smiling. "You still haven't changed."

He still scans for Bubby, frowning a bit with his reply, "Girl what're you talking about?"

"You don't make up. You just act like nothing ever happened."

Keenan says, "That's not just *me*. That's men."

"I'm sorry, Keenan," I say.

"Me too," he says and pulls me through the crowd.

I pull him back and lean to his ear, so he could hear me over the loud music. "I knew Monae was trans and I'm really sorry about that. I had my reasons for not saying anything, but that's one decision I wish I could have back."

Keenan shows exasperation for being forced into this treaty. "You didn't have to admit to anything, Tahj. I already forgave you for everything I *thought* you did. Back then, I was being an asshole, so…" he shrugs, then ushers me along.

I lean again and say, "Fletcher told me you got in his shit about Riley. Thank you."

A nodding Keenan says, "That was fucked up. That's why I'm surprised you're here to support ya boy."

If not for the loud music putting a strain on the conversation, I would have asked what he meant by that. Keenan is an owner too, so why would he phrase it like I'm only supporting Fletcher by being here?

I spot Fletcher in the distance, so I tap Keenan's shoulder and say, "I'll be back."

Fletcher's up at the booth conversing with the D.J. I slide through the crowd. I reach the bottom of the steps at the same time as Fletcher. He looks at me as if he's spotted a unicorn. The speakers are so loud I have to read Fletcher's lips. "What are you doing here?"

I tip-toe for his ear. "That's not the welcome I expected."

He grabs my shoulders like handles. "But you said you wasn't coming."

"We need to talk."

Fletcher looks around, perhaps scoping for Riley, then guides me around the corner, down the hallway past the restrooms, and through the back exit.

We sit in his car, which is turned on with the heat blowing. I splay my hands by the vents to knock off the chill.

Fletcher seems emotionless, even agitated when he asks, "So, what do you want to talk about?"

Hesitantly, I say, "Has she 'given you a reason' yet?"

His head dips; his mouth wanting to speak.

In the many renditions I'd rehearsed in front of the mirror, never did I say, "Jay's gonna ask me to marry him tomorrow."

Fletcher stares ahead and says, "Damn… I always felt like you and me – somehow, someway – would end up together. How naïve."

I look forward and huff. "I tell you that another man is about to ask for my hand in marriage and you just accept defeat?"

"He's better for you."

"And yet here I am."

Fetcher closes his eyes and says, "You sat across that table from me and said that you was decided. You didn't even blink when you said it."

"Let *me* talk for me, Fletcher. How do *you* feel?"

Fletcher uses the crook of his finger to steer my face to him. "Don't ever wonder how I feel about you." With just that whispered confirmation, I'm speechless. I'm his to do whatever he pleases and yet he speaks, "Our love is so deep, I feel like it's been here before. It's like we've already grown old together in a past life. And now we're here, you and me, oblivious… questioning things, entertaining other people. We should be together. No question. But the thing is, you see…"

I whisper, "No. No buts."

Fletcher pulls me to him and we engage in a long kiss. I know we're just two people kissing in a car, but it feels like the euphoria of that previous lifetime that Fletcher had alluded to. We were probably kissing just like this a century ago, on a chuck wagon during Reconstruction, or at a train station during Prohibition, and now we are reunited here in this meaningless era, as witless lovers, parked outside of a nightclub, just now figuring out why we can't be without one another.

Fletcher turns slightly away and whispers, "What're we doing?"

"Sealing our destiny." I lean forward and turn my head to look him in the face. "What were *you* doing?"

He rubs his thumb along his bottom lip and says, "I can't break her heart."

"Who, your rapist? The same chick who forced herself on you the moment you came into money?"

"It's not like that – even if it *started* like that. I can't rip her heart out. It scares me to think what would happen to her."

I raise a hand to my mouth. "Oh my God. I saw this in a dream… But wait, think about what you're saying. This is our last chance, and you'd throw it away because you're afraid that Riley would end up like…" I touch his hand. "Fletcher, look at me."

His head lifts, grief wrinkled in his brow. He says, "She talks about hurting herself."

With a wide, gladless smile, I say, "And that's how she's controlling you. Your soulmate is looking you in the face, and you're paralyzed with the fear, worried that Riley is Meek all over again?"

"I'm worried about what would happen to me! I can't take another one, Tahj. I can't. You know my condition. I would be so far in the sunken place, there'd be no coming back."

I hesitate because I really can't fix my mouth to ask the man to possibly destroy himself to be with me. "Well, why tell me how you really feel about me, just now? You would've been better off telling me you don't love me no more."

"Would you have believed me?" We sit in silence for a spell. Fletcher says, "I need stability more than I need love."

I huff and look away.

The club's back door swings open. Out comes some guy with his phone out, and then Bubby, looking like a rapper in a white fur coat and a big gold chain. He spots Fletcher's car because it's on and humming. He sees Fletcher and me inside. He starts towards us with a fist to his mouth, repeating, "Oh shit!"

I sigh and complain, "I'm *so* not in the mood for Bubby, right now." Besides it's embarrassing being caught sneaking around like the other woman, and nothing runs me off quicker than shame. "We'll talk later," I tell Fletcher.

I step one foot outside and Bubby's loud ass is right there, talmbout, "Tahj to the rescue, cuh! *Talk* to this nigga!"

I fold my arms against the cold and say, "What're you even talking about?"

I should've been able to tell by the exchange of looks between Fletcher and Bubby, that they realized that I was in the dark about something, but the cold has me more concerned about getting inside as soon as possible.

Bubby yells behind me, "So, you're here by coincidence? Even better!"

I figured I'd thaw out at the bar, before leaving. A young man gives up his seat for me as the bartender sets down his drink. He says, "Have the drink too, baby girl, you look like you need it."

I take a sip of what tastes like jet fuel, burning away the lining of my throat. One eye claps shut while the other blares open. The young man just laughs but doesn't try to make conversation or get my number; sweety.

Bubby sneaks up and surprises me with a side hug. "Look at you. Girl, you *know* you bad."

I swivel my barstool to him and say, "Sorry if I was rude out there. How's your ribs? Not good, if you're away from the team, I guess."

"They're letting me heal up until the first round of the playoffs." He looks off, as if making eye contact with someone. I turn and see Keenan in the distance, suddenly stuffing his hands in his pockets.

"Hey Tahj," says Bubby. "I need to talk to you outside."

I frown. "It's cold outside."

"She filed for divorce."

"I'm sorry to hear," I say.

"That's why I need to talk to you outside." Bubby begins removing his coat. "Take my chinchilla."

He drapes the coat over my shoulders. "Heavy," I say. "Feels good, though."

We start heading out front, zigzagging through the people coming in. Just as we reach the door, the music cut and the crowd stirs. I hear the microphone being unholstered; the cut sound isn't a technical issue. The voice I hear, is Fletcher's, *Testing, testing. Can yall hear me in the back?*

I stop and turn. Fletcher says, *Thanks for coming out to the second annual Peach Bowl Bash. There will be many more, but none as special as this.*

Bubby waves me on. "Come on, Tahj. He ain't saying nothing."

I take only two steps toward the exit before I figure things out — why Keenan thought I was here in support of Fletcher; why Fletcher seemed so thrown off that I showed up; why Bubby's in such a hurry to get me outside, and why Fletcher's now announcing that this day is so special. I tug Bubby and say, "Tell me what's happening!"

"I told you it's nothing, damn."

"Is this nigga about to propose to Riley?"

The gig is up. Bubby's head swerves away. "My boy ain't wanted you to see all that."

"I'm okay." I suck my teeth and square my shoulders toward the stage like any other spectator.

"Are you sure?"

"I need to see this." To make me hate Fletcher and love Jay without any regrets.

Bubby looks straight ahead as he says, "What was yall talking about in the car?"

"Let's just say that, after what we talked about, I'd be surprised if Fletcher could still go through with this."

"He can't back out," says Bubby. "Riley's expecting it. She orchestrated it." Bubby's head shakes. "My boy being pressured by her parents. They tryna get him to convert religion… all kinda shit. They got him in a cult."

I say, "I warned him about that church."

"Fletcher's like o'boy in the movie Get Out. Have you really listened to him lately?"

"We haven't been talking…" I hush as Fletcher welcomes Riley to the stage, with her list of accomplishments, "…Miss Georgia finalist, fashion model, author, podcaster…"

I frown. "Riley has a podcast?"

He returns, "And it's straight gahbage."

Riley comes to the stage acting all surprised as if she hadn't orchestrated this herself. I look over at Bubby; no words, just cut eyes and twisted lips.

Fletcher gives an emotional speech, thanking Riley for her help in putting the Peach Bowl Bash together, then he gets personal. "Y'all just don't understand what this woman means to me." What pisses me off is how Fletcher recalls certain memories with Riley at the center instead of me. "…When my car got balled up… I wasn't supposed to survive that, but this woman… this woman was praying for me." How could Fletcher fix his mouth to say Riley saved his life when she's the one who put his life in danger in the first place. Then Fletcher drops down on one knee, presenting the ring. He says, "I already owe you my life, so I'm giving you my life, right here and now…"

Bubby looks me over and says, "You a'ight?"

I smirk like I'm unbothered. "Of course I'm alright."

I'm not alright. My head gets light like it's evaporating away, my knees buckle, and then I wither to the floor, stretched out in an oversized white chinchilla with a disco ball spinning above, which Bubby's face eclipses like the sun. "Damn, Tahj," he says. He dips a finger in his cup then wipes it under my nose. The rank of Hennessey brings me to.

Bubby picks me up and carries me in his arms through the crowd and up the steps to his VIP section. By the time I'm sitting on the wall couch with a cold bottled water, Fletcher and Riley are officially engaged and making their rounds through the crowd like they've won a pageant.

I hang around for a while thereafter, kicking it with Keenan and Bubby, until Keenan pulls me aside and says, "You don't have to hang around just to prove to us that you're okay. It's okay to not be okay."

He's right. I hug the bros and decline their attempts to walk me out to my car. As I go down the steps, Fletcher coming up. He looks at me as if he'd seen a ghost. He says, "Hey, uh…" I shoulder past him without a word.

I walk around the dance floor, taking the outskirts on my way out, when I hear Riley's voice. The newly engaged Riley, who has the ears of a few young women who seem to look up to her, for having done twice what they can't seem to do once. She's been engaged to one star athlete and is now engaged to a former professional athlete who is also rich, by their standards. Riley is like a missionary to thirsty young groupies bearing cleavage and moose-knuckles.

I hide with my back to a pillar, listening as Riley preaches, "This might sound crazy, but the way to stand out is to cover up. All of a sudden you're different; you're rare. This puts him in your maze, trying to figure out how to get to you." The girls hang on her every word. "You think these young men are out here looking for sex, but what they really want is intimacy; sex is just the only expression of intimacy that they know. You ever prayed for a man? Now, *that's* intimacy. As soon as he hears amen, he will open his eyes, gazing at you like you just gave him the best top he's ever had in his life."

And this is who Fletcher plans to marry. I leave in disgust.

I check my phone. Jay hasn't called or texted since midday.

I drive through the city listening to love songs, refusing to steer home until there's that one song sad enough to cut me open. Adele's *Someone Like You* delivers. I pull over with tears streaming down my face, singing with my whole chest.

> *Don't forget me, I beg*
> *I remember you said*
> *Sometimes it lasts in love*
> *but sometimes it hurts instead*

I take my time and finish my cry, hurting myself over and over by replaying, in my mind, the moment Fletcher told Riley that she saved his life; that's *our* thing. And that bitch Riley is making a ministry of how to get a high value man, as if Fletcher is just a plot point in her little gold-digging journey. I pay my eyes dry and take many deep sighs.

Fletcher sends one text. *I'm sorry you saw that*

I reply, *Boy fuck you*

BOOK VI

CHAPTER 31
RITZ CARLTON

It took everything in me to, not tell momma. I held the secret from the New Year ball drop when Jay went down on one knee, until the morning of January 2nd when I'm reopening the boutique after the holiday weekend. I withheld the news – even lied over the phone saying Jay never asked – just so I could pull this lackluster prank.

When momma arrives minutes after me, I'm fanning my face with the ring hand.

Momma almost walks by, but then stops and screams. She damn near yanks my arm out the socket when she pulls my hand to get a better look at the rock.

"You like det," I say.

"When did this happen? Lord look how it sparkle!" She hugs me. "My only daughter is about to be married!" She releases me then asks, "This is what you want, right?"

"Without a doubt, momma."

"If Fletcher didn't propose to Riley, you still would've said yes?"

Our hug releases to just the hands, into which I squeeze assuredness and say, "One hundred percent. Besides, I remember what you said."

Momma shrinks back, leery. "What'd I say?"

"Can't go wrong with a good man. I'm standing on that."

Uncle Sirus arrives with his man purse on his hip, so Momma and me pause the conversation for later. I bum a stick of gum from Uncle Sirus just so I could pop gum all day while standing spring-legged in the middle of the sales floor, determined to get on everybody's nerves with *my fiancé* this, my fiancé that; my repetition game, on level with Plies on his song Ritz Carlton.

As the day goes on, my left wrist aches at the joint for how often I hang that hand to show off my engagement ring.

Around lunchtime, I tell Uncle Sirus, but loud enough for everyone to hear, "Hold it down for me, Unc, while I go have lunch with my fiancé."

I must've finally gotten on Unc's last nerve because he says, "Girl, if you don't getchyo lil narrow behind on somewhere!"

That's precisely what I do; get my behind on, with a smile wide enough to put lipstick in my ears. On the drive to meet Jay at his office, I'm in my mind reinforcing the thoughts I've been having ever since I saw Fletcher propose to Riley. You see, God is partial to babies and fools. I was a fool going to that club behind Jay's back, yet my steps were ordered in such a way that I ended up seeing what I needed to see. I would've never been able to get Fletcher out of my heart had I not seen him propose to Riley and say the things he said. I know he's lying to himself, and dammit, so am I. People have maintained much bigger lies long enough to evolve into their truth.

My love for Jay is renewed and in full bloom. My imagination has been filled with visions of us being together as a married couple, but every time I picture children, I remember that Jay's had a vasectomy during his first marriage. It can be undone, I say to myself. We'll work it out.

Luckily I find street parking half a block away, but there's a slew of police cars and an armored truck on the ground level of the building that houses Jay's office. I hurry out of my car thinking it's a failed robbery.

What I thought was an armored truck is actually a patty wagon with iron bars on the back window. Agents in regular clothing and gun holsters warn people to stand back. One agent, a black woman with a single, large braid draped around her shoulder, looks eerily familiar – even more familiar the closer I get.

When I see the dimples, I know. Skin crawls on my face because I know for a fact that this woman is dead. "Sarah?"

Sarah's splitting image, double-takes and then approaches, saying, "I faked my death." She produces a badge. "Federal Agent Trufant. I was working undercover. I understand that you and Jay are now a couple? Interesting." She scowls. "I *knew* you wanted him."

"Not when you were with him. He really loved you."

"And I really loved him. That's why I was pulled from this case and had to… you know…"

"Jay is no criminal! What is he accused of!"

"I can't divulge that, but I can tell you with confidence that he did it."

I'm in a daze, not even aware that I'm speaking when I say, "I can't believe this is happening…"

"Believe it," Sarah insists. I take no pleasure in breaking you two up, but his bond will be denied for flight risk. He won't see daylight until after serving a long sentence."

"Sentence for what," I yell.

Sarah relaxes. Suddenly, she's all business. "I'm gonna need you to stand back."

Just two days after agreeing to be Jay's wife, I have to stand there and watch him be brought out in handcuffs.

Jay comes out strutting and boasting that the case against him is laughable and that he will single-handedly embarrass the office of the U.S. Attorney General.

I yell, "Jay! What the hell?!"

Jay turns to locate my voice, but finds Sarah's face. His soul leaves his body, it seems. He asks, "How?" When Jay realizes that not only is Sarah really there in the flesh, but she's on the side of those arresting him, his legs give. His handlers hoist him up to his feet.

Sarah walks alongside, tears in her eyes.

Jay asks, "Was it all a lie?"

Sarah's head shakes no.

Jay doesn't even look at me, and I'm standing there watching these two connect in front of a crowd like I'm the other woman at a wedding.

CHAPTER 32
VISITATION

I go on leave immediately and indefinitely – too ashamed, after bragging so much about my fiancé, and now he sits in a concrete room in a jumpsuit.

Instead of a collect call from Jay, I get a direct call from his lawyer who explains that Jay's facing RICO charges. They believe he paid doctors to falsify diagnoses to help him win his cases, resulting in defrauding the government for billions over the years.

The lawyer hopes the charges will be thrown out at the preliminary hearing. If the feds do in fact have a strong case, Jay could still avoid jail time using leverage he has against the state's DA office.

The next day, Jay's bond denies for flight risk. They house him at a minimum security detention center, awaiting trial.

I never imagined me having to visit a man in jail. It all feels so surreal, standing in my closet, trying to piece together an outfit within the visitation dress code. I discard skirts above the knee, low-cut tops, and spandex. By this process of elimination, I end up in the mirror looking like a stud in a turtleneck and pants.

It feels so out of place going into that concrete building, being corralled, and prodded by security guards alongside other visitors who look like they could be inmates themselves.

I try not to be scornful, but this visit shows me that this can never be my normal. To each her own, but I am not the type to hold a man down for no prison bid. No knock on those who do, but prison romances have never been my book genre, so in life with Jay, I see this ending in a jaded DNF.

Not nare nother time will I have armed guards tell me when I can embrace my man – only at departure and at greeting. Even then, it's monitored to ensure that a woman doesn't use a kiss to slip her lover contraband. A guard with a back bigger than her breast hovers while we embrace.

We sit at a numbered table where we update each other on how we've been since the arrest. This ordeal is aging him; there's salt in his beard, and the black filler along his hairline is beginning to fade. After a few minutes of conversation, I finally ask, "Is any of what they're saying true?"

Jay takes a deep breath and whispers, "I'm not gonna lie. Some of it's true. But it doesn't mean that the charges are gonna stick. The doctor who turned information on me was falsifying diagnoses under the direction of the D.A.'s office for years before I found him. He aided them in sending probably hundreds of innocent people to prison. I'm not the big fish; *they* are."

"After all this is over, will you still be able to practice law?"

"Fuck no," he says. "But I have enough money cleaned, to use for business ventures."

"You had money laundered? On second thought, don't tell me. I wanna know as little as possible."

"Good. Because they're gonna question you soon."

"Question me?"

"Of course. You're my fiancé." Jay's eyes close and reopen. "You *are* still my fiancé, right?"

"That hasn't changed," I say.

Jay sees right through me. "Aw shit. How do you expect me to believe that, Tahj, when you look like you don't believe it yourself?"

"Well, I do believe is that I ceased to exist the moment you laid eyes on Sarah…"

"I wasn't looking at Sarah; I was looking at a fucking resurrection. I mourned her." Jay studies me with his fingers rapping the table. "Look, before I forget, there's something I need you to do."

I ask, "Is it illegal?"

"Only if you get caught."

"Then my answer is no. I will not put myself at risk."

Jay leans forward and says, "You are precisely who's at risk if you don't do it. I stored some records in the attic of your boutique."

"You did *what?*" I glance around conspicuously.

"If they decide to search…" His eyes close against the daymare that rises up before him. "I get put away for a long time and you get charged as an accessory."

I look away to shake my head. "This is too much."

Jay smiles. "This is but a small test to your loyalty and you're failing miserably. But I should've known this."

I smile, humored by his attempt at a guilt trip. "Oh really?"

"I almost didn't ask you to marry me, because the day before, you went to see Fletcher."

"I went to see Fletcher? How do you figure?"

"Lie to me," he dares. "Tell me you didn't go to the club to see Fletcher."

"Am I being watched? Do you have eyes on me?"

"Tahj…" He gives a stiff smile. "Do what I asked you to do. Get rid of those records. I'll call you from a cell phone number ending in 5018 to make sure it's done. That's the end of it."

"I'll do it," I say. "But it's over. I love you, but it's over."

Jay whispers, "No, the fuck, it is not over!"

I give him a look like, *Try me.*

Jay changes his tune. "I don't mean it like that, babe. What I mean is that I'm even more determined to put this behind us. You know I don't like to lose, and I'm not about to lose you. In the meantime, just stay away from Fletcher."

Our embrace, at departure, isn't half the embrace that our greeting was. Jay holds me as if the drama makes us stronger. I go along, but with an, *I don't know about all this*, kind of energy.

CHAPTER 33
ACCOMPLICE

I let days go by without removing the records from the attic in the boutique, partly because of the weariness of depression; partly because doing so is a criminal act. The day I build up the energy and the courage, I put on a dark hoodie, jeans, and sneakers, but when I arrive at the boutique, momma's car is still parked there and the lights are on. I drive away, calling Momma as I'd been doing every day since Jay was arrested. She says she can't talk because she's on the phone with I.T. The network is down and she can't submit payroll until it's fixed, so the records remain in the attic for yet another day.

It had to have been during these days when Jay uses an unauthorized cell phone to place a call to Riley. Jay tells Riley that Fletcher's having an affair with me; that way, Riley's insecurity can work to Jay's advantage. Riley wouldn't let Fletcher out of her sight, which keeps him away from me while Jay's legal battles pan out. If Jay knew any better, he wouldn't have to do anything because once I saw Fletcher propose to Riley, I was through with him.

Jay sets up a meeting between Riley and the two boogeymen he had employed to intimidate doctors to continue falsifying diagnoses long past their liking. They meet Riley in the parking lot of a Target shopping center. Maybe Riley demanded this public location for her own safety. She'd later report that they gave her fake names, Dave and Buster.

Riley sits in their SUV while they show her phone pictures of Fletcher and me outside the club. Had a photo of our kiss existed, Jay would not have proposed to me the day after.

I don't know how Riley reacted to the pictures, but the Riley I know would probably have gone into hyperventilation. I also know that the thought of leaving Fletcher never enters her mind; he's her ticket to a life of ease. The only way she'd leave Fletcher is by divorce, when a breakup is lucrative.

Jay's henchmen promise Riley that they'll keep an eye on Fletcher and me, and report everything back to her, while she does everything she can to keep Fletcher on the straight and narrow.

Riley is devastated by the news because she does love Fletcher, by her definition, so when Fletcher returns from the office, he finds her red-faced and crying real tears in the same living room where she took advantage of him months prior.

The next day, I park in the alley by the back door. It's after hours and I'm in a hoodie, to burglarize my own establishment.

I pull the ceiling string and a flight of stairs unfurls. I climb up, using my cell phone for light until I find the string to a single bulb. There's nothing in my attic but surplus material that the builders stashed up here. There's a tar bucket, paint cans, and copper coils. I find the records behind large rolls of insulation. I lug a crate to the lip of the opening, wondering how in the world am I supposed to haul something so heavy while climbing backward down this rickety ladder, but it's either this or jail.

I descend until I'm eye-level with the attic floor, and pull the crate to my chest. It's an awkward grab; too heavy to hold in one arm, so I wouldn't have a hand free to balance against the ladder.

The floor looks a mile down. I take a daredevil's deep breath. I slide the crate onto the top ladder rung.

Each time I step down, I slide the crate down the next rung, praying the whole way – well, halfway because my foot slips and I fall back, an avalanche of papers dumping toward me. My face destined to be smashed under a crate at the bottom of the latter, but my foot gets caught between ladder rungs and hangs me upside down. My back slaps against the ladder so hard, the force causes the ladder to recoil back towards the ceiling. I find myself suspended five feet in the air, screaming in agony because the ankle wedged between ladder rungs feels broken. All I could do is reach for my cell phone.

Riley was so tired of arguing with Fletcher, she sent Phillip to argue for her. Fletcher sits and waits, scrolling through his phone, and checking his watch. Fletcher remembers promising Phillip that he'd never break Riley's heart. They haven't even jumped the broom yet and already there's a cheating accusation. Riley never mentioned the pictures. Fletcher's under the impression that Riley put two and two together: Keenan blocking her from going outside in search of Fletcher; Fletcher coming inside not long after me, and Riley getting a whiff of my perfume as Fletcher placed the engagement ring on her finger.

Fletcher considers Riley's evidence, and concludes that those strings aren't long enough to tie a shoe, much less weave together some cheating accusation – and that's precisely what Fletcher plans to say to Phillip.

When Phillip comes through the door, shedding his peacoat and derby hat, Fletcher's phone vibrates in his pocket. While his future father-in-law's back is turned he checks his phone and sees that the call is from me. He has no idea that it's a distress call until his phone vibrates again as soon as it returns to his pocket.

Phillip, says, "Riley's on the way but she wanted to give us some time to talk alone." Doesn't take Fletcher long to realize that they're not talking; the man's preaching. Fletcher takes the lecture in silence while his frustration, and his concern for me, mounts. Phillip goes on for so long, it surprises Fletcher when the man finally asks for feedback. "Wanna know why she doesn't trust you?"

Fletcher shrugs despondently. The whole ordeal is irritating; this man's love of the sound of his own voice and how he paces the floor of Fletcher's home as if it's his now.

Phillip raises a finger beside his head. "You probably think it has something to do with Gideon, but no. Ya gotta look back further. It starts with her biological father. He left them high and dry, and started passing for white. The other reason is me, her stepfather. She's seen what a man of God looks like. And you, Fletcher, do not compare. Whatever it is that happened between you and this Tish girl–"

"–Tahj," Fletcher corrects, irritatedly. He's been quiet, out of respect, but respect is becoming the stone that the blade of impatience is being sharpened against.

"Let me put it to ya like this: If the *man* in you was overshadowed by the God in you, you wouldn't be having this issue. If you went away to have a private conversation with another woman, Riley would more likely assume that you were praying for that woman. God is not at the head of this house." He looks up and around, his eyes stopping on Fletcher to say, "Young man, God isn't at the head on your big ole shoulders either. Riley needs to see you, in daily devotion. She needs to see you working in ministry – not just praising the Lord, but serving."

Fletcher looks away tight-lipped.

Phillip says, "Don't get bashful on me now. You wasn't bashful when I went out on a limb for you and took you to see the Prophet who healed you of depression."

Fletcher raises a hand to say, "Honestly, when that man touched my head, I just fell back because I didn't wanna embarrass him."

"You're not the first to say that. What did you expect, cherubims, nigga? Look at what happened afterward! You are now ten times the man I met. *Just* like that," Phillip says with a snap of his fingers.

"Lemme ask you this," Fletcher says, with folded arms. "Do you let people tell you how to run your marriage?"

Phillip avoids the question as a way to avoid the punchline that would follow. "Obviously, you don't know the lengths a father would go for his daughter. When she comes to me crying there's nothing I won't do. So I'm asking – nicely this time – that you two push the wedding date forward. Because the other reason Riley doesn't trust you is because you're not getting sex from her, so she's afraid you'll go and get it from lil hoeing ass Tasha!"

Fletcher, through clenched teeth, says, "The name is Tahj, nigga!" Fletcher is more surprised than Phillip, by the outburst, but since it's already done, Fletcher figures he may as well get some more off his chest. "I'll bet Tahj got less bodies than your daughter."

A confused Phillip squints so hard it flexes the bags under his eyes. "Wait, what is bodies? I don't speak thug. Explain it to me, boy."

Fletcher, by now, is fully committed to cursing Phillip all-the-way-out, so he can storm out of his own house and come see about me. "Nah, *you* explain to *me* how you think your daughter is still a virgin when she lived with a dude for a few years. You can't be that dense, man."

Phillip, with a straight face, says, "I know my daughter's a virgin because the prophet restored her virginity."

Fletcher sucks his teeth. "Do you hear yourself, bro?"

"Wait…" Phillip looks down in confusion, then looks up to ask, "Are you two having sex?"

Fletcher smirks and says, "Every which way, up in this house. Front, back, sideways, you name it!"

The man raises a rigid finger. "You betray me! You tempted her!?"

"I ain't even asked her, bruh! She took it! So before you start telling me about Riley, try getting to know her first." Fletcher marches toward the door. "I'm gonna get outta here so when Riley shows up, you two can talk amongst yourselves."

"I should force you two to marry tomorrow morning! But I'm gonna give you a month or else!"

Fletcher stops in front of the door, and turns like that Ike Turner meme. "Or else what? You can't do nothing to me that ain't already been done, bro."

Phillips steps forward with this grim face issuing a death wish. "I will have you shunned!"

Fletcher laughs. "Shunned? Go right ahead."

"Laugh *now*," says Phillip. "But you'll see… When the prophet removes his covering from your life, you'll return to that sad musclebound freak who ain't fit for a dog, much less my daughter."

The way Fletcher's smile disappears from his face lets Phillip know that his arrow hit its mark.

Still, Fletcher leaves, slamming the door behind him.

As soon as he gets in his truck, he checks his voicemail. If it's not an emergency, he'd go back inside, but hears me crying in pain. Fletcher's so triggered, he yells, "Tahj! What's happening?! Where are you?!" He then curses himself for talking to voicemail.

CHAPTER 34
LET IT BURN

Since our phone call, I was able to release my ankle. Still suspended midair, I had to hunch and bounce on the ladder to force it down. Moments later Fletcher's at the back calling my name. "Tahj!"

I call his name, "Fletcher!"

He runs toward me and I hobble toward him. He grips my shoulders. "How'd you get down? Are you okay?"

I reply. "The ankle's not broken, but it's not okay. Hurts to bear weight."

Fletcher sits me down and goes hunting for something. He rips material from one of the industrial sewing machines and returns with a few safety pins in his mouth. He begins wrapping my ankle. "Dis nigga got you committing crimes and shit?"

"Crazy. I know." Suddenly this feeling comes over me. It feels like we're in an action movie, lovers on the run; Fletcher bandaging my ankle as we hunker down, our dialogue setting up the suspense yet to come. I spot a gun in Fletcher's waist. "What're you doing with that?"

"You were hysterical. I had no idea what was happening."

"But what are doing with a gun in the first place?"

"I got one in the house. This one I keep in the truck. Riley's dad made me get them to keep his daughter safe."

My head shakes.

Fletcher pulls the bandage tight. "Ah," I say.

"Sorry. I had to tighten it." He secures the makeshift bandage with safety pins. "I was gonna call you… after I heard about what happened… with Jay and everything."

"I'm glad you didn't. I didn't want to hear from you after you say you love me, but propose to Riley."

"But the first person you call in a crisis?" With the same energy that I had spotted the gun in Fletcher's waist, he spots my engagement ring. "You said yes, huh…"

"With my whole heart," I say, defiantly.

Fletcher comes in closer. For a kiss? No.

"Hug my neck," he says. He picks me up in his arms like a damsel, my legs lapped over his forearm. He carries me to the toppled crate at the foot of the ladder. His phone rings. We know who it is. He ignores the call. He tells me to brace on the ladder. While Fletcher's stuffing the papers back into the crate, he says, "I'm gonna load this in my car. I'll take it to a burn pit out in the country."

"You *do* know there's twelve more crates up there?"

Fletcher just sighs and lumbers up the ladder. He starts bringing the crates down two per stack. All the while he complains, "I shouldn't even be doing this tonight. How am I gonna explain being gone all this time?"

When he loads the crates in the back of his SUV, he says, "I got some shit going down at my house right now. I had to curse Phillip out just to be here." As I follow him inside, Fletcher grows a smirk and says, "The nigga said the church is gonna shun me–"

"–Shun you?"

"–If I don't marry Riley in a month."

"Wait. She pregnant?"

"No," Fletcher frowns. "They think I took her virginity."

"Virginity!" I suck my teeth. "And what kind of church forces people to marry?" I glare, so Fletcher would realize that I'm not asking a question, but that he's the horse I'm leading to water. "A cult – that's what kind. That's how they're controlling you, Fletcher. Even Bubby said it. The only one who can't see it is you."

"Bubby only said that because I don't drink no more," Fletcher says. He goes back up the ladder and comes down with two more crates.

We continue the conversation over the span of four more trips from the attic to his truck, with me limping the whole time. "If you're afraid of being shunned, maybe you *are* in a cult."

Irritatedly, Fletcher says, "Could you quit it with that word please? Who said I was afraid? Did *I* say I was afraid?"

"Maybe it's marrying Riley that you're afraid of?"

"Not marrying her is what I'm afraid of."

I suck my teeth. "Because you think she's gonna bug out and kill herself?"

"It's not just that, Tahj. She's a good woman." I could see this glazed-over look about him as he speaks, convincing himself of the lie that keeps him committed to someone he doesn't truly love. I can identify the look because I've seen it in the mirror, while convincing myself that Jay was the one. Fletcher adds, "She's almost too good. She tends to my needs. She doesn't complain or push back on anything. Sure, she got her ways about her, but she's working to be a better person in the eyes of God. The only thing that bothers me is her trust issues."

"You forgot to mention *that*, in your heartfelt proposal."

"I didn't mean for you to see that."

"But you meant to kiss me, right before. You meant it when you told me that I'm the love of your life, but you still went through with the proposal."

Fletcher scratches the back of his head. "I couldn't back out of the proposal. Riley may have acted all surprised, but she planned it – *we* planned it."

"You said it right the first time."

By now Fletcher's phone has vibrated in his pocket about seven times since his arrival. He closes his hatchback for the final time.

I tail him out to the country. We stop at a gas station where he buys a gas can and fills it at the pump. Next, we go down a long dirt road where there are no light poles, and the night is so thick our headlights slice through it like long, lighthouse beams, spotlighting the pine trees that line this long winding corridor.

We stop at a large dirt clearing. The night is alive with crickets and frogs chirping, bats shrieking, and an owl hooting. To scare me even more, Fletcher smirks and says, "Better watch the ground for snakes."

I stick close by, limping as Fletcher hauls all the crates onto a burnt trash heap. He soaks the crates of documents with gas and throws the canister on top. He lights a piece of paper and tosses it. The flames catch, to the sound of fluffing a giant bedsheet. I throw my arm around Fletcher's waist, and watch the fire.

Fletcher captures his nose with praying hands, which slides down his face. "I wasn't gonna say anything about this, until I'm absolutely sure, but… Remember when I told you that I wasn't gonna end the relationship unless *Riley* gave me a reason?"

I turn, speechless.

"Well… Riley's movin' funny, right now. She movin' *real* funny."

I crane back. "Not your perfect little Riley. Funny how?"

"She's suddenly paranoid about her phone."

"Does she keep it locked?"

"We have a policy: no locks. She keeps it clutched, though." Fletcher sees my eyes widen, so he adds, "But it doesn't stop there. Suddenly, she's getting calls she won't answer around me. She'll leave the room, or all of a sudden she gotta go. Then I see her pulling out of the driveway with the phone to her ear. I think there's someone else."

Not too enthusiastically, I say, "I wouldn't put it past her."

"Me neither, come to think of it. She tried me, when she was still with Gideon."

"While you were in the NFL?" His silence confirms it. With all the sarcasm I could muster, I say, "I distinctly remember you saying that it was only two friends having lunches occasionally."

Fletcher rubs his jaw like he just took a punch. "All I can say right now is that I'm sorry."

Fletcher walks me back to my car. I about-face to thank him, and find him all up on me. A smiling Fletcher says, "I could go to jail for this."

I crane back, frowning to make sense of this invasion of my space. "So, you suggest I repay you, how? Not like this. I would love to be that bitch's karma, but that's not me."

Fletcher's head shakes. "See how you be runnin' out? I was going to hug you good bye."

"But first," I say. "Thank you. You freaking rescued me, today. That million you owed me in love, you just paid it back, and then some." My heart is full of gratitude for the man I have loved for so long, proving his loyalty to me despite the damage it would cause his relationship. "I love you Fletcher." I'm not even thinking when I tiptoe, kiss his lips, and say, "Fuck outta here."

I slip away from him and get in my car. He's framed by my driver's side window, the fire blazing behind him as he stands there looking all confused with palms up. He says, "Could you be any more confusing, right now?"

I sigh in feigned exasperation. "What, bro? Go home to your fiancé," I say, which confuses him even more.

I tail Fletcher towards the city and veer off once I know my way back.

CHAPTER 35
DISTRESS CALL

Fletcher knew the day would come when he'd catch Riley slipping; he didn't think it would be the very next day.

The night before, when Fletcher stormed out of his own home and returned with an obvious lie about where he'd been, Riley pretended to believe him. She pretended as if she wasn't bothered one bit. Now, all of a sudden, come morning, she has this bright idea to spend the day at the office with Fletcher, her controlling insecurity disguised as quality time.

Keenan's out of the office and it's a couple hours until end of day. On the desk that used to be mine, sits Riley's purse. The phone inside of it gets a text alert. Fletcher looks. Riley doesn't.

Fletcher hits print on a fifty-page document and politely asks Riley to retrieve it for him.

Riley disappears in the printing room. Fletcher sneaks over and fishes the phone out of Riley's purse. The message staggers him.

Riley, still at the printer, vents, "Great *day*, Fletcher. How many pages are you printing?"

Fletcher appears at the entrance with her phone held out, displaying a message that he angrily narrates, "Hey ma, I need you to sneak away from your man!? I got something for you!!" Riley holds her gut and braces against the printer, as if she's having the biggest premenstrual cramp of her life. Fletcher demands, "What the fuck is this!"

Riley gulps air. "Before you go jumping to conclusions…"

"Don't explain shit to me! It's over!"

"Nooo," Riley wails. "Just give me time… to explain!"

"The truth don't need time." Fletcher sets Riley's phone down and marches out of the office and down the hallway. Heads poke out of doorways to see the commotion.

Fletcher abouts face in the elevator and the doors close on the image of Riley running down the hallway towards him. When the elevator hits bottom, Fletcher runs out into the parking garage.

He's driving off when he sees Riley, in his rearview mirror, hurrying towards her car.

Fletcher's anxiety builds. He's haunted by the outcome of his last car chase, yet he hits the accelerator, tires squealing as he exits the parking garage, thinking if only he could turn at the first block before Riley exits, he'd lose her, and maybe there wouldn't be a high-speed chase.

I get this call from Fletcher. He's so worked up I could hardly understand him. Momma leans in, asking me what's happening. I take off, saying, "I gotta go. It's Fletcher."

Just one day after Fletcher really came through for me, I'm coming through for him. I refuse to get off the phone with him until I arrive.

His distress call was for the fact that he'd turned to drinking. Being chased by another scorned lover took his anxiety over the edge.

He's at the same bar where we met after settling the debt. I walk straight to him, no pleasantries, no greeting. I snatch the drink. Tough love, but love nonetheless.

Buster – or maybe Dave, says, "Can you stop all that crying please Miss Riley?"

Riley's in the passenger seat with Kleenex in her lap. Her eyes are red and swollen from crying.

From the back seat, the other thug explains, "It's a broken heart, fool. Ain't nothing ya can do *but* cry." He looks away and bats his eyes as if to abate a soft breeze. "I can't stand to see a woman cry."

Dude in the drivers' seat jerks around to check his partner in crime. "Nigga, is you crying?"

Riley blasts, "This is all your fault! Why would you send such an obvious text like that?"

The man's eyes widen with minstrel levels of confusion. "I dunno, call me crazy, but I assumed y'all was like normal couples who keep their phones locked."

"How about, hey, Riley, I have some documents pending your review?" Riley swallows hard. "What'd you wanna show me anyway?"

"Oh yeah," he recalls. "I was trying to tell you that we put a tracker on his car."

Riley swats him. "So, why the hell are we sitting here! Let's go find him!" The same arm Riley swatted, she now claws. "Scratch that! I got a better idea." Riley looks down and shakes her head at herself for what she's about to say. "If he's with that bitch Tahj, I can't show up. I can't let him know that I know. What would he think of me, if I knew, but still stayed with him? Look, I know you guys work for Jay, but there's something I want you to do for me."

The men look at each other and then back at Riley.

Riley asks, "Can you tell me where he is right now?"

The man pulls out his phone. "He's not in a residential area. He's on Ponce De Leon Ave."

Riley cuts her eye at him for a few seconds then says, "I want you teach him a lesson. Can you do that?"

"It'll cost you a band."

"No problem," Riley says. "When you do it, I want you to tell him to stay the hell away from Tahj. I'm gonna go back to his place and wait. Y'all let me know when it's done. And hey… don't hurt him too bad."

CHAPTER 36
LOVERS CHASE

We have no idea that there are thugs combing the city looking for Fletcher. He babysits a sweating glass of water. I tell him, "Drink, bro. You gotta sober up."

Fletcher swats my comment. "I ain't drunk. Tipsy, maybe."

"As if that's okay. You shouldn't be drinking at all."

"Why is that the topic?" Fletcher frowns. "We should be talkin' about us."

I give him a stiff look and a stiff, "Really?"

Fletcher looks me over while shaking his head. "I don't get you. Didn't you just kiss me last night?"

"I shouldn't have."

With arms wide and a grandiose smile, Fletcher says, "I'm a single man now."

"Since an hour ago."

"Is it that? Or is it Jay?"

I show the back of my hand. "Do you see a ring on my finger? He's not who I thought he was."

"Riley wasn't who I thought *she* was, so you should understand. Ain't no going back."

"But it sounds like you never gave her a chance to explain. What if the text was innocent?"

"Innocent or not, all I needed was a reason. I could always say that *that* was the reason and not that *she* was the reason." Fletcher reaches across the table. I give him my hands, but not without lazy eyes and a sigh of reluctance. Fletcher says, "*I* know we're supposed to be together. *You* know we're supposed to be together. Why complicate things?"

I say, "If you were a woman, you'd understand that you don't just get out of one man's bed and jump into another's. Besides, I got questions."

"Questions like?"

"Are you gonna start back drinking?"

Fletcher sighs. "No." Fletcher gets up out of his chair and walks around to me. "Never." He takes my hand, and lifts me out of my chair. He pulls my arms around him and then puts his arms around me. I allow all of it, but at the same time, giving him an eye of distrust. Fletcher says, "Maybe I need to try a different approach." He ducks his head to kiss me, but I turn away.

"I'm telling you, Fletcher. I'm not going there with you."

Fletcher smirks and says, "When you're all alone, giving yourself some self-love, who are you thinking about, huh? I know who *I* be thinking about."

"You're drunk. Unhand me," I say, but I'm smiling.

He pulls me tighter. "You know you miss this dick."

The words run through my body like an electrical current. I figure if I don't get out of this embrace, it's gonna be Pound Town for sure. I start to push away by planting my hands firmly on his chest. And why did I do that? Just the feel of those strong pecs makes me tremble. Fletcher knows he has me where he wants me, but still he lets me push away. I wanna slap him for not taking the pussy.

"Don't make me have to chase you," says Fletcher as he licks his lips.

I wag a finger and sing, "No fair. Don't do that."

"Don't do what," he asks, as if he doesn't already know.

"Do not lick your lips at me."

"Why not," Fletcher says. "We both know why you brought me here."

"I had to get you away from that bar." I wouldn't let him drive behind me because he'd been drinking, which is why his car is still parked at The Bookshelf Pub.

I back away slowly, glancing down at that hard pant print like it's a shotgun. He stalks forward. I turn and run, even on my tender ankle. Fletcher takes off after me, chasing me through my own house.

When the chase is over, I'm on my bed with no way out. Fletcher blocks the doorway, grinning. "Ran straight to the bedroom, huh… You ain't slick."

It's mask off for us both. Fletcher's unbuttoning his shirt and I'm crawling to the foot of the bed. If I didn't have something to say, I would leap for his dick with my mouth open like a striking snake. He looks down, gazing into my eyes. He moves in for a kiss, but I stop him with a hand on his chest. I'm kneeling on the bed, but I'm standing on business, when I say, "Let's get one thing straight. If we do this, we are *together*, hear me?"

"That's the whole point."

"And no matter what, whether Riley's innocent or not, you are not going back to her."

Fletcher huffs and says, "How are you acting like you're the one coming up with this stuff? I already said that."

I kiss his lips and say, "So we're understood?"

"I'm about to *make* you understand…"

I'm panting through an open-mouthed smile when I say, "This is sooo messy. That's why it's turning me on."

We move in closer, smiles fading, dead-ass serious when tongues slip in mouths.

The thing I remember most about the lovemaking on this day, is the trash talk. Oddly, it all starts with me, when Fletcher has his face buried in my breasts and I say, "You miss that? Huh baby?" With a full mouth, he gives a deep, *Mmm, hmm*. I grab the sides of his face and say, through grit teeth, "Look at me."

His eyes pop open. Via telepathy, he says, *Is that what we're doing?*

He kisses my lips, while below, he probes for the sweet spot. He says, "You don't want no smoke."

I whisper, "I want all the smoke."

As soon as the tip pops in, he's shook. He sighs in pleasure. He whispers in my ear, "I miss you so much."

"Ditto," is all I could say because his girth has me in a chokehold. Our kisses only let up just enough for whispers of gratitude. "I should've never left you," I say. Then Fletcher hovers before the next kiss, to reply, "I should've never given you a reason."

Missionary was about gratitude and personal accountability, our words echoing how being apart has humbled us and made us realize what we had.

But when I turn my back to him, there's a change in theme. Instead of gratitude, we chastise each other for ever thinking we could love anyone else.

Fletcher grips my cheeks and pulls me back into him. I sing, *oooh*.

Fletcher taunts, "Oh, you forgot?"

I sharpen my arch and start backing into him. I use his words against him. "See how this thang got you talkin'? Don't play wit me bro…" Fletcher lets me talk my shit for a few minutes but then he takes over, breaking me down with a long, slow, piping; each stroke, a direct hit. My arms give, one by one, folding under me until I'm face down in the pillow, bawling in pleasure.

"Dafuq you thought," Fletcher says.

He has me moaning like a porn chick, the way he puts a swirl in that stroke. He picks up the pace, talkin' 'bout, "Who da GOAT?"

I look back. "A'ight, now. You' doing too much."

"I'm doing too much? I'm about to *show* you too much."

He picks up the pace, stirring my macaroni. "I asked you…" He rows in and out like a well-oiled machine. "Who the GOAT?"

I sob in pleasure, "You baby!"

"Me what!"

"You the GOAT, baby. You!" I can laugh about it now, but for the sake of my insides, I had to repeat it, or he'd go even deeper, and it had been a long time since I had this much man inside of me.

Since Fletcher made me yield, so to speak, he considers his work done. He unsheathes ever so slowly, then he lay on his back. He's kind enough to let me go out on top. As I reach under me to work him inside, I glare at him and say, "You was talkin' real tough back there." I warn, "Just remember, you did this to ya self."

Fletcher isn't having it, though. He tries to dominate from the bottom, got me hopping like a pogo stick and moaning to the ceiling, but suddenly power shifts to me when I have a thick gush and my lips swell around him, fastening its grip. "Awe baby," Fletcher keeps saying, *Aw baby*, over and over – each repetition more unhinged than the last, as he climbs toward orgasmic epilepsy.

I lower half-staff and start twerking on that D like, bop, bop, bop, bop – all the while I'm talking my shit. "Don't you ever! In your life…"

His eyes go cattle wild.

I go, "Riley who?! Boy whet?!" I got him going bonkers, trembling under me. If he were standing upright, his big musclebound self would be doing Tina Turner's frenzied Proud Mary shuffle. "What's my name," I demand.

He drones, "Taaahj!" He's erupting, so he tries to buck me off of him. I sit tight in the saddle and grind every last drop out of him.

Afterward, he still quakes and glitches under me as we kiss and talk about how much fun we just had. Then we play in the sheets, debating who won.

The topic of the five milliliters of nut oozing out of me, as we speak, never comes up; he assumes I'm on birth control. Fact is, I've been off of birth control because Jay had had a vasectomy ever since his first marriage.

My head lay on Fletcher's chest while I ask, "Should we go now, to get your car?"

He pulls me tight and says, "Nah, let's just enjoy this."

I ask, "Are you spending the night?"

"I would love to," he says. "But I got some business to take care of – gotta get the locks changed."

That's the last thing I remember us saying before we drift off to sleep.

I wake up to Fletcher calling my name. I have no idea what time of night it is. Bright lights shine through the blinds like heaven opened up just outside. Fletcher's spying at the window with his back against the wall, like a soldier ready to hurl a grenade. I shade my eyes and say, "Who's that with their high beams on my house?"

The headlights are too bright to see the driver, but Fletcher says, "I'm almost sure that's Riley's car. She know where you live?"

"Not that I'm aware of."

Fletcher starts getting dressed. I throw on a T-shirt and hop into a pair of leggings. I slip one foot into a pair of slides but change my mind, opting for sneakers and then I grab a belt off the dresser in case I have to beat a bitch.

Fletcher's halfway up the buttons on his shirt when the doorbell rings. He looks up and sees me fully dressed. "What do you think you're doing!"

I say, "Have you thought about what it would look like if you go out there? I don't want all that drama at my doorstep, so I'm gonna go tell her you're not here."

Fletcher accepts my explanation, but upon second thought, he inquires, "Wait, what's the belt for?"

I scurry out of the room and go out front. I open the door, but with a firm grip, so Riley can't force her way in. I made Fletcher think I'd be cordial, but I'm onery from the go. "What's your problem, Riley? Got your high beams on my house like a damn Bat Signal! Are you slow?"

"Where's Fletcher?"

I slip through the door and close it behind me. I lean, to study her audacity from a fresh new angle. "No hello? No 'sorry to disturb you'? Where's your manners?"

Riley looks emotionally drained, with the disposition of a wayward zombie, and it seems as if tears would be falling if she had any left. I actually begin feeling sorry for Riley – that is – until she makes praying hands and rotates them forward at me to say, "Bitch I'm gone ask you one more time…"

"Bitch?" I turn an ear, as if hard of hearing. "Who you callin' a bitch? Bitch!"

Riley's eyes thin a me. "I'm not gonna stand here and let you play in my face. You could've just said you don't know where Fletcher is."

"You're right. I *don't* know where he is because he didn't say where he was going when he left my house."

Riley's head bows. Instead of saying grace, she says, "If Fletcher *was* here, it's not because he wants your ole ugl'ass!"

"Ugly?! Bitch I look way better than *you* and I got the test to prove it…"

This hits a nerve. Riley, goes on a tirade, with a knife-hand dicing on the palm of the other hand as she screams, "Bitch I have known Fletcher half my life and I have *never* seen him with another bitch as black-up as you! You are not his type, bitch. *I* am."

I smirk and say, "Well, he dumped you, didn't he?" I unfurl the belt, adding, "And if you don't take it down a notch, you gone end up getting your man took *and* your ass beat on the same day!"

Riley gives a straight face, bled of all affect. "First of all – as a rule – I don't fight ugly bitches because the first thing y'all wanna do is go for the face."

"What's with you calling me ugly?! Bitch your Down Syndrome-lookin' ass! Casper! Peeled-orange face ass bitch!"

Riley pinches the air, continuing, "*Secondly*, you didn't take my man. Is that what you really think happened?" Riley tosses her head back as if to brandish the long, silky hair that I don't have. "Lemme break it down for y'ole black, *bald*-headed ass…"

She doesn't get through her explanation without a slew of interruptions from me, though, but for the sake of clarity, I'll keep her tirade together, but just know that, all the while, I'm giving this bitch a baker's dozen, calling her names, and clowning her about Gideon, a color-struck man who gave Riley's color-struck ass what she deserved because fair skin meant so much to him that he dumped her for a porn slut. At the same time, Riley's tirade is ongoing where she says some things that, admittedly, cut me deep. She rants, "Even if Fletcher *was* here… Even if y'all had sex… that doesn't mean he chose you! You are just the chick he runs to when he hits rock bottom. You was the pet chimp tugging on his arm throughout high school. You were just one of the guys, until that fatal accident. Because you stuck by his side, he repaid your loyalty with a relationship, so don't get all delusional, bitch, you should thank him. *I'm* the one he seeks out when he's at his best; after he's in the NFL or after he becomes one of the top sports agents in the city. Do you get it now? Is it clicking? Since Fletcher's car is parked at a bar right now, that tells me he's at a low point. Maybe he resorted back to drinking, so he resorted back to you. He was never truly your man."

I laugh. "My man? Bitch try fiancé!"

"Cap," Riley spits. "Fletcher ain't never put no ring on your black ass finger."

"Well, he did put a ring on my black ass finger." I snap the belt. "And *furthermore*, you can go ahead and get the fuck outta my yard before I wear your ass out with this belt."

Riley counters. "That's the smartest thing you said yet… because what I look like, standing here, going back and forth with a bitch who has to *work* for a living!"

"Fashion isn't work!" I clap out my next four words. "It's what I do! That's the difference between me and you: my ex-fiancé had more money than Fletcher and Gideon combined and it never even occurred to me to stop doing fashion."

Riley lights up and swats a hand, "Oh I forgot. You *did* get a high-value man outside of Fletcher, but he's old and he's a jailbird. Now it's back to fry cooks and cable installers, bitch." Riley rears back and laughs so loud it drowns out my clapback. Riley then adds, "Fashion may be your field… but a *field* nonetheless. *Field* nigger!" Riley's wordplay impresses even herself, it seems, how she looks me up and down in two head flicks, adding, "Now take *that* to the bank!"

"I'm about to take this belt to your *ass* if you keep running that mouth." I cock the belt back.

Riley sets her hands on her hips. "Bitch I dare y–"

Pow! That belt-slap against her thigh shocks the shit out of her. I cock the belt back again. "I told you to get the fuck outta my yard, Riley! Get, *bitch!* Get, *dog!*"

Riley pretends like the lash didn't hurt; she wouldn't give me the satisfaction. I swing the belt again and miss. Seeing how desperately Riley scoots out of the way of my second swing, I realize how bad the first one must've stung.

Riley resets her stance with her fists balled at her sides warning, "*Hit* me one more time, see what I do to you."

My eyes stretch like, Oh really? I rush her like an angry mother into the junky room that she told her children to clean, metering my words with each swing, "Bitch-I! Told-you! Get-yo, ass…"

Riley backpedals swinging and missing. She stops to kick. My belt pops her arm like a firecracker. Her kick only grazes my hip, but enough to stop me in my tracks. Riley starts taunting as if she's up.

"Yeah, bitch," she says as she hurries and jumps safely into her car as if to secure the win. "And that's just a *sample* of what I could do to you."

"Bitch I stung the fuck outta you. Look atchya, rubbing your arm right now," I laugh.

Riley starts backing out of the driveway saying, "The next time you see me it'll be in third person. So, when you get dealt with, just know that it was me."

I figure she means karma – not thugs for hire.

I come forward saying, "That's right! Run!"

Riley backs out into the street and stops with the steering wheel cut, calling me names like she did in middle school. "Whatever ugl'ass! Better move 'fore I run you over, ugl'ass! Get back in ya house, ugl'ass!" She peels off and waves. "Bye ugl'ass!"

Once Riley's rear lights are red in the distance, I become aware of the neighbors watching from their blinds and some outside, giving the only black woman on the street, the same look they gave me when I was moving in, like, there goes the property value.

I was so blinded by anger that I forgot Fletcher was inside. He comes out and puts a hand on my shoulder.

I yank away, "Getchyo *fuckin'* hands off me!"

I march inside. A baffled Fletcher follows. He shuts the door behind him and asks, "What'd I do?"

"Nothing! That's what you did: absolutely nothing!"

Fletcher explains, "I would have, but y'all ain't do shit. That was the safest fight I ever saw in my life."

I swipe my keys off the counter, and say, "I'm taking you back to your car!"

We pull off in my car. For half the ride, Fletcher's quiet. I yell, "Why are you not talking!"

"Because I know you," he counters. "There ain't no talking to you when you're like this."

"So, there was nothing you could've done differently?"

"Y'all hardly touched each other."

"It's not about that!"

"Fuck the guessing game, Tahj. Just tell me!"

"You let that bitch say all those things. You should've came out and defended your love for me!"

Fletcher looks down and sighs, then he says, "Y'all wouldn't have been talking in the first place if you just let me go out there like I said I was gonna do."

"That's beside the point," I say. "You heard all those things Riley was saying, right?"

"Yeah, but I didn't think for a second that you were believing it."

"All these years you had me looking stupid. If you loved me – I mean really loved me – you would treat me in such a way that no one could piece together some bottom-bitch narrative about me."

"Hell, *Riley* couldn't! She was just saying things to piss you off."

"What-the-fuck-ever! How does she not know that we were engaged, Fletcher? Explain that."

Fletcher dips forward with wide eyes, "You don't remember? For one, she was in California then. Number two, we had to keep it on the low because of Keenan."

"*After* that! You were in a whole relationship with this woman and it never came up in conversation?"

"How is that a question," says Fletcher. "Did you tell Jay that I'm your one true love? Huh? Did you tell Jay that I got the best dick you ever had in your life? No! You probably told him what he needed to hear, just like I did for Riley."

One thing I truly dislike about Fletcher is that he's too good at arguing. He's starting to make sense, but fuck that. I raise a finger and say, "And it was *only* after you got with Riley that you became the man I always needed you to be."

Fletcher grabs his head and rakes his hands down in frustration. "Man what the fuck, bro! Why is it that I'm always the one who gotta prove myself! Ain't nobody proving shit to *me!*" Fletcher sighs and shakes his head. "You know what…" I don't, because he didn't finish his sentence.

We arrive at the Bookhouse Pub. I park in a spot that's a block away from Fletcher's car. I put the car in gear and say, "We should not have had sex. We should've waited. Now I feel like I need time just to think straight."

"Time," Fletcher mocks.

"Time," I assert. "And I'm not so sure that we'll come out of this okay."

Fletcher strokes the back of my neck and says, "Let's talk about it tomorrow; let cool heads prevail." After no response from me, Fletcher leans for a kiss, but I turn away.

Out of anger, I drive away as soon as Fletcher gets out of my car. Had I waited for him to get safely to his vehicle, I would've been there to see the goons trying to head Fletcher off before he could get to the gun that he keeps in his glove compartment.

CHAPTER 37
JACK & MACY ALL OVER AGAIN

After dropping Fletcher off, I return to my living room with my internal voice on speaker, venting to the universe, spazzing out and breaking things until every surface but the floor, is clear. Then, I'm out of breath, hands on hips, yelling demands, from an imaginary Fletcher, to pay back every bit of the million he says he owes me in love. I slap the shit out of a lamp, for the absence of Riley.

For lack of something else to break, I start cracking my knuckles. That's when I get a call from Keenan saying Fletcher's in the ER. My rage pivots to distress. I flee from my house then barrel through the city like a bat out of hell.

Meanwhile, Fletcher's laid up in the hospital. Riley's in the waiting room, shedding crocodile tears. Her stepfather, Phillip, paces the waiting room floor, mumbling prayers and speaking in tongues.

Fletcher's mother is on the phone with her sister, reporting the status, "…Another concussion, sad to say. Yet I'm grateful because it could've been much worse. The lady who called 911 reported that

Fletcher was putting a hurting on those boys until one hit him in the head with a gun butt… No, not yet; they say the nurse prac will come escort us to the room in a few minutes…"

Lew stares into eternity while nervously bending his cap in his hands until Phillip's pacing plucks his last nerve. Lew says, "Won't you sit down in one of these seats, man? You making *me* nervous."

Lew gets a sharp nudge from his wife, who pardons, "Don't pay him no mind, Phillip."

Phillip explains, "I'm just so messed up about this. It's all my fault."

Lew gives his hat to his wife with a no-look pass. "You're saying it's your fault that my son's laid up in the hospill?"

Only Leslie can see that Lew is ready to go off. She rubs his back to transfer calming energy.

Riley, the person who paid the goons to jump Fletcher, looks over to say, "Don't be silly, Daddy. This can't possibly be your fault."

Phillip turns to Riley and says, "When you called me crying today, I went straight to the Prophet. I demanded that he remove his covering from over Fletcher's life. That was just hours ago and already this?"

Leslie inquires, "You say Riley was in tears? What happened?"

"It was nothing," Riley blurts. "Couples go through things."

Phillip elaborates, "There was an argument…" He stops when he sees me enter the waiting room escorted by Keenan who had met me out in the parking and escorted me in.

I correct, "It was more than just an argument." All eyes swim over to me. "They broke up," I say.

Riley recovers from the sight of me, and blasts, "Oh please, Tahj! What're you even doing here?"

Before offering a reply, I hug Fletcher's father and mother and then I wave at Phillip as I lower into a beige row chair. "What am *I* doing here? Shouldn't I be asking you that?"

The tension is electric. We're being watched by everyone within earshot – Fletcher's folks, Keenan, Phillip, the receptionist with the crooked wig, a slim tattooed man who coughs like it hurts, and a brunette with her injured child.

Riley raises the back of her hand to show off her engagement ring. "I'm Fletcher's future wife. Why wouldn't I be here?"

I reply, "Well since you're here, maybe you should have them look at that welt on your leg."

Riley counters, "I thought *you* were only here because you got lost on your way to see your man in jail."

Leslie says, "Isn't this familiar?" She looks at her husband then at us. "My son, in the hospital… two women bickering… You young ladies nowadays make a mother wish her son was gay."

I apologize immediately. "Forgive me, Mrs. Lewis, please," I say. "I let my anger get the best of me."

Mrs. Lewis squeezes my hand and says, "I know, Tahj, because that's not like you." She adds, "My mentor always says be mindful on the front end, so you won't have to apologize on the back end."

Riley glares at Leslie and me, two women on one accord, as if we're the ops. "You know what," Riley says, and nothing more. She snatches up her purse and marches out of the waiting room.

Leslie pulls me aside and asks what happened between Riley and me. I slept with her soon-to-be wedded son, and I don't know how to tell her. My explanation pivots each time I think of how this mess would sound to this exemplary woman of God. "Well, you see um… Your son Fletcher… and Riley, they um… They're engaged, right? No wait, Fletcher came to me… as a friend… saying that Riley was cheating…"

"Cheating? What brought him to that conclusion? Because Riley may have her ways about her, but she doesn't strike me as the type to…"

"Fletcher found texts on Riley's phone, and…"

"He told you this, when? Where did this conversation take place?"

I'm standing knock-kneed and wringing my hands. "Well that's the thing, you see. We were at…" Just thinking of how it would sound, to Leslie, that I had Fletcher over at my place, ties my stomach in a bow. "We were at a bar," I blurt. "Yes, this bar downtown. And Fletcher was drinking, so I wouldn't let him drive."

Mrs. Leslie tilts and says, "Tahj? Why do I feel like you're making this up as you go along?"

It feels like a knife jicks me in the gut. I sigh twice. "Miss Leslie, it… might sound that way because… maybe I'm ashamed of myself."

Leslie covers her mouth and says, "You and Fletcher?"

"We're kinda together now." I smile in hopes that Leslie might smile with me. She does not. She leaves me hanging, with my mouth spread and my teeth feeling long.

"Do you realize how crazy this sounds?"

My head lowers. "Yes, now that I'm explaining it to you."

Leslie's name is called from across the room. It's Lew signaling the arrival of the nurse practitioner who's ready to escort us to Fletcher's room.

Phillip objects, "There's one more, actually. She stepped out for a second."

The nurse answers, "The fiancé? I met her on my way out. She's in the room already."

Under my breath, "The bitch."

I'm quiet on the way to the room, though wishing I could run ahead. I hear our collective feet walking down the hallways, panel lights on the ceiling passing over us, and all I can do is wonder what Riley is saying to Fletcher right now. He's had a near death incident; he may be vulnerable. I wonder if Fletcher may feel regret for leaving her so suddenly and now she's the only one at his bedside, like I was, years ago.

When we enter the room, Riley's caressing Fletcher's face with the hand that still wears the engagement ring. She smiles and reports, "Everything still works. He has all of his wits about him."

Fletcher says, "Y'all need to be worried about the dudes who jumped me."

His body language toward Riley is as if they're still together. I reserve judgement but grind my teeth.

Fletcher's mother and father approach. Riley doesn't come away; she still crowds the bed. Lew comes to the other side of the bed with a handshake but keeps Fletcher's hand. "You alright son?"

"I'm straight, big dawg." He then looks up and says, "What's good, Kee? What's up, Tahj?"

I lean away so he can literally miss me with that casual greeting – as if he was not balls deep in me earlier. Keenan, noting my distress, tilts to me and whispers, "You a'ight?" Keenan doesn't know. I stand there, grinning and bearing the disrespect of Fletcher not acknowledging our relationship. Fletcher's mother and father ask him questions and it seems odd how Riley keeps helping Fletcher with the answers.

Fletcher starts explaining the situation to his father, and then he says something that surprises us all. "The funny thing is, though, I distinctly remember getting in my car and driving home. So, it was crazy to me, waking up on the concrete with people standing over me."

Riley crowds him and says, "Remember you told the doctor that you remembered the fight, how you first tried to take out the bigger of the two?"

"I didn't say that. You said that."

Riley looks quite desperate in the face, as she scans the room and says, "My man is still trying to digest it all." There's this nervous giggle she does when she's lying. "It all happened so fast." She leans in and kisses Fletcher. Leslie's gaze rotates from that kiss to me with a look that calls everything I told her, into question.

My eyes cut away from Leslie and to Riley. Sharply, I say, "Riley. You need to back up off of my man, okay?"

The shock brings on silence. Riley has this look like her world is about to come crashing down.

Fletcher, however, looks genuinely concerned about my mental health. "Tahj, are you okay?"

Riley looks relieved, and no one sees it but me.

I plead, "You don't remember? You caught Riley cheating and you came to me–"

Riley interrupts. "Maybe they need to check *you* for a concussion, girl."

I look around at everyone. "He's not right. He can't remember!"

Leslie says, "Something happened for sure. Phillip? Didn't you say it was bad enough that you went to see your prophet? Tahj isn't crazy."

Riley blasts, "You're just saying that because you like Tahj. You never liked me."

Fletcher looks left and right as if to a tennis match.

Fletcher's mother stares Riley down and says, "Have I ever said a cross word to you?"

Riley points with a lift of her chin. "You insult me so elegantly, don't you? But I know how to read between the lines."

Leslie sucks her teeth and turns away, her eyes landing on Riley's stepfather. "*Talk*, Phillip! What happened?"

Fletcher says, "I remember everything just fine, though. I remember walking Tahj to her car. We had a conversation, and then I was on my way back to my car when I guess I got jumped. Am I right?"

I counter, "You didn't walk me to my car. We pulled *up* in my car, and you got *out* of my car."

Suddenly too many people start talking so no one is heard. I yell, "What y'all don't understand is that Fletcher has CTE!"

Everyone hushes. Fletcher looks at me as if I'd betrayed him. Lew asks, "That true?"

Fletcher sighs and says, "I didn't want anybody to know."

Leslie says, "You wanted Tahj to know. You told *her*."

Riley yells, "You told her! Not me! Your fiancé?"

"Because you were never the one," I say. *Dayumn*, Keenan punctuates.

Riley starts marching for the door, "I'm gonna have you removed!"

I say to Fletcher, "Do you, or do you not remember making love to me today?" Everyone in the room gasps as one, stopping time. Riley frozen with a hand on the doorknob, looks back.

Fletcher frowns like it's the craziest thing he's ever heard. "No," Fletcher denies. "Why would you even say something like that? Why are you doing this?"

Riley exits for reinforcements. Fletcher says, "We kissed, Tahj. That's all we did. And you know it."

A hand leaps to my chest. "You've got today confused with a different day. We only kissed the previous time we were at that bar."

Phillip wears the smile of a hyena. "You say you kissed her? You went behind Riley's back? You bastard."

Fletcher's father turns to Phillip. "You call my son a bastard?" (For the life of me, I'll never understand why Uncs have to repeat the offense.) Lew adds, "Open your mouth again, you gone find a fist in it."

Riley returns with a long-nosed security guard who's telling everyone to get out. Seconds later, the doctor comes in, informing the security guard. "Not everyone. Just one."

"*Her*," Riley points. "The black-up one!"

He holds out a hand and says, "Come on nicely now."

Fletcher protests, "Wait! Can we talk about this?"

Brazenly, the guard replies, "I'll take you too, if ya want."

He immediately regrets those words when Fletcher gets up and he sees how big he is. Fletcher reaches for me but the guard snatches me quicker. I stumble into him and he wraps me in a bear hug. Fletcher lunges.

Lew, Phillip, and Keenan can't hold him back, but where three men fail with muscle, his mother prevails with only the sound of her voice. "Fletcher! Calm down right *neow!* I didn't raise no pit bull; I raised a man."

I'm screaming as the security guard forces me down the hallway. He grips my elbows and gives a whispered threat like an angry parent in church. "Calm yourself down, right now, or I'm calling the police to take you downtown."

I comply. Down the hallways and out to the waiting room, every head dials with the advance of my escort, as if murmurs of the incident had preceded me. I gather what little pride I have left, square my shoulders, and hit my stride, turning my perp-walk into a catwalk.

CHAPTER 38
WHAT HAD HAPPENED WAS

As agreed, I leave the hospital premises, but with the mindset that this shit is *not* over with. I return to the Bookhouse Pub and park behind Fletcher's truck, waiting… My last text is still on read. I try again and get a text fail error once, and then three more times. I blame the signal. I call, expecting a push to voicemail, but instead, I get a prompt that the phone number is no longer in service. I bang a fist on the console.

Apparently, Riley has used Fletcher's admission to kissing me as leverage to force him to call into customer service and change a phone number he's had since high school. I can see Fletcher allowing it because he doesn't remember getting back with me.

Fletcher's memory is a book that's missing the page of the day he caught Riley cheating and reconciled with me, so thinks he's still engaged to Riley.

I couldn't reach Fletcher, so I begin texting Keenan back and forth. He says the hospital released Fletcher shortly after they escorted me out. I've been wasting my time sitting behind Fletcher's truck because if they were going to retrieve it, they would've done it already.

I spend all of three seconds trying to figure out what to do, but the answer's clear; I gotta pull up. In the dark car interior, my lit phone screen makes an inverted mirror of my side window. I see my opaque reflection rolling the steering wheel under my palm, as I pull into traffic, tight lips reading a mother fucker spoken under my breath.

On the way there, I call Riley's phone and we start cursing each other out until she hangs up in my face and blocks me.

I pull up in Fletcher's driveway and begin honking the horn and watching the windows of neighboring homes light up all the way down the street. Their dogs howl. Not one single fuck is given by me. For all I know, Riley and Phillip's backwards ass could be pressuring Fletcher to get married tomorrow morning at a courthouse.

Fletcher's front door swings open, Riley bursting out. I start to get out, but then I notice that Riley has what looks like a knife-sharpening rod in her hand. I get back in my running car, holding the door open, one foot out, as I hit the gas to meet her at the bottom of the steps, my brights blaring yellow on her frightened face. Fletcher snatches Riley back. I hit brakes. I'm so enraged I nearly ran both of them over. Fletcher pounds the hood of my car, yelling, "Fuck is you doing!"

Riley uses the opportunity to try sneak around him, but Fletcher turns, scoops Riley up, and carries her inside on his shoulder like a sack of potatoes. The front door is still wide open so I see him sit her down, and yell, "Don't you come back through that door, you hear me! I am *not* playing with you!" I could tell that Riley has never seen him this angry, how she just sits and nods like a scolded child.

Fletcher then comes down the steps with his arms spread in nonverbal *what the fuck*. "You were gonna fucking run her over?"

"You have amnesia, Fletcher! Riley cheated. And she knows it. She's taking advantage of your memory loss."

"What memory loss though?"

"Who got the concussion? Why question my memory and not yours?"

"Because you're the only one saying these things, Tahj."

"Do you really think I'm out here, on your front lawn, disturbing the whole neighborhood over something that never happened?"

"How come the only things I forgot are the things that you're saying? Me? Forget sex?"

"Can't you tell? I bet your balls are empty, right now!"

Riley, from the doorway, mocks, "Talkin' about empty balls… You know the bitch is crazy, Fletcher. She ain't been right since she passed out in the club – looking all stupid in Bubby's big ole coat. If you ask me, I think she's fucking Bubby… steady flying out to Philly…"

Riley speaks uninterrupted, only because I wait, with bated breath, on a response from Fletcher, whose brows are uneven, as if he's now wondering how his balls got empty (if that's how it works for men).

I plead, "You know she was shady with her phone. You finally found a text from a guy asking her to sneak away."

Riley marches towards us like Sophia through the corn crop. "Fletcher! How much longer you gone listen to this crazy bitch?"

Fletcher cuts his eyes. "Watch ya mouth, Riley."

Riley fixes her hands on her hips. "She come over here disturbing the peace of your home, and you tell *me* to watch *my* mouth? Have you forgot who you're engaged to?"

"Tahj and me was engaged once, too."

The way Riley shut right up, tickles my insides.

Fletcher may have silenced Riley but it doesn't mean he's siding with me. He tells me, "I remember the night at the boutique. I remember taking you out to the country… the fire… everything. Like I said, my memory is good."

Riley says, "So that's where you were that night you went missing? You were with *her!*"

Fletcher turns his whole body around and says, "Riley, I swear, it wasn't like that."

I turn Fletcher back to me with a tug of his arm, and say, "It was like that *today*, though. That's why Riley pulled up on me and we were fighting in my yard."

Fletcher looks off, frowning, "Fighting in your *yard?*"

Riley shouts. "That *never* happened. *Never!*"

I counter, "Okay, then, ask her how she got that welt on her leg!"

Riley starts ranting as a way to drown me out. Fletcher's arms flail as if fighting a swarm of bees around his head. "*Shut up,*" Fletcher booms.

It's so quiet, we hear my idling car and dogs barking from afar, but that's not all we hear. Police sirens whir in the distance. I feel my one chance slipping away. My throat fattens, and tears fall as I petition for Fletchers love and dry snitch in one breath, "When we were sitting in your car, kissing just before you proposed to Riley…"

Riley tries to talk over me, to deny me Fletcher's ear. I yell too, like an announcement at a middle school assembly, telling Fletcher, "You said I'm your soulmate, and you were marrying Riley because you were afraid that she'd kill herself…"

The sirens increase. Fletcher yells, "Let me talk, alright! Everybody's talking but me." We hush. He then peers into my eyes then says, "Why do I feel like you're not lying about any of this?"

I answer, "Because you know how you feel. You said it yourself that you were looking for any reason for us to be together. And she gave you one."

Fletcher's eyes close and his head shakes. "What I mean is that… whatever you think happened was definitely real *to you*. I remember everything *except* for the things you're saying."

That's when I feel the deadening melancholy of defeat. My throat is a knot and I'm speechless while staring at his face, which begins strobing in blue light as squad cars converge on the property. Fletcher backs away slowly. I turn around to face the police. It feels like the scene of a movie, two broad-shouldered cops getting out of their squad cars, me standing there in tears, waiting to be taken away, with all my pride gathered in my bosom.

Riley yells, "There she is, officers! Come get her!"

The lead officer says, "We got a call about a domestic disturbance."

One officer questions me while the other questions them. Riley answers loud enough for me to hear. "I don't know why, mister officer! Maybe it's because she's *been* jealous of me ever since high school." I ignore Riley. Fletcher tries to quite her, but she keeps going. "I made the cheerleading squad while she had to settle for the flag team. I was Valedictorian, Miss Georgia finalist… She's always been under me, so I don't know why she's surprised that Fletcher picked me over her ugl'ass!"

My patience breaks. I start yelling back at Riley, and the officer grabs me, maybe a bit too aggressively, and tells me to calm down. "For what," I plead. "For doing the same thing she's doing? It didn't become a problem until *I* started doing it too!"

The beady-eyed officer barks, in his backwoods accent, "Mam, you're too busy yappin' to know what's happenin'." He points at the others and says. "They're about to put restraining orders against you. By the time their wet signature is on that document, and you're still standing here sassing me… You will be in violation of that restraining order, and I'll be taking you downtown for a free night's say at motel Fulton County."

Not another word needed to be said. I don't play with the police, so I hop in my car and hit reverse, but I down the window to yell at Fletcher, sobbing, "You son of a bitch! You would do me like this? Don't ever speak to me again. Good luck with that fake bitch!"

As I drive away the rearview mirror shows the shrinking image of Fletcher and Riley, embraced on the front lawn because he doesn't remember leaving her.

Electric blue lights oscillate over them and the house as they shrink with distance like a cinematic camera panning out of the final scene of a romantic thriller. My angry eyes are a chilling indicator of a sequel; this is not over.

CHAPTER 39
PLAN BE

All I could do is hope that Fletcher remembers before the wedding, which is highly unlikely. I'd been reading up on Dissociative Amnesia, which is what Fletcher has — whether he knows it or not. The chance of remembering is next to none, and if so, who knows when? It could be tomorrow or fifty years later, Fletcher old in his rocking chair, staring into the memory of playfully chasing me into the bedroom. He'd remember Riley's texts, and peer into her old, wrinkled eyes with the realization that their entire marriage has been a lie. But that's neither here nor there.

Since I can't contact Fletcher due to the restraining order, I've been writing to get things off of my chest. In a month's time, I've barreled through three hundred pages. Somewhere along the line, I realized that I was writing a book.

If Fletcher hadn't lost his memory, and his wedding were not two weeks away, it would've been the sweetest little friends-to-lovers romance, but reality doesn't allow for it.

Unlike an author writing fiction and playing God with forces like fate and destiny, I'm bound to the events of real life. Oddly, it was real life where I foolishly tried to be the author, and put destiny in a box, a happily ever consisting of Fletcher and me.

I write furiously, day and night. I start the story as far back as me being teased as a little girl, with a dark skin, quick-tongued momma who covered me with affirmation and trained me to be a master at the dozens, so that any who tried to clown me would end up finding the clown paint on their face.

When the pages finally catch up to the present, the cursor blinks for hours. I figure the only way I can generate an ending is to return to real life. I've been thinking about turning the boutique over to momma, moving to another city and starting a modeling agency, where I could see this story ending with a new beginning, maybe with me smiling at a first client that looks like me. Or I should write children's books for dark-skinned girls who don't have the support of a mother like mine. For now, I return to my boutique, just to get my legs under me.

It's midday when Joslyn, Riley's friend and confidant, pulls up to my boutique. I have no idea this woman is sitting in my parking lot, contemplating whether she should go through with what she came to do.

All day, Momma's been pretending like nothing's amiss. I talk to her every day; she knows I'm not okay. She pulls me aside and tells me I'm resilient for coming back to work.

I reply, "I'm at work because I have a restraining order against me. I'm at work because I can't be alone in my house without my thoughts looping, to where I can't concentrate on nothing else."

"That's because you're stuck on the idea that you and Fletcher are supposed to be together. I kept my mouth shet all this time waiting for you to figure it out for yourself, but you won't let yourself see that that boy chose Riley over you."

"But Momma, that doesn't make sense."

"It don't have to. People do things that don't make sense every day. Fletcher ain't no forgot. He looked you dead in the face and lied. He's using that concussion as an excuse to back out of a decision he made when he was drunk."

"Explain to me, then, momma, why he would wanna go back to a cheater?"

"Because she red! That's why!"

Everything stops. I hear my own heartbeat and feel blood coursing in my face.

"These lil red bitches get away with murder. We may not speak on it, but we not gonna pretend like it don't exist."

I cut my eyes, "This ain't the eighties and nineties momma. Things have changed."

With a side eye, Momma quizzes, "As soon as these niggas get they hands on lil money, they get them a light-bright. That's why all their wives could pass for sisters."

"Jay has money."

"I'm talking about Fletcher."

"You said all men."

"*Fletcher* ain't never had money – and you – at the same time."

"He left Riley *for* me."

"Bitch, I–"

Our eyes widen. Momma's mouth clamps shut and she covers it with a hand, which she snatches down to say. "Did I just…?"

I just nod yes, my eyes still stretched. I know she didn't mean it, but I consider stamping off and making her feel guilty for it.

Momma says, "You know I didn't mean that." She hugs me. "I'm sorry baby. You just don't understand how that issue gets to me, and that makes me double mad about how Fletcher did you. Do Jesus." Momma releases the hug and holds me at arm's length. "You're too blessed to feel like the world is ending. God's shown you too much favor, to think that the best He can do for you, is a scatter-brained nigga with a big dick." I almost laugh, but I button my mouth because Momma's serious; dead serious, as she waits for me to fix my face. "You *are* where God wants you to be: clothed, in your right mind, and using the gifts He gave you. As far as a man to spend this life with? That'll fix itself because baby you got mo legs than a gazelle, and mo beauty than a face is supposed to hold."

I'm standing there smiling, appraising her with the suspicion that she's pulling my leg. "You tell me anything, Momma."

"And you keep falling for it," she says, lovingly, as she palms my cheek, her thumb smearing a lone tear. "You got this, baby. You got this all by yourself." Momma lowers her hand and walks away, saying. "But if you need me, I'm here."

She refuses to let me be a wreck. I swear if Momma was a corner man, she could inspire any boxer to fight like a world champ. I feel that imaginary boxer's robe slip off my shoulders as I walk onto the sales floor, ready to take on life; ready to put Fletcher behind me.

And then Joslyn enters.

I recognize her, but can't place her. She covers the work badge on her lanyard, calls me by name, and then waits for me to identify her. She's sneaky gorgeous – so easy to miss in a crowd, but when you really set your eyes upon her, she begins to shine like jewel. "I remember you from campus. You and Mimi were like this," meaning, like my crossed fingers. "Joslyn, right?"

"Yup."

"Nice seeing you. What're you up to, nowadays?"

"I'm in pharmaceuticals, senior chemist."

"Whoa." My fingers sprinkle all the money she must be making, which she shrugs off modestly.

I usher her further inside and ask, "So what brings you in, today? I got a peach-stone colored maxi dress that'll bring out the tone in your locks and make that melanin pop."

She smiles, shyly. "Maybe later," she says. "What brings me in today is the fact that I don't have your number. None of your old friends got your number either."

"Money changed everything."

"Amen," she says with a head still nodding and veering away as if she doesn't quite know what to say next.

I ask, "Do you still keep in touch with Tia and them?"

With a coy smile, she says, "Only Riley."

My heart stops. "So, you were trying to get in touch with me, for what reason?"

"I don't have time. I'm on my lunch break and I can't use my phone at work, so let's meet up tonight." She hands me her phone. "Lock in your number."

While dialing myself from her phone, I ask, "Can I at least know what this is about?"

Joslyn takes her phone from my hands. "I've got the receipts to prove that Fletcher has amnesia," she says, while backing towards the exit.

I start hyperventilating. Fate itself reverses field. Having an ally within the wedding camp, unlocks a new possible ending to the story of Fletcher and me.

Riley watches as the seamstress buttons Fletcher up in a sea-glass blue tux. The seamstress tugs the hem, flattens his collars, and centers his bowtie while she and Riley discuss Fletcher's look, as if he's a Christmas tree they're decorating.

Fletcher gets a text from a name he knows all too well, but doesn't remember ever adding to his contact list. The text says, *Running a little late*, which means there's a meeting that Fletcher doesn't recall ever scheduling. Fletcher gazes at the screen with his mouth open, wondering how, on earth, could he have forgotten a meeting with all-star NBA player Brandon Fuller.

Riley scolds, "Fletcher. Would you put the phone down for a minute please?"

Fletcher raises a number one to put Riley and the seamstress on pause. He hits the call button. He answers, timidly, "Brandon? I just got your text that you're running late. I won't hold it against you, brotha… You *do* remember where we're supposed to meet at right," Fletcher asks, because *he* doesn't know. Fletcher can't ask directly because forgetting a meeting is a surefire way to lose a client.

Fletcher's laughter seems riddled with stress. "Of course, *I* know where. I'm already here, waiting on you, man. The question is, do *you* remember?" Fletcher laughs a vein into his forehead as he paces away.

Finally, Brandon Fuller gives-in to Fletcher's little game and names the meeting place they'd agreed upon a month ago. Fletcher, hearing that the destination is across town, he ends the call.

Fletcher lowers the phone and says, "I gotta go." He doesn't even have time to change out of the tux.

Riley takes off to get Fletcher's clothes, but when she comes out of the dressing room with an armload of clothes, her fiancé is nowhere in sight.

"Dammit," Riley says. Fletcher hasn't been out of her sight since the mugging, and now he's driving off in *her* car, which doesn't have a GPS tracker on it.

Fletcher speeds through town, punching the steering wheel and cursing himself. "How could you forget something like that, bro," he says to himself, but then it dawns on him: maybe he does have amnesia.

At closing time, Momma and Uncle Sirus just set the alarm and exit the store when an out-of-control car comes galloping through the parking lot, heading straight for them. They try to run away but run into each other. There's only time to hug each other tight and brace for the bang that would launch them back into the store with a hailstorm of glass.

But the car screeches to a halt. Fletcher jumps out. "Where's Tahj?"

Momma blasts, "Boy you scared the hell outta me!"

Uncle Sirus puts his hands on his hips and says, "Talmbout, where's Tahj? Where's your fucking sense?"

Fletcher comes forward, pleading, "Where is she?"

Momma taps Uncle Sirus and points. "Big block shoulder bastard comin' up here in a got-damn tuxedo."

"*Girl*," Uncle Sirus laughs.

Momma says. "I wish I might tell you where Tahj is, when all you've done is hurt her!"

Fletcher twirls the key chain in his hand and says, "Is she home? I'll just go to her house."

Momma yells, "She's not there!"

"I'll sit there and wait, then."

Fletcher turns and marches toward the car.

Momma stammers for something to say, something to stop him in his tracks. "But she don't want you no more."

Fletcher ignores her and makes the car chirp.

Momma mumbles to Unc, "If he get her alone he gone put that thang on her and it's over."

Uncle Sirus, the trusty sidekick, adds, "Boy you' dumb as you look, if you finna go Tahj's house in your fiancé's car."

Momma whispers, "Good one."

Fletcher pauses with a grip on the door handle. He asks, "Can you call her for me?"

Momma's neck swerves on the words, "Your hand broke?"

"I left my phone," Fletcher says. His phone rings in his pocket, calling him a liar.

"You said you left your phone, so what's that?" Momma squints. "Oh, I get it. You can't call from your phone because Riley's monitoring your calls."

Fletcher sighs and says, "Mrs. Thompson… Look, I don't blame you for feeling the way you feel about me. Tahj is a mess because of me, but at the same time, I'm a mess because of her. You think I'm jumping in and out of her life as I please, but it's the other way around. On the night that I was set to propose to Riley, Tahj sought me out. When Jay was arrested, Tahj called me, and I risked my freedom for her."

Momma places her hands on her hips, "So y'all been messing around?"

"Nothing happened between us that day, but what I've learned, is that every time I look at Tahj, I start freefalling all over again."

My crazy momma claps once, then again, as if she's killing mosquitos, but the clapping cranks up faster, escalating to an applause. Her eyes are full of fake, but convincing gratitude for Fletcher's heartfelt soliloquy. Unc claps too.

Momma says, "Seriously, though, I appreciate you opening up your heart like that, Fletcher, but the thing is, you can tell everybody in the world how you feel, but it doesn't mean a thing if you don't tell–"

"–Tahj knows exactly how I feel," Fletcher says.

"Not Tahj, stanka-butt! I'm talking about Riley. Until you tell *Riley* that Tahj is your one true love, this is always gonna be a mess."

Fletcher's head hangs as he says, "It's not that simple."

"The truth is simpler than lying. Can't you see? Lying got you scared to use your own damn phone!"

Fletcher sighs. "So, you're not gonna call Tahj for me?"

Momma looks at him like he'd just turned dumber right before her eyes.

Uncle Sirus asks, "Young man, was there a breakthrough with your amnesia or something?"

Fletcher replies, "I just left a meeting that… for the life of me, I can't remember ever scheduling. Turns out, I spoke with that client on the same day that Tahj says we were together. This is the first bit of proof I have that some of my memory is missing."

Momma says, "Damn a memory, Fletcher! Tahj is done! She's talking about moving to another city so she'd never have to see your face again! You're a selfish son of a bitch!"

"Calm down, Letha." Uncle Sirus tries to comfort Momma, but she reels away, nearly throwing herself off balance. "No, lemme go, Sirus! I'm not finished!"

Momma points and says, "If you had any amount of decency about you, you wouldn't be looking for Tahj in the tux you're about to marry Riley in. Real men are not this fickle! A man doesn't only think about what *he* wants! This feeling you can't seem to control, real men know how to put it away, and do what's best for everyone involved. Give Riley the wedding she always dreamed off, and let Tahj move on with her life; that's all that both of them wants!"

Fletcher's already backing away, a frog in his throat. He gets in his car first, but he's the last to leave. He sits in the parking lot for a long while, rethinking life.

I had left the boutique a little early to meet Joslyn at an upscale soul-food restaurant called The Renaissance where they serve fried chicken on white cloth tables and slow-roasted oxtails with truffle butter.

Before Joslyn reveals her receipts, she insists on explaining, in intricate detail, how she's actually a good person and would never betray Riley, or anyone, without good reason. The reasons go back to CAU. "She always thinks people jealous of her. That's why those girls had set her up and jumped her over there by Phiefer hall–"

"–I remember. I helped Riley," I say. "I was up in there bammin' too."

Joslyn cuts her eyes at me. "You? Bammin'?"

"Well, I was swinging my purse, but one of the girls pushed the *shit* outta me and said I better stay my ass over there before I get fucked up, so that's what I did. Riley should've kept her tail out the face of these girls' boyfriends."

We high-five. "Preach," Joslyn cosigns. She adds, "That's why nobody liked bringing their man around her. You get a different Riley when there's men around. She starts posing and slinging her hair," Joslyn says, mocking with a sling of her locks.

I add, "Then outta nowhere, a bitch bowlegged too!?"

Joslyn rolls a fist next to her head. "You noticed?"

We come down from our laughter before Joslyn continues. "Riley will never see her ways. Her problem is, she thinks the center belongs to her – even at *my* birthday party… Bitch damn near blew out my candles. She thinks people are supposed to be in awe of her–"

I twirl a finger. "She thinks *black people* should be in awe of her. At modeling events, when the room is white, she's fine with being the scenery to their experience. She's not competitive with them; she's a fan."

Joslyn just sits there with an open mouth.

"It's not her fault, though. She got issues. You do know about her real dad, right? He Brian McKnight-ed their ass – left Riley and her mom for a white woman with a bunch of kids."

"Sad," Joslyn says. "Riley still loves that man to death, although he would never send for her."

I ask, "Are we hating? Because it feels like we're hating."

Joslyn rears back. "No, bitch, we're plotting – there's a difference. She fucked your man, and she fucked mine."

"What?" I slap the table.

"Mm-hmm," Joslyn nods. "This happened a while ago, but I just found out *after* I agreed to be her maid of honor."

"And you're *still* her maiden of honor?"

"Tuh," Joslyn says with a lazy look-away. "I never was, in a true sense. I'm just the closest thing she has to a friend. When she moved to Arizona, I was glad to have her out of my hair."

"Ain't it though!"

"The whole time she was gone, she may have called me maybe twice? But when Gideon sent her packing, she started calling me every day. So, in her mind, we have a bond."

I clap with impatience. "Can you get to the part about your man, though?"

Joslyn says, "This was back in college, senior year. Remember that time Riley went vacationing with a mystery man and she was posting pics of only herself?"

"*That* time? You mean, *which* time."

"The Bahamas."

"All vacays look alike to me, unless it's mine," I say. "I figured Riley was out with an older guy. She always liked them established… Daddy issues, I guess. So Riley was on a cruise with your man?"

"My ex, so, technically she didn't sleep with my man. She didn't sleep with him at all."

"Are you sure about that?"

Joslyn nods, sadly. "That's what pisses me off so bad. He paid to take Riley out the country but got me paying for my own abortion?"

"Whoa," I say. "Did Riley know about the abortion?"

"She knew. A real friend would see him as off limits, but not Riley. All those times Riley was getting chummy with my man, she was just planting seeds."

"She did that with Fletcher."

"Oooo, that bitch," Joslyn says, over a clenched fist. "I almost recused myself as Riley's maid of honor, but no. I realize that I'll never have a better opportunity for my get-back." Joslyn crosses her legs and says, "I even thought about trying to give Fletcher some pussy."

I perk up, my ideological bell rung. "But that's not you," I say. "As momma always said, 'Act cheap and cheap shit happens.'"

"Tahj, I know that you're the one Fletcher really wants. Wanna know how I know?"

"How," I wait with bated breath. One time, Riley confided in me that Fletcher was having nightmares – that he would spring up in the middle of the night hollering your name."

This hits me like an arrow. I cover my face then spread the tears back toward my ears, revealing a face raging with vengeance. "Let's get to the receipts."

We huddle over Joslyn's phone viewing messages from the day where Riley says Fletcher broke up with her, and later that night that he was *over at that bitch, Tahj's house*. Riley texted Joslyn all day. Her chat thread is as detailed as a transcript. It verifies everything I've been saying and everything Riley denies.

Joslyn scrolls and points. "Here's where Riley said that y'all had a fight at your house, where she fucked you up good."

I laugh, my head shaking. "Girl, I wore her ass *out* with that belt. I would go beat her ass right now, if I didn't have a restraining order."

"You don't," Joslyn says. "Fletcher talked her out of it. He said as long as you thought there's a restraining order it achieved the same thing."

I wave for the server and tell Joslyn, "Screenshot all of the messages."

"But Tahj… Put your hand down. That's not all. Did you know that Jay contacted Riley?"

My hand comes down and covers my chest. "What?"

"Jay put Riley in touch with two guys that worked for him. Those men were following you. They showed Riley pictures of you and Fletcher on the night he proposed to her."

"So *that's* how Jay knew!"

Joslyn pierces me with her eyes, "The text Fletcher saw, came from them. But is it coming together though? Two guys showed Riley the pictures. Two guys attack Fletcher. *Two…*"

My breathing stops. "So, Riley…? But that doesn't make sense. Why would she have Fletcher attacked?"

"To scare him. But Fletcher ends up with amnesia and can't remember the men warning him to stay away from you."

I'm ready to take action. "Just send me the screenshots!"

"The messages don't show that Riley was behind the attack."

"Just send me the screenshots, Joslyn!"

"They may show that Fletcher and Riley broke up, but it also proves that Riley didn't cheat. We need to show that Riley was behind the attack. For that, there needs to be an investigation. That's where you come in."

"Why me?"

"Because if it's me, my name might come up when they question Riley, then I'm out of the wedding, which makes plan B impossible."

"Plan B," I smile. "I'm impressed."

"But for plan B to work, we need one more person. So, I've been talking to the best man, Bubby…" Joslyn looks down and blushes, then recovers. "Well, Bubby seems to think the wedding is a mistake."

"Wait, what's all this blushing about?"

Joslyn sighs dreamily and says, "Ya boy can't seem to keep his eyes off of me."

I lean in. "Bubby? Can't keep his eyes off you? Or the white girl standing next to you?"

Joslyn's head shakes as the blushing continues. "I'm not wrong about this, Tahj." She holds up her phone screen. "This man has been texting me paragraphs."

I just look with my mouth open. "So, now I gotta ask you: are you really into my friend, or is it the money?"

"I like him, like… You should see, during wedding rehearsals, how he's been really going out his way for me. He says he got married to someone who wasn't his friend, so he says he wants us to be friends and see where it goes."

I warn, "Don't do that friend shit. I'm telling you. That was the problem with Fletcher and me. It creates a boundary that you never know when and how to cross it. I say haul off and kiss him. That way there's no going back. Show him your tits – something."

We laugh for a spell, then I bring us back on topic. "If Bubby isn't down to help us… As a matter of fact, even if he is down, I got one more person who I know will be down. I raise a number one and start calling the person who says, to this day, that it's on site with Riley.

I call Monae twice and each time it's answered by voicemail, which is normal, if she's with Keenan, but she always responds to texts.

Four messages in, with no response, I begin to worry. "She always responds to text." I signal for the bill, explaining, "I'm worried because Monae is in an abusive relationship."

Joslyn asks, "You think something's happened to her?"

I take Joslyn's hand and say, "I'm gonna need you to come with me."

An upset Keenan says, "Turn that damn phone off."

"But Kee," Monae whines.

Kee says, "When Fletcher was blowing up my phone a minute ago, didn't you make me turn mine off? They just wanna pull everybody into whatever drama they got going on, like the world revolves around them."

Monae explains, "But that wasn't even Tahj just now. It's been a half hour since her last text."

Keenan un-pauses the movie. Monae rolls over in bed and lays her head on his chest.

The doorbell rings.

"That's DoorDash, I bet." Monae rolls out of bed, slips on a robe, and straightens her bonnet on the way out.

Outside, I ring the doorbell a third time. Joslyn's right behind me, second-guessing the whole thing. "Let's leave, Tahj. I don't wanna get caught up in no mess."

Monae opens the door, looking for her food. I snatch the knob. "Are you okay?"

Monae yells in whispers, "Girl, why is you here? My man is right there in the room!"

"Are you safe?"

"Yes! Dafuq? Kee will *flip* if he knew you were here."

Keenan yells from the back, "What's going on out there?"

Monae yells over her shoulder, "Jehovah's Witness!" She then faces forward and proceeds to assure Joslyn and me that Keenan has not put his hands on her since the beginning. While Monae urges Joslyn and me, in whispers, to kindly get the fuck on, Keenan enters her background. He comes out, pulling a t-shirt down his body. He walks well into the living room, believing he's fixing to show Monae how to get rid a couple of old ladies, but when he realizes that the Jehovah's Witness is me, it gives him a jump-scare.

I blurt out, "I knew already."

Monae turns. "Oh shit!"

Keenan blasts, "She knew?! What the fuck, mane?!"

"I've known for a while now."

"W-w-w-w-w-w…" *Wait*, is perhaps the word Keenan struggles to get out. The stutter snowballs into rapid blinking. Keenan short circuits so bad, I watch for smoke leaking from his ears.

Monae mocks, "W-w-w… There go the helicopter."

Keenan blasts, "Wait a damn minute! What d-d-do you *think* you know, Tahj?"

Monae tosses her hands in despair, "Are you still trying to deny this, Kee? You're barefoot, right now."

"You know good and hell well, I'm here about that money you owe me," Keenan says. "I'm barefoot because I sometimes t-t-take my shoes off when I'm on the toilet. You was kind enough to let me use your bathroom, Monae, and I thank you for that."

Monae's foot taps nervously. "What room did you come out of Keenan? The guest bathroom is down the hall. You came out of the bedroom."

Keenan points a stiff finger. "Look, b-b-b…"

"I got your bitch, right here!" Monae hauls off and slaps Keenan.

I throw myself in front of Mo, pleading. "Keenan, please don't beat her!"

Keenan's eyes move from Monae to me, from anger to confusion. "Girl what the hell is wrong with you?"

I shrug. "I thought you… Well ya see…"

Monae steps around me, saying, "He don't beat me. I beat him. Watch." She shoves Keenan. Monae then draws a hand back, threatening, "Deny me again, and see what happens to you!"

Keenan says, "I ain't… puttin' up with this shit. Where my shoes?"

Keenan stamps off into the bedroom. Monae chases, berating him the whole way.

I look back, and there's no one behind me. I call, "Joslyn?"

She comes up the steps with the DoorDash package. Kee marches out of the bedroom with Monae hot on his heels. "Do you think we're supposed to be on the D.L. forever?"

Keenan glitches when he sees Joslyn. "Damn, not her too!" He goes to the door and backs out of it for a last word. "Don't y'all repeat a word of this! She lying!"

"I'm lying?" Monae shuffles around looking for something to throw at him.

I grab her, saying, "It's not worth it, Mo."

"On God, that man makes me sick!"

It takes a while to calm Monae down and begin discussing our revenge plot.

Plan A is me taking Joslyn's texts to police. If there isn't time or evidence to arrest Riley for her role in the attack on Fletcher, we go with plan B and crash the wedding.

Monae suggests, "Skip plan A altogether. I wanna put hands on the bitch!"

We're laying out the plan, when I stop everything to say, "Do y'all smell that?"

"What," they say.

"That smell." I cover my nose and point to the DoorDash bag on the coffee table. "It's that! What is that?"

Monae says, "Fried fish, girl. You don't like fish?"

"I like fish," I say. "But that smell is making me sick, right now. Can you take it away please?"

Monae takes the bag to the kitchen and returns to the huddle, neither of us giving it a second thought.

CHAPTER 40
WEDDING-GATE

I'm late. I call in sick. For lying, God makes me sick for real, or maybe the nausea is Him warning me to, not go cut a fool in His church.

My belly is in coils while I stuff myself into a corset, praying I don't shart. I spend an hour in the mirror getting my makeup just perfect; gotta upstage the bride.

I have never, nor will I ever again, do anything this crazy. I've only seen wedding crashes in viral videos, and every time I side with the bride, calling the other chick thirsty, desperate, or crazy; now I am her. Lord knows I tried everything else.

I took the evidence to Fulton County police. They recovered Jay's cell phone. They found texts between Jay and the two men he employed to stalk Fletcher. Their mugshots appear on the news, but only in connection with Jay; fingered as the boogiemen who intimidated the doctors. They found texts between Riley and the goons, none referencing the attack; therefore, Riley still walks free unless wrongdoing is uncovered in statements given by the men she allegedly hired to attack Fletcher.

I harassed the lead detective every hour of every day. I tried to convince Joslyn to pull Fletcher aside during wedding rehearsals, and just show him the texts – problem solved – but no. Joslyn argued that our evidence proves that Riley didn't cheat, so it's unlikely to stop the marriage. Joslyn, as a result, could get banned from the wedding, making plan B impossible. On pure logic, I couldn't argue her point, but I suspected that Joslyn, lowkey just wanted the bomb to drop on Riley's wedding day, to sweeten her own revenge.

I had asked Monae to look in Keenan's phone and get me Fletcher's new number, so I could tell him myself. That was not an option because Keenan hadn't come around since their relationship was exposed.

I'd tried everything I could, all the way up to the wedding day, but to no avail; therefore, plan B – as wild as it may *be* – is now imminent.

Not only am I running late, Monae isn't where she's supposed to be, which sets us back further. While driving across town to get Monae, I stop at a CVS Pharmacy to get something for my stomach and to use their restroom while I'm at it.

The texts keep coming in from Joslyn and Bubby, updating us that the guests have been seated, the flower girl has marched, the bridesmaids and groomsmen are in place, and the ringbearer is in position.

As I hit the last turn, Riley had already come down the aisle, and the vows have begun.

Security guards cover the door; Riley planned for fuckery, but Joslyn had already made us aware of this. I throw the car in park and text Bubby the signal to fake pass out, as a way to distract security.

I get a call.

Monae's eyes stretch as I answer the phone. "What're you doing? We're late as it is!"

I cover the phone. "It's the detective."

The detective says the men in custody gave statements that Riley hired them to attack Fletcher. I'm too nervous to celebrate. My eyes are on the church. Lo and behold, the security guard leaves the door to go inside and check on Bubby who has collapsed.

Monae taps my knee. "That's our queue!"

I cover the phone and say. "They're gonna arrest Riley."

I uncover the phone and ask, "When?" The detective's answer stuns me so bad I have to repeat it. "Sometime next week?! She's in the church getting married to the man that she had attacked. Can't something be done?"

Monae holds up a finger and says, "With or without you." She gets out and starts speedwalking through the parking lot. I end the call and go, but can't catch up to Monae in her jumpsuit because I'm in a corset and heels.

I'm really doing this. I'm really walking fast across the parking lot to crash a wedding. My throat closes, my breathing quickens. A hundred wedding guests could turn on us; people could get hurt. Ahead of me, Monae grabs two handles and throws the double doors open. I'm not half as brave as her.

My adrenaline kicks in and everything slows down; rather my mind speeds up. I scale the concrete steps and get a clear line of sight through the vestibule and the open-door sanctuary as Monae enters; it's an all-white wedding. I assess the scene in an instant.

Fletcher sweats at the altar. He is not okay. Riley makes for a beautiful bride, but the oleander's beauty makes the flower no less deadly.

Keenan blanches at the sight of Monae marching down the aisle, assuming she'll out him in front of an assembly of his peers. Keenan breaks formation to get ahead of her, pointing, announcing, "What is this person doing in here?"

Wedding guests stir.

Riley swats the distracted bishop on the arm. "Focus!" She wants the vows rushed.

One security guard pops up, leaving Bubby to pursue Monae, the radio to his mouth, barking numeric codes.

Bishop raises a hand as if it holds the staff of Moses. He commands everyone to calm down; no one does. He would've gotten the same effect if he'd kept his hand down and mouth shut. The second security guard guides the bishop away to safety. Riley protests, but to no avail; the man is more important than her wedding vows.

Only seconds have transpired since Monae barged in, and now me, and she's cleared the aisle, and is converging at the altar step with a security guard and a bridesmaid who had kicked off her shoes and ran, while holding up the front of her dress.

In case Maone gets past the security guard or the vigilante bridesmaid, Fletcher guards the altar like a soccer goalie.

This all-white wedding rises from their pews like a pelican flock roused before the mass migration.

The bridesmaid gets to Maone first, grabbing her by the hair. The bridesmaid yanks so hard that when the wig slips off, she tumbles backward, cutting down two would-be heroes like bowling pins.

Monae, with her wig gone, comes away spinning like a running back evading a tackler. Keenan tenses with conflicting passions, to either protect his manhood or protect his lover.

She's slipped the bridesmaid and security, but out of nowhere, Riley's father comes running, as if shot out of a cannon, yelling, "Oh no you don't!"

Phillip jumps on Monae's back and rides her to the ground.

I hurry up the aisle, unnoticed, since I'm dressed in white like the wedding guest. Monae spots me. Although she's now trapped in a clutch of arms, she winks because everything's going according to plan.

Joslyn positions herself next to Riley, ready to restrain her while I show the evidence to Fletcher, but I've got something better than evidence.

Our eyes meet. Fletcher and I become entranced.

In a perfect world, or rather a fictional one, Fletcher and I would run to each other in slow motion to an inspirational score. What happens pales in comparison.

I hear Riley before I see her. Joslyn, instead of holding Riley back, Joslyn points me out like a traitor.

Riley's eyes widen as they zero in on me. "You bitch," she screams, and dashes for the steps; that's when Joslyn steps on the train of Riley's gown, causing her to tip forward and belly flop on the floor.

I call, "Fletcher!" I dig in my purse. They scatter, thinking it's a gun, a scorned lover going postal.

I yell, "I'm pregnant!" I raise the pregnancy test I took in the CVS bathroom on the way there.

I hear the sound of a hundred gasps, and somebody's grandmamma, yelling, "*Do* Jesus!"

Riley un-plants her face, her jaw still on the floor. "For who!"

I hand the test to Fletcher. He squints in disbelief. I hand Fletcher my phone with the screenshots and wait for him to see that he did, indeed broke up with Riley and that I wasn't imagining things when I said that we made love that day.

Fletcher doesn't lash out at Riley, and whisk me away in his arms. His head hangs as he takes it all in.

In the background, Joslyn apologizes for 'accidentally' stepping on the gown and helps Riley to her feet, but Joslyn pretends to trip up, and rides Riley back to the floor. Joslyn puts a hand to her mouth and says, "Did I do that?"

Riley starts kicking and screaming. "Get off of me Joslyn!" Riley rises to her feet, and yells, "You're not helping!"

For Joslyn, it's finally mask-off. She says, "I wasn't trying to help, bitch!" She clocks Riley with a straight right that makes Riley stagger with her eyes crossed, on a straight flight to La-La Land. Joslyn exclaims, "And that's for messing with Xavier behind my back!"

People rush to the situation; bridesmaids, groomsmen, and wedding guests alike. Joslyn kicks off her shoes one by one and gets in a fighting stance, shuffling back and feinting to keep attackers at bay. One girl gets too close and Joslyn drags her down by her hair as a warning to the next booshy bridesmaid who tries it.

Bubby comes to Joslyn's defense, on his toes, in a slick southpaw stance, two fists waving. "*Touch* her," Bubby warns. "I'll put *all* yall niggas to sleep!" The altar looks like a Jerry Springer stage.

Meanwhile, Fletcher says, with a quiet grin, "I'm gonna be a daddy."

Just then, Lew comes up, places his hands on us, and says, "Let's get outta here first, *then* talk."

Out of nowhere Riley appears and punches Fletcher in the back. "You cheated on me! How could you!"

Fletcher's glare hardens. "How could I cheat on you, when I broke up with you." Hearing that I catch a three-second Holy

Ghost. Fletcher adds, "You were texting the same dudes that jumped me?! You told them to attack me?!"

Riley pleads. "No! That's not true!" Riley looks at me, and uses the pull on Fletcher's arm to slingshot around him, enroute to me. "You lying bitch! Why I should–"

"–Should what," says Fletcher's mother, who steps in to block her. "If you attack a pregnant woman, I'll be forced to show you that I wasn't always saved!"

Riley grits her teeth, then marches back to the altar to announce, "The wedding is *off!*"

Fletcher cups a hand to his mouth and says, "Ya think?"

In the distance, Joslyn hugs Bubby, seemingly to thank him for protecting her, but the hug doesn't release. They share a smiling gaze, face to face. I've never seen Bubby so awestruck by a woman as dark as Joslyn, and definitely not a woman with locks. The look on Bubby's face resembles Jay, when he realized that Sarah was the one. Bubby runs his fingers through Joslyn's locks and kisses her then savors it.

Keenan and Monae are MIA. Half the church is outside in the parking lot, awaiting the police.

Fletcher and I descend the steps in all white, holding hands, married – in a sense – by the baby growing inside of me, but there's no thrown rice or blown bubbles in our path. The word bitch is thrown about. I'm the villain. They hate Fletcher too, for supposedly doing what he did to Riley.

He looks over at me and says, "I better get you outta here before police gets here."

"Being an uninvited guest isn't a crime. Who did I assault? Who did Monae assault? They assaulted *her.*"

Fletcher's head shakes. "Ya can't make this stuff up."

Sirens approach.

Bubby and Joslyn come outside together. I walk toward Joslyn asking about our third partner in crime. "Have you seen Monae?" Joslyn scans the surroundings then shrugs.

Fletcher and Bubby bump fists then shoulders. Bubby raises a hand and announces, "Anybody get this on video? I'll pay fifty bands to anybody who got the footage."

With the men distracted, I give Joslyn a look, so she knows that I saw the kiss. Joslyn returns a cheeky smile that tells me they're official. Her hand swats limp as she says, "We'll talk."

We get out of the way because we hear Riley's sobbing long before we see her. Her parents flank her as she exits the church. Riley's mother comes towards me in a tirade, most of it, incoherent drivel, but she clearly calls me a porch monkey.

Riley cries in the background while Phillip approaches Fletcher, yelling in his face about how he knew his daughter was too good for him, and how they're going to shun him from the church – when out of nowhere, Keenan appears.

Keenan taps Phillip on the shoulder, then patiently waits, his hands clasped in front. Phillip turns and says, "Young man, can't you see I'm busy?"

A dead-faced Keenan says, "So you like to hit women, huh?"

Only then do I see Monae behind Keenan, crying and nursing her wrist. On the subject of hitting women, I could say Keenan's the pot calling the kettle black, but I keep my mouth shut. Keenan's anger is as deep as that night at the club when he wanted to hurt Monae; that anger now resurfaces to protect her.

Keenan and Philip face each other in a stare down, Phillip's enthusiasm noticeably dimmed, as if wondering what evil lurks behind Keenan's eyes.

Bubby points. "Yo, Kee. Twelve." Squad cars pool in the entrance. Bubby's eyes thin. The way he wipes a hand down over his mouth, I just know he's about to say something slick. "Yo Kee… Ain't that shawty from the club that night? That's who you' fighting for?"

Like a spun bottle, Keenan turns and stops on Bubby. "Why? You got a problem with that?" Keenan pivots to Fletcher, saying, "You, Fletcher? You got somethin' to say?"

Fletcher backs away with his palms up.

"That's what the fuck I *thought*," Keenan booms. He points back at Monae. "Yall see this beautiful young lady right here? That's me!"

Keenan clubs his chest. "And if anybody got a problem with it, we can get it poppin' right now!"

I've never been prouder of Keenan.

Riley, again, materializes out of nowhere. "Fletcher? Fletcher!"

He ignores her.

"You're just gonna stand there and watch me cry? Do I mean nothing to you?"

Phillip shakes his head as if his daughter is hopeless.

Riley approaches. I step between them, my back to Fletcher, facing Riley, who balls up her hands, as if with every intention to throw them. "Oooh, I should punch you right in your face."

Bubby's says. "All her shit done come back on her. Now she can't take it."

Riley's focus never leaves me. "You swear you' something, you ole black bush-baby! Yo ugl'ass!"

I withhold my pimp-hand and even a reply, so the two officers approaching won't mistake me as the aggressor.

The officers stop at her rear and say, "Riley Purlieu?"

Riley points at me, saying, "There she is officers! That's the woman who crashed my wedding."

One officer tips his hat to me. "Howdy." He then informs Riley, "Being uninvited at a wedding idn't a crime, but Criminal Facilitation is."

The look on Riley's face as they slap the handcuffs on her wrists, makes all the drama worth it. Riley's parents, a flabbergasted duo, swarm the officers with questions. One officer answers, "We've got the two men who attacked Fletcher saying Riley paid them to do it."

They drag Riley kicking and screaming every ugly name under God. I nestle Fletcher's chest and suck my thumb, just to fuck with her.

Fletcher and I head to our first doctor's appointment. I'm driving because Fletcher's on the last few pages of my manuscript. I had converted it to a Mobi file so he could read it on his phone; he said he's keeping his mouth shut until he's done. The silence is killing me, plus I'm irritated that Fletcher plans to go to work right after our first time meeting our baby via ultrasound. I'm more irritated at myself for telling Fletcher it was no problem… He shouldn't have asked in the first place. He should've just taken the whole day off.

Look at him… coming to our first appointment in a damn suit and hard bottom shoes… I already know I'm about to start some shit, so I get right to it. "You make me sick, you know that?" He keeps reading. I say, "And then, look at your shirt. That's a formal shirt, you don't wear that with a regular suit… Lookin' like you're fixing to go lay down in a casket."

Head still down, he smiles big and wide, and I wonder if it's my joke or my book.

Speaking of my book, the rejection letters from publishers have been piling up. Most of them are vague, saying it's not a good fit for their readership, but a few of them are specific. One says there's no trope for our story. Another says the sex scenes are too explicit. Another says it fails as a romance because Fletcher and I entertain other relationships when there should be no happiness outside of being with each other. They recommend rewrites, but I'm not changing a thing. Actually, I did change a thing or two, only because I wanted to, or perhaps reading the critiques over and over made me believe them, in some respect, so I cut out the first chapter, which starts with me being teased as a child. I also cut the club scene where Chris Brown's security denies me entry to his VIP section, citing his "No darkies" policy. It happened, but it was more aside from Fletcher and me, and our crazy relationship.

Fletcher drops his phone in his lap and sighs. He says, "I didn't know you could write this good, babe."

"Thank you again. You said that before."

"I guess I didn't think you could maintain it for the duration… but…"

"But what?"

"How you got me lookin' like I'm some wild animal?"

"Where's the lie?"

"Another thing, I don't even like the name Fletcher. Do I look like a Fletcher to you?"

"I can't use real names. What do you want me to do, get sued? Aside from that, though, what do you think?"

"I'd read it in just two and a half days, so what does that tell you?"

"Not enough."

Fletcher raises a finger. "I'm gone say this one time, and then I'm gonna leave it alone…" Fletcher bites his lip then adds, "Just the other day when we went to the Annual Players Association Conference, what did you see?"

Keeping my eyes on the road, I say, "What did *you* see?"

"I saw rich athletes and their wives, about 80, 90 percent of the women on their arm were light-skinned or white. I think you gave brothas a pass. You made (Riley) the villain when really it's the color-struck ass brothas who enable women like her."

"I was advised to stay away from social commentary… What else," I say, as we arrive and I shift the gear in park. "Did you enjoy it?"

"You know I did. You just want to know what parts I didn't like. One thing: I think sometimes you overshare. Sometimes you even put yourself in a bad light." Fletcher pauses for a while and runs his tongue along his cheek. "I knew (Bubby) had feelings for you. I knew it all along."

I suck my teeth. "Man, get out the car."

We argue somewhat playfully on the way in, and while sitting in the waiting room.

The subject is on pause while we're in the dark room, my belly slathered in cold jelly as Doctor Eilene moves the sonogram over my stomach, her eyes on the screen. "It's too early to hear it, but do you see that little flicker there? That's the heartbeat."

Fletcher grips his face and weeps. I touch his arm and he kneels next to the exam table and tells me how he loves me and how he'll be the best dad ever. I start crying too. When we leave the doctor's office, Fletcher's still got the sniffles.

He drives, this time. He keeps checking his phone, saying before he goes to work, that there's something he wants me to see. He's been secretive lately; I suspect it's a new house.

He looks over and tells me, "Fuck what them publishers say, though. It's the best thing I've ever read. You got a knack for putting the reader right there, in just a few words."

"Thank you," I say. My face isn't big enough for my smile.

"It was hard, though, reading about you and Jay."

I shrink in my seat. "That's so embarrassing."

"I need you to promise me something, though."

"I'm not taking those scenes out."

Fletcher looks over with a smile and says, "I think you low-key those scenes in because you want me to learn what Jay was doing to you."

My mouth makes an O, through which I laugh like Santa. If I were white, I'd be red from blushing. "But you're way better than him."

"Not at *that* part."

"He had to be, because he couldn't really follow it up."

Fletcher smiles and shakes his head. "Look at how we're talking. When I say we can talk about anything, babe… Do you really think other couples have conversations like this?"

My head shakes no as I look out into the world, but then I notice where we're headed. "Are we? Are we going to Indian Creek Park?"

"The home of our first kiss." Fletcher swallows hard and says, "While reading your book, the one thing that stood out to me, is the fact that you wanna feel cherished. I'm ashamed of myself that someone else made you feel that way and not me."

I counter, "But when you left the NFL and our relationship was new, you actually did a good job of that…"

Fletcher quiets me with a number one to his lips. We get out of the car. The weather is so fine it doesn't feel like weather at all. I hear the drone of a single-engine airplane. In the distance, people are seated in front of an altar of white roses. I point, saying, "Aw… I wonder who's out here getting married in our spot?"

Fletcher points. "Says it right there in the sky."

There are words written in smoke. I lip sync as I read, FLETCH & TAHJ 4EVER.

I buckle. Fletcher catches me and raises me up in his arms. My face tingles and stretches with astonishment. "You're kidding! That's my wedding?"

I churn in Fletcher's arms and point. "Those people…? That's… That's my daddy right there!" They wave because they see me pointing.

My legs quit on me again. Fletcher legit has to carry me down the path to the stream. A beautiful woman plays the piano and sings on a carpet of green grass. I recognize the tune. It's a slow and soft version of Hey Ya.

Thank God for mom and dad
For sticking two together
Cause we don't know how
Hey, yah… Hey yah

Momma has a gown already made.

The piano plays softly as the women in my family take me away. They bring a chair for me to sit. They huddle around while Micha, my beautician, works on my hair. Cousin Yolanda, who has worked the Sears counter for thirty years, does my makeup. They shield me as I change into my wedding gown. There's not one eye dry, yet not one mouth frowning, only warm smiles and whispers; small words speaking to eternal things. I've seen them like this during holidays in the kitchen, bonding while working, knowing they're preparing much more than a meal. A breeze picks up as if God Himself sends His love. Leaves skid across the grass. Treetops dance under a blue sky; the stream trickles, and the soft piano changes its tune.

I gather the front of my gown. The circle of women open up and my daddy is there, smiling with his forearm out for me to take. Two follow us to raise the train.

Fletcher's at the altar with a borrowed handkerchief to his face because he's crying so hard that Bubby has to hold him up. When it's all said and done, we face each other before a black-robed reverend and recite our vows. At the final I do, we kiss and someone pulls a string to release something from above. And this is how this story ends; with Fletcher and me kissing in matrimony, with white rose pedals snowing down on us.

EPILOGUE
ANGEL

I turn the shop over to Momma and hire someone to help her manage it because Uncle Sirus declined. Like Jay, Fletcher doesn't want me to work, but not only do I have a fire in me, I also have, in my belly, a little girl that will, in all likelihood, be dark-skinned like myself and my mother, so I wanted to do something that would make the world a more inviting place for her.

I started a modeling agency-slash-marketing firm, with a mind to later go into film. I love all aspects of fashion, but I realized that my purpose is in fashion agency, thanks to Bubby. He says being close to me for so many years is what reprogrammed the way he sees beauty, and I realized that this is what the world needs.

I can best serve this purpose through agency, where I can realize the other definition of the word agency, and be the intervention that affects change.

I turned one of the back rooms of Momma's boutique into a studio. The old brewery was so big that despite a large storefront, and four industrial, programable sewing machines in the back, we still had plenty of space to play with, even after the studio was finished.

I'm at an onsite photoshoot with my models, my tribe, ideal representations of melanin rich beauty. For too long we've been tokened and niched.

So, we're in the studio modeling momma's upcoming fall lineup. They sport long flannel skirts, scarves, and cute caps in front of the green screen.

I'm getting on their nerves as I direct the shoot because this is my dream; modeling is their dream, and clashes are bound to happen when many dreams occupy the same space.

They're in a group shoot, busy hitting their poses when all I said was, "Angel. This is flannel, not leather. It's not time to be fierce, right now. Go softer."

Angel storms out, saying, "I'm not up for this today, Miss Tahj. You always got something to say!" She swears I'm jealous of her.

The other girls gasp. Naya vents, "Why she gotta be such a diva!"

I'm the only one who's not upset.

Me, knowing exactly where Angel has run off to, I go looking for Momma. Angel done pulled my momma aside, giving her an earful.

"Angel," I say. "How you gone try to pit my own Momma against me? You think she gone take your side over mine?"

Angel's head turns to Momma. Momma's head turns with the synchrony of a fallen domino, where she says, in lazy-eyed admission, "I do kinda take Angel's side sometimes."

I sigh. "Come on Angel, let's talk."

Momma puts a hand beside her mouth but whispers loud enough for me to hear, "When y'all done, come back and fill me in on the bullshit, okay?"

I roll my eyes at Momma then walk Angel to the office. Behind a closed door, I ask, "Wanna tell me what's going on?"

Angel just resets her folded arms and stares at a wall.

"Maybe it's better that you just listen," I propose.

Angel replies, "Why? So you can talk like you know me when you don't?"

"I don't have to know you. I live in the same world you live in. I'm wearing the same skin, and we're in the same industry. You know my resume."

Me and my pregnant belly waddles around to face her. "I know that, outside of here, you can be the most beautiful girl in the room, but be treated like you're an extra. Someone who looks like me or you, tries to stand out, and they treat you like you're a background singer trying to upstage the star."

Angel rolls her eyes and says, "Can we go now?"

I'm smiling when I say, "Don't try me, trick. Because my pimp-hand itchin' already." That's how we roll on our good days; threats subverted to endearment. Angel looks away to hide a smile. I continue, "I want your experience in this industry to be better than my experience. My hair was down to my shoulders; they cut it off. They always gave me some loud eyeshadow or lipstick to make me look weird. And for the longest time, I was convinced that they were trying to make me look exotic to help others look more ideal. In fact, I *know* that's what they were doing. But I didn't have the power to say or do anything about it. But now? Me, heading this agency? Me, hand-picking models that look like you and me? Me partnering with companies that are open to dark-skin models being the centerpiece? This is me finally saying and doing something about it." I pick Angel's hand from out of her folded arms and she looks me in the eyes. I say, "I know what you're up to."

Angel swirls her neck. "What am I up to, then? Since you know so much."

"You know that this agency looks and feels different. And when you act out, half the time you're not even upset. You're merely exercising the freedom you don't have outside this agency. You know this is a safe space where you can act spoiled; you can have an attitude, and you can be a diva, but you will *not* be shoved off of your pedestal because of it."

Angel throws herself into me and squeezes me.

That's when I realize that I am doing my purpose.

About Those Nightmares

One night I'm up in the wee hours… baby doing Kungfu in my belly. I look over and watch Fletcher toss himself awake, hollering my name.

I ask him about the dream, but he shuts me down, denying it. And that's when I lose my shit. "Fletcher, I am carrying your got damn baby! You don't get to keep secrets!" Pregnancy has magnified my emotions times three.

Fletcher sits up and rubs his eyes. He sighs as if he doesn't know how to begin. "These dreams… They're all pretty much the same dream… just different situations. I'm dead each time. You've moved on… I'm there, but you can't hear me or see me… I'm a ghost… This time, you was at a concert, Usher… Usher picked you out of the audience and started grinding on you. And you was loving it. I started screaming your name and you couldn't hear me."

I cut my eyes and say, "Stop playing."

"That's the dream, babe. I don't know what else to tell you."

"Ain't no way you hollering like you done fell off a cliff, over that?"

Fletcher looks at me as if he's truly mad at me and says, "You was twerking on him and everything, babe."

I can tell that he's telling the truth, and because of it, he's feeling big and simple, so I comfort him while holding my laughter.

ABOUT THE AUTHOR

Son of a carpenter and a nanny, Rod Palmer was born in a historic Gullah Geechie community in Charleston, SC where storytelling was the life-blood of their culture. He received his degrees in creative writing and Afro studies at the University of South Carolina. Rod Palmer is a dedicated husband and girl-dad who enjoys coastal living and travel.

Other works:

A Pimp In The Pulpit
The Work-Husband Caper
The Harvest
Karma Wears Versace
KWV II: Man Eater
The Waymaker
The Things We Bring to the Table
Della: The Ballerina and the Billionaire

9 7989 8642 8260